I0650809

SEXICO

Volume 1

Written by William Cering

Copyright © 2025 William Cering
All rights reserved.

ISBN 979-8-9988683-0-6

This is a work of fiction. Names, characters, places, and incidents are either the product of the author's imagination or used fictitiously. Any resemblance to actual persons, living or dead, or actual events is purely coincidental.

No part of this book may be reproduced, stored in a retrieval system, or transmitted in any form or by any means—electronic, mechanical, photocopying, recording, or otherwise—without the prior written permission of the author, except in the case of brief quotations embodied in critical articles or reviews.

For permissions, licensing, or inquiries, contact:

sexiconovel@gmail.com

*"Sometimes the only way out is through the fire —
and sometimes, you bring the damn gasoline."*
— Kael Torres

*"You don't need a past when you're the one ending
everyone else's."*
— Grant Comstock

*"Love doesn't make you weak. It makes you load the
second magazine."*
— Marisol Cárdenas

*"When God stopped answering, I bought a shotgun and
started preaching."*
— Padre Luis

"Do I look like I came here to negotiate?
— Natalia Ortega

"When you see me, it's already too late."
— Grant Comstock

*"You ever get turned on during a firefight? No? That's
sad."*
— Valeria Cortez

"I don't do romance. I do war with eye contact."
— Marisol Cárdenas

*"The world ended three times already. We just didn't get the
memo."*
— Kael Torres

*"Amen, motherf***er."*
— Padre Luis

"I'm not here to play ghost. I'm here to bury the living."
— Grant Comstock

"CIA calls me a liability. That's fair — I prefer freedom over rules."
— Grant Comstock

"I only fall for two things: women and explosions."
— Valeria Cortez

"You haven't really lived until you've strangled someone with a rosary."
— Padre Luis

"She saw the monster in me-and kissed it anyway"
-Kael Torres

"My therapist says I suppress emotion. I suppressed her, too."
— Grant Comstock

"Touch me like I'm the last thing you'll ever hold— because I might be."
— Marisol Cárdenas

"I don't believe in safe love. I want the kind that could burn cities to the ground."
— Marisol Cárdenas

"Some men fight for God. I fight for the woman who made me believe in one"
-Kael Torres

Table of Contents

Prologue-Broken Arrow

PROLOGUE

Broken Arrow

The desert wind screamed as if it already knew what was coming.

Kael Torres sat in the turret of the second Stryker, boots braced against the steel, palms slick against the grips of the .50 cal. They were running escort for a convoy of Kurdish fighters—four Strykers in total, packed tight and rattling down the fractured spine of Highway 80.

The air was electric. Tense. Wrong. Kael's eyes scanned the horizon with a rhythm born of instinct, not training. A low throb of dread coiled in his chest. He'd been in enough firefights to know the difference between bad luck and the kind of silence that carried teeth.

Then—

WHUMP.

A thundercrack of light. A 120mm rocket-propelled IED exploded under the lead Stryker. The sound was too big for the brain to process. The vehicle lifted, then disintegrated into a storm of fire and blood.

Kael's mouth filled with iron. A piece of someone's ribcage slammed into his chest plate. Blood—someone else's—splashed across his face and down the side of the turret like paint.

The Kurdish fighters screamed. Their radio chatter dissolved into a wail of panic, a sound so raw it pierced Kael's spine.

One man was cut in half. Another's head rolled to a stop by Kael's boot.

Kael whimpered. The breath in his lungs hitched, catching on something primal.

Then he started shooting.

THUMP-THUMP-THUMP.

The .50 cal thundered from his hands like God's own wrath. He pivoted fast, cutting down a wave of black-clad ISIS fighters storming the ridge. Dust and shrapnel spun like locusts. His rounds carved through bodies like scissors through linen.

He could barely see through the smoke. Could barely breathe through the stench of burning flesh, charred plastic, scorched diesel.

But he kept shooting.

Screams over the comms. Command shouting. Static. The squad leader was gone. The driver of the third Stryker was sobbing into the radio. One of the Kurds was still alive, crawling with no legs, dragging a trail of blood behind him like a worm across gravel.

Kael's best friend, Eli Vargas, tried to climb out of the troop bay.

SNAP.

A sniper's round cored him through the eye.

Eli dropped like a puppet with its strings cut.

Kael screamed, but the sound was swallowed by the Mark 19 grenade launcher hammering behind him. The world devolved into chaos—smoke, fire, brass casings, the stink of burning oil and shit and death.

His finger cramped from the trigger, but he didn't stop.

He couldn't.

Because this was what he was made for.

Because this was the moment the rest of his life would orbit around—the fracture in his soul he could never outrun.

Kael jumped down from the turret mid-burst, landing hard on the scorched tarmac beside the half-ruined third Stryker. His boots skidded through blood and soot. He yanked Eli's body back by the shoulder strap, half-hoping he was wrong. Half-hoping that his friend's eye wasn't dangling from its socket like a popped grape.

But Eli was gone.

Kael's throat locked. The world tilted.

Then the screams came again.

"CONTACT! EAST WALL!"

Rounds pinged off the hull behind him. Another explosion—smaller—a mortar maybe, or a suicide vest—bloomed behind the convoy.

He turned.

A child.

A boy, no older than ten, sprinted toward them barefoot, face blank, eyes glassy. He clutched a duffel bag tight to his chest.

Kael froze.

One second.

Two.

"He's wired!" someone shouted.

Kael raised his rifle. Hesitated.

The boy didn't.

He kept running.

Kael pulled the trigger.

The child dropped mid-stride. The bag hit the pavement, rolled, and ruptured.

It wasn't a bomb.

It was full of medicine.

Kael collapsed to his knees. The breath in his lungs turned to glass. His eyes stung with smoke— and something else.

A young Kurdish fighter ran past him screaming, only to take a round through the jaw. Kael's blood-soaked fingers clenched around his M4, shaking.

He was done.

Not dead—but done.

The firefight raged for another 19 minutes. Minutes that bent time, stretching it like hot metal. Every breath was a betrayal. Every heartbeat, borrowed.

When the dust cleared, 11 were dead.

Six were civilians.

The medevac came late. The paperwork came fast.

Kael took the fall.

A reprimand. A discharge.

No trial. No court-martial.

Just silence.

The kind that sticks to your bones.

He stood at the edge of the blast zone long after the medics had cleared the bodies. Ash drifted like snow. The sun dipped low, bleeding through the haze, casting the world in gold and crimson. Kael didn't move.

He just stared at the place where the boy had fallen.

The place where he had died, too—just not all the way.

Later that night, alone in the back of a medevac with dried blood caking his jawline, he reached into his pocket and pulled out the boy's duffel tag. It had somehow gotten caught on his gear during the chaos. There was a name written on it. In Arabic. Smudged, almost unreadable.

Yusuf.

Kael stared at it.

Then folded it once. And again. And again.

He tucked it into the inside pocket of his armor and zipped it shut.

He wouldn't forget.

Not the name.

Not the smell.

Not the fire.

Outskirts of Mosul – Dusk

Kael crouched low behind a cracked concrete barrier, eyes sweeping the skeletal remains of a bombed-out apartment block. Three teammates remained—Ramirez, "Duke" Donahue, and Falah, their Kurdish interpreter. The rest were dead or missing.

Dust swirled in the air like ash shaken from the lungs of the city. The call to prayer drifted through the air, warbled and broken by distance and ruin. But here, in this final scrap of a forgotten rooftop, it was only the sounds of men trying not to die.

They were down to one belt of 7.62 for the M240, six frags, and whatever rounds were left in their mags. Kael had duct-taped a tourniquet around Duke's thigh to slow the bleeding, but the gauze beneath it had gone from red to maroon.

"Still with me, Duke?" Kael asked, voice dry as bone.

Duke gave a weak grin. "Still kicking, motherfucker. Don't count me out yet."

Kael didn't respond. He was scanning the street below. The shadows were moving. Fast.

A low, ominous buzz grew louder. Drone.

Kael checked his wrist display. A flickering thermal feed showed dozens of heat signatures encroaching from three angles. Insurgents. Dozens of them.

They were boxed in.

Kael's back slammed against the sandbag wall of the U.S. outpost—a forward position long since forgotten by the brass and left for dead in the Mosul suburbs. They'd fallen back under fire, dragging Duke and Falah's body behind them, their ammo almost gone, their chances worse.

Then came the voice.

Low. Raspy. Arabic-accented English.

It cut through the comms with chilling calm:

"American pig. You killed my brother in Raqqa. Today, you die by my hand."

Kael's spine stiffened.

The Black Vulture.

An ISIS commander known for dismembering captured Marines on live feed. CIA thought he was dead.

Kael thought he killed him personally.

"I should've cut deeper," Kael whispered.

Another mortar hit outside the wall. Dirt rained down. Ramirez fell to a knee, cursing, hands bleeding.

Kael raised the mic again.

"Kael," Falah said, crouching beside him, voice quiet and urgent. "They're using civilians. Mothers. Teenagers. As shields."

Kael's stomach turned to stone. He peered through the scope of his M4. He saw it—an older woman being pushed forward, arms raised, trembling. A fighter behind her with a rifle pressed to her spine.

His finger hovered above the trigger.

"Don't," Ramirez whispered. "You shoot her, they've already won."

"Then what the hell do we do?"

CRACK.

The report of Ramirez's rifle echoed across the rooftop.

A sniper fell from the northwest minaret. A clean shot.

"One at a time," Ramirez muttered.

Then a scream. Then a roar. Another explosion shook the foundation of their perch. Dust filled their lungs. Falah shouted something in Kurdish.

"We're out of time," Kael said, already pressing the comm to his ear.

"This is Raider One," he said, voice level. "We are surrounded. Requesting immediate fire mission. Danger close. Full package. Broken Arrow. I say again—Broken Arrow."

The words ripped through every U.S. comms channel across CENTCOM, EUCOM, and the Pentagon. Alarms flashed in the Situation Room. A two-star general slammed his fist on the table.

"Get everything airborne—NOW."

From the Med, F/A-18 Super Hornets screamed off the deck of the USS Abraham Lincoln, loaded for bear with JDAMs.

B-1 Lancer bombers were diverted from Ramstein.

And from Kuwait—two CH-53 Super Stallions tore through the sky, flanked by AH-1Z Viper gunships, missiles hot.

There was a pause.

Then chaos answered.

Above Mosul, the heavens opened.

A Spectre AC-130 roared overhead like a wrathful god, its massive bulk cutting through the clouds. The 25mm Gatling cannons spun up first—

BRRRRRRRT.

Like thunder chewing through steel, the barrage stitched a row of explosions along the enemy's approach. Bodies flew. Dust spiraled skyward. Shouts turned to screams.

Kael ducked his head as tracer fire lit up the night. He could feel the gunship's voice in his bones—each strike a drumbeat of destruction.

Then came the 105mm howitzer.

CLANK.

BOOOOOOM.

The shell hit the courtyard two buildings over, vaporizing the insurgent squad that had flanked them from the west. Shockwaves rippled through the rooftop, knocking Kael against the barrier.

"Jesus Christ!" Duke rasped.

"They heard us," Kael muttered. "They fucking heard us."

Two AH-6 Little Birds screamed into view, zigzagging over rooftops like hornets. Their miniguns spun to life, unleashing a hellish chorus that lit up the night like a rave in hell.

BRRRRRT-BRRRRRT.

Enemy lines buckled. A technical truck exploded into a ball of flame. Fighters scattered in every direction, trying to retreat, regroup, vanish. But there was no vanishing from this.

Kael rose, lifting the M240, body trembling from adrenaline and blood loss. He laid down suppressive fire in the alley as Falah dragged Duke toward a corner for cover.

Ramirez stayed prone, methodical. "Snipers on the east—two buildings over."

CRACK.

"Correction. One sniper."

A voice cut in through the comms, calm and unmistakably American.

"Raider One, this is Havoc. We've got you. CH-53's inbound. Thirty seconds. Pop green smoke."

Kael blinked. He knew that voice.

"Comstock," he said under his breath.

He pulled a green smoke canister from his belt, yanked the pin, and rolled it toward the rooftop's edge.

Below, a gunship strafed the street, carving a path through a wave of reinforcements. From the north, the CH-53 appeared—low, fast, blades carving the night.

Ropes dropped. Operators descended in a blur of motion—black kits, NVGs, silenced weapons. Ghosts made flesh.

One of them rushed forward, crouched beside Kael.

It was Comstock.

Cigar in his mouth, sleeves rolled, blood on his knuckles.

"You boys look like you've been through hell," he said. "You want a ride?"

Kael didn't smile. Just nodded once.

"We're pulling Duke and Falah first," he shouted over the rotor wash. "Ramirez, go!"

As they moved, Comstock leaned in. "When this is over, Torres—we talk. Clock's ticking."

Kael slung Duke over his shoulder, staggered toward the ropes. Rounds cracked past his ears. An RPG flew overhead, missing the CH-53 by inches. The gunners returned fire, shredding the launch site.

"GO!" someone screamed.

Kael was dragging Duke's limp body toward the LZ when a burst of enemy fire dropped him flat. His ribs buckled.

Three rounds to the chest plate.

He rolled, coughing blood.

Ramirez was dead. Falah was dead. Comstock was wounded—shoulder and thigh—but still firing.

The CH-53 touched down hard.

Gunships sprayed the approach with chain gun fire.

Operators poured out—black kits, night optics, fire in their veins.

Kael threw Duke onto the ramp and turned.

He saw The Black Vulture in the chaos.

Limping. Screaming.

Then came the Little Birds—two AH-6s strafing the alley with miniguns, cutting ISIS fighters down in streams of glowing tracer fire. The Vulture's men scattered like ants under napalm.

One of them ran—taller, hooded.

Kael squinted.

"Vulture's on foot," he growled. "GIVE ME THE FUCKING RIFLE."

Ramirez tossed him a scoped M110. Kael dropped to prone, sighted in, took a breath.

BOOM.

The round hit center mass.

The Vulture tumbled into the dirt like a sack of hate.

Inside the chopper, Kael sat between Comstock and the door gunner. Blood dried in cracks on his knuckles. The wind tore through the cabin. Comstock couldn't help himself standing next to the door gunner dropping another 30 rounds with his SR-25 into the enemy as they flew away.

Behind him, the rooftop burned.

Below him, Mosul crumbled.

Above him, salvation waited—but not forgiveness.

Ramstein Air Base – Germany

Kael came to under fluorescent lights.

Comstock was on a gurney beside him, oxygen tube in his nose, chuckling despite the blood-stained bandages.

"Jesus, Torres. You really know how to throw a goodbye party."

Kael ignored him. "Where's Duke?"

"Stable. Med-evac'd to Landstuhl."

Kael tried to sit up.

He couldn't.

His chest felt like it had been hit with a sledgehammer.

A doctor rushed over. "You've got three cracked ribs, a bruised sternum, and a punctured lung. You're lucky your plate caught the rest."

Kael coughed, blood dripping from the corner of his mouth.

"I'm not lucky," he whispered. "Just… not dead yet."

He passed out.

Three days later:

Kael woke to sterile white light. He didn't remember falling asleep. Didn't remember the flight. I didn't remember anything but fire.

The room was quiet except for the rhythmic hiss of oxygen and the soft beeping of heart monitors. The kind of soundscape that didn't belong to the living—it belonged to ghosts still clinging to their vessels.

A voice cut through the fog.

"Well, hell. Look who finally decided to come back."

Kael turned his head.

Comstock sat beside the bed, one arm in a sling, his shirt half-buttoned and spotted with old blood. A cheap cigar rested between his fingers, unlit. His boots were still dusty from the field.

"Germany," Comstock said. "Ramstein. You made it. Barely."

Kael tried to sit up, but a white-hot pain seized his chest.

"Easy," a nurse said from the door. "You've got two fractured ribs, a bruised sternum, and your lung looked like it got stomped by a rhino. You move too fast, you'll drown in your own blood."

She adjusted the IV and left.

Kael looked back at Comstock.

"Duke?"

"Alive. Stabilized. They've got him at Landstuhl with the rest of the critically. He'll limp forever, but he's still got that pretty face."

Kael exhaled slowly.

"Falah?"

Comstock hesitated. Then shook his head.

Kael closed his eyes.

"They gave you the medal, by the way," Comstock said. "Silver Star. For bravery under fire, heroism, all that crap. Pentagon wants to frame your story as a win. A clean one. The kind people back home can swallow with their morning coffee."

Kael stared at the ceiling.

"I shot a kid."

"I know."

"It wasn't even a bomb."

Comstock didn't respond right away. Just flicked the cigar back and forth between his fingers.

"You think you're the first?" he finally said. "You think war waits for clarity?"

"I don't want the medal."

"Doesn't matter. They've already printed the fucking citation."

Kael turned his head toward the window. Snow fell gently outside. The base was silent. His reflection stared back at him—pale, hollow-eyed, stitched and bandaged like a broken thing that hadn't been thrown away yet.

"You didn't come here just to deliver news," Kael said.

"No. I came to offer you a way out. Or maybe a way deeper in."

Comstock leaned forward, voice lowering.

"There's work. Real work. The kind where you don't wear a uniform and no one calls you a hero. You'd be off the books. You'd answer to no one except me. You interested?"

Kael didn't speak. His hand opened and closed under the hospital blanket. He thought about the duffel bag in his jacket back in the barracks.

Yusuf.

He thought about Eli. About Duke. About the rooftop, and the flame, and the rage that hadn't burned out.

He looked at Comstock dead in the eye.

"I'm not coming home."

Comstock nodded once.

"Didn't think so."

He stood. Lit the cigar. And left.

Kael stared at the ceiling until the tears finally came. Quiet. Slow. As if his body could no longer tell whether it was mourning or just emptying itself of the weight.

The wind outside howled like a memory trying to claw its way back in.

Chapter 1

New Beginnings

Kael Torres leaned over the railing of the cruise ship as it glided toward Old San Juan, Puerto Rico. The pastel buildings of the centuries-old city gleamed under the Caribbean sun, framed by crumbling fortresses and lush hills beyond. The salty breeze tousled his hair as he took in the view, a stirring deep inside him — a restlessness he hadn't been able to shake.

This was supposed to be a vacation. A decompression. After years of living in high-alert mode as a U.S. Marine Raider, Kael had tried everything to find a new normal: road trip fishing excursions, even drifting along the California coast where he had grown up. Nothing had worked. He still woke up at night ready for a firefight.

He had boarded the cruise ship out of impulse, hoping the endless horizon would quiet the battles raging inside him. But now, as the vessel idled into the historic harbor, Kael felt something different. Something alive.

The ship finally docked. Slinging his old canvas backpack over his shoulder, Kael meandered into the heart of Old San Juan. The cobblestone streets shimmered in the heat. Bright façades rose around him like a fever dream. Music floated from hidden courtyards. Laughter spilled from open windows. He wandered aimlessly, hypnotized by the pulse of Puerto Rico. It wasn't just the city's beauty—it was its soul. Unpolished. Raw. Real.

Kael returned to the ship to speak to the captain and crew.

"I'm not coming back," he said simply, shaking hands with the few deckhands he'd come to know.

"Tell the cruise director thanks, but... I've got to find something here."

Nobody argued. They saw it in his eyes: the man had already left.

Before this new chapter, Kael's life had been anchored in the small mountain town of Chester, California. Summers were spent fishing in Lake Almanor, riding his bike down dusty trails, and tubing the wild, playful waters of the Feather River. His mother, Renata, a San Jose State nursing graduate, had raised him alone after a short-lived marriage to a man who lived back east.

Kael and his mom built a humble life. She worked double shifts at the Chester Community Hospital as an RN, saving every penny for the occasional trip to Boston, where Kael would visit his distant father. But it was Chester that shaped him: the quiet strength, the bone-deep connection to the land and water, the understanding that real life did not give you anything you didn't fight for.

Life in Chester was simple, but it taught Kael everything: resilience, loyalty, and the thrill of risking everything for something better. Traits that would serve him now, as he traded the familiar for the unknown, stepping fully into the hypnotic rhythm of Puerto Rico.

In the breeze, he thought he could hear it already — whispers of the El Conquistador Resort in Fajardo, where destiny itself was preparing to change his life forever.

The drive from Old San Juan was a sunlit blur of turquoise bays and emerald hillsides. A polished black Range Rover cut smoothly down the coastal road, its tires whispering over the asphalt as it approached the gates of El Conquistador Resort. Kael Torres sat in the back seat, his banker's laptop tucked safely in his backpack, watching the world change with every turn.

At the resort's grand entrance, Kael's breath caught. A row of gleaming Lamborghinis, Mercedes G-Wagons, and oversized Range Rovers lined the valet lane—chrome and horsepower glinting in the afternoon sun. Well-heeled guests strolled past, designer sunglasses in place, smartphones raised, ready to capture the next perfect sunset.

He stepped out, adjusting his pressed white linen short-sleeve shirt against the warm breeze. A valet offered a polite nod, whisking his backpack away on a silver trolley. Kael's eyes swept the scene: manicured palms arching overhead, bougainvillea climbing stucco walls, and scattered art installations— vibrant murals, hand-carved wooden totems, and a fountain sculpted from black lava stone that murmured softly in the courtyard.

Inside the lobby, marble floors stretched under his boots. Glass cases displayed local crafts: filigree jewelry, carved wooden masks, hand-woven hammocks. A brass-rimmed bar glowed warmly, its mahogany counter lined with stools inlaid with mother-of-pearl. Gentle Spanish guitar drifted from hidden speakers. Kael paused by a carved teak table stacked with tropical-scented travel guides, his fingers brushing the glossy pages.

He found the check-in desk, framed by a mosaic of reclaimed driftwood and ocean glass. The clerk—a woman with perfect posture and an effortless smile—scanned his passport without missing a beat.

"Welcome to El Conquistador, Mr. Torres," she said, "Your suite overlooks the marina. Enjoy your stay."

Kael nodded and drifted away, curiosity buzzing. He spotted a narrow passage draped in soft lantern light—an exhibition of local artists—before it opened onto a secret courtyard brimming with orchids and koi ponds. A hidden nook held a row of cushioned daybeds: a private oasis beneath creeping jasmine vines. He made a mental note to return.

A few hours later, Kael found himself on the terrace where an infinity hot tub perched like a jewel above the yacht club. Steam curled into the sky, marrying with the last tendrils of daylight.

He slid into the warm water, letting it rise to his chest. Below, sleek yachts bobbed in the marina. Beyond, three distant silhouettes—Palomino, Culebra, and Vieques—floated like dreams on the horizon.

The heat wrapped around him like a balm. He leaned back, the edge of the tub cradling his shoulders, and let his mind drift. For the first time in months, maybe years, the noise inside him softened.

Birdsong echoed faintly across the bay. The smell of jasmine and salt stirred a memory: his mother's homemade herbal soap back in Chester. He could almost feel the porch swing beneath him, the creak of rope as Renata read from a book...

...she never finished. A stillness he hadn't felt in years returned to him—not peace, but the shadow of it.

A buzz from his phone broke the spell. A client. A hedge fund report gone sideways. He stared at the screen, thumb hovering over the reply button.

"Even here, I can't escape," he muttered.

He typed quickly: Handled. Back online tomorrow.

He set the phone down, exhaled slowly, and leaned back again.

"I paid for this escape," he whispered to the sea. "I'll pretend tomorrow never comes."

For a long moment, Kael simply breathed. Then, as the jets loosened his shoulders, a memory surfaced:

He was ten years old, drifting on a greasy black inner tube down the Feather River. His mother laughed beside him, her ballcap askew, her voice

4

echoing under the old bridge downtown. The smell of pine and wood smoke, the rush of water, the wide-open freedom of endless summers... Chester, California, stitched into the fabric of who he was.

The river carried him not just downstream, but into dreams of distant worlds—places he could never yet name, but always somehow knew were waiting.

Another flash: Kael, wind in his hair, coasting past Chester Middle School on his battered Schwinn, his feet off the pedals as he chased the sun.

A pool server appeared as if summoned by thought, balancing a tray with elegant precision.

"Your cocktail, sir," the server said. "Compliments from the ladies."

Kael raised an eyebrow. "Ladies?"

The server gestured discreetly toward the pool deck below.

There they were—four women in gauzy beach dresses, draped over cushioned loungers beneath flickering tiki torches. Their laughter rippled through the night air like something practiced but still sincere. One of them, a brunette in a flowing coral wrap, raised a glass of red wine in his direction.

Kael lifted his drink—a frosted Blue Hawaiian that sparkled like tropical glass—and gave a playful salute. The women cheered softly, their glasses clinking in reply.

But he only had eyes for the one at the center.

She was not smiling like the others. She did not need to. Her poise made silence feel magnetic.

Dark hair fell in loose waves over her bronzed shoulders. She sat with a calm elegance that made her surroundings blur. Her eyes, almond-shaped and shadow-kissed, locked on his—not with hunger, but curiosity. Awareness.

She tilted her head. Just slightly.

Kael felt it like a current behind his ribs.

He looked away. Not out of fear—but out of strategy.

He let the drink touch his lips, savoring the sweetness and sting, and then set the glass aside. The jets pulsed beneath him. Lanterns around the terrace flickered to life, casting gold on his damp skin.

His thoughts drifted again—this time not toward war or memory, but her.

Who is she? he wondered. Not just her name, but her presence. She carried something. Legacy? Power? Danger?

He did not know.

He only knew this: something had shifted. Not outside him—within.

Across the water, the sky deepened to violet and gold, streaked with clouds like brushstrokes from a forgotten god. Tiki torches flared. Somewhere below, a steelpan band began tuning up—notes metallic and soft, promising the night's heat was just beginning.

Kael stood, water cascading off his torso, and grabbed a towel.

"This place has more stories than the ocean has waves," he thought, drying his arms. Kael walked over to the poolside changing room. He put on a pair of black tailored trousers-lightweight, just formal enough, cut to drape clean over his frame. Over his shoulders, he threw on a crisp short-sleeve camp shirt, dark silk with a subtle palm-leaf pattern that caught the low light. The kind of thing that said he didn't need to try hard to look sharp.

The woman was still watching him.

So, he moved—down the steps, across the patio, toward the ballroom glowing in the distance—toward her orbit.

The ballroom of El Conquistador came alive like something out of a fever dream—velvet heat and gold light, music pulsing through the marble bones of the resort.

A DJ spun a seductive blend of Puerto Rican house and Caribbean disco, the bassline a heartbeat beneath the laughter, clinking glasses, and the sharp gleam of chandeliers overhead. The floor shimmered—lit from beneath in shifting hues of pink, amber, and sea-blue, as if the ocean had crept indoors and decided to dance.

Kael stepped into it like a man passing through a veil.

The crowd was diverse and radiant: linen suits in pastels, silk dresses clinging like secrets, bronzed skin kissed by spotlight. Couples spun lazily beneath the light grid, bodies moving with the casual abandon of the elite—those who had nothing to prove and everything to taste.

Kael did not head for the bar. He did not look for a table. He walked straight toward the heart of the floor.

There was something meditative about the movement. The rhythm found him, coaxed his muscles into subtle motion—feet loose, shoulders fluid, hands relaxed at his sides. He didn't dance like a man trying to be seen. He danced like a man unburdened.

His linen shirt clung to his chest in places, fluttered at the arms. His jaw was stubbled; eyes alert but dreamy. He didn't smile. He did not need to.

In a corner lounge flanked by candlelight and velvet drapes, Marisol sat with her friends.

They watched him.

Her glass of wine tilted slightly in her hand, untouched from the moment she had seen him step onto the floor.

She did not need to ask who he was. She already knew. Not the name. Not the background. But the signature—what moved beneath the surface of him.

Kael.

She felt it.

"You're watching him like you've already decided," one of her friends teased.

Marisol smiled faintly, never taking her eyes off him. "Maybe I have."

When Kael finally turned and caught her gaze—really caught it—it was like a switch thrown inside both of them. A spark in the open air.

He made his way toward the lounge without a word. Slow. Unrushed. When he reached her table, he did not ask to sit.

He just stopped, offered his hand.

"Mind if I learn your name?" he asked, his voice velvet over gravel.

She did not answer right away. Instead, she rose—smooth, graceful, the room curving toward her like a compass needle.

"I'm Marisol," she said, placing her hand gently in his.

"Kael," he replied, his grip warm, steady. "Kael Torres."

She stepped into his space like she was born there.

"I should warn you, Kael Torres," she said, letting her fingers lace through his as he guided her toward the floor. "You look like trouble I might enjoy."

He leaned closely, smiling just enough. "You have no idea."

They moved together—not showy, not rehearsed, just in tune.

His hand found the small of her back. Her palm pressed to his chest. Their steps were not steps at all—more like drift and gravity, two bodies orbiting a center no one else could see.

Her hair brushed his jaw as she turned. His breath caught.

"Where are you from?" she asked.

"Nowhere lately," he said. "But before that—California."

Her brows lifted, curious. "What brings you here?"

"I wanted silence," he said. "But I think I found something louder."

She smiled. "You're bold."

He brushed a kiss to her temple. "You're the one who sent the drink."

She tilted her head. "You noticed?"

"I notice everything."

She laughed softly. It sounded like something dangerous breaking open.

Around them, the music deepened, the room fell away, and a thousand stories narrowed into one.

The song faded, but Kael and Marisol didn't stop moving. They lingered in the rhythm like it belonged to them now—like it had always been written for this moment.

Around them, the ballroom spun back to life. Couples swayed. Glasses refilled. The DJ slid seamlessly into another tropical beat, but Kael and Marisol were already in their own silence.

"Do you want to sit?" she asked.

"No," Kael said softly. "Walk with me."

He kept hold of her hand—not tightly, but with certainty—and guided her from the dance floor. They moved past linen curtains fluttering at the edge of the lounge, past the golden bar with its polished mahogany glow, and down a side corridor lit only by low sconces and the occasional flicker of candlelight.

Their footfalls were soft against the marble.

"Do you always move like that?" Marisol asked. "With no plan. Just… forward?"

Kael's mouth curved faintly. "Only when it matters."

They stepped through an open archway onto a moonlit veranda. Below, the marina was alive with soft clinks of rope and metal, the quiet slap of tide against hull. The sea looked black and endless, peppered with light. Warm breezes rolled over them like breath itself.

Kael rested his forearms on the balcony rail. Marisol stood beside him.

The silence stretched—not awkward, not empty. Just full. Charged.

"Why here?" she asked, watching his profile. "Of all places."

He thought for a long moment.

"I think I was waiting for something I didn't believe in," he said finally. "A moment. A reason. Maybe new beginnings."

"Did you find it?"

He turned toward her. "I might have just now."

She looked at him, not blinking.

"I don't do this," she said.

"What's this?"

"Meet strangers. Dance. Let myself be seen."

Kael tilted his head. "Why not?"

"Because once I let someone see me, they usually want something."

Kael took a closer step. "I'm not here to take."

"Then what are you here for?"

He didn't answer. Instead, he reached out and gently tucked a lock of hair behind her ear. His fingers lingered—not to flirt, but to remember what it felt like to touch someone without armor.

Marisol closed her eyes briefly. When she opened them again, they were softer. Warmer. More dangerous.

"Kael," she said, as if trying out the name again in the dark.

He smiled. "Marisol."

"Goodnight," she whispered, stepping back.

But before she turned, she leaned in and kissed his cheek—slow, deliberate, right at the hinge of his jaw.

He watched her walk away, the sound of her heels swallowed by the night.

Kael stood alone, staring out at the water. The sea moved endlessly below him. Behind him, the music drifted like smoke. Ahead, something unseen waited—something irreversible.

And Kael felt it in his chest like a tide turning. This was not just the beginning of a night. It was the beginning of everything.

Chapter 2

Drift to Palomino

The marina shimmered beneath a blue jay sky, the kind of perfect morning that looked like the gods had airbrushed it. The sun was already warming the polished decks of the luxury yachts lined up along the private dock behind El Conquistador. The water was so clear and still it looked like you could walk across it.

The scent hit him first—sea salt, teak oil, and sunscreen. Then the sound: gulls circling above, the soft lapping of tide against fiberglass hulls, and the quiet clink of rigging against aluminum masts. It was morning in paradise, and everything was too perfect.

Kael Torres stepped onto the boarding ramp of the 64-foot Azimut yacht, chartered daily by the resort to ferry guests to Palomino Island. He wore dark aviators and a white cotton button-down with the sleeves rolled up. A pair of tan canvas pants sat low on his hips, casual, relaxed—but under the surface, Kael was clocking everything.

He always did.

The movement of the dockhands. The tightness of the ropes. The cameras hidden in plain sight.

A crew member in a branded polo offered him a chilled towel and a mimosa. Kael waved it off, shaking his head politely but without warmth. He moved toward the starboard rail, resting one forearm against the cool stainless steel, scanning the open water like he was expecting something to rise from it.

He wasn't here to make friends.

He wasn't here to relax.

This was supposed to be a day trip, but in his gut, it already felt like a dream.

Kael had spent too long in places where calm was a lie, and paradise came with a body count. And yet... the Caribbean had a way of seducing even the most armored men. It wasn't just the beauty, it was the illusion of safety, and the danger of letting go.

Then he saw her.

Marisol.

Seated near the bow with a cluster of other women, mimosas in hand, their laughter light and unfiltered. She wore a white wrap over a black bikini, sunglasses perched low on her nose. Her hair was loose, catching the sun like silk. She hadn't seen him—yet.

Kael's eyes lingered on the group for just a beat longer.

One of the women didn't quite fit.

While the others wore coordinated coverups and giggled in rhythm, this one sat straighter, apart—not aloof, just… watching. Her tattoos were visible even under her linen shirt. Not the delicate kind Marisol had on her ankle, but older, darker. More like Kael's. Symbols meant for memory or warning.

She laughed when the others did, but a second too late.

Kael filed it away.

He shifted his stance slightly, adjusting the weight on his heels like someone preparing to move if necessary. The yacht's deck crew untied the last mooring line and waved toward the bridge.

The Azimut eased out from the marina, slicing the turquoise water with effortless grace. It was a stunning vessel—sleek, three decks, teak floors, and chrome details that shimmered in the sun.

Kael let the hum of the twin diesel engines vibrate through the soles of his feet as he watched the coastline drift away.

Then, Marisol saw him.

And within seconds, she was excusing herself from her friends. Mimosa in hand, hips swaying in sync with the gentle sway of the boat, she approached from behind.

"Are you always this quiet in the morning?" she asked, her voice brushing his neck before he turned.

Kael managed a dry smirk. "Only when someone sees me two days in a row."

She raised an eyebrow. "Are you saying I'm bad luck?"

"I'm saying I didn't plan on seeing anyone I danced with last night before noon."

Marisol sipped her drink, eyes not leaving his. "And yet... here we are."

She didn't break eye contact. Kael noticed the way the corners of her mouth moved slightly—not a smile, but the suggestion of one. A woman like Marisol didn't waste full smiles. She rationed them, offered them when she chose.

"You're a hard one to read," she said.

Kael shrugged. "That's the idea."

"Military, banker, divorced?" Marisol asked.

His brow lifted behind the glasses. "You always guess strangers' secrets?"

"No," she said. "Only yours."

They stood in silence as the yacht pushed out into open water, the sun rising higher, casting gold across their skin. Below deck, music played softly. Wind tugged at strands of Marisol's hair.

Kael watched her out of the corner of his eye. Not for beauty—that part was obvious—but for something else. Something underneath. Her presence felt sculpted, like a statue built to distract from the vault hidden behind it.

He was drawn to it. But not blindly.

"Tell me something true," she said, out of nowhere.

Kael hesitated. "I'm not as relaxed as I look."

"I know," she said softly.

He glanced at her. "And you?"

"I'm not as wild as I seem."

He nodded. "I don't believe you."

She smiled. "Good. You shouldn't."

The yacht sailed forward, Palomino Island growing slowly in the distance like something out of a myth. And between them—beneath every line, every silence—was something beginning to burn.

The rest of the ride passed with light banter and stolen glances. As they neared Palomino, the island rose from the sea like something from a painting—powdered sugar sand, lush palms, and water so clear it looked more like crystal than ocean. But to Kael, even paradise had shadows. He could feel the tension humming beneath the surface, low and indistinct, like a faraway drumbeat. Still, when Marisol stood beside him, hair trailing in the wind, the edge softened.

By noon, the group had scattered—some snorkeling, others sunbathing. Kael and Marisol found a shaded spot beneath a palm, drinks in hand. Conversation drifted between teasing and truth, silence, and spark.

Their drinks arrived a few minutes later—a Blue Hawaiian for him, tropical and over-the-top; a Paloma for her, classic with a twist of lime and something unspoken. Kael didn't say much.

He just opened a worn paperback, leaned back against a beached log, and let the world fade into surf and salt.

Marisol did not mind. She liked the silence. The confidence in it. Most men could not handle being ignored by a woman like her—they either fidgeted, bragged, or drowned in awkward chatter. Kael seemed to crave it. He wore silence like armor, not avoidance.

So, she watched him instead.

The way his thumb dragged slowly down the edge of the page. The way his jaw shifted when he was thinking, not speaking. How he never once checked his phone.

Minutes passed like waves. Unhurried. Warm. Intentional.

Marisol sipped her Paloma and let herself melt into the moment. Not just the view, not just the breeze—but him. The rare man who did not try to possess her, impress her, or predict her.

He just existed. And somehow, that made him even harder to forget.

She thought of her father—of his endless warnings. Of the types of men to avoid. Kael didn't fit any of them, but he also did not feel safe. Not because he was dangerous—but because something about him made her want to be known.

And that was the most dangerous thing of all.

Kael finally looked up from his book. "Good story?" she asked.

He nodded. "Old Hemingway. He writes like the world's about to end. I like that."

"You always carry books like that?"

"Only when I need to remember something real."

She tilted her head. "And do you?"

His gaze lingered on her. "I do now."

The air thickened between them, sweetened by heat and sea. A soft hush had fallen over the beach as guests disappeared into their own rhythms. There was something unspoken building between them—just under the surface. Like the moment before a wave breaks.

Around 2 p.m., an hour before the yacht was scheduled to depart, Marisol rose from her towel.

"Swim with me," she said, offering her hand.

Kael did not hesitate.

They waded in until the water reached their chests, the current gentle, the world far away. Sunlight rippled across their skin as waves lapped softly between them. Kael leaned back, letting himself float slightly, eyes closed for half a second—until he felt her.

Marisol slipped her arms around his neck.

Her body pressed into his with sun-warmed ease, her legs rising, wrapping lightly around his waist. She moved slowly, confident, the way someone does when they know you're already theirs.

Her lips found his.

A kiss that started soft and grew hungry. Her fingers threaded through his hair. He gripped her thighs, anchoring them both as the water shifted around them, gently rocking them like a lullaby. Petting, kissing, the tension of days crashing like silent waves between them.

They floated there a moment longer, suspended between sun and salt, between what had happened and what hadn't yet.

Kael's eyes drifted toward the horizon.

A small fishing boat sat about two hundred yards offshore. It looked casual enough—sun-bleached, with rust around the motor housing—but something was off. One man sat in the back, listlessly bobbing a fishing rod over the side. The other stood, motionless, holding a pair of binoculars trained toward the island.

They weren't looking for fish.

Kael's jaw tightened slightly. He marked the boat's position, the tide, the line of sight. He wasn't alarmed yet—but he was paying attention.

"Everything okay?" Marisol asked, fingers trailing along his chest.

He blinked, then let it go. "Yeah. Just thought I saw something."

"You did." She leaned in. "Me."

Kael smiled, but part of him stayed watching—mentally drawing lines between dots that weren't supposed to connect.

Yet.

Marisol let her fingers drift again across his chest, trailing small circles in the water.

"So… if you're more of a relationship guy, what does that mean for tonight?"

Kael tilted his head, watching her through narrowed eyes. "That depends."

"On?"

"Whether or not I see you on the dance floor."

Her smile turned playful, almost daring. "You mean you'll be there first?"

"I was there last night," he said, a low smirk curling on his lips. "Your move tonight."

She bit her lip, just a little. Enough to let him know she was already thinking about what she'd wear. About the music. About the way he'd look at her in the dark, with all that rhythm between them.

"Fine," she said. "But don't expect me to behave."

He leaned in, lips close to her ear. "Wouldn't dream of it."

Back on the boat, Marisol rejoined her friends, giggling and glowing, their laughter trailing behind her like perfume. One of them elbowed her lightly. Another whispered something that made them all burst out laughing.

Kael stood near the rail again, sunglasses hiding the flicker of something real. But his hands were clenched tighter than they had been before.

As the yacht pulled away from Palomino, the island shrank behind them.

But the feeling?

That stayed.

Chapter 3

I Dissolve in You

Night fell over Puerto Rico like a silk sheet—warm, soft, and full of promise. The El Conquistador resort pulsed with life, the open-air lounge glowing in amber lights, the beat of Caribbean disco thumping through the air like a second heart. Laughter floated on the breeze. Ice clinked in glasses. The dance floor shimmered under the moonlight, a blur of hips, heat, and desire.

Kael stood at the edge of it all, drink in hand, sharp in a button-down he had not planned to wear. The top two buttons were undone, sleeves rolled up just enough to show off forearms dusted with old ink. He looked calm, unreadable—but beneath the surface, his blood was already moving faster.

He was not waiting for a woman.

He was waiting for her.

And when Marisol appeared—he knew.

She did not walk in. She arrived.

Skin glowing, dark dress hugging her like a secret. It split at the thigh just enough to catch the light. Her heels clicked like she owned the floor before she even touched it. Hair loose, lips dark, eyes locked on him.

Kael watched her approach slowly and sure, drink forgotten in his hand.

"You came," he said, low enough that only she could hear.

"You asked."

They stood face to face, music swirling around them, the heat of the island night sticking to their skin.

Kael held out a hand. "You ready to dance?"

Marisol didn't take it right away.

She leaned in instead, lips brushing his jaw as she whispered, "Only if you're ready to misbehave."

Then she took his hand.

He pulled her onto the floor, into the music, into him.

They moved together like they had done it in a hundred lifetimes—sweat-slicked skin, fingertips grazing, hips pressed close. Not fast. Not wild. Intentional.

Every movement was a promise.

Every touch was permission.

She laughed when he spun her. He groaned when she rolled her body up against his chest.

They were surrounded by people, but all he saw—all he felt—was her.

It was not about sex.

It was about wanting.

Deep, slow, and dangerous.

As the music shifted into something slower, sultrier, Marisol curled into him, one hand sliding up the back of his neck, her lips close to his ear.

"Still a relationship guy?" she teased.

Kael's hand gripped her waist tighter. "Starting to think this might be the beginning of one."

"I Dissolve in You" by Costa and Maria Nayler

The final slow notes of the previous song faded into the air, and for a heartbeat, the ballroom stood still — a suspended breath.

Then a new melody began to rise, low and slow, like a heartbeat beneath silk sheets.

"I Dissolve in You" whispered from the speakers, a sound so haunting and beautiful it curled around everybody still left in the room.

Kael's eyes locked onto Marisol across the dance floor.

She didn't say a word — just stepped forward.

He met her halfway.

Their bodies slid into each other's arms like two halves, finally fitting back together after too long apart. Kael's hand found the small of her back, firm and claiming. Marisol's fingers traced up the column of his neck into his hair, tangling there.

The world blurred around them.

They moved as one, slow and hypnotic, hips brushing, breathing shared between barely parted lips. Kael leaned down and kissed her — a kiss so light at first it felt like a prayer.

Marisol melted against him, her hand roaming under the crisp fabric of his shirt, fingertips grazing his skin as they swayed.

The dance wasn't polished or practiced — it was desperate and raw, a silent confession of everything they were too afraid to say aloud.

Kael's thumb stroked the side of Marisol's ribcage, feeling the rapid flutter of her heart beneath his touch. She arched into him instinctively, her mouth finding his again — longer this time, mouths opening slightly, breaths mingling, tasting.

The beat of the music thrummed through their blood, matching the racing of their hearts.

They danced like no one was watching.

They danced like the world was ending.

Bodies pressed together, sliding gently, communicating through every whispered graze of skin and sigh of longing.

As the vocals soared — "I dissolve in you…" — Kael slid his forehead against hers. Their noses brushed, their lips ghosted kisses again and again, lazy and lingering, too drunk on each other to stop.

Neither wanted the song to end.

Neither cared who saw.

In that moment, they were nothing but two souls dissolving into one.

The song faded.

But they didn't let go.

Not even when the lights came up.

The night air wrapped around them like silk— warm, laced with salt, and pulsing with the rhythm of crickets and coquí frogs echoing from the trees. The stars blinked in the Caribbean sky, and the world felt slow, quiet, waiting.

Kael and Marisol walked side by side, silent, but nothing about the silence was calm. It was a storm in stillness—buzzing in their veins, tugging at their skin. Every brush of an arm, every glance, was a loaded touch of promise.

They reached the funicular, the glass-walled lift gliding down the steep cliffside toward the marina and yacht club below. Lights danced off the ocean as it moved, a slow, glowing descent.

Inside, Kael pulled Marisol gently by the hand, then turned her, guiding her back against the cool glass. The lights of the resort shimmered outside, casting golden ribbons across her skin.

He stepped in, one hand at her waist, the other finding her cheek.

Marisol's breath caught.

Kael's lips met hers—not like earlier.

This wasn't careful.

This was claiming.

A kiss full of heat and quiet control, lips brushing, tasting, coaxing. Marisol melted into him, fingers sliding into the collar of his shirt, tugging him closer, like her body had been waiting all night for this exact moment.

The funicular landed.

Marisol asked Kael if he was still a relationship guy, her voice low and grinning.

Kael replied, "Tonight for you, I'll make an exception."

They walked to his room like the night pulled them forward, opening the door with a single swipe, stepping inside with a silence that roared.

The moment the door clicked shut, it all broke.

Kael pressed her back against it, their mouths crashing together, hungry, raw, addictive. Clothes came off in pieces, hands exploring like a map they were desperate to memorize. His mouth traveled her collarbone, her neck, her breasts. Her hands roamed his back, his chest, the inked reminders of a past she didn't know but ached to understand.

They collapsed onto the bed—no hesitation, no fear.

Only instinct.

Only need.

They moved like they'd known each other for years. The touches were firm, fingers trailing, teasing, guiding. He massaged her thighs as she arched beneath him, slow and reverent one second, deep and grinding the next. Their first time wasn't about control—it was about giving in.

The second was something else.

After, skin slick with sweat, muscles twitching, Kael lay beside her, brushing fingertips over her hip like she might disappear if he let go.

But she didn't.

She turned to him, kissed him again, and pulled him back with a force that felt like gravity.

And this time, it wasn't just about lust.

It was fire.

It was fusing.

Their bodies tangled, breaths mingled, and somewhere between the arch of her spine and the way he whispered her name like a prayer, something broke open.

They lost track of time. Of thought. Of everything but each other.

By the time the sun began to rise over the sea, spilling soft gold across the sheets, Marisol lay in his arms, her cheek against his chest. Kael's hand traced the curve of her back in lazy, possessive lines.

Neither spoke.

They didn't need to.

Because in the glow of that first Caribbean sunrise together, something had shifted.

And neither of them would ever be the same again.

Outside the open sliding glass door, the night murmured with the gentle sounds of coquí frogs and lapping surf. A warm breeze moved through the curtains, stirring the quiet with the scent of salt and hibiscus.

Kael's gaze drifted past Marisol's shoulder, out toward the dark terrace.

That's when he saw it—just for a second.

A small object, maybe the size of a football, buzzed silently across the treetops. A red LED blinked once in the dark—a signal, not a warning.

It hovered for a moment, then zipped higher, vanishing into the sky like a ghost.

A drone.

Kael's brow furrowed.

Could've been some kid with a DJI Mini. Tourists flew them all the time—scanning coastlines, filming resort pools, chasing the sunrise.

But something about the flight path felt too clean. Too... intentional.

He didn't move.

Didn't alert her.

Just filed the unease in the back of his mind—where all the old instincts went to sleep with one eye opened.

Chapter 4

A Week of Yes

Kael woke slowly, the Caribbean sun slipping between the curtains, golden and soft on his skin. But it was not the light that stirred him, it was the weight of Marisol's gaze.

She was propped on her elbow, sheets tangled at her waist, eyes locked on him like she could read every secret behind them.

"You're staring," he murmured, voice thick with sleep and sex.

"I'm memorizing," she said softly.

Kael smiled, still halfway dreaming, and said, "You are so… SEXICO."

She blinked. "Sexico? What the hell does that mean?"

He turned toward her, dragging his hand lazily through her hair, brushing fingers along her jaw. "Sensual. Erotic. X-rated. Intimate. Compassionate. Orgasmic."

Isabel burst into laughter, throwing her head back, but before she could get out a comeback, Kael rolled over and hovered above her, grinning.

"You forgot shameless," she whispered.

He leaned down and kissed her—deep, slow, and consuming. Her hands found the back of his head, fingers tangling in his hair as their bodies slid together again. Heat bloomed fast and reckless, limbs wrapping, hips grinding, skin slick and sensitive from the night before.

What began as a playful moment became afternoon delight—a tangle of moans and murmured words and slow, exquisite pleasure. They moved like they knew the contours of each other's bodies from another life—familiar yet still exploring with wonder. The way her fingers curled into his lower back as she came undone, the sound she made when he pressed his mouth to the spot behind her knee—Kael memorized it all.

They didn't leave the room until well afternoon.

And when they did, they decided—together—to say yes to everything that week had to offer.

They strolled through Old San Juan, hand in hand, eating piraguas under the sun, dodging pigeons in the plazas, whispering things into each other's ears that had nothing to do with history and everything to do with heat. Isabel teased him about the way he squinted at street art; Kael admired how she read every plaque out loud like a storyteller.

They danced on cobblestone corners when a guitarist strummed something aching and beautiful. Isabel sang along—off-key and proud—and Kael spun her into his arms with a mock bow, kissing her in front of gasping tourists.

They climbed the ancient fort, her back against the stone, his mouth on her neck, until the tour group turned the corner. She bit her lip, eyes wide with thrill. He smirked against her collarbone.

They hiked the rainforest, sweat glistening on their skin, boots muddy, until they found a secluded waterfall. And when Marisol pulled off her top and tossed it over a rock, Kael followed without a word. They kissed in the pool, naked and breathless, the sound of water crashing around them like thunder. It felt ancient and holy—like their bodies belonged to the jungle for those stolen minutes.

When voices approached—other hikers—they scrambled behind thick brush, laughing, half-naked, slipping into their clothes and into each other's arms again like they hadn't just been caught red-handed. They held each other under dripping leaves, laughing too hard to breathe.

They golfed one afternoon—Isabel in oversized sunglasses and a sun hat, pretending to know what she was doing. Kael wore a backward cap and chased the ball without care.

"This game makes no sense," she said, squinting at her ball.

Kael lined up a shot. "It's therapy."

"For whom?"

He didn't answer. Just swung. The ball soared. She watched him—not the shot. His jaw set, his brows twitching. The flicker in his eyes when he watched it disappear into the trees—not joy, not victory. Something heavier. Something she didn't push.

They drank Moscow Mules and Cosmos from Stanley cups in the cart, racing down the fairways like rebellious teens. She drove like a maniac. He laughed harder than he had in years. He told her about the first time he drove a Humvee. She told him how she used to sneak her father's Escalade out of the estate at sixteen.

They cooked dinner barefoot one night in the casita kitchen—burnt garlic shrimp and sticky rice. Marisol smeared butter on his nose. He carried her onto the balcony over his shoulder in revenge. They ate by candlelight with no music, no phones, no filter.

That night, it rained.

They stood outside on the terrace, skin slick with mist, drenched and kissing. Lightning forked over the ocean. Kael pressed her back against the wall and kissed her slowly, like the world could wait. Her hands slid under his shirt, tracing every scar like Braille.

"Who hurt you?" she whispered.

Kael didn't answer right away.

He looked out past the terrace, into the black expanse of sea, the sky above it carved with thunder. His breathing slowed, but his eyes didn't blink.

"I've seen things I can't forget," he said finally. "Done things I never wanted to survive."

27

Isabel cupped his face. "You don't have to tell me everything. Just don't lie when you do."

He nodded.

And when she kissed him this time, it wasn't to claim or possess it was to pull him back from wherever he'd gone.

They undressed slowly under the storm's echo, skin warming skin, the rain washing away everything that wasn't them. The way Kael held her that night was different—not with hunger, but with reverence. Every touch a vow. Every breath shared like it might be their last.

They didn't speak for hours.

But everything important was said.

Later, in bed, her fingers rested on his chest, over his heart. His arm draped over her hips.

She whispered, "What scares you most?"

Kael thought about it—really thought. "That I could lose you before I even understand how I found you."

Isabel turned into him, kissed his jaw, and said, "Then don't waste time trying to understand. Just feel it."

Outside, the coquí frogs sang like a lullaby, and the rain tapped a soft rhythm against the glass, as if the island itself had stopped to listen.

That night, back in the room, tangled in sheets and sweat and words unspoken, Isabel turned to him.

"So... what are we?"

Kael didn't hesitate. "We're together. Long distance or not."

Her lips were curved.

"One week a month?"

"Minimum," he said. "I'll make it work. I want you."

And when he kissed her again—slow and deliberate—it wasn't just about sex.

It was about belonging.

She rolled on top of him, palms on his chest, eyes studying him like a scripture. "Promise?"

Kael met her gaze. "I've broken a lot of promises in my life. But not this one."

They made love again—slower, reverent, like everything had been leading to that moment.

And afterward, as she lay half-asleep on his chest, her breath warm against his ribs, Kael whispered something to the ceiling he didn't mean for her to hear.

But she did.

"Mi hogar está aquí."

My home is here.

She closed her eyes, heart thudding.

A quiet kind of forever settled between them—not spoken, not even fully understood—but felt, deep in the marrow.

Outside the open sliding glass door, the sea breathed against the shore. A warm breeze stirred the curtains. The rain had passed, but the sky still glistened from the storm.

Inside, Kael and Isabel slept wrapped in each other, neither knowing that this would become the memory they clung to when the world began to burn.

They had rented a Boston Whaler for the day—a rugged little vessel with twin outboard engines and enough power to outrun boredom, if not time. The plan was simple: take it across open water to Culebra Island, leave the world behind, and find a corner of sand no one else had touched. Just them, the horizon, and the kind of silence that said more than words ever could.

The sea that morning was glass—a still, mirrored skin reflecting everything they felt but hadn't yet spoken aloud. Marisol stood barefoot on the sun-warmed deck, her dress clinging to her from the light sea breeze, the edges fluttering like a promise. Kael watched her from the galley, half-hidden in shadow, but unable to take his eyes off her. There was something in the way her hair danced, in the way her fingers dipped into the salty air, that made his chest ache.

He walked up behind her slowly. Quietly. Until his chest was flush with her back and his arms circled her waist. She didn't speak. Neither did he. The moment said everything. "I wish we could stay like this," she whispered finally. "Out here. Away from the world."
Kael pressed his lips to the edge of her neck. "We can. We are."

She turned, her eyes burning gold from the rising sun. Her hands slid up his chest, over his shoulders, into his hair. And then she kissed him—fierce, deep, and aching with a hunger only silence could explain. The kiss didn't ask permission. It took. It devoured.

Later, on the bow of the Boston Whaler, wrapped in linen sheets and each other's limbs, Marisol traced her finger down the hard line of his jaw.

"You scare me," she whispered.
Kael looked at her, eyes narrowing slightly. "Why?"
"Because the last time I loved someone this much, they didn't come back."
Kael exhaled through his nose, jaw tightening. "I'm not them."
"I know," she said, pressing her forehead to his. "That's what scares me."

They spent the next hour in silence, tangled in conversation and skin, their touches shifting from gentle to desperate and back again. Every kiss tasted like a vow. Every glance asked a question the other wasn't ready to answer.

In a freshwater cove tucked behind a ridge about a mile inland from the beach on the fourth day, they swam naked. The waterfall splashed against their bodies like thunder, and he caught her mid-laugh, lifting her into the air and holding her there like some sea-soaked goddess. Her thighs wrapped around him instinctively, lips crashing onto his as the jungle echoed with the sound of them.

"I don't care about your past," she whispered, panting. "I want every breath you have left."

"It's yours," he promised. "All of it."

They made love there, half-submerged, steam rising from skin and water and the space between them. It wasn't fast. It wasn't soft. It was savage and sacred and soaked in something older than either of them.

By the sixth day, the word "yes" had stopped needing to be spoken.

It lived in her eyes. In the way she let him pull her hair when he kissed her. In the way she climbed onto him at night like she couldn't stand being apart. In the way she laughed without hesitation, danced barefoot in the rain, and woke him up with her mouth on his chest and her name already moaning in his ear.

He had become her compass. And she—his flame.

On the seventh night, they lit the fireball. The bottle went up in smoke and laughter as they sat under the stars, her head on his shoulder, his hand in her lap.

"I'm going to ruin you," she whispered.

Kael chuckled. "Too late."

They dined under the stars in Isabela, barefoot beneath a canopy of string lights and ocean breeze. The restaurant sat on a cliff's edge, where candles flickered against the salt air and wine glasses clinked like lullabies. Marisol wore a linen dress that whispered against her skin. Kael couldn't stop staring at her, the way the light hit her collarbone, the way she laughed without apology.

After dinner, they danced. Not to music, but to the rhythm of the waves crashing below. The wooden deck creaked beneath their steps, but they didn't care. Marisol leaned into him, her fingers brushing the back of his neck, her lips inches from his ear. 'This moment,' she whispered, 'belongs to us.'

Later, they strolled the moonlit beach, shoes in hand, the tide kissing their ankles as if blessing their joy. Marisol leaned down and drew a heart in the wet sand with her finger. Kael knelt beside her and wrote their initials inside it. 'What if it washes away?' she asked. Kael kissed her temple. 'Then we write it again tomorrow.'

They found a hammock strung between two palms and curled into it, tangled together, the stars blinking their slow approval. The world didn't exist beyond that beach. There was no worries, concerns and no war—just skin, breath, and the slow surrender to something bigger than both of them.

Chapter 5

We Were Just Dancing

The terrace was wrapped in gold, the kind of light that made everything look softer, dreamier, touched by something divine. Marisol spun slowly beneath a canopy of string lights, laughter on her lips, her wrap fluttering like a second skin. Kael leaned against the bar, drink in hand, watching her with a look that wasn't guarded for once. It was open. Almost gentle. For a few rare moments, they were just two souls orbiting closer, pulled together by rhythm, heat, and the hush of paradise.

She reached for him without a word. He stepped into her gravity like it was the most natural thing in the world. Their hands met—palm to palm—and they began to move. Not rehearsed. Not perfect. Just real. The music wasn't just playing—it was part of them now. And as Kael's hand slid to the small of her back, guiding her through the sway, Marisol looked up at him like she'd always known him. Like the night had been waiting for this exact moment. Time slowed. The world blurred. And they danced.

The music was still going—loud, electric, and pulsing through the open-air terrace like a living heartbeat. Marisol swayed, hips rolling gently as her eyes locked on Kael's. The world had fallen away around them, and all she could feel was the gravity pulling her toward him.

It was like drifting—weightless, effortless. The heat of the Caribbean night kissed her skin, and the bass beat of the Puerto Rican disco blurred into the rush of her blood.

Kael watched her with fire in his eyes.

His heart was pounding—not from the music, not from the drinks, but from her. The way she moved. The way she looked at him like she saw every dark, jagged piece he tried to hide—and wanted him anyway.

Then the world cracked.

Gunfire.

A sharp, deafening pop-pop-pop, so fast it didn't register at first. Screams tore through the terrace as people hit the ground, knocking over tables and drinks. The DJ ducked. Bottles shattered. Chaos took over like it had been waiting.

Kael didn't think—he reacted.

In one swift, controlled movement, he grabbed Marisol, wrapped his arm around her waist, and threw her down behind a heavy planter, shielding her with his body.

"Stay down," he growled into her ear, low and commanding.

Her heart was thundering. Her breath came in short gasps. But she nodded.

Another shot cracked—closer.

Kael's eyes flicked toward the source, scanning fast and sharp. One shooter—black jacket, bad stance—was moving through the scattering crowd, eyes locked on them.

Too direct. Too trained.

Kael's body coiled like a spring.

The shooter stepped forward.

Kael moved.

Like a trained machine, he was up, grabbing a heavy liquor bottle from the bar and hurling it. It smashed against the attacker's shoulder just as Kael lunged. He slid across the bar counter, his hand snatching a steak knife off the cutting board. The attacker swung—but it was too slow.

Kael drove the knife deep into the man's ribs in a single, clean strike. A grunt. A stumble. Blood on Kael's forearm. He twisted the blade and dropped him silently to the floor behind the bar.

He turned—and saw the second man.

This one was closer to Marisol.

That's when Kael saw her friend—Lena—the one with the sleeve tattoos and eyes that never quite matched the group's rhythm. She had dropped low, hand in her purse. When she came up, it was with a Glock 43.

She fired three shots into the night, tight pattern, sharp control.

The second assassin ducked and returned fire. Glass shattered everywhere.

Lena moved fast, pushing Marisol down and keeping her head low as Kael closed the distance. A flying knee, a punch to the solar plexus, then a violent twist—the second shooter was down too. Not dead. But not a problem.

Kael kept moving.

A third shooter burst through the terrace archway, this one carrying a suppressed MP5, and wearing a comms earpiece. Professional. Kael's eyes tracked him instantly.

"Left side!" Kael shouted.

Lena ducked behind an overturned table. The MP5 lit up the air with a suppressed snarl, stitching bullets into the bar's wood facade.

Kael slid across the floor, scooping up the second gunman's pistol, and fired twice—center mass.

The third shooter stumbled back, hit but not dead. He was wearing body armor. Kael aimed for the head and fired again. The man dropped.

A scream rang out from behind a broken column. A fourth attacker—young, erratic—began firing wildly into the crowd.

"Shit," Kael muttered.

He sprinted toward the shooter, vaulted over a tipped chair, and slammed into him shoulder-first. The two crashed into a table, sending shards of glass and silverware flying.

The attacker clawed for his weapon. Kael pinned the barrel with his forearm and headbutted him—once, twice—until the younger man went limp. Then Kael grabbed the assassin's SIG pistol and two full magazines, then dragged Marisol up from behind cover.

"Time to go," he said.

The crowd was still panicking, but the music had finally stopped.

Kael stood over the scene, breathing hard, blood on his shirt, knife still in hand.

He glanced back. Marisol was still down, eyes wide, shaken but alive.

He exhaled.

Then his jaw clenched as he looked at the body.

This was not a random act.

This had intent.

This had a purpose.

And Kael had seen that kind of hit before.

Someone had just tried to send a message.

And Marisol? She might have been the message.

The air was thick with panic, screams still echoing as Kael grabbed Marisol's hand and pulled her through the shattered terrace doors of the El Conquistador. The heavy beat of music had been replaced by chaos—broken glass, toppled chairs, bodies crouched low in fear.

But Kael didn't hesitate.

He moved like a man who'd done this before—eyes scanning, calculating.

"We need to move. Now," he said, his grip firm but careful around Marisol's wrist.

They burst into the lobby, Kael pulling her low, zigzagging through stunned tourists and panicked staff. A second shooter might be coming. He could feel it in his gut.

They reached the valet stand, and Kael spotted the first running attendant.

"Dame las llaves!" he barked.

The kid froze.

Kael stepped in, took a ring of keys off the stand, and hit the unlock on a nearby SUV. A black Range Rover blinked in response.

"In," Kael growled, shoving the door open for Marisol.

As they peeled out of the valet circle, tires squealing across polished stone, Marisol glanced back just in time to see a dark sedan jump the curb behind them.

Her eyes locked with Kael's. "We're being followed."

"I know," he said, jaw tight, eyes already scanning the narrow roads of Fajardo ahead.

The chase was on.

They shot through the twisting roads leading down from the cliffs, Kael maneuvering with skill that screamed military precision. The Range Rover drifted around a curve, tires kicking up dust and gravel, Marisol gripping the door with one hand and the dash with the other.

Behind them, the black sedan gained ground, headlights glowing like predators in the rearview mirror.

"Who the hell are they?" she demanded.

Kael didn't answer.

He slammed the wheel left, cutting through a narrow street lined with pastel-painted houses and cracked sidewalks. Dogs barked. A woman screamed from a balcony. The chase tore through the heart of Fajardo, turning the quiet fishing town into a war zone.

The Range Rover roared down Calle Unión, tires shrieking as Kael swerved between parked scooters and fruit stands, bullets punching through the rear windshield like thunderclaps. Marisol ducked low in the passenger seat, her hand gripping the door as shards of glass rained around her. Behind them, a matte-black SUV surged forward, one shooter leaning out the window, firing bursts from an M4. Locals scattered, screaming, as Kael clipped a corner, sending crates of mangoes flying across the road in a burst of orange and panic.

"Up ahead—Plaza Pública!" Marisol shouted, pointing as they careened past a colonial stone church. Kael spun the wheel hard, drifting around the plaza's fountain, tires skidding over cobblestones slick with ocean mist. He yanked his Sig from his waistline, rolled down the window with his elbow, and fired three clean shots behind them—one cracked the SUV's headlight, another sent the shooter ducking for cover. Marisol grabbed a second pistol found beneath her seat, exhaled, and leaned out just enough to empty a mag toward the front grill of their pursuers.

"Hit the tires!" Kael barked.

"Trying!" she snapped, squeezing off another round as sparks flew.

They shot through the archway toward the ferry docks, engines howling, the sea flashing beside them like a silver blade. Kael took a sharp left onto an alley barely wide enough for the SUV, metal scraping against stucco walls. The pursuing vehicle clipped a pole and spun out, crashing into a row of mopeds with a fiery blast. Kael didn't look back. He downshifted, punching the gas, and the Range Rover launched forward like a beast unchained. Marisol was breathless, blood running from a scratch on her temple, but her eyes were lit.

"That all you got, Fajardo?" she whispered to the night, adrenaline still surging.

Kael glanced at her, cracked a crooked grin, and said, "Buckle up."

Kael glanced in the rearview.

"Two in the car. Driver's calm. Passenger's armed."

"How do you know that?"

"Because he hasn't shot yet," Kael said. "He's waiting for a cleaner shot. Which means they want you alive."

Marisol's stomach twisted.

Kael made a sharp right onto a stretch of back road leading toward the forest edges of the El Yunque foothills. The city lights thinned behind them.

The sedan followed.

"Hold on," Kael warned.

He veered suddenly off the paved road onto a dirt trail, the Rover bouncing violently as trees closed in around them.

The sedan wasn't far behind.

They raced through the dark, headlights bouncing off palm trunks and overgrown brush. Then Kael slammed the brakes, spun the wheel, and skidded behind a grove of trees. The car stopped. He killed the lights.

Breathing heavy.

Marisol turned to him, eyes wide, adrenaline still spiking through her blood.

"You knew how to do all of that," she whispered.

Kael didn't look at her. Not yet.

"I told you," he said. "I'm more than just a financial advisor."

The silence stretched between them, thick with tension and tropical heat. Outside, the jungle breathed—cicadas humming, leaves rustling, as if untouched by the chaos they'd just escaped. Kael's hands were still tight on the wheel, his knuckles pale, his breath slowing from a sprint to a controlled exhale.

Marisol reached out, her fingers brushing his forearm gently. "Are you always like this?" she asked, voice low. "Calm while the world burns?"

Kael finally turned to look at her. The shadows made his features sharper, more myth than man. "Only when I'm with someone worth protecting."

The air shifted.

She studied him for a beat longer, then leaned in, close enough to feel the heat radiating off his skin. "So... is that what I am to you?"

Kael hesitated—but not because he didn't know the answer. He just wasn't used to saying it. "You're not what I expected," he said. "But you're exactly what I was running toward."

Marisol let out a breath she hadn't realized she was holding. Then she smiled—not the flirtatious one she wore like armor, but something softer. Something real.

"I thought I was the one running."

"You still can," he said. "But I'll be right beside you."

She reached across the console, threading her fingers through his. For a moment, the storm outside was just a memory. The SUV was a cocoon, a hideaway. A place where two people who didn't believe in fairy tales suddenly started to wonder if maybe—just maybe—they were inside one.

Marisol's voice was almost a whisper. "This is insane."

Kael smirked. "Yeah. But so was last night."

She laughed, a quiet sound that curled into his chest like a match catching fire. "So... what now?"

Kael glanced at the darkness ahead—the trail winding through the jungle, the stars overhead sharp as diamonds. "Now we disappear for a little while."

"Together?"

He turned toward her fully; his hand still wrapped around hers. "Always."

And just like that, the danger faded behind them. All that remained was the rush of escape, the heady promise of something wild and alive.

Something they hadn't dared to name but could already feel.

Together, they drove deeper into the night.

Chapter 6

The Jungle Doesn't Sleep

The stars above the jungle were barely visible through the thick canopy, but Kael didn't need light. His instincts had taken over—just like they used to when the mission turned south, and survival meant trusting your gut.

The SUV was well hidden in the brush. The two of them had trekked on foot until Kael spotted an empty vacation casita, half-swallowed by vines and humidity. Long abandoned. Quiet. Safe—for now.

They'd hiked for over a mile under cover of darkness. No flashlight. Just ambient starlight and Kael's memory of topography and trails. The jungle floor was slick with decay, leaves sticking to their boots. Every few minutes, Kael would stop, raise a hand, and listen. Once, a far-off burst of automatic gunfire cracked through the night. Another time, headlights flickered through a distant grove below the ridgeline. A car. Then another.

"They're still looking," Marisol whispered.

Kael only nodded.

Eventually they crossed a small arroyo and ascended toward a rise cloaked in strangler figs and wild palms. That's when he saw it—the casita.

The casita sat on a hill crest overlooking a dense wash of foliage that stretched for miles. A winding trail choked with overgrowth led up to it—a path only someone like Kael would notice. The clay tiles on the roof were chipped. One of the shutters hung crooked. But the structure held. The foundation was solid. It was the kind of forgotten place that no one remembered, which made it perfect.

They reached the entrance in silence. Somewhere, deeper in the jungle, a howler monkey barked, then went still. The moon above was fractured by trees, its light shifting like smoke across the forest floor.

Inside, the air was thick with damp heat and the sound of coquí frogs croaking in the night. The walls were covered in peeling paint and old family photos bleached by time. A broken ceiling fan hung limp. In the far corner, a rusted mini fridge gave a weak hum before going silent again.

Kael checked the windows—shards of dusty glass in warped frames. He shoved a chair under the doorknob and kicked a couch against the entrance. Then, and only then, did he turn to face Marisol.

She stood in the center of the living room, moonlight striping her skin, her arms wrapped around her waist like she was holding something in. Her dress was torn at the hem, a streak of dried blood on her ankle from the chase. Her hair was wild; lips still parted from the adrenaline.

He stepped closer, voice low. "You okay?"

She exhaled. "No. And... yes. I think I need to tell you something before I lose the nerve."

Kael's body stilled. He could feel the shift.

She looked up, glassy eyed but hard-edged.

"My father is Salvador Cárdenas. The head of the Cárdenas cartel."

The silence cracked like a branch underfoot.

Kael's brows didn't move, but his jaw did—tight, restrained. "That explains the bodyguards. The tailored life. The constant shadows."

"I'm not part of it, Kael," she said quickly. "I don't want anything to do with it. I've spent my life trying to carve out something clean—something mine."

"Yet here we are," he said.

Marisol nodded. "There's no escaping the name. The money. The threat. They find me no matter how far I run. And maybe this... this thing that

43

just happened—it was for me. Or maybe it was for you. But it always comes back.

Kael paced once, twice. Then he stilled again. "You know what kind of men your father deals with?"

She nodded. "Worse than the ones who came tonight."

Kael watched her. He should've walked away then. Should've reminded himself he wasn't built for this anymore.

But instead, he said, "You ever feel like you're a cheetah stuck in a cage with gout?"

She blinked. "What?"

"I've been limping for years, Marisol. Slowing down. Telling myself I'm done with the adrenaline, the missions, the danger. But tonight—when the shots rang out, and I grabbed you, I remembered who I was. What I am. That fire? That instinct? It's not dead."

Her eyes flickered.

"You feel alive," she whispered.

"I feel like the cheetah just remembered how to run."

She walked to him, slowly. The jungle pressed against the windows with its nighttime hum—coquís, rustling leaves, distant thunder like a drumbeat in the earth.

The space between them caught fire.

Adrenaline turned to heat. Heat turned to hunger.

Kael stepped forward. Marisol met him halfway. And when their lips crashed together, it was desperation. It was claiming. It was two lives spiraling into one collision they couldn't avoid anymore.

He grabbed her like she was his anchor and his sin. She pulled him close like she was drowning, and he was the only thing keeping her above water.

They devoured each other—wild, primal, and unrelenting. Like lions feasting, tearing away the layers of fear and secrets and lies. They didn't speak. Didn't explain. Didn't slow.

Kael lifted her up against the wall, lips at her throat, her thighs clenching around his hips. Her hands roamed under his shirt, nails dragging against scars she couldn't name but already felt bound to. They moved across the casita like a storm—knocking over a dusty lamp, scattering an old chessboard, collapsing onto the worn cushions of a sun-faded couch.

There was nothing gentle about it.

Not this time.

This was passion with claws. A surge of tangled limbs and bitten lips and gasping mouths. Clothes fell in pieces. Furniture was creaked in protest. The night outside roared

with frogs and crickets and leaves brushing the casita walls—but inside, they only heard the symphony of each other.

They didn't make love.

They survived each other.

At some point, Kael broke away, breathless, chest heaving. He opened the old mini-fridge and found nothing but condensation and rust. Then, behind a warped cupboard door near the kitchenette, he spotted it—an old dusty bottle of white rum, its label faded and foreign. Next to it, a half-drunk bottle of red wine, cork jammed back in sideways, and an unused candle barely clinging to its wick.

He held them up, raising a brow. "Looks like the universe isn't done with us yet."

Marisol smiled—something soft and disarming amid the chaos. She lit the candle with a cracked match she found in a tin. The flame flickered, casting golden light across the walls, turning their shadows into dancing ghosts.

They sipped the rum first. It burned, but it made them laugh. Then the wine—lukewarm, metallic, and somehow perfect. Marisol curled beside him on the couch, legs drawn up under her, her head resting against his shoulder.

Kael took her hand, tracing circles on her wrist. "You ever wonder what it'd be like—if none of this existed? If I wasn't who I am, and you weren't her?"

"I think about it all the time," she whispered. "But then… would we still find each other?"

Kael looked at her, brushing a thumb along her cheek. "I think we were always going to find each other. The fire just burns that way."

She tilted her face to him, their lips meeting again—not with hunger, but with something deeper. A slow burn. A surrender.

He carried her to the floor by the shuttered window. Moonlight spilled over their bodies in silver fragments. She kissed the hollow of his collarbone. He traced a line down her spine.

Their bodies moved again—slower now, deeper. No less intense. But something shifted. A reverence. A recognition.

When it was over, they collapsed in a tangle of sweat and heartbeats. Not a word was spoken.

They didn't need to.

Because in that moment, they weren't enemies or secrets or mistakes.

They were fire and storm and the wild thing that lives in the dark.

Outside, a distant gunshot echoed across the jungle—faint, but real.

Kael's eyes opened.

He didn't move.

Marisol stirred slightly in his arms, then stilled again, her breath steady against his chest.

But Kael didn't sleep.

The jungle didn't either.

He listened.

To the jungle sounds that weren't quite natural. To the coquí calls that paused for just a breath too long. To the rhythmic chirps disrupted by something heavier. Boots? A shifting branch? Or maybe just his ghosts.

He let Marisol rest, brushing a strand of hair from her cheek. Her warmth kept the cold edge of his instincts at bay, but not by much.

He whispered so softly it wasn't meant for her to hear. "If they come again… I won't miss."

Marisol murmured in her sleep, her body curling tighter into his. The jungle hissed outside like it was watching, waiting.

Kael closed his eyes for just a moment—but even in the dark, he didn't let go of her.

Not tonight.

Not ever.

Chapter 7

What The Moon Forgot

They had fled the jungle casita before dawn, slipping down the back trail on foot until Kael found the SUV he'd stashed under a collapsed palapa. It still ran. Barely. He drove without headlights, weaving through backroads and old sugar routes that had not seen traffic in years. Every airport, ferry terminal, and major road out of Fajardo was guaranteed to be under surveillance by now—either by authorities or by whatever cartel faction had sent the assassins.

They needed a way off the island. Fast. The only option left was the sea. And Kael knew of just one place that offered the kind of vessels fast enough to outrun radar, quiet enough to slip past patrols, and remote enough to, just maybe, not already be burned.

The night air was thick with salt and secrets as Kael and Marisol crept along the edge of the marina at Puerto del Rey. Moonlight glinted off the still water, casting silver streaks across the decks of million-dollar dreams.

They had not planned to come here. Not at first.

After the firefight at the resort, Kael knew the roads would be locked down—too many federal checkpoints, too many eyes looking for fugitives that matched their faces. The airports were out of the question; every tarmac from Fajardo to San Juan was likely crawling with DEA, customs, or worse. He didn't trust the highways either, with cartel watchers stationed on every bypass and overpass.

But the ocean? That was different. The sea did not ask questions. It didn't check passports.

And if you had the right vessel, the right heading, and the right storm cover, you could disappear between waves, and no one would know until it was too late.

That is why he picked Puerto del Rey. Tucked against the northeastern coast of Puerto Rico, it was one of the largest marinas in the Caribbean—rows upon rows of yachts, catamarans, and pleasure cruisers. A place built for escape, even if it did not know it. Kael had been here once before, years ago, when a retired DEA agent tipped him off to a ghost-runner boat stashed in the far end of the marina, something fast, quiet, and anonymous. He just prayed it was still there.

They moved quietly now, boots crunching over gravel and seaweed. The air smelled like diesel and wet rope, laced with the faint hum of generators and the distant thump of music from a docked party yacht.

Two men stood at the gated entrance to the yacht slips—hard eyes, tactical posture. Too alert for simple dockhands. They weren't marina staff. They were not police either. Kael could smell it.

Cartel.

Kael held up a hand, signaling Marisol to stay hidden behind the low sea wall. No words, just instinct.

Without a sound, he slipped into the water. Cold. Quiet.

He swam beneath the surface, flanking them from the dock's far side. The water was dark and still, broken only by the occasional flicker of moonlight reflecting off submerged ropes and barnacled pillars. Each movement he made was deliberate—silent as the tide itself.

He emerged silently behind them, water rolling off his skin like armor. In one smooth motion, he struck. The first went down fast, choked into silence, eyes wide, struggling, then still. Disarmed and incapacitated in under four seconds.

The second turned, too slow.

49

Kael snatched the pistol from the first man's holster. A silenced 9mm. He fired once clean into the second man's thigh. No sound. Just shock. Collapse.

Both men were on the ground in under thirty seconds.

Kael crouched, gun ready. "Who sent you?"

The wounded man gritted his teeth. "Ramos. Southern faction."

Rival cartel. The ones looking to take Marisol's father down—and her with him.

Kael looked down at him, gaze cold. "You're lucky I don't send you back in pieces."

He quickly scanned their bodies—radio, cash, a burner phone in one of the pockets. He pocketed the phone and yanked the earpieces from their collars.

Kael knew the truth: there were more. Still circling the island. Still hunting.

He stood and turned just as Marisol emerged from the shadows.

"You could've killed them both," she said softly, eyes searching his.

"I could've," Kael said. "But what's the point? Their bosses will know either way. No need to take life unless I have to."

Something about that answer struck deep in Marisol. His restraint. His control. His unwavering focus—on her.

He wasn't just surviving. He was navigating. Calculating. Protecting.

He was getting his SEXICO off this island.

They bound the men, gagged them, and dragged them into a supply shed. Kael used nylon dock lines to restrain them and shoved empty tool crates around the bodies to slow any potential discovery.

The marina was quiet now—eerily so. The scent of diesel and salt hung heavy. A few halogen lamps buzzed overhead, casting pale gold pools of light across the walkway.

They moved fast and quietly. Marisol kept watch while Kael broke into the marina supply shack with a crowbar. Inside: MREs, bottled water, tools, old flare guns, a handheld VHF radio, and a paper grocery bag with $25,000 in clean bills—likely cartel payoff money stashed for emergencies.

Kael tossed the bag over his shoulder.

Twenty minutes later, they were crouched behind a row of dock lockers, soaked, silent, scanning rows of darkened hulls. Most of the vessels were too luxurious—sleek white yachts with polished chrome and security cams blinking red on the stern. Others were too exposed, too close to occupied slips. Kael dismissed each one with quiet precision.

They needed something unassuming. Something functional. A vessel that would not be missed for at least a month or two—but that could still handle open water and outrun trouble.

They searched four boats.

The first had a dying battery. The second was too big and sat like a floating palace. The third was spotless—too spotless. Kael didn't trust boats without a single scuff mark.

Then they found her.

A 38-foot Leopard catamaran with matte paint and a faded name barely visible on the side: The Commodore.

She was tucked behind a larger cruiser, slightly obscured, and moored like she hadn't moved in weeks—but not abandoned. The Fenders were tied properly. The sails were stowed right. A half-empty bottle of Havana Club rum sat in the galley sink. The wine fridge held 24 bottles of chilled wine. Whoever owned her had left in a hurry or was planning to return. Either way, she was not locked down.

Kael climbed aboard first, putting out his hand guiding Marisol onboard. He popped the hatch and ducked inside. The interior smelled like old teak and warm electronics. Systems were dated but clean. Diesel levels were good. Engine lit up on the second try.

He poked his head back up.

"She'll do," he whispered.

Marisol exhaled. "What's she called?"

Kael glanced at the weather-worn letters. "The Commodore."

She smirked. "Fitting."

He didn't answer. He was already scanning the stars, plotting their heading.

"Is this the one?" Marisol whispered.

Kael nodded. "She'll get us to Saint Martin if we keep her light and clean."

They boarded quickly—Kael disabling the dock security sensor, Marisol checking below deck. The catamaran was fully stocked: charts, life jackets, extra diesel. And a surprise—beneath the mattress in the starboard cabin, Kael found a waterproof case.

Inside: a .45 ACP Glock, an old sat phone, and a photo of two smiling men with the inscription: Never sail alone.

Kael stared at the picture for a long second. "This boat has stories," he said.

Kael moved to the fuel gauge and squinted. A third of a tank. Not enough.

They needed at least another fifty gallons to make it to Saint Martin without drifting into a maritime death trap. The currents between here and the Leeward Islands could be unforgiving, especially if you were running low and had enemies behind you.

He cursed under his breath and climbed off the boat.

"We don't have enough fuel," he told Marisol.

She tensed. "So, what do we do?"

"We borrow some."

Kael grabbed a length of siphon tubing from the Commodore's emergency locker, slung it over his shoulder, and began moving down the docks—methodically, silently. Most of the larger yachts had auxiliary tanks, and Kael had done this before—in darker places, under darker skies. He kept low, choosing boats that were shielded by others,

Targeting the ones with similar engines. He siphoned twenty gallons from a charter fishing boat, another ten from a private cruiser, and a final fifteen from a long-range trawler with a full tank and no lights.

He worked quickly, breathed steadily, ears tuned to every creak and echo.

By the time he slid the last capped jerrycan into the Commodore's stern locker, his shirt was soaked with sweat and diesel. The horizon had started to lighten—just a whisper of deep blue behind the eastern clouds.

They had two hours until full sunrise.

And less than one hour before the first dockhands or patrol boats would start their rounds.

Kael climbed back aboard, wiped his hands, and looked at Marisol.

"We go now," he said.

They fueled her. Loaded gear. Cut the lines.

Just before dawn, with the sky painted in soft hues of pink and gold, they untied the last rope.

The Commodore pulled away from the dock in silence, slipping into the vast unknown.

A light breeze rippled the water. Marisol stood at the stern, watching the marina recede. Her hair moved with the wind, her hands tight on the rail.

Kael stood at the helm. One eye on the open sea, the other on the horizon. He adjusted the sail and charted their course southeast.

They were headed toward Saint Martin. A slow route. A cautious one. Hugging islands and hiding in harbors, circling slowly toward Mexico.

Toward Tampico.

Toward the fire waiting at the center of Marisol's world.

But for now, they had the sea.

And each other.

Below deck that evening, Kael lit a lantern and laid out the items they'd collected. A map. The burner phone. Cash. Rations. He studied the chart for an hour, then handed Marisol the sat phone.

"We'll need to make contact in the next forty-eight hours," he said.

"With whom?" she asked.

He paused. "A man I once trusted. He owes me."

Marisol didn't ask questions.

Instead, she knelt beside him, brushing damp curls from her face. "When we get to Mexico… will it be this again? Guns? Running?"

Kael looked at her, voice like smoke. "It'll be worse."

She swallowed. "Then why are you still with me?"

Kael leaned in, touched her cheek. "Because I never knew who I was until you made me choose."

Outside, the Caribbean stretched out like a secret—dark, deep, and endless.

Inside, two spirits once apart. But now combined drifted across the tide, haunted by pasts they could no longer outrun.

But for now, they sailed forward.

Together.

Chapter 8

In Simpson Bay We Melted

The light shifted on the water like liquid fire, dancing in soft ripples around the catamaran moored in Simpson Bay—two hundred yards off the coast from Simpson Bay Resort Villas.

It had been five days since Kael and Marisol slipped out of Puerto Rico under threat and chaos, chased by bullets and shadowy enemies with no names and no rules.

Now, the rhythm was different. The days bled together—sunlight, salt air, late afternoons with cheap rum and fried conch in paper baskets. They took the water taxi into the marina each day, blending in among tourists and locals, pretending—if only for moments—that they weren't fugitives.

Marisol had a weakness for coconut M&M's. She'd stuff a pack into her beach bag like a kid on summer break. Kael teased her about it, once calling her the "most dangerous woman he knew with the palate of a piña colada." She just smirked, popped a candy in her mouth, and winked.

For the rest of the day, they drifted toward Maho Beach, the legendary stretch of white sand at the edge of Princess Juliana International Airport. They sipped mojitos from sweating glasses, the mint cool on their tongues, the rum lazy in their blood.

Above them, the planes came in low—so low you could almost touch them. Each arrival and departure felt like a punch to the chest, the roar of jet engines shaking the sky itself.

Kael leaned back against the sand, one arm behind Marisol's shoulders, watching a KLM 747 taxi into position for takeoff. The engines screamed to life, a thunderous surge that battered the beach in a wall of hot air.

Laughing like kids, Kael and Marisol were tumbled backward into the sea, splashing and sprawling through the surf like they were young and foolish again.

When they came up—drenched, breathless, laughing into each other's mouths—Marisol brushed her wet hair from her eyes and said, "God, I wish it was that easy."

Kael smiled, chest heaving from the rush, forehead pressed to hers.

"It is," he said quietly. "With you, it is."

For a few rare moments, as the saltwater burned their lips and the world blurred into noise and color, they forgot who was chasing them. They forgot what was waiting over the horizon.

For a few rare moments, they were just two souls chasing freedom under the roar of the open sky.

As Kael and Marisol jumped onto the catamaran from the water taxi, Kael froze. He noticed a shorty dive suit, scuba gear, and a face mask resting near the cabin steps. A voice yelled out:

"Don't fucking shoot me, kid. I brought a care package for you."

They're sat Grant Comstock.

"Damn kid," he said, eyes hidden behind black lenses, voice smooth and half amused. "What kind of mess have you gotten yourself into?"

Grant tossed two heavy duffle bags across the deck. Kael caught them with both hands.

"Two hundred and fifty grand," Grant said. "All clean. Untraceable. There's a Sig Sauer P226, twenty-four mags. An HK94, folding stock, ten-inch barrel with a dozen mags. Consider it your new per diem."

Kael cracked the zipper, saw the stacked bills, the glint of steel.

"I guess I work for you now," he muttered.

Comstock gave a dry chuckle. "Isn't like you're going back to that bank job, not with a seven-figure bounty and a love interest straight out of Narco Weekly."

Kael froze mid-step. Marisol reached his side, still dripping from the swim.

"Who the hell is this?" she asked, breathless, her hand instinctively brushing the grip of her borrowed pistol.

Grant tilted his head, giving Marisol a once-over. "That right there is the daughter of Salvador Cárdenas," he said, whistling low. "Which means, Kael... you've officially graduated from complicated to biblical."

Kael didn't blink. "You followed us."

Marisol frowned. "Who are you?"

He smirked. "The guy who kept him alive in Mosul. The guy who can get you out. And the guy who just burned three favors with three-letter agencies I hope to never see again."

Kael stepped forward. "How'd you find us?"

Grant leaned back against the rail, posture relaxed but words sharp. "The whole damn shootout in Fajardo was caught on multiple CCTV angles. Gas station cams, traffic cameras, even a Nest cam from a vacation rental. Took Langley two days to scrub it all. You and her? You're on every agency's radar."

Kael's jaw flexed.

"The DEA wants to 'debrief' you. The CIA wants their pound of flesh. And Cartel Nueve Vidas?" Grant let out a low whistle. "Those crazy bastards want to split-roast you over an open flame and eat the seared meat off your bones. In front of your girl."

Marisol's eyes narrowed.

Kael said nothing.

Grant continued. "Once the analysts got a bead, they followed the breadcrumbs. Last confirmed sighting was a marina camera showing you slipping into Puerto del Rey. After that, it went cold... until satellite footage flagged a catamaran leaving port in a hurry. One boat. Predawn departure. All other sail traffic was logged."

He gestured up at the sky.

"FORTE-11 and FORTE-12. Two Global Hawks. Running 15-hour loops at 65,000 feet. One tasked by the Senator, the other by your sins."

Kael looked up instinctively—nothing but stars and the curve of the Milky Way.

"You've got about 72 hours before someone figures out your next move," Grant added. "Make it count."

They walked outside of the cabin onto the deck. Comstock put on his scuba gear. Then he pulled his mask down, winked once at Marisol, and flipped backward off the catamaran—vanishing beneath the surface with barely a splash.

Only the sea remained.

Kael stared at the ripples where Comstock had vanished, the weight of truth heavier than the duffle in his hands. Marisol stood beside him, her jaw tight, eyes scanning the dark horizon. The Commodore rocked gently beneath their feet, but the world around them had just shifted.

They were fugitives now. Global Hawks circling above. Three-letter acronyms hungry for answers. Cartels sharpening knives.

That night, The Commodore became their sanctuary. Anchored in the inky stillness of open water, miles from the nearest harbor light, it felt like they were adrift in another world—untouchable, invisible, and alone together.

Below deck, Marisol opened a concealed panel beside the galley and grinned.

"Well, someone stocked this for more than just emergency rations."

She pulled open a compact wine fridge built into the cabinetry and withdrew a bottle of Silver Oak Cabernet with a reverent smile. "This one's for you." Then she reached deeper and retrieved a chilled Veuve Clicquot champagne. "And this one's for me."

They brought both up to the deck along with two glasses and a faded wool blanket.

The sea was calm—so smooth it reflected the moon like polished glass. Marisol kicked off her sandals and padded barefoot across the wood, her white shirt billowing open at the collar, Kael watching her like a man witnessing a hallucination he never wanted to end.

They drank slowly at first. Then freely.

Laughing. Letting the bubbles and the tannins warm their blood and loosen their tongues.

They drank and laughed.

The moonlight turned the Caribbean silver—so bright and still it looked like they could step off the hull and walk across it.

And then they did the only thing that made sense in a world unraveling—they made love under the stars.

It wasn't hurried, or desperate. It was deep. Intimate. Reverent. A collision of two broken things that somehow fit when pressed together.

She kissed the scar on his shoulder. He brushed the hair from her face like it was sacred.

And when it was over, they fell asleep right there on the deck—naked, tangled, and finally quiet.

The next morning, The Commodore rocked gently at its mooring in Simpson Bay, the pastel hues of sunrise casting long shadows across the calm water. Kael was already up, shirtless, standing at the bow with a mug of strong black coffee. Marisol emerged behind him, stretching in his oversized t-shirt, her hair a tousled halo in the morning light.

"We should stretch our legs today," she said, looping her arms around his waist from behind. "We've got maybe another day—two if we're lucky— before we need to vanish again."

Kael nodded, eyes on the coastline. "Let's make it count."

They took a water taxi to shore, slipping back into the rhythm of locals and tourists without drawing attention. Everything looked deceptively peaceful— sunburnt couples snapping selfies, steel drums playing faintly from a beach bar, and the scent of grilled fish curling through the air.

Marisol flagged down a rusted old Nissan taxi with peeling decals. "Loterie Farm?" she asked the driver.

He grinned. "Best place on the island to lose yourself."

Forty minutes later, they arrived at the lush foothills of Pic Paradis, where the jungle swallowed the path and time seemed to pause. Loterie Farm was part sanctuary, part playground—equal parts luxury and nature's wild heart.

They rented a private cabana, tucked into the foliage, draped in linen, with a plunge pool carved from stone. Marisol slipped out of her cover-up, revealing a white bikini that shimmered like moonlight. Kael let himself smile for the first time in days.

They toasted with tropical drinks laced with fresh mint and dark rum, laying side by side in the filtered sun. It felt like they were in a forgotten world—one where war, cartels, and shadows didn't exist.

But the real thrill came next.

They signed up for the zipline course, climbing rickety ladders high into the jungle canopy. From platform to platform, they flew laughing, breathless, wind ripping past their skin. Marisol screamed joyfully as she launched herself into the green, Kael just behind her, keeping pace like a shadow. At the final station, she spun in midair and stuck the landing with a grin that stole his breath.

Later, back at the cabana, they stripped down for a couples massage—side by side beneath flowing white sheets, oils of lavender and ylang-ylang sinking into their sun-warmed skin. Marisol sighed as skilled hands worked the tension from her shoulders. Kael almost fell asleep beneath the rhythmic pressure, lulled by the breeze, the birdsong, and her presence beside him.

For a moment, it felt like they were just two lovers on vacation. Not fugitives. Not targets. Just human.

Afterward, they lounged in the water of their private plunge pool, bodies entwined, sipping coconut water and watching the sun dip lower.

"Let's stay here," Marisol whispered against his collarbone.

Kael smiled. "You know we can't."

"But maybe we can pretend just a little longer."

He nodded, brushing a damp strand of hair from her cheek. "Just a little longer."

The illusion wouldn't last—but in that hidden jungle escape, wrapped in each other and the taste of paradise, they let it live a few hours more.

Kael and Marisol made their way back towards the marina. They lingered on Welfare Road as the afternoon waned into golden hour. A warm breeze danced along the boulevard, stirring up scents of jerk chicken and sugarcane rum. Laughter spilled from the open patio of NoWhere Special, where locals and tourists clinked glasses in a kind of soft, collective denial that danger ever existed on an island this beautiful.

Kael and Marisol moved in sync, slipping from bar to boutique, ducking into a record shop just to hear vintage vinyl scratching out Latin soul. Marisol tried on sunglasses she didn't need. Kael bought a folding knife he didn't trust the local ones to carry. They shared a rum ice cream cone and a kiss in the alley behind Captain's Rib Shack. It tasted like sweat and heat and memory.

They weren't just pretending anymore, they were borrowing time.

"Let's not talk about leaving," Marisol said, her voice softer than the breeze.

Kael gave her a long look, then nodded. "Just for now."

As the sun dipped lower, they made their way down to the water's edge. A small wooden dock waited beyond a row of market stalls closing for the night. Kael signaled a water taxi—an old Yamaha-powered skiff piloted by a Rasta in wraparound shades and a weathered straw hat.

The ride back was silent. Not cold—just reverent. The sea was a sheet of liquid copper under the dusk light. Shadows curled along the hills of Saint Martin like sleeping gods. Marisol leaned against Kael's shoulder, her fingers laced with his, watching the sky bleeding colors.

When The Commodore came into view, moored peacefully off Simpson Bay, the Rasta cut the engine.

Kael reached into his pocket and handed the man a folded fifty. "We were never here."

The Rasta grinned, tapped his temple once, and pulled away without a word.

They climbed aboard. The deck felt like home now—salt-worn and silent. Marisol kicked off her sandals and walked barefoot to the stern, trailing fingers along the rail. Kael followed her, the hush of the coming night pressing close around them.

Above, the first stars blinked into existence. It was too perfect.

And that's when the engine noise came—low and distant but growing.

Kael sat up and pulled her into his lap, wrapping his arms around her waist as they watched the orange-pink sky melt into the glistening Caribbean. The moment was still—until it wasn't.

A sudden ripple of engine noise cut through the morning calm. Kael's eyes sharpened instantly. Off the port bow, a white patrol boat skimmed the water, slowing as it passed near the resort docks.

Marisol tensed. "Is that them?"

Kael's hand slipped from her waist to the small compartment beneath the bunk, pulling out a pair of binoculars. "Not cartel. Local authorities. But that doesn't mean they're not looking."

He handed the binoculars to her. "Get dressed. Quietly."

She nodded and slid from his lap, grabbing her sundress from the cabin hook. Kael pulled on board shorts and a linen shirt, still damp from the night air.

As Marisol moved past the galley, Kael noticed a blinking red light on the nav console. A message.

Grant Comstock.

Encrypted Transmission: U.S. Territory Authorities Tagging In. Assume Your Position Is Known. Hostile Networks Competing. Avoid Mainland Contact. Rendezvous Soon.

Kael's jaw tightened.

"They're working together now. Rival cartels… corrupt law enforcement… international flags on the table."

"Kael…" Marisol said, now behind him, her hand on his shoulder. "What does that mean for us?"

He turned and faced her, his voice lower, steel in his tone.

"It means no ports. No customs. And no mainland. We play dead until I say otherwise."

He cupped her face gently.

"But I'm not letting anything happen to you. Not while I'm breathing."

She kissed him slowly, hungry, and aching with trust. He lifted her onto the galley counter, the morning sun casting golden halos over her shoulders. They moved together, not hurried, but needing—like the world outside didn't exist for the moment.

Later, still breathless and tangled, Marisol laid her head on his chest.

"We can't stay dead forever," she murmured.

Kael closed his eyes.

"Then we find a place where even fugitives can rest."

After they cleaned up and the authorities had drifted past without boarding, Marisol moved to the cockpit, the wind gently teasing her hair as she tapped into an encrypted communication app on her satellite phone—one of the few pieces of tech they trusted.

Kael watched her from the cabin door, towel draped over his shoulders, still shirtless.

"You making a call?" he asked.

She nodded without turning.

"There's only one person I can trust. She's worked for my father… but she was always more loyal to me."

The call rang twice. Then a click.

A woman's voice came through, smoky and edged in grit.

"Marisol Cárdenas. Either I'm dreaming or you're about to drag me into hell again."

Marisol smiled softly.

"Natalia Ortega Henacho. I need you."

There was a pause.

"You alive, mami? I saw the news. Heard whispers. Fajardo was a warzone."

"I'm alive," Marisol said. "We're off the grid. In the water. Near St. Maarten."

Another pause.

"And the man you're with?"

Marisol glanced at Kael. He raised an eyebrow. She looked back to the sea.

"He's the only reason I'm still breathing. Former CIA and Military. Lethal. Loyal. And not afraid of the dark."

Natalia gave a short laugh.

"Sounds like my kind of broken."

"We need an extraction. Discreet. You still have access to La Furia?" Marisol asked.

"I do," Natalia replied, her tone shifting to serious. "I'll be within range in two weeks. But Marisol…"

"Yeah?"

"If your father finds out I helped you, I'll be a ghost too. You sure this is worth it?"

Marisol stared into the horizon, wind tangling her hair, Kael standing behind her now, hand on her shoulder.

"She's worth it," Kael said, answering for her.

Natalia paused once more.

"I'll see you in two weeks. Don't die before I get there."

The call ended. Marisol stared at the sea, the silence after the call heavier than gunfire.

Kael stepped beside her.

"Who is she?"

"Natalia?" Marisol said, her voice was flat and nostalgic. "She's not just a sicario. She's a storm wrapped in red lipstick and a switchblade. Grew up in the same shadows I did. She saved my life once when I was seventeen. I think she's about to do it again."

Kael nodded slowly.

"Then let's be ready."

That night on the catamaran, the breeze carried the scent of grilled fish and salt. Marisol sat barefoot on the deck, legs tucked beneath her, sipping a dark rum over ice. Kael leaned over the map table, tracing a route southwest with his finger.

"Ambergris Caye," he murmured, his voice low. "Quiet. Remote. It gets us closer to the Yucatán… and closer to home."

"Safer than open waters," Marisol added, her gaze steady on the horizon.

The Caribbean shimmered like a liquid sapphire under the mid-morning sun.

Kael stood at the helm of the catamaran, the wind whispering through his hair, the salt of the sea kissing his skin. Marisol leaned against the rail, her sundress fluttering like a flag in the breeze, her eyes reflecting the endless horizon.

And though the storm hadn't come yet, they could both feel it gathering—just beyond the blue.

They held hands in silence, eyes locked forward.

Together.

Toward the fire. Toward freedom.

Toward the next war.

Chapter 9

The Caribbean Shuffle

They had slipped away from Simpson Bay at first light, slicing southward through the Lesser Antilles, sailing free — or so it seemed.

Every ripple of water, every glance over the shoulder carried an undertone of danger. But here, alone at sea, it was easy to believe the world had shrunk down to just the two of them.

The catamaran was a vessel of freedom — and passion.

Six days passed like a fever dream — passion, planning, whispered fears, and reckless hope twined together under the stars. Each moment felt suspended outside of time. They danced in the galley to old songs from Kael's playlist, fed each other fresh mango slices, and played cards long after the sun dipped behind the horizon.

The cargo net stretched between the twin hulls below became their sanctuary. At sunset, with the sky painted in fierce streaks of gold and crimson, they made love on the cargo net — suspended over the sea, waves brushing against their bodies. The rhythm of the ocean matched the rhythm of their hearts, their souls colliding in a storm of need and tenderness.

The breeze wrapped around them like silk, warm and salt kissed. Marisol's fingers laced into Kael's hair as he kissed the hollow of her neck, her breath catching with each whisper of wind. The ocean rocked gently beneath them; a lullaby made of waves and desire. Below, the water shimmered with light reflected from the dying sun, a kaleidoscope of red, pink, and deep indigo.

They took their time — exploring, teasing, discovering each other all over again. Every sigh, every moan became a hymn to freedom, to survival, to the fragile bliss they had carved out between danger and exile. Kael kissed her slowly, reverently, as if committing every freckle and scar to memory. Marisol arched into him, her body pliant and alive, matching his every movement with fierce, graceful hunger.

Above them, the sky deepened. The first stars blinked into view as if drawn by their fire. The catamaran swayed gently, creaking in rhythm, as if nature herself gave them privacy. Their bodies tangled together like seaweed in a tide, raw and beautiful, completely unafraid.

When they finally collapsed into each other's arms, breathless and slick with sweat and salt, Kael pulled her closer and kissed her temple.

"I don't care what waits for us," he murmured.

"Neither do I," she whispered back, tracing lazy circles on his chest. "If the world ends tomorrow, I'll still have this."

They lay there as twilight bled into night, the world hushed but for the sea's eternal song and the beating of two hearts refusing to surrender.

They would occasionally flip on the boat's AM and FM radio — a relic from simpler times. Sometimes, in the early hours or right before dusk, they'd pick up scratchy transmissions. For an hour or two, faint voices would break through the static: snippets of cartel violence tearing through Tampico, news of new tariffs gutting local economies, hints of Chinese operatives landing in Central America. One fragment even mentioned Veloxyn by name. The quiet out there felt unnatural. Too still. Kael had learned long ago that calm didn't mean safety-it meant something was coming. Something always was. Shadows moved in silence. Enemies sharpened their knives in moments like these.

They had to reach South Water Caye soon — to regroup, to plan, to survive.

But none of it felt real — not here. Out on the open ocean, where the water stretched like silk in every direction and the stars spilled across the sky like spilled sugar, those grim dispatches felt like they came from another planet.

They looked at each other and smiled. The chaos was distant. They were safe, alone in their own floating world.

Kael knew their time on the open water was limited. There were whispers — of cartels tightening their grip, of men hunting him for reasons that tied him to a past he could never fully escape. He knew it not only in instinct, but in the cold shiver of that radio static, in the garbled warnings drifting through from a civilization on the brink.

But for these few stolen days, Marisol was not the daughter of a powerful man.

Kael was not a haunted soldier.

They were just two souls at the mercy of the sea — and of each other.

The days were languid, and sun kissed. Marisol would wear his old military tee, hem pulled tight at her thighs, skin glowing with sun and salt. Kael would cook breakfast shirtless at the galley stove — eggs scrambled in coconut oil, fresh mango slices, black coffee brewed strong and bitter. They'd eat on the deck in silence, their connection deeper than any conversation.

One morning, after a long silence and a shared smile, Kael reached into the under-seat storage and pulled out two collapsible fishing rods. "You ever catch your own dinner?" he asked.

Marisol raised an eyebrow. "Only if tequila and charm don't count."

They rigged the lines and cast off the stern, drifting slowly on gentle waves. Minutes passed. Then an hour. They drank coconut water straight from the shell, talked about nothing and everything.

Then—

Kael's rod dipped suddenly.

But it wasn't his line.

"Marisol—your reel!" he shouted.

Her rod bent like a bow. The line screeched out as something massive fought against it.

She stood, legs braced wide, squealing with laughter and panic. "It's a monster!"

Kael sprang to her side. "Hold steady — don't let it snap!"

She fought the fish like a warrior, the rod bowing violently. Ten minutes passed. Then fifteen. Sweat glistened on her brow as she clenched her jaw and reeled.

With a final heave, a massive flash of silver exploded from the water.

"A tuna!" Kael exclaimed. "That's sixty pounds easy!"

Together, they hauled it up, flopping and gleaming on the stern deck. Marisol dropped to her knees, breathless and stunned. "Holy shit. I caught that."

Kael bent beside her. "You caught it. That beast is all yours."

She whooped and threw her arms around his neck. "We're eating like pirates tonight."

They gutted and filleted it right there, saltwater rinsing the blood away. Kael packed half into the fridge and sliced the freshest cuts into sashimi. Marisol fetched a bottle — no, a magnum — of red wine from the cooler.

Back on deck, they laid out a makeshift picnic. Chilled tuna, soy sauce, wasabi, and the wine breathing bold and heavy in the humid air.

"To my pirate queen," Kael toasted.

"To tuna and tequila hearts," Marisol laughed, clinking her glass to his.

They got drunk fast, laughing and feeding each other pieces of fish, fingers brushing lips. Marisol climbed into his lap, nuzzling against his neck. "I've never been this happy," she whispered.

Kael kissed her slowly, then deeper.

They stumbled below deck, knocking into cabinets, stripping clothes as they went. The afternoon was thick with heat and wine and want. They made love with the abandon of storm-chasers — unashamed, reckless, and alive.

Later, tangled in the sheets, skin damp and satisfied, Marisol murmured, "Best sushi I've ever had."

Kael grinned. "And the wine?"

"Dangerous," she said, kissing his shoulder.

They dozed, wrapped around each other as the sun dipped toward the horizon.

In the afternoons, they dove off the stern, bodies cutting through the turquoise water like dolphins. Marisol would surface laughing, her wet hair slicked back, treading water as Kael floated beside her. Once, she pulled him under, kissing him beneath the waves, the salt stinging their lips as they tangled like sea creatures.

At night, they'd lay out on the top deck with an old wool blanket, watching the stars. Kael would trace constellations on her stomach with the tip of his finger, naming each one — Orion, Scorpius, Cassiopeia. Marisol listened like a child hearing fairy tales. She told him about her childhood in the mountains, the scent of lime trees, the hidden rivers where she learned to swim.

They shared stories they'd never told anyone.

Kael spoke of the day his best friend bled out in a Humvee beside him, how the radio screamed but no one answered. Marisol revealed she once wanted to be a painter, had even applied to a school in Barcelona

— before the cartel shut down that dream like a fist closing over light.

The past lingered between them, fragile and heavy. Yet instead of driving them apart, the confessions wove them closer. They didn't flinch from each other's darkness — they cradled it. Every scar they shared became another bond sealed by moonlight and truth. For once, there was no need to pretend. No war face. No masks. Just two survivors clinging to each other in the eye of a slow-moving storm.

The ocean had given them shelter, but it was also a reminder: no escape lasted forever. And somewhere beyond the waterline, reality waited with sharp teeth and greedy hands. But tonight, that shoreline shimmered like a dream.

When they finally neared South Water Caye, the island rose before them like a secret whispered only to lovers. Palm trees bent with the wind, casting long shadows across ivory sands. The catamaran slowed as Kael took the helm and Marisol tossed lines to the weathered dock.

After tying off the catamaran at the rustic dock of South Water Caye, Kael and Marisol stepped barefoot onto the soft sands. The warm Caribbean water lapped at their ankles as they strolled the shoreline, the sun lowering in molten gold streaks across the sky.

They found a small, open-air beach bar nestled under a canopy of palms, the glow of string lights beginning to flicker alive. Inside, an old disco playlist spun through battered speakers, the rhythm pulling them closer.

Over the hum of music and the clink of glasses, they fell into a deep, vulnerable conversation — no masks, no guarded glances. They spoke of family, of the ache for something real, of love, peace, and the freedom to live beyond the shadows that haunted them.

Kael told her about the time he buried his teammate in Mosul, how he sat by the body for eight hours until the sun came up, whispering stories just to keep his own soul from collapsing. Marisol shared the ache of losing one her sister at thirteen, the silence that swallowed their house, the quiet expectations of a cartel dynasty pressing in around her like a tomb.

Moved by a surge of boldness, Marisol pulled Kael into a slow dance, pressing herself into him with the effortless grace of a woman unafraid of her power.

Their eyes locked.

"Kiss me," she commanded softly.

Kael, his voice thick with mischief and desire, replied, "Only if I can French kiss you... in Spanish."

They both laughed, the sound raw and unfiltered, a release of everything binding them.

The dance stretched on, heat building between them. Kael kissed her shoulder, then her collarbone, then her jawline, savoring the taste of sea and sugar on her skin. People around them faded into silhouettes.

After the dance, half-tipsy on rum and possibility, they hatched a plan:

Call Natalia.

Arrange for her to meet us in Ambergris Caye in three days.

There, they would finalize their next move — a move that could free them... or doom them.

Later, under the ink-black sky pricked with stars, they wandered the village's edge and found a tattoo shack. The artist was an old Rasta named Elijah with a silver beard and eyes that had seen too much. He spoke in riddles and blessed them both before touching needle to skin.

The place smelled of sandalwood and sea salt, lit only by a flickering kerosene lamp and a hanging string of dim blue lights. Marisol sat first, her legs crossed, eyes locked on Kael as Elijah prepped the needle.

"You sure you can handle a little pain?" she teased, lifting her shirt just enough to expose her hipbone.

Kael smirked. "I've been stabbed, shot, and ghosted by three women. I think I can handle you."

"You can't handle me," she said, voice like smoke. "You survive me. There's a difference."

Elijah chuckled slowly. "This one's got fire. Careful, soldier."

When it was Kael's turn, Marisol leaned in and whispered near his ear. "If you flinch, I'm going to tell Elijah to ink a dolphin on your ass."

Kael didn't flinch — but his breath hitched when her fingers slid just under the waistband of his shorts while she watched.

"Don't distract me," he murmured.

"Oh, but that's my specialty." She leaned in and nipped his earlobe.

Impulsively, they decided to get matching ouroboros tattoos — the ancient symbol of a serpent devouring its own tail, eternal rebirth. Marisol chose her left hip. Kael chose the back of his right shoulder.

When it was done, they stood side by side in the mirror, their skin still raw, their eyes glowing.

The tattoos were branding, a silent vow.

They belonged to each other, no matter what came.

Outside, the stars above South Water Caye blinked in approval as Kael pulled Marisol into the shadows behind the shack. Her laughter was soft and wicked.

"Let me guess," she said, wrapping her arms around his neck, "you're feeling brave now that you survived the needle."

Kael kissed her, slow and deep. "I just inked forever into my skin. You think I'm scared of a little sin?"

Her response was a moan and the scrape of fingernails down his back as the night swallowed them whole.

As they returned to the catamaran, something shifted. The night was too quiet.

The boat was dark — too dark.

Inside the lounge area, Grant Comstock waited, cloaked in shadow.

He had already delivered the duffel days ago: cash, a Sig 9mm, and a modified HK94 — not just as a gift, but a burden. And now, Grant Comstock was back.

This time, he didn't come bearing gear. He came with something heavier.

Kael and Marisol found him on the rear deck of the catamaran, leaning against the rail, his expression taut, arms folded tight across his chest. No cigarette. No forced calm. Just tension wound so tight it made the air hum.

Kael's voice was low, cautious. "You weren't supposed to show your face again so soon."

Grant didn't move. "I wasn't supposed to need you again this fast."

Marisol crossed her arms. "Then something went wrong."

Grant nodded slowly. "Something's going very wrong. And not just the usual cartel theatrics."

Kael stepped closer. "Talk."

Grant turned, his eyes darker than usual. "I've been monitoring communications along the Gulf and Caribbean corridors. There's a new player pushing through the cracks — offshore, highly resourced, and untraceable. Not Chinese military, not even the locals. Think: ghost ops with blank passports."

"Private military contractors?" Kael asked.

"Possibly. But I think it's bigger than that. Multiple encrypted signals are bouncing between eastern Cuba, the Baja peninsula, and the southern

Yucatán. Three major arms drops have hit Mexican soil in the last month — all routed through shell companies. No manifest. No oversight. And none of its Cárdenas-controlled."

Marisol's jaw tensed. "Rival cartels?"

"Yeah," Grant said. "But these guys are getting help. I've seen high-grade tech — drones, NV scopes, even next-gen comms. Stuff that shouldn't be in cartel hands unless someone's backing them from the outside.

He stepped closer, lowering his voice. "The border's destabilizing. U.S. agencies are on radio blackout. Chinese recon units have been spotted near Chiapas. And I've intercepted chatter about sleeper assets in Veracruz. The whole southern corridor is heating up."

Kael's face tightened. "How much time do we have?"

"None. That's why I'm here."

Grant reached into a dry pouch strapped to his belt and pulled out a photo — grainy, black, and white, snapped from a low-orbit drone. A fortified jungle compound, flanked by guard towers, camouflaged netting, and heavy antenna rigs. "This is where the last signal came from. Northwest of Corozal. Deep bush. Off-grid. High encryption. Whatever they're working on, it's not drugs. It's organized, military, and not sanctioned."

Kael took the photo. "You want me to go in."

Grant nodded. "I need eyes. I need someone who can ghost in and out without tripping their surveillance. You're the only one I trust with both the skill and the conscience."

Marisol cut in, voice sharp. "And what about me? You want me to just let him walk into that hell alone?"

Grant met her gaze.

"If you go, it's as his shadow." Maybe some help from the shadows — but not guaranteed. This isn't a rescue op anymore. This is about stopping a collapse — one that could make the cartel wars look like border skirmishes."

Kael said nothing for a long moment. Then: "If we do this, we do it our way. No satellites. No handlers. No backup."

Grant gave the faintest of nods. "Wasn't planning on bringing any. You two are it."

Marisol looked at Kael. "Ride or die?"

He answered without hesitation. "Sexico forever."

Grant turned back toward the water, his voice barely audible. "Then you leave at first light. And pray the storm doesn't reach you before you reach it."

The waves below slapped against the hull, the night silent but for the promise of war brewing in the dark.

He would do anything for his Sexico.

Grant vanished into the night, leaving only the heavy scent of salt and danger behind.

Kael and Marisol clung to each other, the world outside a rising tide of chaos.

Their hands explored in gentle worship — petting, teasing, breathing each other in — until exhaustion pulled them under like a lullaby.

In the deep of night, Kael lay awake, one arm draped over Marisol, listening to the gentle slap of water against the hull. He knew the storm was coming. Not just weather — the kind of storm that rearranged lives. He whispered her name into her hair, and she stirred, eyes fluttering open.

"I'm not afraid," she whispered. "Not with you.

Morning broke.

The sails caught the wind.

South Water Caye shrank behind them as they pushed toward Ambergris Caye — and toward the storm waiting on the horizon.

Chapter 10

The Ambergris Betrayal

The water had begun to change, as if the ocean itself were signaling their arrival.

From the deeper navy hues of the open sea, it shifted now to an impossible turquoise — a clear, liquid silk beneath their hull. As Kael cut the engines, the catamaran slowed and drifted in twenty feet of pure, crystalline shallows, the sea floor a soft, white canvas stretched out below them. Ambergris Caye shimmered in the distance under the Caribbean sun, mirage-like, rising from the ocean like something imagined — too beautiful to be real.

Marisol stood at the bow, barefoot, her sundress flaring slightly in the warm breeze. Her eyes were locked on the island ahead, but Kael watched her instead. There was something different in her posture — not just anticipation or wariness, but something tender. A quiet resolve.

Kael set the throttle in neutral and let the catamaran coast. He turned to look out across the water, resting his forearms on the rail. A stretch of silence settled between them, thick and contemplative.

"We've made it," Marisol said softly, more to the sea than to him.

"For now," Kael murmured.

Without another word, he peeled off his shirt and dove overboard in a clean arc. He sliced through the turquoise like a blade, disappearing into the liquid world below. Marisol watched the ripple of bubbles rise before diving in after him, her laughter bright, unburdened — a rare sound lately.

They dove deep, retrieving conches and spooking a small school of reef fish. Kael surfaced beside a sunken boulder and pointed — two fat lobsters huddled in the shadow of a coral shelf. He gave her a quick nod and descended. Kael took out an old fishing knife found on the boat earlier and stabbed the lobsters. When he surfaced again, one lobster clenched in each hand, Marisol threw her arms in the air and cheered.

"You're a goddamn sea warrior," she shouted through her snorkel, eyes wide.

Kael grinned, teeth flashing against the sunlit water. "You can just grab them if you know how to hold 'em right."

"Show-off," she teased, kicking toward him. "Next time I'm bringing a spear."

"You don't need one," he said, pulling her close. "You already got me."

She rolled her eyes, laughing into the sky. "Cheesy, but effective."

They swam back to the catamaran with their haul in a net bag, saltwater dripping from their bodies like sequins. Kael climbed aboard first and reached down to help Marisol up. Her hand slid into his, wet and strong, and as she rose onto the deck, she pressed her slick body against his.

"Still think you're the alpha hunter?" she whispered.

Kael leaned in, his voice low. "Only when I'm not being hunted."

They laid the lobsters and Conche on a cutting board near the galley, laughing as one tried to crawl off. Marisol gave it a gentle tap with a spoon.

"Stay," she said. "You're dinner, not a guest."

They ate barefoot on the deck, dipping chunks of lobster into a dish of melted butter, sipping cold white wine straight from the bottle. Marisol fed him a piece with her fingers, licking the last drop of butter off her knuckle.

Kael groaned. "Careful. I might not make it to dessert."

"Oh, you'll make it," she said, eyes gleaming. "You just might not survive it."

For a moment, they weren't fugitives. They were just lovers, barefoot and wet, caught in the thrill of discovery and saltwater.

Marisol toweled her hair, watching him as he opened the weapons cache left behind by Comstock — matte black Sig Sauer 9mm, custom HK94 carbine, and dozens of full mags for each.

He held one of the pistols out to her.

She hesitated, then stepped closer.

Kael's voice was steady. "Thumb here. Grip firm but not strangling. You're in control. Not the weapon."

She followed his instructions, adjusting her grip. He stepped behind her, guiding her arms, his breath against her neck.

"Now breathe in. Slow. Focus on that crate at the stern."

Kael stood behind her, his voice low and steady in her ear. He adjusted her stance, nudging her elbow just slightly.

"Front sight focus," he whispered. "Sight alignment… then trigger squeeze."

Marisol exhaled and pulled the trigger. The shot cracked, sending a neat hole through the crate's center.

She blinked in surprise, then turned to grin at him. "Looks like I've got a knack for it."

Kael gave her a crooked smile. "You're a natural. Sexy and lethal. My favorite combination."

She exhaled and fired again.

The crack echoed off the water. The bullet punched clean through the crate.

A thrill rushed through her. Not from the shot — from the way Kael looked at her afterward. Proud. Trusting. Equal.

Again.

Again.

Again.

The pistol emptied with confidence she didn't know she had.

Marisol wasn't supposed to love it.

But she did.

Not the killing — the claiming. Of her own strength. Of her own fate.

And Kael… he didn't just let her have that moment. He gave it to her.

He holstered the Sig and pressed a kiss to her temple after she emptied four full magazines into the crate.

"You're better than most men I trained," he whispered.

She smirked. "Good. I don't plan on being a sidekick."

Later, she sat on the deck with a piece of bread and butter, feeding chunks to the seagulls and pelicans that hovered nearby. Kael cleaned the weapons with the quiet rhythm of ritual; the kind of discipline that kept a man like him alive.

They were drifting toward the edge of the known world, and yet somehow it felt more grounded than anything else they'd lived through.

Kael's gaze wandered to Marisol again. She was watching the gulls, but her expression had softened into something distant — the kind of stillness that comes after breaking a fever.

She caught him looking and tilted her head. "What?" she asked.

Kael shook his head. "Just wondering what the hell I did to deserve you."

Her smile didn't reach her eyes. "We deserve each other. The broken parts. The wild parts."

Kael walked over and knelt in front of her.

"No," he said quietly. "You're not broken."

She blinked hard, caught off guard by the gravity in his voice.

"You're brave. And dangerous. And more alive than anyone I've ever met. You're just finally being seen. That's not broken — that's waking up."

For a few moments, neither of them spoke.

The catamaran drifted.

The sun slanted lower.

And then Marisol whispered, "When we hit shore… it all changes, doesn't it?"

Kael's jaw clenched. "Yeah."

"Then let's have one more moment," she said.

He rose, offered his hand, and led her into the cabin.

The sun dipped lower as the catamaran approached the marina at Ambergris Caye. The sky flared with molten oranges and violent streaks of crimson, a painter's apocalypse unfolding in the west. The ocean beneath them burned gold, every wave a flicker of firelight rolling toward shore.

A stillness settled over the boat — not calm, but a charged quiet, as if the wind itself was holding its breath. Marisol stood near the bow, her hair swept back by the breeze, her eyes locked on the coastline that shimmered in the distance like a mirage. Kael watched her, sensing it too — that subtle, electric shift in the air.

Even nature seemed to whisper everything's about to change.

The rhythmic slap of water against the hull slowed, more deliberate now, like the beating heart of something ancient. The closer they got, the more the island felt like a threshold — not just another waypoint, but a crossing. From sanctuary to storm. From lovers at sea to fugitives at war.

Kael gripped the wheel tighter. Marisol turned, met his gaze, and nodded. No words. Just understanding.

And ahead, the docks waited — sun-soaked and silent, the last breath before the next descent.

Kael stood at the helm, jaw tight, eyes scanning the harbor with a soldier's instinct.

He recognized the figures on the dock before Marisol did — six men, three women. One of the women stood with her arms folded tight across her chest, a sleek silhouette in tactical pants and combat boots, black hair pulled into a no-nonsense bun. Natalia Ortega Henacho.

Marisol emerged from the cabin barefoot, hair still damp from their swim, her expression soft until her eyes caught the dock. Then everything in her shifted.

"Father. Natalia."

Her voice broke like surf over a sharp reef, full of undertones.

Kael noticed the slight falter in her breath. It wasn't fear. It was something else.

History. Heat. Memory.

He watched her posture tighten as she stared at Natalia. The world didn't exist for a beat. Not the island. Not Kael. Just Marisol and the woman on that dock.

Kael's hand instinctively went to the grip of the Sig holstered at his hip, not out of threat, but reflex. Something electric had passed through Marisol. Something intimate. And Kael knew what that kind of silence meant.

She had once loved Natalia.

No — worse. Marisol had once belonged to her, even if for a moment.

Six years ago. Cancún. A storm rolling in over the jungle. Rain steaming off tile roofs and thunder shivering the windows of whatever villa had been their cage.

Kael didn't need to hear the story to see it unfold in Marisol's eyes.

He saw the ghost of the kiss that had wrecked her.

The shame.

The ache.

But she pulled it all back into her spine — the resolve returning like armor being redressed.

"Father! Natalia!" she called again, louder this time, smiling like she meant it.

Kael didn't move. He simply watched.

Marisol descended the dock ladder and ran barefoot across the wood planks toward the two most complex figures from her past.

Salvador Cárdenas stood tall and unflinching — silver at the temples, a linen shirt rolled at the sleeves, a presence that made even well-armed men defer to him without a word. His arms opened and Marisol crashed into them.

Behind him, Natalia gave a guarded nod. Her expression was unreadable.

Kael followed more slowly, the Sig still clipped to his waist, the HK slung across his back beneath a weathered linen shirt. When Salvador's eyes met his, there was no warmth. Only assessment.

"Mr. Torres," the cartel patriarch said flatly, his accent clipped and formal. "So. This is the man my daughter risked everything for."

Kael didn't flinch. "I didn't ask her to."

Salvador's lips curved slightly. "And yet here you are. Still breathing. That says something."

Natalia stepped forward, offering a hand to Kael. Her grip was firm, dry, surgical.

"Welcome to the next chapter of the storm," she said.

Kael nodded. "I hear you've been busy."

Her eyes flicked to Marisol, then back to him. "You have no idea."

They rode in silence in a line of black SUVs through the winding edge of town. Marisol sat between Kael and her father. Natalia took the front seat, hand on her Glock, scanning intersections as if she could taste the trap before it sprung.

Kael leaned closer to Marisol and whispered, "What happened with you two?"

Marisol didn't look at him.

"Don't ask me that," she said quietly. "Not now. Not when we need to survive."

Kael leaned back. His mind didn't race. It calculated. He wasn't jealous of her, he was adjusting. Natalia wasn't just a bodyguard or ally. She was a fault line in Marisol's past, and that meant one wrong step could crack open something deeper than betrayal.

They arrived at a cantina with peeling green paint and iron chandeliers that hadn't held electricity in years. El Infierno Verde.

Inside, the scent of grilled meats, lime, and sweat clung to the air like perfume. Beers were passed. Bottles of rum set down hard on tables. It was loud — too loud. Laughs quickly came, and stories were told in reckless tones.

Kael stayed near a wall, half-listening as Salvador told a story about bribing a customs official with a yacht and a Venezuelan mistress. Marisol laughed, though her eyes kept scanning the windows.

Inside, Salvador stood and raised a toast.

"To blood. To the truth. To whatever comes next."

Glasses clinked.

Valeria was the only one who noticed the man slip out through the back kitchen door. A Cárdenas bodyguard. Casually dressed, but too lean, too calculated in his exit.

Her instincts went razor-sharp.

She stood quietly, eyes narrowing as she ghosted after him, sliding through the cantina's side exit without drawing attention. No backup. No radio. Just grit.

Outside, the late afternoon sun cast long golden shadows across the narrow street. The air was thick with summer heat, and the light had that slow, honeyed hue — deceptive in its beauty. The world looked calm. It wasn't.

The bodyguard moved fast, ducking into an alley two buildings down.

Valeria followed at a distance, boots silent on the cobblestones. As she neared the corner, she slowly listened.

"...they're all here. She brought him. Yeah. The American. I've got eyes on Salvador too..."

Her stomach clenched.

She stepped into the alley, rifle up, stance low.

"Drop the phone. Hands where I can see them," she barked, her modified M4 leveled at his chest.

The man froze, turning slowly. His face shifted from surprise to calculation.

"Valeria," he said carefully. "You don't want to do this."

"Too late," she growled. "How long?"

"A year," he said with a shrug. "Since Tampico started going sideways. Nueve Vidas made a better offer. Less chaos. More structure. Fewer bodies on our side."

She took a step forward, rage building. "You called them?"

"They were already in the air hours ago," he replied. "Two Cessna 208 Caravans. Twelve per plane. Full load of sicarios and heavy muscle. They all just landed."

Her finger twitched near the trigger. "You sold out your people."

"I survived," he hissed. "You can't win this war."

Then he lunged.

She wasn't ready.

He slammed into her, pushing her into the wall. The M4 twisted between them. She snarled and held on, wrestling to keep in control. He tried to jam a knee into her ribs, but she slammed her forehead into his nose. He reeled.

She kept the rifle.

But he was gone before she could level it again — sprinting down the alley, vanishing into the sun-drenched shadows.

"Shit!" she cursed, breath ragged.

She stormed back into the cantina, chest heaving.

"They know," she shouted, cutting through the music and conversation. "The bastard called them. Two planes. Twenty-four sicarios. We've been burned. We need to move. Now."

The room fell silent.

Salvador stood up from the back booth, stone-faced. Natalia was already halfway across the room, her hand on the grip of her sidearm.

"Who?" Salvador barked. "Who betrayed us?"

"It was Rafa. Skinny, quiet. The one always watching the exits. Said he's been working with Nueve Vidas for a year."

"How long do we have?" Natalia asked, sharp and fast.

Valeria shook her head. "Not long. Two Cessna Caravans. Twelve in each. Armed. Coming in hard. He said they're already landed."

Mateo Cardenas cursed under his breath. One of the younger sicarios grabbed a rifle from under the bar.

Salvador's hands trembled just slightly. Then he threw his glass against the wall. It shattered like a gunshot.

He pulled his pistol and chambered a round.

The room responded like a chorus.

"Move."

The SUVs were still idling, but the street around them had emptied like the eye of a storm.

That's when it hit.

A sharp crack of gunfire split the air, followed by a roar of engines from the side alley.

Kael shoved Marisol behind the nearest vehicle and drew both weapons — the Sig in one hand, the HK94 slung forward in the other. He could already see them — two trucks barreling down the side street, the beds loaded with sicarios in black vests and knockoff tactical helmets.

"Down!" he barked.

The next few seconds were a blur.

Natalia's team of sicarias and sicarios responded like thunder — pulling weapons from hidden compartments in the SUVs, using the vehicles as cover, firing short, controlled bursts that lit up the late evening sky with staccato muzzle flashes.

Marisol huddled low, grabbing her father's collar and dragging him behind a concrete planter. The old man didn't argue. He just grunted and checked the pistol hidden in the waistband of his slacks.

Kael moved like water — shifting positions, firing two quick shots through the windshield of the lead truck, killing the driver instantly. The vehicle swerved, crashed into a utility pole, and flipped sideways, trapping two men beneath.

Another truck came around the bend. Kael turned his HK94 toward it — but a shot cracked from far away, high, and clean.

The passenger's head exploded. Blood sprayed against the window like paint.

Kael didn't have to look.

Grant Comstock.

Only he fired like that. Only he hit at that angle.

Kael Whispered Comstock's name.

Then Kael's satellite phone buzzed.

"Comstock. You here?"

A pause. Then the cool, gravel-dipped voice Kael knew better than his own breath.

"Cover's blown. Took the high perch at 300 meters. Dropping targets. Move your people. You're in the open."

Another sicario tried to flank them through the cantina kitchen. Natalia turned and dropped him with a double tap before he hit the ground.

The SUVs peeled out, engines snarling as bullets riddled the frame of the third car. Marisol screamed as the rear window shattered, glass slicing across her cheek.

Kael crawled over, checked her wound — shallow, bleeding. He wiped it with his shirt and nodded. "You're good. Go."

More rounds ripped through the air.

Across the street, Comstock's position became obvious only by the way people kept dying when they moved toward Kael. One by one, clean shots dropped the enemy — chest, neck, shoulder, and head. Always just before they could fire.

389 yards.

Comstock didn't miss.

Kael returned fire with the HK, taking out two men trying to flank from the rooftops. His shoulder throbbed from recoil, sweat pouring down his temples.

Then — silence. The kind of silence that feels like something holding its breath.

"Move," Comstock said again, calm but urgent. "Reinforcements incoming. Get to the damn airstrip. I'll clean up here."

Kael grabbed Marisol's hand. "We have to go."

"But Natalia—"

"She knows. She'll catch up."

Marisol hesitated, torn.

Then another shot rang out, closer this time. A round slammed into the SUV's hood, and they moved — sprinting to the last vehicle.

As Kael climbed in and started the engine, he caught one last glimpse of Comstock standing alone on the rooftop, SR-25 in hand, his body still, his eyes scanning for the next kill.

A god of precision. A legend on overwatch.

The road to the airstrip was a gauntlet of shattered pavement and smoking ruins. The final SUV — its windows spiderwebbed with cracks, its tires wobbling — growled as Kael pushed it past 100 kph. Natalia sat in the back, one arm around Valeria, who was losing blood fast, her head lolling slightly. Luciana lay across their laps, eyes closed, whispering prayers between clenched teeth.

Salvador Cárdenas clutched a shortwave radio, barking Spanish commands to the surviving Cárdenas security units scattered across the region. Marisol's hand gripped Kael's thigh, blood smeared across her fingers from the cut on her cheek.

The closer they got, the blacker the sky became — not from nightfall, but from smoke.

The airstrip was on fire.

Literally.

The Nine Lives Cartel's Cessnas burned at the far end of the runway — an inferno of twisted metal and scorched flesh. The smell hit them first — burning fuel, cordite, blood.

Marisol gasped as they rounded the last bend.

Two pickup trucks lay overturned. Bullet casings carpeted the tarmac. A half-dozen bodies, friend and foe alike, were strewn across the perimeter fence. A fire team of Cárdenas loyalists had set up a barricade behind an empty tanker truck, trading bursts of gunfire with the last remaining sicarios. A helicopter buzzed overhead but didn't fire — likely out of ammo or on the verge of retreat.

Salvador's Citation Latitude sat at the edge of the runway. The plane's nose was intact, but the right engine smoked and sputtered, coughing like a dying animal. A mechanic waved frantically from the stairs.

The Citation Latitude could hold only nine passengers at maximum capacity—and they had already flown in overloaded. Now, with one engine out and trailing smoke, there was no chance of taking everyone. Hard choices had to be made.

"We've got maybe one shot at this!" Salvador shouted. "Get aboard!"

Natalia kicked open the back door and helped Valeria out, draping the woman's arm around her shoulders. She moved fast, but Kael could see the pain on her face — the kind of pain that had nothing to do with bullets.

Marisol hesitated.

Kael turned to her. "You go with them."

She looked at him like he'd just torn her open. "No."

"Marisol—"

"No!"

But there was no time. Salvador grabbed her by the elbow and pulled her toward the plane.

"You'll slow him down," he said. "And he'll never leave if you don't go."

Kael's voice cracked. "I'll find you."

Her eyes filled instantly, but she nodded. "You better."

Gunfire popped again, closer now. Natalia turned and laid down a wave of suppressing fire as Kael covered them both. Comstock's voice crackled once in Kael's comms.

"They're breaching the west fence. You've got sixty seconds. After that, I can't hold the perimeter."

Kael cursed and ran after them, guiding the wounded aboard, ducking under the whine of the sputtering engine.

At the top of the stairs, Marisol turned. She looked at him like she was trying to memorize his face.

Kael stepped up behind her. Their foreheads touched. One breath.

"I love you," he said. "You're my way out."

"I'm your way home," she whispered.

Then Salvador pulled her inside. The stairs hissed upward.

Kael jumped back as the turbines shrieked to life.

Bullets clipped the edge of the fuselage.

Kael ducked behind a concrete pylon, firing blind as the jet rolled forward. The tires screeched on the torn tarmac.

The plane wobbled once — just once — and for a second Kael thought it might explode.

But it didn't.

The battered jet lifted off, clearing the runway with only feet to spare. A burst of flares followed as it disappeared into the smoke-stained sky.

Kael stood frozen, chest heaving, smoke in his lungs, heart pounding like war drums.

Natalia grabbed him by the collar.

"They're coming back," she said. "We move. Now."

He looked up at her, hollow.

But nodded.

The SUV they commandeered was a bullet-riddled Toyota Hilux, one of the few vehicles on the tarmac that could still move under its own power. Kael hotwired it while Natalia loaded Valeria into the backseat, her body limp but alive. The engine wheezed, then caught.

Kael floored it.

Behind them, smoke curled into the darkening sky. The last of the Cárdenas jet's flares still blinked like dying stars in the distance.

The road to the marina was littered with the wreckage of the ambush — blown-out tires, glass, and a single motorcycle spinning in slow circles against the curb, its rider nowhere to be seen. Sirens wailed in the distance, but none approached. The authorities were either bought, scared, or both.

"Valeria bleeding out," Natalia said, pressing down hard on her friend's shoulder. "She needs a medic."

Kael didn't answer. He just drove faster; teeth gritted against the blood in the air.

They made it to the marina at the edge of Ambergris Caye just as the last sliver of sun disappeared into the Caribbean. The Commodore waited in her slip, sails furled, decks clean, engines primed. But they weren't alone.

Comstock stood on the dock in full tactical gear — his SR-25 across his chest, the sidearm holstered, radio clipped to his shoulder. Around him were six men — all ghost operatives like him. Former Delta, CIA ground branch and DSS. Off-books warriors who didn't exist on any roster. They were loading crates of weapons onto a second smaller boat, a modified SURC vessel bristling with mounted gear.

When Kael pulled up and stepped out, Comstock simply nodded.

"You cut it close."

"Had to," Kael replied.

Natalia looked around, stunned. "You called in your own team?"

"No," Comstock said, stepping forward. "I am the team."

Gunfire cracked from the far side of the marina.

"Here we go," one of Comstock's men muttered, raising his rifle.

A convoy of three trucks screeched around the far corner. Sicarios with AKs and homemade armor piled out, screaming orders, wild-eyed and high on adrenaline and rage.

"They want to finish the job," Kael said, lifting his HK94.

Comstock turned to him. "Then let's show them how that ends."

The dock became a warzone.

Kael fired first, dropping the lead shooter with a burst to the chest. Natalia dragged Valeria onto the Commodore and laid her flat on the deck, then grabbed her rifle and returned fire from the bow.

Comstock's team didn't miss.

Controlled, methodical shots — one after another.

The enemy tried to flank from the left side of the harbor. Two divers surfaced near the fuel line.

"Divers!" someone called.

Comstock didn't hesitate. He lobbed a flashbang into the water, followed by two suppressed shots from his sidearm. The water boiled red.

On deck, Kael moved from rail to rail, laying down cover for Natalia as she repositioned. Bullets whipped through the rigging, punched through sailcloth, and ricocheted off the dock pylons.

Then came Rafa Medina.

The traitor himself.

He appeared at the far dock, an old M4 in hand, screaming in Spanish — curses, threats, prayers. He aimed straight at Natalia.

Kael saw it too late.

But Comstock didn't.

Two sharp cracks from his SR-25.

Two shooters — faces unfamiliar but clearly cartel muscle — dropped instantly. One tumbled over the railing, disappearing into the sea with a splash. The other crumpled beside a rusted oil drum, weapon still clenched in his lifeless hands.

Silence followed, punctuated only by the echo of distant waves.

Rafa had vanished into the chaos moments earlier. But the damage he'd done would echo far louder than any rifle shot.

A breathless, blood-soaked silence.

The surviving sicarios ran. No orders. No loyalty. Just fear.

Comstock slung his rifle and gave Kael a look.

"You've got twenty seconds. I'll hold the dock."

"You coming with us?"

"No," he said, gently. "You've got a future to chase. I've got a cleanup job."

Kael hesitated. "You'll die here."

Comstock smirked. "Wouldn't be the first time."

Kael nodded once. A salute in everything but form.

He climbed aboard the Commodore. Engines ignited. Lines snapped free.

As the catamaran pulled away from the dock, Comstock raised his rifle again — not to fire, but in farewell.

The last Kael saw of him was a silhouette haloed by firelight, standing alone on a splintered dock with the wind in his face and ghosts at his feet.

They hit open water by nightfall.

Natalia collapsed beside Valeria, who groaned softly but managed a thumbs-up.

Kael set course south, heart still pounding. He turned to look at the stars — the same ones he and Marisol had watched just days ago, suspended in peace. She was out there now, somewhere above the clouds, or grounded in another country already, waiting for the next move.

He didn't cry.

He just gripped the wheel tighter, and whispered to the wind:

"I'm coming for you, mi SEXICO."

Chapter 11

Ashes in the Sky

The bullet-riddled Citation Latitude limped through the sky like a wounded animal.

What should have been a smooth flight — or at least a secure exfiltration — was now a coffin with wings. The fuselage creaked with every shift of air pressure. The right engine had been hit on takeoff and now coughed every few seconds, belching black smoke. The left-side port wheel assembly was failing, one tire visibly peeled and flapping with each drag of the undercarriage. Inside the cabin, oxygen masks swung like pendulums. Blood smeared across the walls. The stench of gunpowder, sweat, and death hung heavy in the air.

The pilot had died instantly — a bullet to the neck, mid-ascent. His blood had sprayed across the dash, a grotesque red canvas that had yet to dry. The copilot had shoved the body aside with shaking hands, gripping the yoke as if it were the only thing keeping his soul tethered to the earth. His voice was a cracked, breathless whisper over the comms.

"Mayday, mayday... we are hit... two souls dead, multiple injured, requesting immediate permission to land... anywhere."

Salvador Cárdenas sat beside the satellite phone with blood crusted across his temple, the muscles in his jaw locked tight. His eyes never blinked as he listened to the latest intelligence.

"We lost five in Veracruz," one voice crackled through. "They hit the convoy disguised as soldiers — Chinese uniforms, but the weapons were cartel-issued."

Another voice followed. "The Progreso docks are gone. Two of our captains switched sides. We think they took the payment and ran north."

Salvador said nothing. He merely adjusted the phone, one hand resting on the thigh of a bodyguard whose pulse was fading by the minute.

"You stay with me, mijo," he whispered in Spanish. "You hold on. You hear me? Don't let go."

The boy's eyes fluttered, then closed. His fingers twitched once. Gone.

Salvador didn't curse. Didn't scream.

He just picked up the satellite phone again.

Across the aisle, Marisol sat numbly beside a shattered window, her fingers trembling as she rubbed dry blood from beneath her nails. Somewhere beneath the chaos of the past twenty-four hours, she still felt Kael's arms around her. Still heard his voice whispering that she was at his home.

But was he even alive? Was Natalia? Was anyone?

Every bump in the air made her clench the armrest. She had seen death before — the calculated, businesslike executions that came with cartel life. But this was different. This was survival by inches. The kind of escape that demanded something sacred be traded — faith, innocence, humanity.

The copilot turned back, eyes wide.

"Runway in sight! Brace!"

Marisol gripped the seat in front of her and whispered a prayer she didn't believe.

Outside the window, the Tampico countryside unrolled like a frayed carpet — stretches of green farmland, thin jungle strips, and a single, cracked landing strip that looked like it had been carved by machete out of the earth. A half-dozen black pickups and SUV gun trucks ringed the airfield perimeter, men in tactical vests standing with rifles raised. Friendly — maybe.

The moment the wheels hit dirt, everything went to hell.

The left tire exploded. The plane lurched, screeching sideways. A second later, the nose gear collapsed, slamming the fuselage into the ground with a thunderous crack. Marisol's shoulder slammed into the window frame. Sparks roared across the dirt. The jet spun in a full circle, then another, before groaning to a halt.

Silence.

A hiss of smoke from the brakes. A pop of hydraulics.

Then doors burst open, and Cárdenas soldiers poured in like a SWAT team descending on a hostage scene.

"¡Vamos! ¡Vamos!" one of them screamed.

The wounded were pulled first. Some of the dead dragged out second. Marisol stumbled out with her father's arm over her shoulder. Her knees nearly buckled as she stepped onto solid ground. Heat waves danced across the airfield. The world felt like it was melting.

Then she heard it.

"HERMANA!"

A figure sprinted through the dust.

Santiago.

Her other brother.

Tears leapt unbidden from her eyes as Santiago collided with her, lifting her off her feet in a crushing hug.

"You're alive," he whispered, burying his face in her neck.

"I made it," she choked.

Another younger brother reached them slower, quieter, always composed. He placed a firm hand on her shoulder and leaned in. "We thought you were dead."

"So did I," she said.

Behind them, Salvador moved at half-speed, supported by two men. His lips moved in a slow mantra, eyes distant.

Emilio "Bruto" Díaz — six feet of merciless instinct, the man they called El carnicero de Chiapas — spotted the trembling copilot still inside the aircraft, hands shaking as he reached for the cockpit's emergency beacon.

Bruto drew his pistol. One shot. Clean. The copilot collapsed, slumped over the console.

Salvador exploded.

"¡¿Por qué hiciste eso?!"

Bruto holstered the weapon with a shrug. "We can't trust anyone not born inside the house."

No one disagreed.

Not openly.

Marisol turned her face away, bile rising in her throat.

The Cárdenas convoy moved out fast — like a creature made of steel and shadows. Thirteen armored SUVs and pickups snaked through the lowland countryside, engines rumbling like distant thunder. Dust plumed behind them in hazy trails that glowed amber in the setting sun.

Marisol sat between her brothers in the lead SUV. Her hands trembled in her lap, still sticky with blood. The interior smelled of pine cleaner and metal. Mateo, ever the talker, remained unusually silent. Santiago gripped his rifle with both hands; eyes locked on the road ahead.

Salvador rode in the SUV behind them, flanked by Bruto and two paramedics who weren't allowed to speak unless spoken to.

As they drove deeper into Altamira, the landscape changed. What had once been open farmland and ranchland now bore the scars of quiet war. Black scorch marks on roadside checkpoints.

Charred husks of motorcycles. The occasional stench of something burned and long buried.

The silence inside the SUV thickened with every mile.

Marisol finally spoke.

"I thought we had peace here."

Santiago exhaled through his nose. "We did. Until they realized we were still standing."

Mateo added, "The other cartels folded like cheap umbrellas. They went feral. Started offering deals to our lieutenants. A few flipped. A few disappeared."

"They used to call us boring," Santiago said. "Too clean. Too corporate. Too quiet."

"Now they call us dangerous," Mateo smirked. "Because we didn't die."

They pulled up to the outer gates of Hacienda Santa Gracia. Twin wrought-iron doors rose from the dry earth like ancient armor, flanked by tall watchtowers with machine gunners already posted. A palm scanner flickered blue as Santiago leaned out to place his hand.

The gates creaked open.

Marisol leaned forward, catching her first glimpse in a year.

The hacienda still stood — proud, sprawling, like something carved out of myth.

A thirty-thousand square foot estate surrounded by fields, stables, workshops, water tanks, and a private helipad. The architecture was a blend of colonial grandeur and modern security — marble columns and bulletproof windows, a terracotta-tiled roof shielding reinforced concrete. Hidden beneath it all were bunkers, armories, and escape tunnels. It was beautiful. And terrifying.

Memories surged in.

Her mother's laughter echoed off the courtyard walls.

Racing horses with Mateo.

Sneaking past curfew to smoke cigarettes with Santiago in the olive grove.

Now, all she smelled was gun oil.

All she saw were rifles.

As they parked beneath the porte-cochère, staff swarmed the vehicles — some armed guards, some old servants in pressed uniforms who looked at Marisol with cautious eyes, like they weren't sure if she was alive or a ghost.

A new woman met them on the steps. Mid-thirties, tall, with copper skin and piercing eyes.

"This is Jimena," Santiago said. "She runs the estate now."

Jimena gave Marisol a small nod. "Welcome home, señorita."

It felt like a line from a play — scripted, hollow.

Inside, the transformation was even more jarring.

The ballroom had been converted into a war room. The chandeliers remained, but now they dangled above crates of ammunition, tactical radios, and folding tables stacked with field maps. Bulletproof whiteboards displayed Cárdenas family territory, competitor strongholds, recent ambush zones. A large digital screen blinked red in several key regions.

The air was stale, conditioned, and thick with adrenaline.

Salvador entered last, removing his jacket slowly, revealing a blood-streaked white shirt and a shoulder holster still warm from use.

He walked to the center of the room, lit a cigar with shaking fingers, and stood by the massive walnut bar.

Marisol stood behind him, numb.

Mateo grabbed a tequila bottle and took a long pull before collapsing into a leather chair.

Santiago leaned over a map table with Héctor Suárez, the cartel's veteran strategist.

The room grew louder as lieutenants poured in. Some were limping. Some were still dressed in mud-caked tactical gear. Others wore silk suits stained with blood.

Only one thing was consistent: they all looked afraid.

And the chairs? At least a third were empty.

Marisol didn't need to ask.

They were gone. Killed. Flipped. Or vanished.

Salvador scanned the room. He didn't speak for a long time.

Finally, he smashed his glass against the fireplace.

"¡Silencio!"

Every conversation ceased.

He lifted his hand and then dropped it again. His voice came low, gravel-coated, and lethal.

"Someone explain what the fuck is happening."

Silence echoed through the ballroom like the moment before a firing squad pulls the trigger.

Every man and woman in the room shifted their weight, glancing at one another, waiting for someone else to speak first. The chandeliers swayed slightly above them, casting fractured shadows across crates of hollow points and blood-stained battle maps.

Finally, one man stepped forward.

Héctor Suárez — seventy-one, built like an oak tree, with a voice that could cut through smoke — stood at the center table. His once-black hair was now a silver crown, and his reputation stretched from Sinaloa to Singapore. He had helped build the Cárdenas empire when Marisol was still in a cradle.

"Señor," he began, voice calm and steady, "this did not begin with bullets."

Salvador stared at him, unmoving.

"It began in Washington," Héctor continued. "When Trump returned to office, he sealed the border tighter than a banker's vault. No more flow — of goods, people, bribes, not even medicine. Tariffs hit hard. The coyotes dried up. Supply chains strangled. The other cartels — the weaker ones — collapsed inward. Their foundations cracked."

He pointed to the map where the territories blinked red.

"They turned on each other. Then on us. Because we were still moving shipments. Still feeding cities. Still breathing when they were choking."

A murmur rose in the room.

Salvador nodded slowly.

"We didn't need the border," he said. "Because we diversified."

That word — diversified — rang in Marisol's mind like a warning bell.

She remembered the glossy reports. The charts. The talk of 'infrastructure-based laundering,' of building generational wealth through legal fronts.

Agricultural conglomerates. Logistics routes. A chain of luxury gas stations across Jalisco. A fleet of charter yachts. Restaurants, hotels, packaging plants. Their money was everywhere. Real.

But the beating heart of it all?

Veloxyn.

DARPA's failed dream. Cárdenas' accidental miracle.

A synthetic compound built for endurance, mental focus, and pain suppression — originally designed for covert U.S. military testing in the early 1960's. Discontinued. Buried. But one sample survived.

Re-engineered in secret. Optimized. Stabilized.

Only one mineral could bind its formula.

And that mineral only existed in the soil under Cárdenas's farmland.

The drug was odorless, tasteless, undetectable. And addictive not in the usual sense, but spiritually — it made you believe you could become something more. Better. A god in your own skin.

And everyone wanted it.

Marisol spoke softly but firmly from the rear of the room.

"They're not just coming for our ports or our routes. They're coming for the land."

Everyone turned.

Mateo looked at her like he was seeing his sister as a general for the first time.

Marisol stepped forward, her voice steady now.

"The Chinese aren't just advisors. They're embedded with our enemies. They're training them. Equipping them. Protecting the harvest sites. And they're trying to replicate the compound."

Héctor nodded. "But they can't. They've tried. Their scientists fail. Their batches collapse. Veloxyn breaks down after 72 hours without the mineral binder. That's why they're here."

"They're not just here," Salvador added. "They're invested."

He walked to the edge of the table and jabbed a finger into the glowing digital map. "We have proof of encrypted comms between Chinese paramilitary groups and Cartel Nueve Vidas. Financial transfers from state-owned Chinese banks to shell corporations run out of Mérida and Campeche. This isn't a cartel war anymore. This is foreign warfare. Hybrid warfare."

He turned to his most trusted: Santiago. Bruto. Goya.

"This is economic conquest."

Bruto grunted. "You want to hit the Chinese?"

"I want to scorch the earth they think they own."

Héctor stepped closer. "We still have friends. Politicians. Journalists. International partners. If we go full revolution, we may lose the few shields we still have."

Salvador's voice dropped an octave. "There are no shields anymore. There are only weapons."

He lit another cigar and inhaled slowly.

"You think the world will save us?"

He gestured around the room — at the bulletproof windows, the encrypted laptops, the broken men.

"They only notice us when we bleed on their screens. So, let's make them look."

He raised his voice.

"Arm the loyalists. Activate the underground cells. Move the weapons from Campeche to Veracruz. Pull the women out of Poza Rica. And burn every mole we haven't verified with family blood."

Mateo stood slowly. "All of them?"

"All of them."

The room shifted. Everyone could feel the line being crossed.

This wasn't strategy.

This was defiance. Righteous fire.

A whisper of revolution.

Salvador turned to the fireplace, staring into the flames as if they might answer back.

"This isn't a war."

His eyes reflected the fire.

"This is a revolution."

Chapter 12

Isla de la Juventud

They had sailed west at first, driven more by instinct than strategy. The map meant little when every coastline was a question mark, and every port a potential ambush. Kael kept the Commodore on a zigzag course, conserving fuel and praying for direction. They needed shelter — not just from their enemies, but from the slow corrosion of exhaustion.

It was Natalia who finally broke the silence. She sat on a storage crate, cleaning the deep graze across her side with rum and gauze, wincing but focused. "We need to disappear," she muttered. "Not hide. Vanish."

Kael didn't look away from the horizon. "Where?"

She glanced at Valeria, who leaned against the mast, arms crossed, eyes distant. "Isla de la Juventud," Natalia said, switching to Spanish. "The Island of Youth."

Valeria nodded. "I have family there. Cousins. Old resistance fighters, fishermen. People who know how to make someone vanish without asking why."

Kael finally turned. "How long can we stay?"

"Long enough to heal," Valeria replied. "Long enough to find out if Cárdenas is still alive."

Natalia gritted her teeth as she pressed gauze to the wound. "And long enough to figure out if this war has already left us behind."

A pause settled between them before Natalia looked up. "Hey, Captain — got anything to drink?"

Kael, still at the helm, didn't turn. "Wine fridge is half full. Take your pick."

Valeria made a face. "Wine? We're Mexican, cabrón. We need something stronger."

Natalia laughed through the sting of her wound. "Yeah, give me something that burns on the way down and makes me forget I've been shot."

Kael chuckled, shaking his head. "There's rum and vodka in the cabinet above the fridge. Knock yourselves out."

Valeria was already moving. "That's more like it."

Kael checked the chart on the navigation console and made a slow turn east by southeast. "There's a reef shoal about six hours out," he said. "I'll anchor there — ten feet of water, calm and shallow. You two get some rest below. I'll wake you when we get there, and you can keep watch through the early morning."

Natalia raised her bottle in mock salute. "Captain, navigator, bodyguard, insomniac... is there anything you don't do?"

Kael gave a half-smile. "Sleep.

The next morning, just after first light, the Commodore rocked gently in the shallows of the reef shoal. The air was thick with salt and promise, the sun was not yet high enough to burn away the velvet mist clinging to the water.

Kael stirred in his bunk, the scent of the ocean and diesel faint in his nose, when a cold piece of metal pressed hard into the center of his forehead.

His eyes snapped open.

Natalia stood over him, her face tight with fury, her pistol leveled squarely at his skull.

"Get up," she said, her voice low and deadly. "Slow. Hands where I can see them."

Kael froze, blinking hard. "What the hell—"

"Shut up," she snapped. "Out. Now."

She backed away as he slid from the bunk, keeping the pistol steady. They moved topside, the morning breeze cutting across the deck as Kael's bare feet touched the sun-warmed planks.

Valeria stood near the mast, arms crossed, silent but watchful.

Natalia jabbed the muzzle into his chest. "I want the truth. All of it. Who the fuck are you?"

Kael swallowed, heart pounding. "You already know—"

"I know you move like a Phantom," she said. "I know you handle a pistol like it's an extension of your spine. I know you were in Puerto Rico conveniently when Marisol needed someone. I know you've used aliases, contacts I can't trace, and I know Salvador trusted you way too fast for someone with no history. So again, Kael Torres... who the fuck are you really?"

Kael's jaw clenched. He looked between them, then exhaled. Slowly, deliberately, he raised his hands.

"I was born in the U.S. My mother was Mexican. She raised me alone — Campbell, then Chester California. I joined the Marines Reserves at seventeen to escape a dead-end life. I received the GI Bill and went to college while I was in the Marine Reserves. When I graduated to college I went to Officer Candidate School and became a Marine Corps Officer. I commanded a Marine MARSOC unit for a couple of years. I bled in Fallujah, almost died in Mosul. After that, I joined a covert unit that doesn't officially exist. For years, I did black ops work across the globe. Then I burned out. Left. Tried to disappear."

Natalia didn't lower the gun.

Kael stepped forward an inch. "I met Marisol at the El Conquistador in Puerto Rico. She wasn't some target. She wasn't an op. I didn't even know who she was until it was too late to pretend, I didn't care."

His voice broke slightly.

"I love her. Not some passing thing. Not lust. Love. I'd give up the life I lived, everything I've ever been, just to keep her safe. I don't work for anyone.

I'm not spying. I'm not here to use her. I'd burn the fucking world to keep her breathing."

Silence followed, sharp and heavy.

Valeria's eyes softened first. Then she reached out gently, pushing Natalia's gun down.

"He's telling the truth," Valeria said quietly.

Natalia stared for a long second. Her finger hovered over the trigger.

Then she sighed, holstered the pistol, and offered Kael a hand.

"I had to know," she muttered. "We've been used before."

Kael took her hand and stood.

"I understand," he said. "Just don't pull that shit again before coffee."

By late morning, stomachs were growling, and the tension had lifted just enough for hunger to take over. Kael pulled the Commodore slowly off the reef and into deeper water, scanning the fish finder until he spotted movement. He grabbed one of the heavy rods from the stern locker and set to work.

Within the hour, they had a bounty — a trio of red snapper and a fat, glimmering snook flopping in the kill cooler. The girls whooped from the deck as Kael held it up like a trophy.

"Looks like dinners on the American," Natalia called.

Kael gave a mock bow. "Finally, something I can't screw up."

He cleaned the fish on a cutting board near the transom, tossing scraps overboard as seabirds circled above. Valeria fired up the galley stove while Natalia pulled down a bottle of rum and a fresh bottle of wine from the cabinet.

They grilled the snapper with lime and garlic, pan-fried the snook, and served it all over day-old rice with diced mango Kael had found buried in the cooler. The three of them sat in the shade of the cockpit tarp, barefoot, salt-skinned, drinking from mismatched mugs.

Kael leaned back and sipped his rum. "Alright. I spilled everything this morning. Now it's your turn. Start from the beginning."

Valeria leaned into Natalia, resting her head briefly on her shoulder. "I was born on the Island of Youth. A village outside Nueva Gerona. My parents were teachers. Not activists, not rebels. Just... good people. When I was thirteen, they were killed. Car bomb. Wrong place, wrong time. I ran. I lived with my grandmother until I turned seventeen, then I left for Mexico. I didn't know what I was doing. Just... moving."

Natalia reached over and took her hand, gently lacing their fingers.

Kael nodded. "And that's where you met?"

Valeria smiled. "At a dive bar in Veracruz. I was broke, bruised, and drunk. She pulled me out of a fight I was going to lose."

Natalia chuckled. "She threw a bottle at a federale. It missed. Hit a mirror instead. I thought, anyone that reckless might be worth saving."

Kael grinned. "So, you recruited her?"

"No," Natalia said, her voice quieting. "I trained her. She had the instincts — the drive. But she needed purpose. I'd been running a small crew back then, working clean-ups for the Cárdenas cartel. They gave me autonomy. I saw something in her. Fire."

Kael looked at Natalia. "And you? Where'd your story start?"

She took a long sip of wine, then leaned back.

"I grew up in Sinaloa. Small ranch outside Mazatlán. Father was a mechanic. Mother ran a cantina. I was the oldest of five. When I was sixteen, a new faction rolled through town. Los Huesos Rojos. They demanded tribute. My father refused."

Kael said nothing.

Natalia's voice sharpened. "They came at night. I was out in the fields when it happened. Came back to smoke and screams. Everyone I loved — gone. I buried them myself. Then I disappeared."

Valeria held her hand tighter.

"I found my way north. Did what I had to do. Eventually, I ended up in Mexico City. Got picked up by a woman named Camila who ran intel for Cárdenas. She gave me work. Then training. Then purpose. I learned about weapons, tactics, counter-surveillance. By the time I turned twenty-five, I was running operations across three states."

Kael looked between them. "You two have survived more than most soldiers I know."

Natalia smirked. "We're not soldiers. We're something worse."

"No," Kael said. "You're survivors. And that's the rarest breed."

They drank in silence for a moment, the sea stretching out around them, the sun beginning to dip again.

Whatever came next, they would face it together.

It had been four days since they escaped the burning ruins of Ambergris Caye.

Four days of open water, salted wind, and the slow, gnawing ache of survival.

Four days since Kael had seen Marisol's face — felt her breath on his neck, heard her call him mi SEXICO with that low, reverent rasp that made him forget everything he ever regretted.

The Caribbean stretched around them like a prayer — endless, sacred, full of danger and promise. The Commodore cut through it like a mirage come to life, its twin hulls slicing silently through swells that shimmered in morning light.

Kael stood barefoot at the helm, the wheel steady under his hand, his body swaying with the

113

subtle rhythm of the sea. His dog tags lay cold against his chest, tucked under a salt-stained T-shirt. He hadn't shaved. Had barely eaten. Sleep came in fragments. Dreams came in her voice.

Behind him, laughter drifted from the galley — not loud, not carefree, but real.

Natalia and Valeria had found slivers of peace in the wreckage. They spent their days sprawled across the catamaran's cargo net, sunbathing, whispering, disappearing into each other like lovers who had seen too much death to wait for anything. They shared a bottle of dark rum from St. Maarten, passed between them like a ritual.

Kael caught glimpses of them when he wandered the deck at night — limbs tangled, soft moans carried on the breeze, their bodies glowing in the moonlight like moving sculptures. One night, he had stepped quietly out of the catamaran lounge and paused as he saw them through the cabin's porthole — Natalia's back arched, Valeria's mouth pressed to her collarbone, their connection so tender and primal it silenced him.

He didn't envy them.

He admired them.

They had each other. A bond forged not just in desire, but in fire, in blood, in battle.

Kael had Marisol — but only in memory.

And memory was a cruel companion.

Every mile they put behind them placed more ocean between them, but Marisol hadn't left him. Not really. She lingered in every gust of wind, every breath of salty air. He could still feel the imprint of her on his chest. The ghost of her fingertips. The ache of everything she didn't get to say when the bullets started flying.

Sometimes, when the wind dropped and the sea went still, he could hear her voice.

"You're my way out, Kael… but I'd go deeper in if you asked me to."

He gripped the wheel harder.

The first sight of Isla de la Juventud came at dawn.

The island emerged slowly from the haze — jagged, green, untamed. It looked like it had been carved from the belly of some ancient beast, the shoreline riddled with limestone bluffs and thick mangroves. Its interior was dense jungle and cane fields, cut with narrow dirt roads and fading colonial remnants.

Kael muttered under his breath. "We're smoke in the wind."

Natalia joined him at the helm, her hair tied back in a tight knot, eyes still sharp even after days at sea.

"If you die," she said dryly, "I'll have to learn to sail."

Kael cracked the smallest smile. "Then I better not die."

They docked at Marina Siguanea, a sleepy harbor tucked in a crescent-shaped bay where rusted catamarans and wooden fishing boats bobbed in lazy unison. No questions were asked. Cash was paid. Slips secured. Eyes averted. That was how things worked here — if you paid enough, nobody remembered your name.

Kael handled the logistics while Natalia and Valeria stretched their legs. He gassed the Commodore, stocked it with dry goods, solar chargers, extra fuel, two backup marine batteries, and a few bottles of Havana Club Rum for good measure. He rechecked the false floor panels and tucked three long rifles inside — suppressed HK416s with adjustable optics. Another crate carried roughly three hundred thousand dollars in cash, rolled tight and vacuum sealed.

He handed the marina manager his burner.

"If anyone comes asking about a gringo on a catamaran," Kael said, "you call that number first. Only that number."

The old man nodded, tucking the phone into his shirt.

Valeria kissed him on the cheek and winked. The old man nearly dropped the clipboard.

They wandered inland through the dusty streets of Nueva Gerona. Children kicked soccer balls barefoot across cracked pavement. Chickens darted between pastel-colored Volkswagen Beetles and bicycles with milk crates strapped to the handlebars. Cuban jazz blared from second-floor windows, bouncing between buildings faded with time.

Kael paused at a corner shop where trinkets and handmade jewelry hung from the strings.

He spotted a beaded anklet — turquoise, with three obsidian stones in the center.

The same kind Marisol once wore back when she laughed more easily.

He bought it quietly, wrapped it in cloth, and slipped it into his pocket.

Valeria stood quietly in front of an old telephone booth, her fingers trembling just slightly as she fed in coins and dialed a number she hadn't used in years. The booth's plexiglass was scratched and fogged, and the handset smelled of rust and sea salt. Kael and Natalia gave her space, sitting at a small plastic table under the shade of a weather-worn umbrella.

They waited at El Rincón del Pescador, a faded little seaside café known for fried red snapper and sweet plantains. Kael ordered without asking — two local cervezas, a plate of ropa vieja, and yuca con mojo, garlic still sizzling in the oil.

Natalia tilted her chair back slightly and studied Kael's face.

"You were willing to die for Marisol," she said after a long pause.

Kael didn't answer right away. He reached for his drink, took a sip, let the carbonation burn its way down.

"She looked at me and didn't see the wreckage- just the man buried beneath it."

Natalia nodded. "You told her everything?"

"No," he said. "I couldn't."

"Why not?"

Kael glanced toward the surf. The waves were slow here, lazy. Rolling in and out like a breath.

"Because it made me less mine," he said quietly. "Made me someone else's son. Someone else's mission."

"And now?"

"Now it explains too much."

They lapsed into silence, the kind you earn after gunfire and blood. Not awkward — just full.

Then Valeria appeared, her eyes wide, cheeks flushed.

"My tío answered," she said. "My abuela is alive. They're in the capital. We can stay with them."

Relief passed between the three like a cool wind.

An hour later, they found a ride — an old 1953 Ford flatbed truck, paint peeling, fenders rusted to the bone. The driver barely spoke but let them climb into the back, motioning for them to sit low.

The road to the capital twisted through jungle and sugarcane, the scent of burning trash and wild orchids drifting in turns. Valeria sat in the corner of the truck bed, hugging her knees, her eyes scanning the horizon like someone remembering and forgetting all at once.

"This island raised me," she whispered. "And almost killed me."

117

Kael watched her as she spoke and the way she moved when she did. He'd seen that look before — in Marines walking back into their hometowns after tours in Fallujah. Love and trauma tangled together. Memory turned into landmines.

When they reached the outskirts of Nueva Gerona's inner district, the streets narrowed. Dogs slept in doorways. The scent of fried garlic and old diesel filled the air.

They arrived at a modest yellow house near the docks — barred windows, banana trees in the yard, and the sound of bolero music drifting from a transistor radio inside.

Valeria's grandmother opened the door before they knocked.

She was tiny, ancient, and fierce — like a bird made of iron. She hugged Valeria so tightly Kael thought she might break ribs. Then came her uncle, a broad man with skin like burnished clay and tattoos that marked time in prison. He didn't ask who they were. He only nodded once and said, "Mi casa es tu casa."

Lisindra Duarte — a cousin about Valeria's age — brought towels, fresh clothes, and a pot of black beans that made everyone go quiet for twenty straight minutes.

For the first time in weeks, they slept in real beds. Clean sheets. Windows cracked open. A ceiling fan that squeaked like an old gate but kept the mosquitoes at bay.

Kael lay awake that first night, staring at the ceiling.

He hadn't dreamt in days.

But that night, he saw Marisol.

Not screaming. Not bleeding.

Just dancing.

Laughing.

Wearing nothing but that anklet.

The next morning, Lisandra pulled Natalia aside while the rest of the house prepared breakfast.

"There's a businessman near the dock," she said. "Owns a warehouse. Sells shipping manifests to tourists. He has a satellite phone."

Natalia looked at her, surprised. "And he'd let us use it?"

"If you ask," Lisandra smirked. "And maybe flash your gun."

The warehouse was a squat gray building near the pier, stacked with boxes of canned meat and fake Lacoste polos. Inside, a desk fan buzzed over spreadsheets and a single battered satellite phone that looked like it had been used in the first Gulf War.

Natalia and Valeria made the calls while Kael kept watch outside, scanning the street like a hawk.

They dialed over a dozen numbers.

Most were dead.

A few rang endlessly.

Then — static, and a voice:

"¿Bueno?"

Natalia sat up straight. "Conejo?"

A sharp breath. Then: "¿Están vivos?"

"Sí," she said. "We made it out."

"¿Y el güero?"

"El güero's here."

There was a pause. A sniff. Then a sound that might have been a choked-off laugh or a sob.

"Dios mío... we thought you were all dead. Most of us are scattered. Salvador's in hiding. But Leandro — Leandro's alive."

Natalia froze. "Where?"

"Mérida. Captured. Being held in an old penitentiary near the highway. Cartel Nueve Vidas is running it. And there are rumors..."

"What kind of rumors?"

"That the police chief there joined El Filo de Dios. Converted. Baptized in blood, they say."

Kael stepped inside the warehouse.

"Then we're going to Mérida," he said.

Conejo hesitated. "You do that, you won't come back."

Kael nodded. "Then we burn everything behind us."

That evening, the air thickened with sweat and smoke.

Lisandra insisted they needed a night out before heading back into hell.

"You're about to run into lions," she said, pressing a crimson halter dress into Natalia's hands. "You should remember what it feels like to be alive."

So, they went — the four of them — to Club Fuego Rosa, a place that was half bar, half strip club, half dance hall, and somehow entirely none of the above.

It was a building with no shame: low ceilings, velvet booths, neon signs shaped like flamingos and devils. The air was perfumed with cheap cologne, rum, and heat. Reggaeton and trap beats pulsed through the floorboards. Ceiling fans spun slowly like lazy vultures. The lighting came in moody shades — hot pink, blood red, sickly purple — and the walls sweated with history.

Kael entered first, scanning the room with a soldier's eyes. Every movement. Every exit. Every potential ambush. His fingers twitched near his belt as if missing a sidearm that wasn't allowed inside.

And then he saw him.

Grant Comstock.

White linen pants. A Cuban shirt unbuttoned halfway down his chest. A tumbler of whiskey in one hand. A dancer on his lap with red sequins and heels that looked like weapons. Her laughter was syrupy, trailing off as Comstock's grin widened.

"I was just about to come find you," Comstock said, pushing the girl gently aside with the kind of charm that made women forgive ghosts.

Kael didn't return the smile. "How the hell do you always find me?"

Comstock took a slow sip, licking the sweat from his top lip.

"Tracker. On the boat. Since St. Maarten. You didn't think I'd let my most problematic asset float into open waters without eyes, did you?"

Kael grunted. "And my dad?"

"Wants an update. Wants to know if his rogue-son is still making waves."

They moved to a quiet corner — a back lounge with velvet curtains and a small table stained with fifty years of spilled secrets. The air was cooler here, filtered through a hidden duct, but the tension between them raised the temperature anyway.

Comstock's tone dropped.

"Washington's watching. Closely. Nine Lives sicarios crossed into Laredo last week. Killed three border agents and a DEA liaison. There's chatter about pulling assets from Europe. And the Chinese…"

Kael cut him off. "They're embedded."

"They're escalating," Comstock corrected. "And your girlfriend's family owns the only thing they can't replicate."

"Veloxyn."

Comstock nodded. "They've spent millions trying. Can't do it. You know why?"

"The mineral."

"Right. And guess where ninety-eight percent of it exists?"

Kael already knew the answer.

"Cárdenas's farmland."

Comstock leaned forward.

"You're standing on the fault line between the old world and the new. And whether you want it or not, you're a goddamn prophet with a gun."

Kael didn't blink. "Then I'll need a few more miracles."

"What kind?"

"Two M240s. Three M249s. Sidearms. RPGs. Grenade launchers. Suppressors. Flashbangs. Thermal gear. And enough ammo to make hell jealous."

Comstock raised his brows. "Jesus, Torres. You're not asking for a care package. You're staging an invasion."

Kael didn't flinch. "Call it what it is."

Comstock knocked back his drink. "Fine. Noon. Meet me at the marina."

The night didn't end there.

If anything, the night had just begun.

The DJ transitioned into a deeper rhythm — trap beats laced with slow, grinding basslines. The walls seemed to pulse with the tempo. Purple strobes flickered like sirens behind gauzy curtains. The air thickened with bodies, perfume, sweat, and unspoken hunger. Shadows moved like myths on the dance floor.

Kael didn't remember when he ended up there — only that he was suddenly in the center of it, shirt damp with sweat, limbs loose but intentional. He moved slowly, deliberately, every motion like a ripple through shallow water. His eyes stayed low. Focused. Detached.

He didn't move to be seen.

He moved to remember he was alive.

The music thumped. People brushed past. A woman in a white dress touched his back and disappeared. Another tried to catch his eye. He didn't bite. He kept breathing in rhythm. He didn't want touch. He wanted stillness. Focus.

But still, the heat came for him.

Natalia found him first — hips rolling like a serpent, hair cascading over one bare shoulder. The crimson halter dress Marisol gave her clung to her like a second skin. In the flashing light, she looked like she was bleeding seduction. She didn't speak. She didn't have to.

She moved close.

So close that her breath tickled his jawline.

Kael turned slightly, his eyes meeting hers. There was something unspoken there. Not love. Not lust. Something more dangerous: shared survival.

Then came Valeria.

She moved like smoke — untamed and precise, hips angled, eyes half-lidded. Her shirt was unbuttoned just enough to blur the line between suggestion and threat. She moved in behind Kael, her hands sliding up his back, then across his chest like she was claiming him for a few beats.

The three of them swayed as one. A triangle of temptation.

Natalia pressed her lips to his neck. Slowly.

Valeria leaned in and kissed his mouth — soft, slow, a flicker of heat.

Kael didn't recoil.

But he didn't move either.

He stood still, letting the moment pass through him like smoke in a crosswind.

"You've both had too much to drink," he said evenly, voice a notch above a whisper.

Natalia's smile curved into something sly. "We're not drunk."

Valeria tilted her head. "We just want to play."

Kael's lips quirked at the corner. The ghost of a smirk. He shook his head.

He stepped back, gently, respectfully — disengaging like a soldier stepping off a minefield.

"No games tonight," he murmured.

He turned and slipped into the crowd.

Not running. Just choosing.

He didn't belong in that moment — not yet. His soul was still tethered to someone who wasn't there. A woman who danced barefoot in a Puerto Rican ballroom and whispered to him like she was casting spells.

They let him go.

For now.

Behind him, Natalia and Valeria watched. No jealousy. No offense. Just the acknowledgment of a man too haunted to be touched.

They clinked their glasses together and drank instead. Night blurred into morning, carried by the hush waves and the clink of unfinished toast. Somewhere offshore, the stars faded slowly, as if reluctant to leave. No one said goodbye. They didn't need to. The air was heavy with the unspoken promises-not made but felt. Kael sat alone for a while, the sounds of laughter and glass long gone, his mind already slipping into the silence ahead. The war and violence would return with the sun. But for a few borrowed hours, they had been human again.

The next morning, the sky split wide open with sun.

The heat hit early — dense and sharp, radiating off the asphalt with a vengeance. The Caribbean shimmered to the east, calm but endless, and the cries of gulls echoed overhead like warnings wrapped in song.

Kael arrived at the marina before anyone else.

He stood at the edge of the dock, looking out over the Commodore — the catamaran rocking gently, the water slapping at its twin hulls like a whisper of things to come. Salt crusted his boots. Sweat trickled down his back. He hadn't slept. Not really. His mind was locked in the rhythm of the approaching storm.

Moments later, Grant Comstock appeared.

Gone was the white linen playboy from the night before. Now, he wore desert-tan tactical pants, boots, and a fitted shirt that clung to his frame like a second skin. Aviators. Sidearm. An earpiece tucked behind his collar. Comstock wasn't smiling now.

Behind him were two massive black crates and a pallet wrapped in camo netting.

A military truck, covered in dust, idled behind them — its bed already empty.

"You weren't kidding," Comstock said, nodding toward the boat. "Looks like you're about to start your own navy."

Kael said nothing. He walked over and opened the first crate.

Inside:

• Two M240B machine guns, belt-fed, barrels greased and glinting.
• Three M249 SAWs, each with fresh cleaning tags.
• Five suppressed sidearms, matte black, matched serials.
• Six RPG-7 rounds in wax-sealed containers.

In the second crate:

• Flashbangs. Frags. Claymores. Thermal binoculars.
• A sealed case of C4 bricks with remote triggers.
• Kevlar vests. Tactical chest rigs. Utility belts. Extra optics.
• Batteries, radio gear, encrypted comm units.

Beneath a false floor:

• Two million dollars in U.S. bills — neatly stacked, banded, and vacuum-sealed.

Kael ran his hand over the cold steel of the M240B, fingers tightening on the grip.

"This will do," he said.

Comstock stepped closer, dropping his voice. No more theatrics. No sarcasm. Just soldier to soldier.

"They want you alive," he said. "For now. But that's changing. Fast. Word's out. The CIA. The

125

Chinese. Every cartel between Sinaloa and Guatemala — they all know your name."

Kael closed the crate gently. Latches clicked into place like final decisions.

"This thing?" Comstock gestured toward the horizon. "It's past agency territory now. This is something else."

Kael looked toward the Commodore, the ocean beyond it-vast, open and unknowable. Somewhere far to the west, across that blue void, the first battles had already begun.

He could feel it in his bones.

A shift.

This wasn't about loyalty anymore. Or survival.

This was about legacy.

Kael exhaled.

"Then we sail into it," he said.

Comstock held his gaze. Then clapped him once on the shoulder.

"I'll be watching."

Kael turned back toward the boat.

And for a few heartbeats, the dock fell silent — nothing but gulls, the crackle of tension, and the distant hum of history preparing to be made.

Chapter 13

Ghost Harbor

It had been four days since Kael, Natalia, and Valeria left the succulent hillsides and emerald water of the Island of Youth. The Commodore cruised west across the Gulf of Mexico, cutting through calm waters like a black blade. The days stretched long and quietly, broken only by routine: meals, weapons maintenance, short bursts of sleep, and the kind of silences that didn't require words.

Kael watched the women fall into rhythm. Valeria spent long hours sharpening knives or tracing routes into her tattered map book. Natalia would disappear into the cabin for stretches, writing coded messages or cleaning her rifle in a ritual that bordered on sacred. At night, they curled together on the cargo net like twin flames burning in the dark — the bond between them tender, feral, and unbreakable.

He gave them space. But he also saw them clearly now — not just as lovers or fighters, but as women shaped by war and welded by love. He admired them. Respected them. And envied their simplicity. His own mind was never still — it circled back to Marisol like a compass unable to find the north without her.

The nights were thick with memory. The weight of Marisol's absence pressed against his chest like a second set of lungs. The way she said his name. The heat of her skin. The taste of her breath. He'd replay it all as he sat at the helm, eyes locked on the horizon.

They approached the Mexican coast just before dawn. A salt-heavy mist clung to the water, and through it, the dark silhouette of the Marina Yucalpetén emerged like the ghost of a drowned city. Kael cut the engines and let the Commodore drift.

No one spoke.

They waited offshore until 3:00 a.m., the deadest hour, when predators stirred and security guards dozed. The catamaran glided between rows of abandoned fishing boats and listing pleasure yachts. Kael guided her into a hidden slip and killed the lights.

The dock creaked under their boots as they tied off the lines.

"It's too quiet," Natalia muttered. Her eyes scanned every shadow. "Too damn quiet."

"Like the town's holding its breath," Valeria added, voice low.

Progreso had changed. Once a thriving coastal stopover, it now stood like a husk — drained of joy and bristling with unspoken danger.

"If we get separated," Kael said, "fall back to the Commodore. We'll push south along the coast toward Tampico."

Natalia nodded, unclipping her sidearm and handing it to him. "You stay with the boat. Lock it down. We'll get intel."

Kael loaded mags, checked seals on waterproof cases, and hid rifles in hollowed compartments below deck. He topped off the fuel reserves and slipped a few thousand pesos to a nervous harbor security guard. The man took the money without a word and vanished into the fog.

Natalia and Valeria disappeared into the streets like ghosts.

Progreso greeted them with dead lights and shuttered windows. The streets had once danced with the colors of market stalls, roaming mariachi, and schoolchildren chasing stray dogs. Now it was silent. Abandoned bicycles rusted in corners. A dog collar lay near an empty food stall, its leash frayed. The air tasted static and old blood.

They bought ponchos from a roadside vendor — the kind meant to blend in. Plain, anonymous.

"What happened here?" Natalia asked the shopkeeper, a weathered man with yellowed eyes.

He didn't answer at first. Then, leaning in with a glance over his shoulder, he whispered, "After El Filo de Dios came, everything changed. Men with guns and robes. They called it holy work. They said Progreso was to be purified."

Valeria's fists clenched. "How?"

"They took our farms. Took the strong for labor. The rest vanished."

They nodded and moved on.

A rusted public phone still clung to the side of a crumbling pharmacy. Valeria fed coins and called in old markers. The line hissed, then clicked.

"Sosa?"

A pause.

"Valeria. You're alive."

"Barely. We need to meet."

"Leandro's alive. But they've got him locked in Mérida. La Casa de Penitencia. They turned it into a fortress."

"Can you meet?"

"Only between three and five. That's when movement shifts. After that, it's lockdown."

"Where?"

"Cantina Cielo Rojo. The old place. It's still ours."

By late afternoon, the cantina's battered wooden door groaned open. Natalia and Valeria stepped into the haze of tequila fumes and dust — and survival. Inside, they were greeted by thirteen Cárdenas loyalists: field workers turned warriors, retired cops, tattooed sicarios with eyes like ice. And Mateo Sosa.

One by one, nods turned to hugs. Hugs to tears. And tears to quiet resolve.

Kael arrived last, a duffle bag of gear on his back, his eyes scanning every face.

Natalia stood at the head of a scarred wooden table.

"How many can we count on?"

Murmurs rose.

"Eight, maybe more from the south farm."

"I've got ten — armed with old pistols."

"Five. Two more in hiding nearby."

"Twelve. Waiting for the word."

Final count: seventy-three. Far from what Cárdenas once commanded, but loyal. Hardened. Desperate.

"Most only have light arms," Sosa said. "We're outgunned."

"That's about to change," Natalia replied, pulling a map from her jacket.

Outside, she dialed Goya.

He answered in a single breath. "You made it."

"We're in Progreso. Seventy-three loyal. Kael's with us."

"Salvador. Natalia's alive."

Then the voice they'd missed most crackled through.

"You've survived worse, vieja."

"Leandro's being held in Mérida."

"There are small caches in a citrus market. Another at Finca del Cielo. The largest though is at Edificio San Miguel. Hidden behind a steel wall . You'll find what you need."

"What about backup?"

"No. Not yet. I need a hammer, not a distress call."

Natalia's lips curled. "Understood."

"Is the güero with you?"

She passed the phone to Kael with a smirk. "You're on."

Kael took a breath.

"Marisol?"

"Kael?"

"Mi SEXICO."

"You're alive," she whispered.

"I miss you. Every second."

"Come back to me."

"As soon as I finish what I started."

"Don't you dare die before I see you again."

"I won't."

The line went silent — but neither hung up for several more heartbeats. Just breath. Presence. Grief.

When the call ended, Natalia rolled her eyes. "We better win. Or you'll never get laid again."

Kael didn't laugh.

He just picked up the map, nodded to the room.

"Let's get to work."

Chapter 14

The Loyal and the Lost

The fan buzzed overhead, stirring stale air and dried blood.

Kael stood over the spread-out city map like it was a war altar — knife tucked behind his belt, eyes bloodshot from a sleepless night. The map itself was riddled with markings: Xs, red circles, arrows in thick Sharpie. It looked less like a diagram and more like a prophecy.

The room stank of sweat, mildew, and spent adrenaline.

Natalia leaned against the wall, arms crossed, her gaze pinned to Lieutenant Mateo Sosa, who sat at the folding table with a stitched wound along his shoulder. His eyes were sharp despite the bruising around his temple, his voice gravel from shouting and grit.

Valeria poured black coffee into a dented steel mug. The liquid steamed faintly as it filled the chipped enamel. She passed it to Sosa, who took it in both hands like it might anchor him.

No one had spoken for five minutes.

It wasn't a silence born of indecision — it was calculation. The stillness that comes before lighting the fuse.

Sosa finally broke it, his voice ragged but firm. "We don't have days. We have hours."

Kael nodded once, the movement was sharp. "Then we move now. But not blind."

He leaned forward, the muscles in his back taut under his sweat-darkened shirt. He pointed to three red-marked locations on the map:

- La Casa de Penitencia
- La Casa Amarilla

• Finca de Cárdenas, eleven miles west

Natalia stepped forward, eyes locked on the map. "La Casa Amarilla is a decoy. I'd bet my life on it. Too much movement during the day — like they want us to watch."

Sosa took a sip of the coffee, set it down, and leaned in. "Intel says El Filo de Dios is guarding the Penitencia gates. But the internal security? That's Cártel Nueve Vidas. And there's been chatter — whispers of Chinese military advisors being embedded inside."

"We recon all three to be sure," Kael said, his finger tapping each mark in turn. "No assumptions. Not with what's at stake."

Natalia stepped forward, her eyes scanning the map with razor precision. "Split teams?"

Kael nodded. "Three targets. Three angles of approach."

He traced a route with the edge of his knife. "I'll take Valeria and three men to La Casa de Penitencia. We'll map guard shifts, patrol rotations, electrical fencing, drone coverage. If there's an exploitable seam, we'll find it. We need to know if they've reinforced the southeast drainage tunnel—the old sewage access marked here."

Natalia leaned in. "What about the other two?"

Kael continued. "Sosa will lead a four-man scout team to La Casa Amarilla. We suspect it's being used as a logistics point—medical or detention overflow. If they're moving prisoners or weapons, we'll see traces: tire tracks, food supply crates, comms antennas. Get photos. Drones if you have them. Don't engage."

Natalia nodded. "I'll take the third. Finca de Cárdenas." Her voice caught slightly at the name. It had once been a safe house. A place where cartel loyalty was a given. "I'll move with two on foot from the west, cutting through the treeline. If it's been flipped, we'll find traces—changed patrol routes, burned Cárdenas's insignia, even an ambush waiting. I want confirmation before we move anything through there."

Kael looked up from the map. "Comms check every 20 minutes. If anyone misses two in a row, assume compromise."

Valeria stepped up beside him, pulling her hair into a tight band, jaw set. "And if we find leverage?"

"Document. Don't act. Not yet," Kael said. "This is recon. Not a hit. We hit after the intel is solid."

Natalia folded her arms. "We've got two hours of daylight left. That buys us a recon window before they lock everything down at dusk."

Kael nodded. "Then we move in ten."

The room shifted with purpose—quiet bodies checking mags, testing radios, tightening laces. No panic. No fear. Just focus.

The kind you only find in those who have nothing left to lose.

Later That Morning – Rooftops Above La Casa de Penitencia

Kael crouched low behind a rusting A/C unit, scanning the courtyard below. The heat was rising, shimmering off concrete and coiled razor wire. The penitentiary looked more like a fortress than a prison — ringed with reinforced walls and littered with makeshift barricades.

Beside him, Valeria steadied binoculars, her jaw clenched. Her knuckles were white.

To their left, Raúl Castañeda — one of Salvador's oldest sicarios, face like granite and hands like butcher's tools — spit into the gutter and muttered a curse.

"Place is crawling."

Kael adjusted the zoom on his monocular.

He counted: Twelve cartel guards pacing the outer wall • Three snipers on the roof • A mortar emplacement tucked behind sandbags near the north stairwell

And then — movement.

A formation of dark uniforms filed out from the east wing. Not Mexican. Not Cárdenas.

Kael's stomach tightened. He inhaled slowly.

"That's Chinese gear."

Valeria shifted beside him, eyes narrowing. "Not cartel?"

"Military," Kael muttered. "At least a platoon. Maybe more."

Tight movement. Clean spacing. Type 95 bullpup rifles. Chinese flag patch, partially covered with tape. They didn't swagger. They advanced.

Raúl's breath hissed through his teeth.

"¿Qué carajo…?"

Kael reached into his pack and pulled out a matte-black Pelican case. Inside: a compact drone, folded tight like a sleeping insect.

"Let's confirm it."

The drone hovered silently over the penitentiary courtyard, its camera gliding between shadows and sunbeams. Kael's eyes didn't blink. His fingers clenched the controller tighter with every passing second.

On-screen: Prisoners in rags • Ritual beatings near a cracked concrete altar • A cartel lieutenant dragging a limp body by the ankle

And then — discipline.

A platoon of trained Chinese soldiers, unmistakable.

Not PMC. Not cartel muscle. Soldiers. Organized. Tactical.

Their uniforms bore no official insignia, but Kael spotted enough: Type 95 rifles • Clean gear rigs •

Platoon commander giving hand signals in Mandarin •
Boots that moved in sync like they'd trained for war.

Valeria whispered, "This isn't support. This is a
foreign army."

Raúl's face went pale. "Those bastards…
they're helping them hold the city."

Kael nodded grimly. "They're not helping.
They're here for the product. Veloxyn."

"This is no longer a cartel problem," Valeria
said.

Kael's voice went cold. "This is geopolitical
now."

The wind picked up slightly, rattling the rusted
vent behind them. Somewhere in the distance, a dog
barked. The city was still holding its breath.

The door slammed behind them. Kael set the
Pelican case on the table and flipped it open. Natalia
and Lieutenant Sosa looked up from the war table,
eyes narrowing as the drone tablet powered on.

"They're not just cartel," Kael said.

Valeria stepped in behind him. "There's a
Chinese military platoon inside La Casa de Penitencia.
Thirty men. Full gear. Command structure. This isn't
local."

Natalia blinked, then straightened. "Are you
sure they're soldiers?"

Kael pushed the drone tablet toward her —
paused on the image of a Chinese officer barking
orders near the staircase. The image was grainy, but
unmistakable.

"Sure, as I've ever been."

Sosa sat forward, the color draining from his
face. "China doesn't send soldiers unless the stakes are
global."

Kael looked at the map. His voice was dry, but
his mind raced.

"We're sitting on something bigger than Veloxyn."

Natalia exhaled. "Then we need to strike now — before this turns into a war we can't win."

Silence again. But now it buzzed with urgency.

Valeria tapped her finger on the finca. "We'll need the weapons stashed here. If we go in light, we die fast."

Natalia swore under her breath. "They're not just running drugs anymore. They're running a goddamn fortress."

Kael stared at the map, then slowly turned toward Sosa. "How accurate is the intel?"

Sosa looked up, weariness etched in his face. "Accurate enough to get us all killed. But we don't have another option."

There was another beat of silence.

Kael's eyes glinted. "We burn down the airport tarmac. Hit their shipments. Let Los Huesos Rojos think they're under siege from every direction."

Valeria let out a short laugh. "We're lighting a fuse that might blow up the entire Yucatán."

Sosa stood slowly. "Then we better pray the blast reaches the right bastards."

Kael looked at each of them in turn. His voice dropped, steady as stone.

"This isn't just extraction. It's declaration. We're not going to be unknown anymore."

And then, in unison, they all leaned closer to the map — not as fugitives, but as a strike team.

The cantina's backroom had turned into a war room.

An old lantern hissed softly on the table, casting pale amber across the map. The fan above spun lazily, barely stirring the humid air thick with sweat, gun oil, and tension. The mood wasn't panic — it was precision.

Kael stood over the city map again, tapping his finger on the quadrant marked "Edificio San Miguel."

"We hit this first. Nothing moves without weapons," he said. "Salvador said there's a full cache in the boiler room — crates under steel plates. Could be enough to turn farmers into a strike team."

Raúl Castañeda adjusted the sling on his rifle and leaned in. "That building's is a graveyard. No traffic. No lights. But that's not peace. That's a kill zone."

Sosa nodded. "I scouted it a month ago. Two side exits, one freight entrance in the back, cameras were off — or hidden. We can come up from the drain channel off Calle 18. No direct approach from the main road. No one will see us."

Natalia crossed her arms. "And if someone does?"

"Then we improvise," Kael said. "Fast in, fast out. Load and vanish."

She shook her head slightly, lips pursed. "You're not going in light."

"We can't afford another daylight op," Kael replied. "We move just after sunset. Use the shadows."

Sosa pointed at the sewer system on the east side. "This junction connects to the back of San Miguel. Old maintenance route. Covers your movement. No overhead angles."

Kael looked at the team. "Alright. Three squads."

He drew a line from the marina to the target, then circled the building.

"I'll lead the entry team. Raúl, I want you on point with me. Valeria already prepped our route — she'll slip in ahead and check the perimeter."

Sosa straightened in his seat. "I can move with support. I'll take two of the younger loyalists. Quiet ones. Give me rear cover and fallback.

Kael nodded. "You'll hold the channel. No one gets behind us."

Raúl tapped the map. "And Padre Luis?"

"We'll put him with Team Three — he knows explosives and he's got steady hands. He'll bring two from the upper fields."

Natalia shifted against the wall.

Kael looked around the room. "We go in quiet. We come out loaded. If we get the arsenal, we change the board. If not…"

"We pray the sea's still open," Sosa muttered.

Kael's eyes were flint. "There's no going back. Not now."

No one disagreed.

Outside, the shadows lengthened over Progreso. Somewhere in the ruins of Edificio San Miguel, the tools of war waited for hands bold enough to claim them.

"I'll hold back," Natalia said, her voice even. "I'll stay here. Prep the rest."

She said it like strategy. Tactical. Unemotional. Just another line in a mission briefing.

But Kael saw through it. So did Valeria — her gaze lingered a beat longer than usual.

This wasn't about tactics.

It was about survival. Her own.

The last ambush had left more than a bruise on her ribs and a scar on her thigh. It had taken something deeper — a part of her faith in control, in planning, in always being one step ahead. Natalia had pulled Valeria from a burning Humvee with bullets singing past her ear. She had watched Cárdenas's blood spill onto cement and jungle floor alike. She had felt the warm slick of someone's life leaving them — and it wasn't the first time. But it might have been the time that finally cracked her.

She didn't want to be numb. Not yet. Not again.

"I can't keep losing people," she whispered, too quiet for anyone to hear. But Kael did.

His jaw clenched slightly, but he said nothing. Just a small nod — not of approval, not even of agreement, but of understanding. The kind only warriors shared.

Natalia turned away, rubbing the back of her hand across her brow like she could wipe the weariness off. She needed to be ready for the final reckoning. And that meant staying whole. At least for tonight.

The silence that followed was not cold. It was heavy — the silence of respect. The kind that comes before movement. The kind that means war is about to begin.

And this time, none of them would walk away unchanged.

War was coming.

And they were done hiding.

Night fell like a curse.

The moon hung low, veiled by haze and faint traces of ash. Streetlights flickered like dying stars, casting broken halos over abandoned cars, shuttered taquerías, and walls painted with blood-red warnings and cartel tags. Mérida wasn't a city anymore — it was a trap wrapped in silence.

They moved like seasoned professionals.

Kael's boots hit the pavement in near silence as he led the column forward.

They moved in staggered formation — three teams, three per unit, spaced a hundred yards apart. No radios. No flashlights. Just hand signals, shadow discipline, and unspoken trust. The city around them was sleeping but not resting. It was dreaming of violence.

Kael led the first team — Natalia on his left, Raúl Castañeda on his right. Valeria had helped prep the route earlier, but Kael insisted on leading the breach himself.

Behind them, Team Two: Lieutenant Sosa, recovering but sharp, flanked by two young Cárdenas's operatives — one with a limp, the other fresh from Veracruz, barely twenty.

Team Three swept the rear: two hardened fighters escorting Padre Luis, the ex-mercenary priest with a silver beard and eyes like carved obsidian. A Saint Jude medal dangled from his pistol grip — taped there like a sacrament.

They slipped through alleyways and burnt courtyards. Past blown-out windows and forgotten churches. Dogs barked in the distance, but no one came to the windows. The city was awake, but silent — watching.

Kael raised a fist. The column froze.

He pointed ahead.

Edificio San Miguel loomed like a tombstone against the pale sky — five stories of concrete, mold-stained windows, and shuttered history. Once, it had been the regional headquarters for a Cárdenas shell corporation. Then the tax records vanished. Then the power was cut. Then it disappeared from memory — except for Salvador.

Kael stepped through the shattered doorway first.

Inside, the building breathed rot and time. Damp ceilings sagged. Paint peeled like old scabs. The air was thick with mildew and dust, but Kael pressed forward — one foot over memory, the other over mission.

Down the stairwell.

Past collapsed desks and rusted pipes.

He remembered Salvador's words clearly:

"Back of the boiler room. Behind the maintenance wall. You'll know it when you see it."

The stairwell ended in a rusted door marked MANTENIMIENTO. Raúl raised his rifle. Kael gave him a nod.

One kick. The door gave.

The boiler room was still. Cold. Long dormant. Shadows stretched over the rusted belly of the boiler. Broken gauges and ancient pipes rattled faintly in the wind coming through a side vent.

Then Valeria pointed.

"There. Back wall. Doesn't match the rest. No rebar seams."

Natalia stepped forward, running her fingers along the plaster.

"This wasn't part of the original structure."

Raúl grabbed a crowbar from the corner. Valeria handed Kael a sledge from the utility cabinet.

They got to work.

Brick cracked. Dust bloomed. Old mortar crumbled into powder.

And then — a hollow sound.

Thud.

Raúl stopped. Stepped back.

Kael gripped the edge and yanked. The panel tore free and clattered to the ground.

Silence.

The room beyond was pitch dark.

Raúl clicked on his flashlight and stepped inside, the beam slicing through years of secrecy.

A steel-walled chamber.

Lined with crates. Floor to ceiling. Neatly stacked. No clutter. No trash. No mistakes.

The air inside was cold. Pressurized. This place had been sealed like a time capsule.

Kael moved first. His boots echoed faintly off the concrete as he passed the first crate — stamped in block lettering:

F88 Austeyr

He cracked it open.

Inside: twenty rifles. Wrapped. Greased. Magazine-fed. Battle-ready.

Next: HK416s — ten of them. Suppressed. Clean.

Further down: AK-47s, thirty total. Wood grips polished like furniture.

Rifles for a regiment.

In the corner — a foam-lined case of Ruger GP100s. .357 Magnum. Hammer-polished. Six-shot revolvers that could stop anything shy of a rhino.

Valeria ran her hand along the inside wall.

"This isn't a stockpile," she whispered. "This is a war chest."

Kael moved deeper — found the cargo container bolted into the back wall.

Padlocked.

Raúl handed him bolt cutters. One snap. Two. The lid creaked open.

Inside:

• 8 RPGs, sealed and factory-fresh.
• 200 RPG rounds
• 2 81mm mortars
• 400 mortar shells
• 5,000+ rounds: 5.56mm, 7.62mm, .357 Magnum
• Tactical vests, medical kits, encrypted comms
• And five duffels stacked in a corner, zippers already half open

Kael reached down. Unzipped one.

Stacks of U.S. cash. Band after band. Brick after brick.

Sosa, just stepping into the threshold, froze.

"Jesus Christ…"

Kael looked back and grinned.

"Now we can do some damage."

Sosa exhaled slowly.

"I may be able to bring thirty to fifty more officers over. Real ones. We've talked about it. But they'll need a reason."

Kael nodded. "How much?"

"Fifty grand apiece," Sosa said. "Maybe less if it's personal."

Kael looked at Natalia. "Still leaves us more than enough."

She smiled, the edge of a blade behind her eyes.

"In cartel terms? This is lunch money. But to the right people — this is revolution fuel."

Raúl slung his rifle. "We won't be able to move it all."

Kael nodded.

"We're not going to."

He turned back toward the room, calculating.

"This building is off grid. Structurally intact. No utilities. No surveillance. Forgotten by everyone but us."

He looked at Natalia.

"We leave a third of it. Food, gear, comms, ammo. We build a fallback right here."

Natalia nodded slowly. "San Miguel becomes our last stand."

Sosa added, "If Mérida falls, this is where we disappear. Where we rise again."

Kael glanced back one last time.

Five million dollars.

Enough firepower to light a war.

A room full of ghosts and gunpowder.

And just the beginning.

Kael scanned the crates stacked along the warehouse wall—guns, RPGs, mortars, and a dozen duffel bags stuffed with ammo. "We need wheels," he said. "Something low-profile. Can't move all this on foot."

Padre Luis stepped forward, brushing dust from his cassock. "There is an old Cárdenas taxi lot four blocks west. Used to run the entire east quarter before the collapse. If the taxis are still there, some might run."

Kael gave a single nod. "Take a team. Quiet and fast. Bring back at least six."

Within minutes, Padre Luis was at the edge of the lot, his group fanned out behind him. The gate hung open, its rusted chain limp. Weeds choked the pavement. The warehouse loomed like a tomb — once busy, now forgotten. Inside, rows of yellow taxis sat in varying states of decay. Some had their hoods popped and engines gutted. Others rested on bare axles, missing tires or windows. But six still looked whole. Luis crossed himself, whispered a prayer in the oil-slicked silence, then turned to the team. "God provides. Let's move." They hotwired what they could, pushed away what they couldn't, and within fifteen minutes, six battered taxis roared to life— sputtering, coughing, but ready. They rolled back through side streets, yellow ghosts returning to life, ready to carry war.

The convoy rolled in without headlights.

Six battered taxis — yellow paint faded, bumpers loose, mufflers wheezing — crept down a narrow alley flanked by old stucco walls and sagging electrical wires. Each vehicle was stuffed with crates that could start a war: rifles wrapped in sheets, RPGs hidden under floorboards, ammunition stuffed in duffel bags.

The taxis rolled up to the safehouse under cover of darkness. Their tires crackled over broken concrete and crushed glass, headlights killed long before they turned the final corner. Rusted frames, faded paint, Cárdenas's insignias barely visible beneath layers of grime — every inch of the vehicles spoke of survival over aesthetics.

Inside the lead car, Raúl rode shotgun with a crate cradled in his lap like a newborn. It was heavy, but he didn't flinch. In the backseat, Kael sat with a stripped-down HK416 across his knees, his forearms dusted with sweat and grease. His eyes, red-rimmed from sleepless nights, scanned the alley ahead like it was a battlefield.

It was almost laughable.

Weapons worth millions moved in cars worth hundreds.

But that was the Cárdenas way now — subtle, quiet, stripped of vanity. The empire was bleeding, but it was still alive.

Natalia stood in the doorway of the safehouse as Kael's team returned.

Their clothes were soaked with sweat and city grime. Kael's shirt was half untucked, his arms streaked with mortar dust. Raúl's boots left prints of black soot across the tiles. Sosa limped slightly, but his posture was straighter now — a man with purpose.

Inside, the air shifted.

The safehouse had felt like a tomb for days — quiet, static, too many ghosts and not enough weapons.

Now?

Now it buzzed.

Kael stepped through the door with a crate balanced on his shoulder and a revolver in his waistband. Natalia looked up from the war table as he entered. She took one look at his expression and nodded.

"You found it."

He set the crate down on the table.

"Better than that."

Valeria moved fast. She popped open the lid — inside, rows of gleaming HK416s. Her eyes lit up.

"Holy shit."

One by one, the others came forward — Cárdenas's loyalists, a few trusted outsiders, even two former mercs hiding from old debts. They gathered around the crates like pilgrims at an altar.

Kael stood at the center, lifting a rifle from the foam.

"This isn't just gear," he said. "It's insurance."

He handed the weapon to a young fighter with shaking hands.

Natalia added, "And what we couldn't carry? It stays behind. Hidden. Deep inside San Miguel. If we fall, if this city burns — that's where we rise again."

Raúl, still wiping dust from his brow, grinned. "Plan B. The ghost bunker."

Sosa stepped forward, nodding toward the rest of the crates now being carried in by hand.

"We'll need to distribute these fast. Quiet. Staggered drops. No patterns. No witnesses."

Kael looked around the room. Men and women opened duffels with surgical care. Ammunition boxes were organized by caliber. RPG tubes checked for seals. Vests sized and matched.

This wasn't just rearming.

This was a resurrection.

Valeria ran her hand over the casing of an RPG. Her voice dropped low, almost reverent.

"It's been a long time since I held something that made me feel dangerous."

Kael smiled faintly. "You were never not."

Natalia crossed her arms. "This is going to change everything. But we need more than firepower. We need shock value."

"We have it," Kael said. "The attack on La Casa de Penitencia isn't about extraction. It's about message."

He stepped toward the map, tapping the red-marked prison with the butt of his knife.

"We hit them where they're sure they're untouchable. We broadcast it. We show the world the Chinese aren't just 'influencing'—they're occupying."

Raúl added, "And when we drag their bodies through the street, the message writes itself."

Sosa stood at the war table; one arm still bound in gauze.

"I've sent word," he said. "Thirty officers. Maybe more. They'll meet us at the rally point tomorrow. Some want cash. Others want blood. They all want a future."

Kael tossed him a duffel. "Fifty thousand each."

Sosa caught it. His eyes flicked to Natalia. She nodded.

"It's not about the money. But it opens ears."

For a long beat, no one spoke.

"Split it." Said Kael

Natalia added, "Tell them the rest comes after the prison falls. Not before."

Sosa nodded. "They'll respect that."

Valeria was crouched over the mortar shells now, checking weight and casing. She looked up at Kael.

"What about air cover?"

"Comstock," Kael said. "He's watching. He'll strike when we get into trouble. But only once."

"Then we better make it count," Valeria muttered.

Kael turned to the map again.

The red circle over La Casa de Penitencia seemed to glow like an ember.

He tapped it once with the flat edge of his knife.

"This is where we open the gates of hell."

Natalia moved beside him. Her voice was low, calm.

Then Natalia placed her pistol on the table and pointed to the map.

"If this is our Firestarter — we need a name for the operation."

Kael's eyes didn't leave the prison mark. "Call it Twin Fang."

Valeria raised a brow. "Why?"

Kael's voice was ice.

"Because we're going in with two bites: the frontal strike… and the one they never see coming."

Kael tossed him a duffel. "Fifty thousand each."

Sosa caught it. His eyes flicked to Natalia. She nodded.

"It's not about the money. But it opens ears."

For a long beat, no one spoke.

Chapter 15

The Bite You See

A tropical storm was moving in from the east — one of those brooding Caribbean tempests that October conjured like clockwork. The radar showed it was still offshore, but the rain had begun. First a drizzle, then a steady cascade, rattling softly against the cracked tile roof of the safehouse.

For once, it wasn't the sound of gunfire. And for the fighters inside, the rhythm of falling rain brought a strange calm. The kind that wraps around your nerves and lulls them into stillness — like a lullaby for people raised in war.

Kael stood in the corner by the window, adjusting the straps of his chest rig. Outside, the wind bent the palms eastward. The air was thick — salted, charged, and full of storm light.

Kael didn't speak. Instead, he reached into the inside of his vest and pulled out something soft — Marisol's scarf. Still faintly scented with jasmine and red wine, the last thing of hers he carried. He lifted it to his lips, kissed it once, folded it, and tucked it over his heart.

The room around him was a slow-motion hive of tension. Natalia walked calmly from table to table, checking gear: flashbangs, grenades, rifle mags, two suppressors, a med kit. Her hands were steady, her face unreadable.

The rain drummed harder now, a steady roar on the roof. Inside, the safehouse felt sealed from time — a war room untouched by mercy.

Kael stood at the head of the table, arms crossed. A printed city map was taped down, its edges curling from humidity. Sosa leaned on his cane nearby, face pale but eyes sharp. Natalia hovered just behind, quiet like a loaded rifle. Valeria clicked a pen beside a yellow notepad of callsigns and gear lists.

Padre Luis entered last — rain dripping from his cassock, rifle slung casually across his back. His eyes, black and still as obsidian, swept the room. He nodded once at Natalia, then at Kael.

"Padre," Kael said. "You sure about this?"

Luis held up his rosary, then his sidearm — a silver-plated CZ pistol with a Saint Jude medal taped to the grip.

"One for God," he said. "One for justice."

Kael cracked the faintest grin. "Alright."

He pointed to three red circles on the map — the penitentiary, the fallback cache, and the east dock.

"We split into three elements. Team, One hits the cache. Get Leandro out. Team Two forms the diversion net. Team Three secures fallback and evac routes."

Natalia cleared her throat. "I'll stay here. Comms. Triage. If anyone needs extraction or medical fallback, they report to me."

"No argument," Kael said. "You're the spine of this."

Sosa grunted. "Then who's going in with you?"

Kael turned on the map. "I am. With Raúl. Valeria prepped the approach earlier, so she's coming too. We take two more — ones who've been through close-quarters hell."

"I'll tap Jairo and Nico," Sosa said. "Jairo cleared safehouses in Sinaloa. Nico's a Ninja in the dark."

"Perfect," Kael said.

Padre Luis stepped closer. "And me?"

Kael looked him in the eyes. "You sure you're not just here to absolve sins?"

Luis smiled, grim. "I'm here to Acollect them."

"Then you're on Team Three. Evac and overwatch. You see us coming out bloody, you move."

Valeria double-checked the frequency bands on the table. "We'll be on encrypted burst—five-second windows only. No comms outside designated slots unless we go redline."

"Copy that," Raúl said, checking his belt grenades.

Sosa straightened up. "I'll lead Fang Two — El Filo compound. Take Tigre, Benito, and the two mortarmen. Hit it fast, burn it down, pull back. That'll draw them west."

Padre Luis folded his hands over the map, then looked up at Kael. "If the devil has a church, better we be the fire that razes it."

Natalia leaned in. "You all know your roles. We don't improvise unless the mission shifts. Primary is Leandro. Nothing else matters."

Kael looked around the room, taking in each face.

"Once we commit," he said, "there's no walking it back."

Valeria nodded. "Then let's make sure they remember who we are."

Kael pulled the scarf from his vest again, kissed it once.

"Let's bring him home."

Valeria was locked in by the radio terminal, issuing final instructions to their satellite teams. "Team Alpha ready. Bravo holding until green light. RPG crews in motion."

Lieutenant Mateo Sosa, already armored and pacing by the table, looked up.

Kael walked over and said, low and certain: "We get him. Or we don't come back."

The static burst from the radio console. A click. A voice.

152

Valeria looked back. "It's Goya."

Natalia crossed the room, grabbed the mic, and spoke fast. "Goya, we're locked. The plan's in motion. Diversions go live in forty. Leandro is the primary. We'll need the fallback cache from San Miguel if we take too many hits."

Goya's voice came in dry, strained but sharp. "You thought this through?"

"I didn't plan it," she said.

A pause. Then came another voice — deep, commanding, unmistakable.

Salvador Cárdenas. "Then who did?"

Natalia looked over at Kael and handed him the radio.

Kael's voice was low, but clear. "I did."

"I figured."

"You don't need to back it," Kael said. "But you need to know — this isn't just an extraction. It's the spark."

Salvador's voice was calm. "Why? Why her? Why this?"

Kael paused. The scarf was still warm against his chest.

"Because I've never felt what I feel with her."

"With Marisol?"

"Yes."

Kael looked out the window, where lightning flashed faintly over the rooftops.

"She's not a reason. She's the reason. When I'm with her, time stops. Thought disappears. There's only presence. There's only now. I feel like... like our souls collapse into each other. I'm not fighting for her. I'm fighting because of her."

There was silence on the other end. Then—

"Está bien," Salvador said. "You've always spoken like a man with nothing to lose. Now you sound like a man who finally has something worth dying for."

Another shuffle of sound.

"Wait," Salvador said. "Someone wants to speak with you."

The channel shifted. The static sharpened.

And then—

"Kael?"

It was her. Marisol.

Soft. Breathless. Shaky, like she'd been waiting by the radio all night.

Kael froze. "Marisol."

"Mi SEXICO," she said.

His eyes closed. The storm outside faded to silence.

"Every night," she whispered, "I sleep with your scent still on my skin. Every morning, I reach for your touch. I ache for you."

Kael swallowed. "You, okay?"

"I'm safe. But I've missed you. More than I can say."

"I'm coming," he said. "Nothing stops me. You know that."

"I do." A pause.

"I have things to tell you. Things I want you to hear from me, face to face."

"Then I'll come back. And you'll tell them all."

Valeria gave Natalia a warning nod from the console. The signal intercept risk was rising.

"I have to go," Marisol said. "But promise me—come back alive."

"I promise," Kael said. "You're the only place I've ever wanted to return to."

Then the line clicked off.

Natalia looked over. "We better make this work," she said with a smirk. "How else will you ever see your SEXICO again?"

As the storm thickened outside, the safehouse came alive with final coordination.

Kael unrolled a map of Mérida over the dining table. Raúl, Sosa, Natalia, and Valeria gathered around. Flashlights flickered over red marks.

"We hit them from two directions — two fangs," Kael said. "Simultaneously. While they're distracted, we breach the penitentiary."

Valeria pointed at the east quadrant.

"Fang One: the airport. There's a Chinese tactical aircraft on the tarmac and a black Gulfstream used by Cartel Nueve Vida. We take a six-man team, post them five hundred yards out, hit the aircraft with RPGs and sniper fire, and vanish."

Kael nodded. "They're not to engage beyond that. Fire, vanish, reposition."

Natalia chimed in, gesturing to the opposite side of the map.

"Fang Two: the compound and church of El Filo de Dios. Same structure. Six fighters. Use Molotovs, RPGs, scoped rifles. Their headquarters goes up in flames."

Sosa tapped his finger on the central target.

"La Casa de Penitencia — heavily guarded. Concrete walls, two towers, thirty Chinese soldiers inside."

Kael's eyes hardened. "If both fangs draw their attention, we'll have a window. We enter from below — storm drains. Sewer access. Silent breach."

Natalia nodded. "We go in with six. Me, Kael, Valeria, Raúl, and two others. The rest stand by for extraction."

"What about my men?" Sosa asked.

"We hold them back," Kael said. "All 26 officers you secured — keep them in position. We don't show our full force unless necessary. No grandstand. No flags."

Raúl adjusted his vest, voice low. "We want them to think this was surgical. Not a revolution."

Kael turned to Natalia. "Let's call it in."

Natalia returned to the radio.

Goya answered. Salvador was still on the line.

She detailed the plan — both fangs, timing, fallback cache. Then he handed the mic to Kael again.

"You trust this?" Salvador asked.

Kael's voice was still.

"Yes."

"I hope you're right."

"You're not just getting your second back," Kael said. "You're lighting the match."

The rain thickened into sheets as six Cárdenas fighters belly-crawled through cactus scrub and thorn grass outside the airport's east boundary fence.

Lightning flickered above the tarmac, illuminating two target aircraft: a gray Chinese tactical transport and a cartel-labeled Gulfstream, painted black with tinted windows.

Hidden behind a ridge, their RPG gunner took aim.

"Target one locked," he whispered.

No command was spoken. Just a nod.

THWUMP.

The rocket launched with a plume of fire and smoke.

BOOM.

The Chinese transport exploded, fire blooming against the downpour like an angry god's scream.

Screams and alarms followed. Lights swept the perimeter. Cartel soldiers ran in disarray, ducking as a second RPG streaked toward the Gulfstream.

BOOM.

Secondary explosions rocked the field.

Two Cárdenas snipers opened fire from the ridge, dropping a fleeing guard and blowing out a Humvee's front tire.

The team was gone before the smoke cleared.

Pre-Dawn – Fang Two: El Filo Compound

Six more Cárdenas fighters approached the cult compound — a crumbling colonial church now wrapped in barbed wire; its bell tower covered in blood-red cloth and painted scripture.

Tigre crept to the gate, a Molotov in hand.

He whispered, "For every throat you cut in God's name…"

WHOOSH.

He hurled the bottle through a stained-glass window.

WHOOOMPH.

Flames erupted inside.

Chanting turned into chaos. Cultists poured out in robes, some wielding machetes, others blindly firing rifles. Smoke coiled upward like a signal to hell.

A second firebomb sailed in.

Inside the sanctuary, Lieutenant Javier Montalvo stood calmly on the altar, arms spread.

The glass behind him shattered.

He didn't flinch.

"Let it burn," he whispered.

Meanwhile – Sewer Infiltration Beneath La Casa de Penitencia

Kael, Natalia, Raúl, and three Cárdenas men stood waist-deep in a blackened, moss-rimmed storm channel beneath the penitentiary.

No talking. No sound but boots on metal grates and water sloshing.

Kael held the HK416 tight to his chest. His night vision goggles glowed ghost green. Emergency lights above pulsed red through cracks in the concrete.

Natalia's voice in his ear:

"Diversions hit. We've got three, five minutes before they regroup."

Kael pointed.

Up ahead: a welded grate. The maintenance tunnel. Their entry point.

Raúl moved in, cutting the bolts with handheld shears.

SNAP. SNAP. SNAP.

Kael moved first, crawling up into the darkness. The boiler room above was dim, hot, and quiet. Two guards stood near the back.

Kael fired twice. Thup. Thup. Suppressed rounds dropped them where they stood.

The rest of the team slipped in behind.

They were inside La Casa de Penitencia.

The hallway above the boiler room was a dead zone — long, narrow, silent. A blood-black crucifix was burned into the wooden double doors at the far end.

Kael kicked them open.

They entered a converted chapel.

Candles burned low in broken sconces. Incense wafted like ghost breath. Crimson banners bearing the symbol of El Filo de Dios draped from broken ceiling rafters.

At the altar, in the center of it all, hung Leandro Barragán.

His arms were stretched wide; wrists bound with leather straps to the beams of a wooden cross. Blood trickled from his side. His face was swollen, lips split, but he was conscious.

Barely.

Kael rushed forward, blade already in hand.

"I've got you," he whispered.

He cut the bindings, and Leandro collapsed into his arms.

Behind him, Natalia and the team cleared the corners, taking out two cult guards before they could reach for weapons.

"Valeria," Kael whispered into his throat mic. "We've got him."

Then her voice came back — tense, fast, urgent.

"Kael. New feed. Two American hostages. Being loaded into a vehicle at the east side dock."

Kael's eyes flicked to his drone wrist pad.

Grainy feed. Two men. Zip-tied. Blindfolded. Shoved into a truck.

One of them wore a bracelet with a worn American flag.

Valeria saw the hesitation.

"Stick to the mission," she said firmly.

Kael clenched his jaw. "No."

"You go rogue, we risk it all."

"They're not cartel. They're ours."

"I don't give a damn—"

"They're ours," Kael said again.

Then he was gone.

Off-Mission

Kael sprinted down a lower hallway, boots slipping on wet tile. The truck roared outside as its rear door slammed shut.

Two guards spotted him—one Chinese, one cartel.

Crack. Crack.

Kael dropped them both with the HK416.

He slid under a half-lowered security gate, vaulted a crate, and grabbed the truck's rear latch.

The vehicle lurched forward.

He yanked the door open, leapt inside, and fired twice killing the guard seated with the hostages.

The truck swerved.

Kael shot the driver through the metal partition.

The vehicle crashed into a retaining wall, airbags bursting in smoke.

Kael freed the Americans.

"Can you walk?"

One of them nodded. The other was semi-conscious.

Kael slung him over his shoulder and moved, fast.

The comms crackled.

"Kael?" Valeria's voice. "Talk to me."

"I've got them," he breathed. "Headed to fallback."

Courtyard – Minutes Later

The air reeked of burning plaster and blood.

Kael emerged from the east dock tunnel with the two Americans in tow just as mortars began raining down. The rooftop RPG teams had repositioned and were now targeting Chinese patrol trucks and eastern wall reinforcements.

Flames licked skyward from the chapel roof.

Valeria staggered across the courtyard, blood streaking her arm. Leandro leaned heavily on her, barely conscious. Behind her, Raúl fired methodically, covering their retreat from a flanking squad.

Sosa and Tigre's diversion team converged on the breached northern gate, laying down suppressive fire with salvaged M240s.

Then — from the southeast tower — a stream of machine gun fire erupted.

Valeria dove, dragging Leandro behind a stone trough. Kael ducked low, shielding the hostages with his body.

Raúl didn't duck.

He ran.

Straight into the fire.

"¡Viva la Revolución!" he roared, pulling every grenade from his vest.

A bullet caught his shoulder. Then his leg.

He didn't stop.

He reached the base of the tower, climbed halfway up the steel rung, and yanked every pin.

BOOM.

The southeast tower exploded into flaming stone and shredded metal. Bodies rained down. The firelight washed over Raúl's final smile.

Gate Breach – Comstock's Strike
Valeria's voice came through Kael's comm:
"Comstock's drone just reached the gate. Detonation in three..."
Kael grabbed Natalia and Leandro, dragging them toward the broken archway.
"...two..."
The outer wall was already crumbling.
"...one—"
BOOOOOM.
The gate exploded inward, revealing a collapsed barrier and open dirt road beyond.
Cárdenas motorcycles appeared in the mist, led by a scout waving a black flag.
Kael turned to one of the fighters.
"Take the Americans. Now."
He slung Leandro over his shoulder, vaulted onto a dirt-caked bike, and nodded once at Natalia.
She nodded back, blood soaking her sleeve.
"You bring him back."
Kael revved the engine.
"I will."

Jungle Edge – Escape
They hit the edge of the jungle just as the storm broke again — not a drizzle now, but a torrential curtain of warm rain.
Kael didn't slow. He rode into the trees, branches lashing at his face, Leandro slumped against his back like a ragdoll of blood and breath.
Behind him, motorcycles fanned out. A pickup with the rescued Americans roared through the breach. Fires still flickered in the distance.

Kael tapped his comm once.

"Valeria, patch me through."

A beat.

Then:

"Kael?"

Marisol.

"I have him," Kael said. "He's alive. We're clear."

Marisol exhaled audibly — like she hadn't breathed since the assault began.

"I knew you'd do it."

Kael looked up through the canopy as thunder rolled overhead.

"No," he whispered. "We just lit the fuse."

The chapel still burned.

Smoke billowed through shattered stained glass, rising like a black psalm into the storm-heavy sky. What had once been the spiritual heart of El Filo de Dios was now an open wound — charred pews, melted candles, the altar reduced to rubble.

Colonel Sheng Wu stood under a tactical umbrella at the edge of the courtyard. His uniform was immaculate — gray, unmarked, pressed even in the rain. A single drop of blood clung to the sole of his boot, unnoticed.

In his hands: a military tablet streaming live drone footage.

Beside him: Lieutenant Javier Montalvo, robed in his scorched cassock, the red sash of El Filo still tied around his waist. His eyes burned not with fear — but humiliation.

Wu rotated the drone screen.

Kael Torres, caught mid-sprint on camera, riding out through the broken penitentiary gates with Leandro Barragán strapped to his back. A blood-soaked storm behind him. Fire at his heels.

"You let him get away," Montalvo said, voice low, brittle.

Wu didn't look up. "No. I let him show me what he is."

Montalvo raised an eyebrow. "And?"

Wu froze the video. Kael's face stared back — rain-slicked, half-bloodied, alive with fire.

"He's no longer running," Wu said.

Montalvo lit a cigarette with shaking fingers. "Then we should be worried."

Wu gave the faintest smile. "We should."

Behind them, cultists dragged the dead into neat lines. Chinese junior officers argued in Mandarin over fallback positions and resource losses. Two aerial drones hovered silently overhead.

None of it mattered.

Because Kael Torres had just declared war.

And the men watching knew it.

Chapter 16

The Cross and the Fire

Leandro Barragán sat slumped against a cinderblock wall, his breathing shallow but steady. His torso trembled slightly with each exhale, the weight of broken ribs shifting beneath bruised flesh. Blood crusted the corner of his mouth. His left eye was swollen shut, and his knuckles were scabbed—torn raw from weeks of shackles, interrogation, and resistance.

But he was alive.

Alive was enough—for now.

Natalia crouched beside him with a tin cup of rum, her voice softer than Kael had ever heard it. "You're home, hermano," she whispered. Her fingers gently touched the rim of the cup before lifting it to his lips. Leandro drank slowly, like each swallow had to pass through ghosts.

Kael stood nearby, silent. His arms Not with noise, but with motion. Quiet preparation. Whispers and glances.

Men checked weapons with methodical movements. Some loaded mags by candlelight. Others taped grenades into bundles with duct tape and prayer. Boots scraped concrete. Radios clicked softly between bursts of static. Every corner was filled with hands doing something: sealing ammo boxes, wrapping bandages, sketching new movement maps.

Valeria moved between them like a current wounded but composed, her arm still tightly bandaged from the last fight. She checked their setups with a sharp eye and low voice, never lingering too long. A leader in motion.

On one folding table, near a stack of C4 bricks and a partially disassembled rifle, lay a simple bloodstained cloth—Raúl's armband. Folded. Reverent. Untouched since the day he died saving their escape.

No one spoke of him.

But no one forgot.

Then—

The satellite phone rang.

The sound cut through the safehouse like a shot. Everyone froze. Even the rain on the tin roof seemed to pause.

Natalia reached for it without hesitation, the moment stretching like pulled wire. She pressed the receiver to her ear.

A crackle of static. Then a familiar voice—Goya's—broke through. Rough, full of breath and disbelief.

"Lo lograron… hijos de la chingada… lo lograron."

They had done the impossible.

Then came another voice—calm, heavy, deliberate.

Salvador Cárdenas.

"Kael. Natalia. Listen closely."

Kael stepped forward, his boots quiet on the concrete. "We're listening."

"There's a boat," Salvador said. "A forty-foot fishing vessel. El Susurro. It left Cozumel four hours ago. Packed with crates—medical, weapons, cash. But it can't dock until we take Progreso."

Kael's jaw tightened. "It's just floating out there?"

"It'll stay offshore," Salvador confirmed. "Any closer and it gets sunk. You want your reinforcements? You clear the port."

Natalia's voice cut in, sharp and immediate. "And Marisol?"

A pause.

Salvador's tone changed—lower, became quieter. "She's... not well. She collapsed yesterday after Lunch. Santiago took her to the hospital near the university. She's guarded. Safe. But weak."

Kael's breath hitched. He didn't ask for more. Didn't have to. The ache carved its own shape in his chest.

Salvador continued. "You'll need to move on multiple fronts. Hit them where they don't expect it."

Kael exhaled. "You want a war."

"No," Salvador said. "I want a message."

His words were final. Weighted.

"Stay at Torre Cristal. Let them come to you. Then hit the farm—Finca Sangre Verde—and secure the weapons. Meanwhile, Sosa will move on Progreso with his officers."

Kael glanced at Natalia, then Valeria. They nodded without hesitation—calculating already.

"You've got momentum," Salvador said. "Don't waste it."

The line clicked dead.

No goodbye.

No hesitation.

Just war.

Kael slowly lowered the receiver. The hum of tension returned—louder now, sharper.

Outside, the sky over Mérida began to dim into burnt orange and dense shadow. Storm clouds hovered offshore, roiling like bruises over a sleeping giant. Thunder rolled in the distance—not yet overhead, but near enough to feel it in the floorboards.

Inside the safehouse, the war drums began to beat again soft at first, then louder, building through every glance, every rifle click, every final breath of quiet before the storm.

Torre Cristal hadn't changed.

The windows were still shattered. The walls still bore the black scars of fire and bullet spray. And yet, as Kael stood in the main corridor of the 9th floor, the building felt… different.

Alive.

Men moved with quiet urgency, loading crates into old panel vans and rust-bitten taxis. Each vehicle had been chosen not for speed or firepower, but for how invisible it could be — the tools of the overlooked. Tools of the working poor. The kind of vehicles that passed unnoticed on streets cluttered with loss.

Nobody would question their presence until it was too late.

Kael watched the rhythm of it all, his arms crossed as he leaned against a broken marble pillar. A cigarette smoldered between his fingers, but he hadn't taken a drag in minutes.

Down the hall, a Cárdenas mechanic crouched beside a van, welding makeshift armor plates onto the side panels — old refrigerator doors, road signs, even a chunk of a rusted oil drum. It was brutal ingenuity. Ugly. Effective.

A voice behind him drew his attention.

"Short three drivers," Mateo Sosa said, walking in with a police radio tucked under one arm and grease streaked across his knuckles. "I'll pull some of my boys. Half of 'em are ex-military anyway. They know how to floor it and kill on a dime."

Kael nodded. "And Aguilar?"

"Already sent the message," Sosa replied, flipping open a notebook and scribbling something in code. "Montalvo's crew thinks we're cornered here. Scared. Burning through ammo. They're calling us rats."

Kael's mouth twitched at the corner — not quite a smile. "Then let them come bold."

Sosa grinned. "We'll send their bones back in fruit crates."

Kael didn't laugh.

He turned and walked down the hallway, his boots echoing over the cracked tile, stepping over spent shell casings and cigarette butts that hadn't yet been cleaned up from the last fight. The stairwell was half-collapsed on one side, the railing missing in chunks, rebar like ribs poking out of the wall.

This building wasn't just a stronghold.

It was a challenge.

One floor above, in what used to be an executive office with a corner view of the skyline, Natalia sat on a stained mattress dragged in from a looted hotel. Her rifle leaned against the wall beside her. In her lap, a half-cleaned sidearm glinted beneath the half-light. Her fingers moved over it with precision, muscle memory layered over fatigue.

The room smelled faintly of gun oil and candle wax.

The blinds were warped. The drywall cracked. But it was quiet. For a moment.

Valeria entered without knocking.

Sweat glistened on her collarbone, and her black tank top clung to her frame like a second skin. Her hair was pulled back in a messy bun, and there was a faint smear of soot along her cheekbone. She looked like a soldier and a statue all at once.

Natalia looked up, her eyes tracing Valeria's face as if she were checking for fractures in a precious artifact. "You, okay?"

Valeria shrugged, leaning against the far wall. "Yeah. Just… everything's starting to feel real."

Natalia placed the sidearm down gently and patted the mattress. "Come here."

Valeria hesitated for only a second, then crossed the room and sat. Her breathing was shallow.

The kind that came not from exertion, but from what followed it — memory, anxiety, anticipation.

Natalia brushed a strand of hair behind Valeria's ear, her fingertips lingering.

"You're shaking," she whispered.

"So are you," Valeria replied.

They sat in silence for a long moment. The wind outside pressed against the window, rattling it softly — like the world itself wanted to come inside and watch.

"I used to think I was untouchable," Valeria said, her voice thin. "Like nothing could crack me. Not men. Not guns. Not fire."

Natalia leaned closer, her hand resting lightly over Valeria's wrist. "God made me for you, mami."

Valeria's eyes blurred. She looked away. Then looked back.

And kissed her.

Not desperate. Not hungry.

Deliberate.

Slow and sacred — like they were building something holy from the ashes.

Their fingers laced. Jackets fell. Breath tangled.

Clothes became a memory on the floor as two bodies found warmth beneath the storm.

On that mattress, beneath the broken ceiling and the glow of a failing LED lamp, they weren't sicarias or survivors. They were simply two women who had earned peace — and, for a fleeting moment, let themselves believe it might last.

Downstairs, the scent of fuel and sweat mixed with the sharp bite of ozone, drifting in from the coming storm.

They stayed in each other's arms until the LED bulb overhead flickered twice, then died with a soft pop. Darkness settled over them like a second blanket — quiet, warm, fragile. But fragility had no place in the world waiting below.

A knock came at the door. Two short raps. No urgency, no words.

Valeria was already moving. She pulled on her pants, then her boots, braiding her hair with muscle memory while Natalia buttoned her shirt and slung the pistol belt around her hips. No kisses this time. No promises. Just a glance—one filled with something unspoken, something sacred.

By the time they stepped into the hallway, the storm had broken open above the warehouse. Rain hammered the metal roof in bursts, echoing like distant gunfire. Natalia and Valeria moved through the corridor like returning warriors—calm, armored, dangerous.

Kael saw them as they entered the loading dock. He gave a slight nod but said nothing. Whatever had happened between them was theirs. It didn't need explanation. All that mattered now was what came next.

Natalia appeared at his side, tying her hair back beneath a mesh field cap. She handed him a folded operations sheet. Her voice was low. Precise.

"Valeria and her crew are staged near the airport fence. They've confirmed only two patrols per hour. They'll breach at 19:40 and knock out flight control."

"Perfect," Kael said, scanning the sheet.

Natalia continued. "I'll take 40 and hit Finca Sangre Verde just after 20:00. Sentry rotations are loose. Intel says most of Montalvo's crew left for the ambush tonight. That leaves farmers, techs, a few guards."

"Minimal casualties," Kael said. It wasn't a question.

Natalia nodded once. "Unless they force our hand."

Kael looked at her. "Don't let them."

170

Kael moved through the old loading dock like a general among ghosts. His shoulders rolled with quiet tension, his steps precise. He checked loadouts one by one—metal cases of 7.62 rounds, wrapped bricks of C4, olive canvas bags stuffed with morphine and coagulants. Every crate was weighed, tagged, and sorted like precious cargo.

The men he passed looked up at him the way soldiers look at the man who'll die beside them—no salute, no ceremony. Just trust.

Every one of them knew: tonight was going to be bloody.

A chalkboard leaned against the concrete wall near the bay doors. On it, someone had scrawled in charcoal:

TRES FANGS. UNA NOCHE. NI UN PASO ATRÁS.

Three fangs. One night. Not one step back.

Kael paused in front of it for a beat, his jaw tight, then continued.

Mateo Sosa entered from the south hallway; a phone pressed to his ear and a suppressed pistol in his waistband. "Port recon is done," he said without preamble. "The roads into Progreso are clear, but we'll have to move fast. Two ferry checkpoints. Light arms. Nothing we can't steamroll."

"And the boat?" Kael asked.

Sosa smirked. "El Susurro is floating off the reef like a pirate ship. They've got enough supplies to outfit two hundred men. We clear the port; they dock in twenty."

"Good," Kael said. "Then we let Salvador know the gate is open."

Sosa handed Kael a flash drive. "Encrypted satphone code. For when the port's ours."

Kael pocketed it. "Final briefings in the glass boardroom. Bring your crews."

Glass Boardroom – Torre Cristal

The old boardroom had once hosted suits and shareholders.

Tonight, it hosted warriors.

Half the windows were blown out, the table chipped and fire scarred. A piece of bloodied drywall covered the west wall, now used as a tactical sketch surface. On it: maps of Mérida. Colored tacks. Movement paths. Kill zones.

Kael stood at the head of the table, arms bare, shoulders squared. A black Sharpie in one hand. His voice didn't raise—but it cut through the room like a blade.

"Three waves," he said. "One blow. If we stall, we die. If we splinter, we disappear. This is a precision war—low signature, high consequence."

He gestured at each zone in turn:

• Torre Cristal: "This is our bait. We make noise, draw them in, hold the line."

• Finca Sangre Verde: "Natalia leads the seizure. We get the vaults. We take back our backbone."

• Mérida Airport: "Valeria's team disrupts command and escape. No air support for our enemies."

• Progreso Port: "Sosa clears and holds. The moment it's secure, El Susurro lands. Full reinforcement."

Natalia added, "We hit at dusk. Not before. Not after. We don't fight for land—we fight for the right to exist."

Valeria stood near the back, rifle in hand, calm as still water. "And we leave our mark. No flags, no symbols. Just fire."

Someone asked the question everyone was thinking:

"What if they hit us back tomorrow?"

Kael didn't hesitate. "Then we welcome them."

Dusk — Deployment Begins

Outside, dusk bled across the Mérida skyline like molten steel over coals. The storm offshore was stalled—its mass like a god's hand waiting to fall.

Kael crouched on the rooftop of Torre Cristal, wind tugging at the collar of his field jacket. Below, six enemy trucks rolled into the commercial zone—matte-black Toyotas, engines growling low, cartel flags stenciled in white on the side doors. Each was filled with overconfident killers.

An armored personnel carrier rumbled behind them, painted with hybrid Chinese-cartel insignia. The arrogance of empires.

Kael adjusted the earpiece radio. "Visual confirmed. Targets entering the kill box. All units—hold."

Inside Torre Cristal, Cárdenas's fighters pressed into every shadow—behind stairwells, under counters, between stacks of broken office chairs. Rooftop spotters steadied RPGs beneath tarps. Snipers lay prone behind windows; breath measured to the second.

Two blocks away, a single Cárdenas scout crouched in an alley, his finger hovering over a garage door opener rigged to a street grate wired with trip-mines.

Kael's voice cut over the comm.

"Aguilar. Do it."

Two blocks southeast, the scene unfolded with surgical deception.

Lieutenant Marcos Aguilar stood in the open, sweat clinging to his neck beneath the starched collar of a counterfeit police uniform. His arms were raised in a mock surrender. His stance — wide-legged, jittery — sold the illusion of panic. The cartel would expect fear. He made sure to give it to them.

Behind him, four of his officers waved tattered cartel flags. One held a radio aloft, feeding static into an open channel. A false distress call. A bait signal.

The convoy slowed.

Six matte-black trucks came to a halt, engines rumbling low. Their occupants scanned the windows of Torre Cristal, eyes narrowed, rifles lifted but not readied. They smelled weakness.

That was the trick.

From the lead truck, a Chinese officer disembarked — short, lean, meticulous in every movement. He wore a steel-gray tactical vest and spoke Spanish with a clipped Beijing accent.

"And why are you here, Lieutenant?" the officer asked, squinting toward the tower's upper floors.

Aguilar smiled, slow and wolfish.

"To watch them burn."

He dropped the radio.

Raised his Glock.

Fired.

The first shot caught the officer just below the cheekbone, exiting near the base of the skull. His legs folded instantly. He crumpled like wet paper.

Then — hell answered.

BOOM.

The tripwire mine beneath the rusted street grate detonated, flipping the lead Toyota like a kicked dog. The shrapnel punched through its undercarriage. Screams erupted from inside. One man was ejected, slamming into a streetlamp with a sickening crunch.

In the same breath, the Cárdenas scout triggered the second detonator — a shaped charge buried beneath a storm drain.

KRAKOW.

The explosion tore through the convoy's rear guard, sending the last truck into the air. The street lit with orange flame and bone-white shockwaves.

And then Torre Cristal opened fire.

From the windows, Cárdenas's gunners unleashed a fury they had been waiting months to deliver:
• RPGs screamed from the rooftop and punched clean through steel doors.
• Snipers cracked rounds from the 12th floor, targeting drivers, gunners, anyone who moved.
• Automatic bursts shredded the second and third trucks before the passengers could return fire.

One cartel shooter ran for cover—too late. A burst of 5.56mm rounds stitched his chest and hurled him backward into a shattered shopfront.

Inside the building, Kael moved like vapor, sweeping down stairwells with calculated urgency. He took the east hallway exit, flanked wide behind the smoking convoy. Two cartel footmen, dazed and disoriented, stumbled into his path.

Kael raised the Sig Sauer P226 and dropped them both.

Two shots. Two kills. No hesitation.

Street Level Chaos

Mateo Sosa's men — disguised as loyal police — sprang from alleys and storefronts, rifles drawn. The moment the first shots rang out, they turned their muzzles away from Torre Cristal and toward the convoys.

Betrayal cut deep.

One cartel enforcer gaped in disbelief as a man he had trained beside — a former federale — emptied a magazine into his gut.

Another tried to run, only to be cut down by three rounds from Aguilar's sidearm.

One Cárdenas officer with an RPG ducked behind a trash bin, locked onto the armored personnel carrier, and fired.

BOOM.

The first round scorched the side armor, breaching the fuel line.

The second — fired from the rooftop by Valeria's second-in-command — punched through the engine block and ignited the whole goddamn vehicle.

The APC erupted like a demon's lantern. Flames billowed skyward, washing the corridor in red light. Screams turned into silence. Tires melted into puddles.

By now, only five cartel fighters remained — two injured, three scrambling for cover.

Kael's voice came over the comms: "Clean the block. Stack bodies if you must."

The Cárdenas teams didn't hesitate.

Shots cracked out from the broken shadows.

Bodies fell.

Silence returned.

Smoke drifted through the broken plaza like incense over a battlefield altar.

Aftermath – Torre Cristal

Kael walked the wreckage, stepping over spent brass, smoldering tires, and a man who had died still gripping a grenade that never detonated.

One of Aguilar's lieutenants tossed a scorched cartel flag onto the fire and stepped back as it curled into black ash.

Valeria crouched in the tall weeds just outside the airport perimeter, her HK94 resting across her thighs, breath steady. The chain-link fence ahead was already clipped—cut silently an hour earlier by one of her girls under cover of rain. Now the last patrol had passed, and it was time.

She signaled.

Two sicarias slipped through the gap ahead of her, their footfalls featherlight on cracked tarmac. Valeria followed, eyes sweeping left and right. The control tower loomed in the distance, windows dark, antennas still blinking red. The runway lights had been shut off remotely—one of the techs had breached the network just before their move.

Inside the maintenance hangar, three men sat drinking Tecates beside a dead baggage loader. They didn't see her coming. The first died with a blade to the neck. The second never even stood. The third got a round to the spine before he could raise his radio.

Valeria stepped over the bodies without pausing.

She planted the thermite charge on the electrical junction box, set the timer for twenty seconds, and walked away without looking back. The control grid lit up like a sun flare. Sparks flew. Lights died. The air traffic control system blinked, sputtered, and then fried into silence.

She keyed her comm with calm finality. "Airport is lit. Runways are blacked out. Air control is scrap metal."

Natalia moved like a shadow through the cane rows the moonlight fractured by windblown leaves. Her team fanned out behind her—forty fighters armed with suppressed rifles and blood-deep loyalty. At the edge of the field, the old farmhouse loomed: part storage depot, part cartel checkpoint, part graveyard.

She raised a fist. The line froze. Through NVGs, she spotted the sentries—two guards half-asleep with rifles resting on their laps, more interested in their smokes than their sectors. Amateurs. "Intel says most of Montalvo's crew left for the ambush tonight. That leaves farmers, techs, a few guards."

Natalia gave the hand signal.

Two silenced cracks cut the night. Both guards slumped forward, dead before the cigarettes hit dirt.

They breached fast. No flashbangs—too loud. Just boots, muzzles, and fury. Her team moved with brutal precision, clearing the front room in seconds. One farmer dove behind a stack of crates. Another reached for a radio. Natalia dropped him with a double tap before his finger hit the transmit key.

177

She stepped over his body and into the main hall, her rifle up, heart calm.

In the back room, she found the cache—untouched, just like the intel said. Crates of Veloxyn. Bundles of bills. Maps. Tablets. Stolen tech. She didn't smile. She didn't relax.

She just keyed her mic. "Finca Sangre Verde secure. Cache is untouched. Full inventory in progress."

PROGRESO – NORTH HIGHWAY, 19 MILES OUT

The first ambush came just past the broken toll gate.

Sosa's convoy—two armored pickups, two Humvees, three taxis, and a dented city bus retrofitted with steel panels—was rolling fast when the first RPG slammed into the lead truck. It didn't explode, just punched through the side like a fist into wet clay. The driver swerved and clipped a rusted guardrail, skidding into the ditch.

"MOVE!" Sosa shouted from the second truck, already out the door and firing before his boots hit the dirt. His rifle barked short, controlled bursts. "Left side berm—two shooters!"

The taxis peeled off toward the smoke, its windshield rattling as the gunner sprayed tracer fire across the ridge. Two men dropped. Another tried to run and was folded backward by a round to the spine.

Sosa didn't stop.

He ran to the downed vehicle, yanked open the mangled door, and dragged the driver out by his vest. "You good?"

The man coughed blood but nodded.

"Then get in the bus. You're not done."

They pushed forward—fast and aggressive—through what used to be sugar roads and fishing lanes. Now it was a patchwork of burned-out checkpoints, overturned trailers, and the occasional body left as a message. But none of it slowed them.

12 MILES OUT

They hit a militia barricade near an old PEMEX station. Homemade armor. Hunting rifles. Teenagers in knockoff body armor and soccer cleats. One fired early, panicked. His bullet pinged harmlessly off a windshield.

Sosa raised a megaphone.

"This is your only warning!" he shouted. "Lower your weapons and join us, or I turn this whole street into fucking fireworks!"

One of the teens blinked. Dropped his gun.

The rest followed.

The Cardenas banner was draped across their hood before they reached the marina gates.

PORT APPROACH – 3 MILES OUT

By now, the convoy had grown. Civilians were waving them on. An old priest handed out bottled water. Two retired federales joined with scoped rifles and steady hands.

Sosa's second-in-command leaned toward him in armored truck. "You realize you're starting a militia with every mile?"

Sosa grinned. "Good. I want them watching when we raise the flag."

Then the radio crackled.

"Sniper on the dock tower. Red jacket."

"Copy."

Sosa didn't hesitate. He climbed onto the trucks roof, balanced on one knee, and took the shot himself—one clean pop from his DMR.

The red jacket folded like laundry in the wind.

MARINA GATE – 0.5 MILES OUT

The final push was surgical.

Two Humvees from the original Reyes stash flanked left and right. A Reyes loyalist fired a flare. Smoke poured from the side entrance as a diversion.

179

Sosa led the charge on foot—his rifle up, eyes cutting through smoke and confusion. They met light resistance at the fuel depot—three gunmen in mismatched uniforms guarding crates of stolen cartel ammo. Sosa dropped the first two. The third tried to run and was gunned down by a teenage fighter.

He looked at Sosa, hands shaking.

"You did good," Sosa said. "Now reload."

They cleared the control tower, warehouse, and shipping hub in under fifteen minutes. Minimal casualties.

And then quiet.

Sosa stood on the edge of the dock, chest rising with each breath, rifle still hot. Out on the reef, just past the break line, the outline of El Susurro shimmered into view—a black shape against the silver surf, running lights off.

"She's here," one of the Cardenas scouts said.

Sosa smiled.

"Dock her. Unload everything. Then find me a bottle of Tequila and a radio."

He keyed his mic. "Progreso dock is ours. Boat's landing now. She's beautiful."

Kael turned in a slow circle, the last flames of the convoy reflecting in his eyes.

The wind shifted. Somewhere in the distance, thunder rolled — the storm's first warning growl.

He keyed his mic.

"Then it's done. Cárdenas are home.

The night swallowed Mérida.

Smoke still hung-over Torre Cristal's perimeter, thick and pungent. Sirens wailed in the distance but never got closer — either redirected or deliberately muted. The city was bleeding quietly, too paralyzed to scream.

Kael stood at the rooftop's edge again; boots planted beside a shattered air conditioner. His field jacket flapped in the wind. Below, the street was a mosaic of destruction: charred asphalt, broken glass, dead men still clutching rifles.

But there was no victory dance. No parade.

Only the heavy breath of survival.

He keyed the mic again. The radio cracked.

"Status," he said.

One by one, the voices returned.

Natalia:

"Finca Sangre Verde locked down." We'll have full recon reports by dawn. Five wounded. No dead."

Valeria:

"Airport's blacked. No flights in or out. They'll need satellites and wings to see us now."

Sosa:

"Progreso's clean." El Susurro docked. Crates are moving now—medical, long guns, encrypted satphones, field packs. We even found a damn espresso machine."

Kael exhaled a tight breath through his nose. He could hear the fatigue in their voices—bone-deep, soul-worn—but under it all… was pride.

They were making history with blood and silence.

He looked across the horizon. The storm had arrived — but slower than forecasted, dragging its feet like it wanted to witness the aftermath. Thunder cracked miles away, and the first cold drops of rain began to fall across the scorched city.

The rooftop door creaked open behind him.

Leandro Barragán emerged, walking slowly. A bandage hugged his ribs; his beard still matted with dried blood. But his spine was straight, and the fire in his eyes had returned.

Kael glanced at him. "You shouldn't be up here."

"I shouldn't be alive," Leandro replied.

They stood in silence for a while, both men watching the broken skyline. Fires still flickered near the airport. A faint glow pulsed from the south — the cult's last compound burning into nothing.

"I heard what you did," Leandro said. "Rescued Americans. Took down towers. Cleared an entire street with six men and a homemade bomb."

"I've had worse nights," Kael muttered.

Leandro grinned despite himself.

"You changed the tide tonight."

Kael didn't answer.

Because it wasn't over.

Elsewhere – Hospital Room, University District

Marisol Cárdenas stirred under a thin white blanket. Her skin was pale. Monitors beeped softly beside her. IV bags dripped fluids into a vein in her hand.

Santiago sat nearby, half-asleep in a plastic chair, his suit jacket folded on the windowsill. His pistol lay under a copy of a medical chart, hidden from the nurses but ready.

Marisol's eyes fluttered open. The pain was distant, dull. Her first thought wasn't fear. It was Kael.

She reached for the small radio on the nightstand — the one patched through to a restricted Cárdenas frequency.

Static. Then…

"Cárdenas are home," Kael's voice whispered over the speaker.

Her lips parted.

And for the first time in two days—

She smiled.

Torre Cristal – Just Before Dawn

The rooftop buzz faded into silence.

Kael lowered the radio. Below, Cárdenas's men began collecting bodies, stacking weapons, and drawing chalk symbols near the outer alley walls — warnings to their enemies, promises to their people.

He felt the shift. This wasn't just a win.

This was the turning of the blade.

Natalia joined him minutes later; her jacket soaked from the rain. Her hair was pulled back into a loose braid; a pistol tucked beneath her belt.

"You're quiet," she said.

Kael looked out again.

"I was never supposed to be a symbol."

"Too late."

"I'm not Cárdenas," he added. "Not by blood."

Natalia stepped beside him. "You are now. So am I. So is anyone who stood their ground tonight."

They watched the city together — her hand resting on his shoulder.

Then she turned to go.

Kael remained, rain running down his face like melted steel.

Behind his eyes, he wasn't thinking about empires or tactics or lines in the sand.

He was thinking of her.

Marisol.

Of the way she had said, mi SEXICO.

Of the moment her voice broke through the storm and reminded him what this was all for.

And in that silence, Kael made a vow—

We take it all.

Or we die.

Chapter 17

The Crown and the Vultures

Location: San Felipe de Los Montes – Yucatán Highlands

A quiet mountain town near Hacienda Santa Gracia, protected, loyal, and thought to be untouchable.

The IV drip clicked softly in the corner.

Marisol Cárdenas lay back against the hospital bed, sunlight pouring through the shutters. Her cheeks were pale, her eyes heavy. Bloodwork. Hydration. Nothing serious. Just a moment to breathe after weeks of chaos. The linens smelled of clean cotton and antiseptic, and for the first time in days, the sounds outside the window were birdsong, not gunfire.

Santiago Cárdenas sat in the chair beside her, arms crossed, a pistol holstered against his ribs. He hadn't left her side in two days.

"You'll feel better soon," he said.

"I'm fine," she murmured. "I just... felt light. Dizzy."

He nodded. "You've been through hell."

The moment was quiet. A fragile silence stretched between them—brother and sister, scared and tired. She reached out and rested her hand lightly over his. He didn't move it.

Then the rotor blades came.

Low. Close. Violent.

WHAAP-WHAAP-WHAAP.

Santiago's eyes snapped upward. He stood fast, hand on his weapon.

"Down!" he barked, grabbing Marisol and dragging her behind the bed.

Outside, four black helicopters swept over the tiled rooftops—Chinese Harbin Z-9s, their insignias glinting in the sun. They moved with surgical intent, banking sharply and circling the hospital like vultures ready to dive. The town, once quiet, erupted into chaos.

Windows shattered. Dogs barked. Locals screamed. And somewhere far below, a little boy dropped his ice cream and started crying.

The Lead Gunship — Harbin 3

On board, Colonel Sheng Wu stood at the open door, headset tight, eyes burning with fury. Wind tore at his coat. His fingers flexed around a compact submachine gun, polished and merciless.

"Mérida humiliated me," he growled to the co-pilot. "Progreso bled me. Now we bleed them."

The Cárdenas cartel had taken everything. Now they would pay.

And the key was Marisol Cárdenas—not just Salvador's daughter, but the living bargaining chip for Veloxyn. The synthetic drug that changed everything. A compound so potent, so uniquely formulated, that even the Chinese military's brightest chemists couldn't reverse-engineer it without access to the Cárdenas family's guarded mineral compound and processing techniques.

Wu had tried infiltration. He had tried diplomacy. Now he would try domination.

Veloxyn was only the beginning. The Cárdenas organization controlled more than just formulae—they controlled corridors. Smuggling routes buried beneath the Sonoran border, Caribbean handoff chains, offshore laundering stations, encrypted crypto vaults, and deep alliances with paramilitary cells from Baja to Barranquilla.

Colonel Wu didn't just want Marisol.

He wanted the farm compounds. The chemists. The ports. The covert airstrips. The whole dark web of the Cárdenas empire. He wanted their lieutenants interrogated, their accountants broken, their captains killed or co-opted.

If he could seize Marisol Cárdenas, he could fracture the last loyalist stronghold from within. Turn the crown princess into a pressure point. Or better yet, a tool.

"We take her alive," Sheng said. "Kill the rest."

His men nodded. No questions. No mercy.

The Assault

• Chopper 1 landed on the hospital rooftop, rotor wash blasting debris into the air.

• Chopper 2 slammed down on the street below, crushing a row of market stalls.

• Chopper 3 touched down on the roof of the adjacent town hall.

• Chopper 4 hovered above, machine gun ready, muzzle glowing.

Each bird deployed 7 men — a total strike force of 28.

Some in Chinese tactical gear. Others branded with tattoos and armor patches of the Cartel de Nueve Vidas — The Cartel of Nine Lives. They spilled from the choppers like black ink from a shattered vial, moving with lethal purpose.

Gunfire erupted.

Santiago yelled for the Cárdenas guards to hold the stairwell. The entire hospital shook as the first wave of attackers stormed the halls.

Inside, chaos exploded — windows shattered, nurses screamed, patients scrambled for shelter. Doors splintered. Fire alarms wailed. Bullet holes tore through patient charts still pinned to walls.

Marisol stumbled into a side room, heart pounding. Her bare feet slapped the tile floor as Santiago threw her a bag. A weapon clattered to the ground.

"Take it," he snapped.

She looked down — a matte black Desert Eagle, heavy in her hand.

It felt foreign. Terrifying. Necessary.

Her fingers tightened around the grip. Not because she felt brave — but because she remembered.

The Commodore.

Warm night air. The gentle sway of the sea. Kael's arms around her from behind, steadying her hands, guiding her aim.

"This isn't about killing," he whispered. "It's about control. You point this only when you've already decided what happens next."

She hated the weight of it then. The way the recoil had rattled her bones. But Kael never judged. Just corrected her stance, nudged her chin higher, and whispered, "Again."

Now, standing in this cold unfamiliar room with death clawing at the door, she realized he wasn't just teaching her to shoot — he was teaching her to survive.

She exhaled.

The gun no longer felt foreign.

Just necessary.

The hallway outside howled with gunfire.

Two cartel soldiers crashed through the door— one with a blade, the other with a rifle. Marisol pivoted, raised the Dessert Eagle with both hands—

BOOM. BOOM.

Their chests exploded, blown back into the frame.

Blood sprayed the walls. The smell of gunpowder and copper filled the room.

A third man grabbed her from behind, slamming the gun from her hand. His breath was hot in her ear.

"¡Puta madre!" he spat, smashing the butt of his rifle into her temple.

She crumpled.

As smoke filled the corridor, the enemy team dragged Marisol's limp body across the tile. Santiago rounded the corner, eyes blazing.

"¡ISABEL!" he screamed, firing three shots — one cartel soldier dropped instantly.

Another grabbed Marisol under the arms and yelled, "VÁMONOS!"

They hauled her into the helicopter.

Santiago hit one more. The body slumped from the side of the bird as it lifted.

Marisol, unconscious, disappeared into the sky.

The chapel doors swung open hard.

Salvador Cárdenas stood at the altar, shoulders squared, the glow of candles flickering across his face. He hadn't moved since the report came in. Two silver coins sat in his hand — ancient Spanish pesos — a ritual he only used for executions.

He turned them over between his fingers as if weighing the price of failure.

Goya stepped in, cautious. His voice trembled just slightly. "It's confirmed. Marisol's gone. Extracted by Nine Lives and Sheng Wu."

No response.

"Santiago's alive," Goya added. "Barely. They left six of our men dead. It was fast, brutal—surgical."

Salvador didn't blink. He stared up at the statue of San Miguel — the Archangel posed in triumphant combat, sword driven into the heart of a serpent.

Then he spoke.

"I told them… the ghosts of this world come for blood, not peace."

He stepped down from the altar slowly, deliberately. The silver coins clinked softly in his palm.

"Send word to León. I want him back from Havana."

Goya hesitated. "Sir, we don't—"

"I don't care if he's embedded with the Cubans or dead drunk in a brothel. I want León Escamilla back under this roof. Tonight."

His voice was a gunshot.

Salvador turned and pointed to Goya.

"Seal every road within 50 kilometers of San Felipe. Shoot down any aircraft without our colors. And send a raven to the Chinese delegation in Campeche."

Goya raised an eyebrow. "A raven?"

Salvador nodded. "Yes. A message. Simple. One sentence."

He handed Goya a piece of torn paper with blood smeared across the edge. Written in red ink:

"You touched my daughter. Now watch the world burn."

Darkness pressed against her eyelids like wet concrete.

Marisol stirred.

Her skull throbbed. The world swam. A taste of blood sat at the back of her throat. Her arms were pinned — cold steel shackles locked at the wrists. Her head lolled to one side, resting against cracked leather. A single overhead bulb buzzed, swinging faintly.

The air smelled of piss, dust, diesel, and blood.

She was in a shipping container. Modified. Reinforced. Bolted into the dirt. Deep in jungle country. Somewhere off-grid.

Across from her sat a folding chair and an empty metal table. Blood dried along the floor. This was a room for breaking people.

Her breathing slowed. The pain was sharp, but familiar. The disorientation wasn't new. She had survived far worse.

Focus, Cárdenas. Don't give them your fear.

Footsteps echoed. The door creaked open, scraping against metal. Three silhouettes entered, black against the strip of sunlight behind them.

• One in black tactical gear, Chinese comms rig clipped to his vest.

• One in a button-down shirt, gold tooth, snake tattoo wrapping his neck — Cartel de Nueve Vidas muscle.

• And the third — tall, lean, cruel — walked in last, dragging a chair behind him with a screech.

He sat with a theatrical slowness, like a king assuming a throne of rot.

"You're prettier than I expected," he said in Spanish, his tone sickly sweet.

He lit a cigarette, the flame trembling in the gloom.

"My name is Luciano 'Luzbel' Garza. You've heard of me, no?"

Marisol didn't answer.

"They call me Luzbel because I don't bring pain. I bring clarity."

She spat blood at his feet.

"You're a rat in a knockoff suit," she hissed.

He laughed, clapping once.

"Ah, there she is. The queen of the desert. La hija de Cardenas. You know, I begged them to let me kill you. But Sheng Wu insisted. Said you're more valuable alive. Something about Veloxyn, secret trade routes, logistics and cocaine. Something about leverage."

He leaned closer, the smoke from his cigarette was curling between them.

"But I don't need you alive to make your father scream."

The Chinese officer raised a syringe. Something inside glowed a faint, sickly blue.

Veloxyn. Uncut. Experimental.

"Just a taste," Luzbel said. "Let's see what happens when we feed the dragon to the princess."

The syringe gleamed under the humming bulb.

Luciano "Luzbel" Garza smiled like a man pouring gasoline on a match.

The Chinese officer adjusted his gloves, slowly advancing with the syringe.

"This is the pure strain. Straight from the farm. Unstabilized. One dose in the wrong nerve and you'll hallucinate in six dimensions."

Marisol's breath slowed. Her heart didn't race — it dropped into full combat silence.

She watched his feet. His hands. The rhythm.

Strike first. Win small. Stay alive.

The moment his boot crossed the oil stain on the floor, she moved.

With both hands chained, she kicked her legs upward, catching the officer's forearm and slamming the syringe against the edge of the metal table. Snap.

Glass shattered. Liquid spilled. The needle skittered to the floor.

"¡Puta!" the officer cursed, stumbling back.

Luzbel surged forward and slapped her hard across the face.

"Wrong move, reina."

Marisol's lip split, blood running down her chin. She smiled, slow and feral.

"Do it again," she whispered. "And I'll make you bleed like the last man who touched me."

Luciano froze.

The two cartel soldiers shifted uncomfortably.

The Chinese officer hissed something in Mandarin — urgent, anxious.

Luciano raised his hand.

"Take her to the white room. Strap her down. No drugs. Not yet."

He leaned down, inches from her face.

"We were going to be civilized, you and me. But now? Now we go biblical."

The guards grabbed her — hard — but not before she turned and landed a brutal headbutt to one man's nose, sending him stumbling backward with blood spurting down his shirt.

Marisol didn't scream. Didn't cry.

As they dragged her through the door, shoulders bruised and lip bleeding, she locked eyes with Luzbel and smiled — wicked and unbreakable.

"Mi SEXICO viene por mí."

My SEXICO is coming for me.

The convoy rolled into the ranch gates just before dusk.

The tires were caked in dust and blood. The vehicles dented, smoke scarred. Bullet holes stitched across the doors like tattoos earned in a nightmare. The Cárdenas family's once-pristine fleet now looked like a caravan of survivors from a different world.

Santiago Cárdenas stepped out of the lead truck, his shirt torn, arm wrapped in a bloodied sling. His face was hollow. Haunted. Smoke streaked his hair. A line of dried blood cut across his cheekbone. He had not spoken since the final shot was fired.

The surviving bodyguards moved in silence — their eyes hollow, guns still clutched like children's toys after a nightmare. There was no shouting. No orders. Only the crunch of boots on gravel, and the dull clank of doors swinging open on stiff hinges.

Inside the main house, Doña Teresa — Marisol's mother — heard the gates open and ran to the courtyard.

She didn't need to ask.

Her scream shattered the silence.

"¡Marisol!"

The cry came from a place deeper than grief. A primal rupture of the soul.

She fell to her knees. Her friends pulled her back, sobbing, gasping through clenched teeth.

"No, no, no…"

Santiago stood there — bleeding, silent, unable to speak.

Behind him, one of the guards knelt and whispered to the house priest, who bowed his head and crossed himself. Someone shut off the music in the kitchen. A housekeeper dropped a plate that shattered across the tiles.

Time fractured.

Grief soaked the air like rain.

Salvador Cárdenas poured mezcal into a crystal glass and looked around the room.

Every lieutenant, every sicario captain, every trusted confidant filled the long mahogany table. They sat straight-backed, wide-eyed, wearing sidearms and fresh bruises.

The air was dry and electric, the kind that precedes a lightning strike.

Maps of the Gulf spread before them:
• Mérida: secured.
• Progreso: ours
• Campeche: shaky
• Tampico: fractured
• The Yucatán corridor: bleeding

A storm was coming, and it was not of wind or rain.

Salvador stood slowly, voice level but sharp as broken glass.

"This is not vengeance for my daughter," he said. "This is reclamation. Of our country. Our people. Our dignity."

He walked the length of the table. Every step echoed.

"The rival cartels, the foreign occupiers, the Chinese… they want chaos. They want us to turn on each other. To fall back into tribal madness. But what have we done?"

He stopped. Looked each man in the eyes.

"We brought order. Food. Jobs. Medicine. We gave the villages something the politicians never did — hope. Now they want to take that too."

He raised his glass.

"We retake Tampico. We retake everything."

The room erupted — not in chaos, but in precision. A storm of clipped voices, layered orders, overlapping strategies. Some shouted for León Escamilla. Others for the submarine routes. Ideas sharpened into threats. Threats hardened into war plans.

But Salvador said nothing more.

He walked out quietly, the untouched mezcal still in his hand.

The door creaked open.

The light was soft, untouched. The bed made. Candles burned low. A photograph on the dresser showed Marisol at 15, wearing a white summer dress, arms around a young Santiago.

Everything in the room smelled like her — lavender, sandalwood, the sea.

Salvador stepped inside. He didn't turn on the lights. He moved slowly, reverently, as if each step might disturb her ghost.

He ran a hand along the vanity, pausing at the mirror. His reflection was hollow. A king broken open by a single blow.

Then he saw it.

On the bathroom counter. Boxes. Dozens of them. Some open. Some still sealed. All with the same label.

Pregnancy Test Kits.

His heart stalled.

He stepped closer.

Knelt.

Looked at one.

Positive.

Another.

Positive.

Another.

Twelve tests.

All positive.

Every single one.

He stood with the last test in his hand, trembling.

Not like a drug lord. Not like a patriarch.

Like a father.

And then… like a man reborn with wrath.

The air was thick with storm scent — orange blossoms, wet stone, the faint copper of distant blood. Salvador Cárdenas stood at the window, unmoving, his silhouette cut in half by lightning flashing beyond the arches.

Doña Teresa stepped into the room behind him; shawl clutched at her chest. Her face, regal and weathered, was calm — but her voice carried quiet command.

"You sent for me."

Salvador didn't turn.

"I needed a moment before I said it aloud."

She stepped closer, gaze narrowing.

"What is it, Salvador?"

He turned and held out the test results — folded but trembling slightly in his hand.

She looked at it. Read it. Stopped breathing.

"She's pregnant," he said.

The words echoed in the tiled room like a pistol shot.

Doña Teresa sat slowly, hands folded in her lap, the paper still clutched between her fingers. Her eyes welled, but her posture never broke.

"Marisol…"

Her voice cracked, once.

Salvador knelt before her.

He held up a slip of paper — test results, smuggled from the hospital where Marisol had been treated before her abduction.

"She's still alive. These came from the clinic in San Felipe — before they took her. Bloodwork. Ultrasound. Everything. She's carrying."

"Does Kael know?"

He shook his head. "Not yet. Natalia doesn't either."

Doña Teresa reached for his hand and squeezed it tight.

"Then tell them. And save her."

The door slammed open like a shot.

Everyone turned.

Salvador stood in the doorway, still holding the test in his hand.

The long stone table glistened with condensation from untouched glasses of mezcal. Around it stood Goya, Tigre, Hector, Bruto, and three others — men and women Salvador trusted with the future of the Cárdenas name.

He entered with slow, deliberate steps. No smile. No pleasantries.

He dropped the folded test in the center of the table.

"She's with child," he said. "My daughter. Our future."

Goya flinched first. Tigre said nothing. Goya stared hard at the test, reading every line twice.

"Kael's?" someone asked.

Salvador didn't answer with words. He only looked at them — the kind of look that makes men reach for their rifles.

"We move now," he said. "No more delays. No more debates. I want every corridor in Tampico mapped. I want street eyes awake. I want Natalia informed within the hour."

He turned to Goya.

"Make the call."

"We are not just rescuing a soldier. We are saving a bloodline."

Lightning cracked outside.

The room moved into motion.

His face was steel and storm.

"Move heaven and hell."

Silence.

"I want Natalia or Leonardo on the line — right now."

A storm of movement erupted. Radios were pulled. Satellites calibrated. Runners dispatched. The war had already begun — but now, it had a heart.

Not just revenge.

Not just resistance.

This was bloodline protection.

This was legacy.

This was war made personal.

Back in the War Room — 9:37 PM

The table hadn't cleared. The tension hadn't faded. It had only crystallized — sharpened like a blade on steel.

Salvador Cárdenas stood at the head, still gripping the pregnancy test like it was an indictment from God.

He turned to Goya.

"Recalibrate the offensive. We're not just retaking territory — we're building a shield around a bloodline."

Goya's mouth parted, astonished. "A grandchild…"

Salvador didn't blink.

"She already is."

He grabbed a red pen from the map table and stabbed it into the Gulf region — just south of

Tampico, right over the rumored Nine Lives staging area.

"We level everything between here and Campeche. I don't want prisoners. I want corpses."

The room surged to life.

Men began shouting orders into satellite phones. Logistics teams scrambled to re-divert supply routes. Three teams were dispatched to track any satellite pings that could lead to Marisol's location.

One Cárdenas intelligence officer spoke up.

"Sir — there's chatter out of a jungle sector. Near a decommissioned Pemex station east of Tampico."

Salvador looked at him coldly. "That's exactly where she is."

But Goya replied, " Let's remember it could be a trap and they could easily move her."

Salvador turned to Goya. "Coordinate it with caution and flexibility."

Then back to the room at large:

"No one sleeps. No one hesitates. If she dies... if that child dies... then there will be no more Cárdenas cartel. Only ash."

Goya whispered, "This isn't a war anymore."

Salvador turned.

"No. It's a resurrection."

Chapter 18

The Echo of Blood and Fire

Music echoed off the freshly liberated skyline. Bonfires cracked in steel drums. Cárdenas loyalists laughed, drank, and passed bottles of mezcal like war trophies. Some danced with pistols still holstered at their hips, moving like people who hadn't felt joy in years. Flags bearing the family's phoenix crest fluttered from balconies and broken police stations. Progreso, Mérida, and the Finca Sangre Verde had been reclaimed.

Someone fired rounds into the sky — celebratory, reckless. No one flinched.

Kael watched it all from the rooftop's edge. Below them, the city glimmered like an ember that refused to die.

The city was breathing again.

Local governors crawled out of hiding, issuing statements of peace as if they hadn't been trembling behind bulletproof doors.

Uniformed officers retook checkpoints and apologized under their breath to the Cárdenas operatives who had stormed through.

Civilians reopened shops with shaking hands and cautious hope, mothers clutching children close, old men sweeping bullet casings from their stoops.

It felt like the beginning of a rebirth — not just for the city, but for something older. Something sacred. Something lost long ago in the smoke and blood.

On the rooftops, the survivors shared stories. Men who once fought on opposite sides passed flasks and laughed like brothers. Wounds were wrapped in duct tape and good local Tequila. Scars pressed against each other in celebration.

For a moment — just a breath — the war felt far away.

But not to Kael.

Not with the weight in his chest.

Not with the echo of a name he hadn't heard in days pulsing like a bruise beneath his ribs.

Kael stood near the window, glass in hand. Behind him, maps, comm boards, and radio chatter still buzzed — but quieter now, like a storm had passed and left only the sound of dripping water behind.

His silhouette, backlit by orange cityglow, cut a sharp figure — the posture of a man who'd fought through hell and still wasn't sure if he'd made it out.

Leandro and Mateo Sosa leaned over blueprints for Tampico, hunched over a scarred table layered in layers of dust and blood.

"We've got almost 300 loyalists now," Leandro said. His voice was gravel soaked in smoke. "Ex-military. Some from the old federales. Even a few former rivals. More are coming out of hiding."

Mateo grinned and lit a cigarette with shaking fingers. "And the cops? They're crawling back too. Even the ones who took Chinese bribes. They want to live under Cárdenas law — not Nine Lives chaos."

Kael nodded but said nothing.

He should've been relieved. Should've felt the victory vibrating in the floor beneath his boots. But something in his chest was tight — a storm that hadn't broken.

His fingers tightened on the glass.

He hadn't heard from Marisol.

Not for three days.

And somewhere, in the ache behind his ribs, he already knew something was wrong.

The candlelight in Salvador Cárdenas's private study flickered against the leather-bound tomes and dust-slicked photos of a different era. The room was still — a kind of sacred stillness that came only before great loss or great violence.

Salvador held the satellite phone like a weapon. Not gently. Not casually. Like it might explode in his hand. Or like he might.

His jaw was clenched so tightly the muscles in his neck jumped. A thick vein in his temple pulsed beneath the candlelight.

He had made dozens of these calls in his life — orders, threats, death sentences.

But this call… this one tasted like iron.

"Natalia. Leonardo," he said, his voice low and deliberate. "Listen carefully."

There was a pause on the line. And then the unmistakable click of attention. The sound of soldiers preparing to absorb pain.

"They took Marisol."

Silence.

Not confusion.

Just breath held.

Waited.

Measured.

"Sheng Wu. Nine Lives. San Felipe. They came with gunships. Hit the hospital. Took her." His voice cracked, only slightly, like a chisel tapping stone.

"And…" Salvador hesitated.

Not because he didn't know how to say it.

But because the moment the words left his mouth, the war would change.

"…she's pregnant."

He said it like an execution.

On the other end of the line, the world ripped open.

Natalia's scream cracked through the speaker like a bolt of lightning tearing down a cathedral.

It wasn't a battle cry.

It was a mother's scream. A sister's. A fighter who had just been pushed past the edge of comprehension.

Raw. Primal. Ragged with grief and rage.

Valeria dropped to her knees beside her, arms wrapping around her like armor. Her hands shook. Her lips moved in prayer. Or fury. Maybe both.

"No… no no no no…" Natalia sobbed.

Leonardo said nothing — but his fist shattered a bottle against the wall.

The line hissed with static and the sound of a family unraveling — and becoming something harder.

Something forged.

Kael turned his head slowly.

He had heard it.

Every word.

He had felt it before anyone else.

He walked to the radio table, the celebratory noise behind him evaporating into ash.

His footsteps were slow. Surgical. Each one heavier than the last.

"What is it?" he asked.

Leandro didn't answer at first.

Then, softly, as if the words themselves had weight: "They have her, Kael."

Natalia came into the room. Broken. Shaking. But still holding the blade of her soul.

"They took her from the hospital. She's alive… but they're holding her. And…" The breath she drew was a sob. "She's pregnant, Kael. She's carrying your child."

Kael didn't move.

Didn't blink.

Didn't speak.

He set the glass down with precision — like it was the last gentle thing in the world — and stared out over the city. The skyline of a place they had just wrestled back from oblivion.

His jaw twitched once.

His chest rose.

Then he lowered his head, one hand bracing the edge of the table, knuckles white.

The entire room stilled.

As if the walls themselves were holding their breath.

Like the dead had gathered to witness what came next.

No one dared speak his name.

Because everyone knew what was coming.

And they feared for whoever stood in its path.

Kael sat alone in the corner office. The lights were off.

Only the orange glow of the liberated city painted the walls — a ghostly warmth filtered through shattered blinds, fractured by bullet holes. It danced across his features, carving shadows in the hollows of his cheeks and beneath his eyes.

His rifle leaned against the wall like a loyal dog.

A half-drunk glass of rum sat untouched on the desk, sweat beading down the side.

But Kael wasn't drinking tonight.

He was remembering.

Or maybe dreaming.

Something deeper than memory — something closer to prophecy.

He pressed his palms together and leaned forward in the chair, head bowed, eyes closed.

[Flashback – Mosul, Iraq, 2016]

Smoke curled around a mosque's blown-out minaret.

Kael dragged his bleeding teammate across broken stone, boots sliding in rubble. A belt-fed PKM chattered from an alley up ahead. Bullets screamed past their heads.

"Stay with me!" Kael shouted.

His voice cracked from smoke, grit, and something deeper — the guilt already building.

He was twenty-nine.

Too young to feel this tired. Too angry to care.

He reached for his radio. The words came out cold and trained.

"Broken Arrow. I say again — Broken Arrow."

Spectre gunships circled overhead.

The war didn't pause.

It just got louder.

[Flashback – Puerto Rico, 2024]

The deck of The Commodore.

Moonlight dancing on saltwater.

Marisol laughing in the breeze, her sundress clinging to her hips, hair loose, alive. She spun toward him, barefoot, reckless, beautiful.

They'd just outrun death.

But all Kael remembered was the way she said his name.

Not "Kael."

Not "amor."

But the way she whispered: "Mi SEXICO…"

Like he wasn't a man at all.

Like he was a myth. A legend. A home.

[Vision – The Life That Could Be]

A mountain house.

No guards. No alarms.

A child barefoot in the garden. Small hands brushing the pedals on a flower. A girl with Marisol's eyes. A boy with Kael's silence and intensity. Maybe three children in total Kael thought to himself.

A hammock strung between Douglas fir trees along the feather river.

Laughter echoing through the wind.

Marisol leaning on the porch rail, hair streaked with silver, belly round with another child.

Kael watching them.

His rifle rusting quietly in the attic.

Peace was real.
And he would kill the world to make it true.

Kael opened his eyes.
The city was still burning in places — but it wasn't fire that lit his stare now.
It was purpose.
He stood slowly. Walked to the sink. Splashed cold water over his face. His reflection stared back — older, meaner, carved from the wars he had never asked for.
He did not see a killer.
He saw a father.
And that changed everything.
He dried his face, stepped into the hallway, and did not bother with the rifle.
He did not need it yet.
But when he did... the world would remember.
The war room glowed under the soft buzz of halogen lights. Map tables were still cluttered with intel, satellite printouts, scribbled notes, empty coffee cups, and spent shell casings — reminders that even victories had their cost.
Kael stepped into the light like a revenant walking out of a tomb.
The silence cracked.
Natalia looked up first, her eyes swollen but sharp. She had wiped her tears away, but the grief was etched in the lines around her mouth.
Valeria stood behind her, arms crossed over her chest. She did not hide her fury. Her jaw was clenched, but her stance screamed readiness — like a lioness just waiting for the signal to tear something apart.
Leonardo had a satellite tablet in his hands, but his gaze snapped up the moment Kael entered.
No one spoke.

Kael walked straight to the center of the table, grabbed a red marker, and began circling coordinates on the satellite maps of Campeche, the Yucatán interior, and a cluster of rural roads leading into jungle territory.

His voice, when it came, was low and calm.

But it cut through the room like a blade.

"We're going to find her."

He circled another location.

"We'll burn everything between here and her if we have to."

Natalia stepped closer to the folding table, her hand resting on the edge of the marked-up map. A half-burned cigarette dangled from her fingers, the smoke curling toward the cracked ceiling.

"We've already started scouting jungle routes between San Felipe and the black site corridor," she said, tapping her finger near a line of elevation marks. "Dense terrain. Wu's men use it to run arms and prisoners between camps. If Marisol was moved by air, they did not keep her near the coast. It is too exposed. She is inland — somewhere off-grid."

Padre Luis crossed himself slowly, then spoke in that low, measured cadence of his. "That stretch is cursed ground. I have buried men who wandered into those trees and never came out. The Cartel Nueve Vidas has supply caches and lookouts in the hills above the Pemex ruins. They have got deals with Wu's enforcers — blood for cargo, silence for fuel."

Kael leaned over the table, eyes tracking every route. "If Wu moved her into that network, he is not just using her as bait. He is protecting something bigger."

"Veloxyn," Leonardo muttered, his voice gravel. "Or the labs. Or both."

Sosa exhaled slowly, rubbing his stitched shoulder. "I have still got one loyalist in the foothills — moves coke for the Cárdenas family under ghost sigils. He knows the lay of the jungle and where Nueve Vidas has been seen operating. I can reach out."

"Do it," Kael said. "And see if he has heard any chatter about inbound flights. Fixed wing or rotary. Anything unusual the past week."

Natalia looked at Leonardo. "Do we have anyone we trust with the airstrip maps? If we can narrow where they could have landed—"

"There's an old smuggler strip near Tenosique," Leonardo replied. "Overgrown, but usable. And another near Macuspana. If she is being held near either, we'll need to move fast before she's transferred again."

He just nodded. "Let's look at every airstrip first. They had flown out in helicopters, I'm told, four of them.

He circled another point on the map — an old smuggler's strip buried in the Sierra de Balancán. "Start there."

Padre Luis nodded solemnly. "I can call in favors from the mission clinic near the border. They treat wounded people from both sides — cartel, militia, trafficked souls. If someone saw a convoy, or a helicopter drop, I'll hear of it."

Kael straightened, voice low but firm. "No delays. Sosa, reach your guy. Padre, start the calls. Leo, prep two extraction routes — one east of the ridge line, one south toward the basin. Natalia, you, and I will cross-check drone feeds and heat maps starting tonight. If we catch a trail... we hunt."

Natalia gave a single nod, her voice quiet but lethal. "We find her. Or we burn every jungle in Mexico until we do."

Kael then looked up at Natalia.

Then at Leonardo. Then Valeria.

No speeches. No theatrics.

But the message was clear: This wasn't a rescue.

It was a reckoning.

The room fell silent again.

Not with fear — but with focus. Like the moment before a storm hits.

And then — something rare happened.

He felt arms wrap around him.

Natalia stepped in first. Strong and trembling. Her cheek against his shoulder. Her voice barely above a whisper.

"You're not alone."

Valeria followed without hesitation. She pressed into his other side, wrapping one arm around his back, her breath sharp and quiet.

"You're family now," she said.

Leonardo watched for a moment. Then he stepped forward and pulled them all into a single knot of arms and heat and silence. His hand gripped the back of Kael's neck, anchoring him.

"And we're going to get her back," he said, voice steady. "No matter what it takes."

Kael didn't speak.

Didn't cry.

Didn't break.

But he didn't pull away either.

He stood there — at the center of a circle he didn't ask for but now couldn't live without.

Surrounded by warriors who had become something more.

His people.

His vow.

The rooftop was quieter now.

The fires in the drums had burned low, crackling like dying memories. The laughter had thinned into murmurs. Most of the Cárdenas loyalists had either passed out in corners or retreated into the building to rest for the first time in weeks. Victory had a strange way of turning the fiercest men into children when the adrenaline wore off.

Kael stepped through the corridor alone.

He didn't glance at the mezcal bottles. Didn't pause at the celebratory banners or the graffitied wall that read: SEXICO VIVE.

He walked like a man on a private path to hell.

In his hand: an encrypted satphone. Slim. Black. Military issue. One of only three in the region still linked to the ghost network Comstock used.

He keyed in the number from memory. A number no one else had.

Three rings.

Then a voice, slow and amused:

"Been waiting for this call, brother."

Grant Comstock.

Kael leaned against the steel railing, staring at the bruised horizon.

"I need help," Kael said.

"Figured. I've been tracking Chinese chatter since the hospital hit. Satellite thermal spikes. Infrared images showing enemy movement and trails. Someone's stirring the jungle."

"You know what I'm gonna ask."

"No boots," Kael said. "No flags. No agencies."

"Exactly," Grant replied. "The U.S. can't engage. Not officially. Not while China's still pretending this is humanitarian aid. But Washington's twitching. They see the shadows moving. You've got their attention."

Kael's voice dropped an octave. "I'm going to help the Cárdenas family take back everything from here to Tampico, Find her and bring her back.."

A pause.

Then a quiet chuckle. "You're serious."

"I'm past serious."

"You like suicide missions, Torres."

"Not this time."

Another silence.

Then Comstock spoke again, more measured now.

"Chinese units are embedded in every layer of this mess. Cartels, private banks, ports. They're not just here for influence. They're here for Veloxyn."

"I know."

"They want the formula, Kael. The pure mineral source. DARPA may have birthed it, but the Cárdenas family bred it into something military-grade. Focus enhancement, endurance, no crash. If it stabilizes — it becomes the next nuclear deterrent."

Kael exhaled. "That's why they took her."

"Not just her," Comstock said, his voice low. "Her child. Do you get that yet?"

Kael's spine straightened.

"You're not just rescuing your lover. You're protecting the bloodline of the only family left in the world that controls the most valuable synthetic enhancement on Earth."

"Then I need you here," Kael said.

"You'll have me," Comstock replied. "I'm bringing three with me. Old friends. All off-grid."

"Where are you now?"

"Outside Cancún. Two hours out from the coast. We'll go dark and slip through the blockade. Be there in two days."

"No slip-ups."

"I taught you, remember?"

Kael allowed himself a breath. Not a smile. But something close to it.

Then, just before he hung up, he added:

"One more thing."

"Go."

"Call the senator."

A beat of silence.

"Your old man?"

"Tell him… he has a grandchild on the way."

The silence on the other end was thunderous.

"Well," Comstock finally said. "That's going to change a few things."

Kael hung up without another word.

The wind rolled across the rooftop like a whisper from the sea.

Behind him, the war was waiting.

But now… so was blood.

And legacy.

Chapter 19

Inheritance of Flame

Three Days latter the horizon shimmered under
the weight of heat and tension. Cicadas sang in the
trees like a distant alarm, pulsing in sync with the
oppressive heat. The wind was still, chilling with the
coming storm. Insects hovered above the cracked
asphalt, and in the distance, the brush swayed with
uneasy rhythm.

At first, it was just a shadow. A black smear in
the late afternoon sky, slicing low across the Yucatán
brush.

But the sound gave it away. Wub-wub-wub-
wub...

Every head turned skyward. Eyes squinted.
Hands shaded brows. Soldiers paused mid-load.
Civilians leaned from rooftops. Even the children in
the street fell silent.

Kael stepped out from the Torre Cristal
compound, squinting against the sun. The silhouette
came fast, a shark cutting toward shore. Low.
Aggressive. Like a hawk zeroing in on a kill.

A Bell UH-1Y Venom skimmed the treetops,
its rotors slicing the air with low, surgical menace. No
decals. No numbers. Just matte black silence.

"He's here," Kael muttered, and there was
something like relief in his voice. A confirmation that
the cavalry had finally arrived — even if it was a
cavalry of misfits and hooligans.

The chopper flared at the edge of the building,
slowing to a whisper-hover just above the rooftop.
Dust kicked up in sheets. Rotor wash slapped the
faces of those nearby. Men shielded their eyes. Flags
rattled. Doors swung open with hydraulic precision.

First to jump was Grant Comstock — dark
amber colored shades, low beard, an SR-25 slung

across his chest like it had grown there. He hit the rooftop in a crouch, stood tall, and swept the horizon like he already knew where the bullets would come from.

Behind him, 5 oversized duffel bags tumbled out for men to see:
• Grenade launcher • Thermite grenades • Breaching gear • Surveillance drones • Enough ammo to start or end a war

Comstock stood tall, boots crunching broken glass, and took in the rooftop like a returning general.

Behind him, three others followed fast — shadows in human form.

The first: a stocky woman with a braided mohawk and a nose ring, carrying a modified AA-12 auto-shotgun on her shoulder. On her thigh, a Glock 18C with full-auto capability. On her back, twin sheathed tomahawks wrapped in paracord. She smirked at Kael like they'd survived the same war — maybe not the same side, but the same scars.

Her name was Sergeant Reva "Sawtooth" Guerra — close-quarters specialist, breacher, and clandestine recon out of Panama.

The second: tall, lean, face veiled in a sand-colored shemagh. Slung across his back: an M249 SAW with a scorched heatshield and a 200-round box mag. Suppressed HK VP9 on his hip. Combat knife strapped upside-down across his chest. He moved like he could disappear mid-step.

Corporal Elias "Ghoul" Navarro — suppression and overwatch, ex-FARC defector turned Tier 1 contractor.

The third: a wide-shouldered Cuban man with sleeve tattoos and a devil's grin. M79 grenade launcher in hand — the "Thumper." Suppressed MP7 on his back. Bandolier full of high explosive, smoke, and thermobaric grenades slung across his chest.

His name was Ángel "Boomer" Valdés —
demolition expert, ex-Cuban naval special forces, once
charged with blowing up oil rigs. Now freelance angel
of destruction.

Kael was the first to reach him. They didn't
speak at first — not with words. Just a short embrace,
tight and brief, not of friends but of men who had
bled in the same mud and crawled through the same
hell.

"You brought the Motley Crew?"

Comstock looked at his team. The Hellpack.

"I brought hell with a silencer," he said flatly,
brushing dust off his shoulders. "Let's take back a
city."

"Good to see you vertical," Grant said, clapping
him on the back.

Natalia stepped forward next. She didn't offer a
handshake. She punched him once, hard, in the
shoulder. Then hugged him.

"Been a while, gringo," she said, voice flat but
eyes warm.

Valeria followed with a smirk. "The legend
lives."

Leonardo shook his hand, eyes narrowing in
study. "Heard you were just a rumor."

"I am," Grant said, still smiling. "Just one with
excellent aim."

Kael motioned toward the steel stairwell that
led down beneath the rooftop. "There's a place we can
talk."

Comstock gave one final glance to the rooftop.
"Nice view. Hope it looks this good when I leave."

Kael led the way.

"Let's plan the retaking of Tampico."

The old marble table was cracked down the
middle, but it still stood like a relic of power — a
scarred altar now devoted to revolution. The windows

were blacked out. A generator hummed like a distant heartbeat.

Kael, Grant, Natalia, Valeria, and Leonardo circled the table like warlords preparing a funeral for the old world. The room reeked of sweat, gun oil, and coffee.

Overhead, a battered projector flickered to life — casting satellite imagery, heat maps, and real-time drone feeds across the wall.

Grant Comstock dropped his rucksack beside the table, unclipped a black hard case, and popped the latches with a soft click-thump.

"Alright," he said, rolling up his sleeves. "Let's get surgical."

Inside the case:
• A foldable satellite modem
• Printed infrared overlays on polymer sheets
• Magnetic counters for unit placements
• A humming thermal drone the size of a hawk
• Thumb drives marked with the Cárdenas sigil

He handed Kael a fresh coffee. "You're gonna need it."

Kael took it, eyes locked on the glowing wall.

"You've all been busy," Grant said, nodding toward the handmade tactical maps already plastered across the board. "But you're gonna love this."

He unrolled a heatmap of Tampico — vibrant in color and violence.

The room fell silent.

Red pulses lit up across the screen like fresh wounds.

Grant's Intel Drop

He pointed at three glowing clusters, each more inflamed than the last:

1. Tampico Naval Port — under partial Chinese military control, reinforced by Nine Lives logistics teams. Container stacks had been weaponized.

2. Customs Office Compound — cartel-occupied. Converted into a fortified HQ with anti-drone tech and command bunkers.

3. Hospital Barracks — high-risk zone. Reinforced concrete. Likely site of detainees. Intel suggested foreign operatives and cartel advisors were holed up inside.

4. The airport and control tower.

"These are your four zones of control," Grant said. "We take these, we take the city."

Natalia leaned closer, jaw tight. "Any sign of Marisol?"

Grant nodded toward the hospital sector. "Possible. Signals were scrambled two days ago. But we picked up a drone image. Looked like a woman matching her frame being escorted through the southern wing. Can't confirm yet."

Kael's knuckles whitened on the edge of the table.

Grant continued. "Now the good news — most of the Chinese are pulling out. They're under diplomatic pressure. Shifting toward Veracruz. The bad news?"

He tapped the glowing heart of the customs compound.

"What's left behind are PLA special units. Hardened. Elite. The ones that want to stay."

He pulled up a separate overlay.

"And here's the kicker."

A thin red line appeared — barely visible, tracing from the harbor across the city.

"We confirmed a subterranean network — tunnels. Old cartel infrastructure co-opted by Nine Lives and El Filo de Dios. It runs from the port all the way to Iglesia de la Cruz Final."

Valeria hissed softly. "They're hiding in churches now?"

Natalia's voice was ice. "Then we'll bury them under the altar."

Leadership Vibe Check

Kael leaned over the map, scanning it like a surgeon before a procedure. His finger hovered over the path from the dock to the hospital.

Leonardo lit a cigarette, exhaled slowly, and muttered, "This is going to be bloody."

Valeria tapped her blade sheath against her thigh like a metronome, watching Kael's eyes.

Natalia traced a line from the hills south of Tampico to the western bridge. "We use the terrain. We bait their attention and cut under it."

Grant looked at Kael. "You've led trained teams before. What's the play?"

Kael didn't blink.

"Divide and decimate," he said. "Three fronts. One night. No hesitation."

He moved the magnetic markers on the table:

• A strike at the port
• A breach at the hospital
• A descent on the customs HQ

"And Marisol?" Natalia asked.

Kael's voice dropped. Rough. Absolute.

"We get her out. Alive."

The light from the satellite projector bathed the room in hues of pale green and red. The city outside was quiet — too quiet. Like it knew what was coming.

Kael, Grant, Natalia, Valeria, and Leonardo stood around the glowing map like survivors planning an exodus. Or an apocalypse.

Grant pointed to the red zones along the northern approach road to Tampico.

"They've got numbers. Enough to bury a city. The intel estimates over three thousand fighters split across three cartel factions — Los Huesos Rojos, Cartel Nueve Vida, and El Filo de Dios. But it's more than just bodies."

Kael nodded grimly. He already knew.

Enemy Force Breakdown

Cartel Presence:

• Los Huesos Rojos – positioned at the industrial fringe, known for mortars and psychological warfare.

• Cartel Nueve Vidas – entrenched near customs and docks, using shipping crates and cranes as cover.

• El Filo de Dios – embedded in churches, schools, and government buildings, masking war with religion.

Each group had their own colors, tactics, codes — but they answered to the same masters now.

Chinese Detachment:

• ~400 elite PLA troops

• Stationed in mobile units with thermal drones, anti-air systems, and long-range comms

• Backing Nine Lives leadership "unofficially"

• Engaging when provoked — and always with precision

"They're playing peacekeepers on paper," Leonardo said, "but they're moving like shock troops."

"And they're not here for charity," Valeria added. "They're here for Veloxyn, cocaine, logistics and the Yucatan Peninsula.

Grant's Deception Plan

Comstock slid a convoy token across the map — a black rectangular piece labeled 'Tampico Front.'

"So we give them what they expect: a parade. A decoy convoy — full of Cárdenas fighters, old vehicles, mounted guns. Nothing subtle. Just loud, proud, and impossible to ignore."

Natalia smirked. "A battering ram."

Valeria glanced at the map's scale and let out a low whistle. "Five hundred and eighty miles. That's assuming we don't get detoured or hit."

Sosa shook his head. "We can't make that kind of push with half-dead pickups and AKs. Not with what we're facing out there."

Leandro leaned in, voice low. "We'll need real armor. Humvees, DPVs, mounted weapons. Something that can take a beating and give one back."

Natalia looked to Kael. "I don't care where they come from — military surplus, Comstock's ghost network, hell, even the black market. We need those vehicles before sunrise."

Valeria looked at Kael. "We can't roll across half of Mexico like it's a funeral procession. If this turns into a firefight halfway there, we'll lose people."

Kael's jaw tightened. "Then we roll heavy. We prep for war."

"Exactly," Grant nodded. "It keeps eyes on the main road while we slip in through their blind spots."

He tapped the east coast of the digital map. "Bahía de Tampico. We come by sea."

Kael leaned forward, eyes narrowing. "The Commodore?"

"Your old flame," Grant said with a grin. "Already being fueled and rearmed. She'll lead the flotilla. We've got three more vessels—one disguised as a shrimp trawler, another mocked up like a civilian ferry, and a third retrofitted rusted Cuban Coast Guard cutter we quietly lifted out of Havana years ago."

"Just four boats?" Valeria asked, skeptical.

"Four's all we need," Grant replied. "They won't see us coming."

"Where do we land?" Kael asked.

"El Dorado Marina," Grant said, pointing at the satellite overlay. "Farther down the coast. Less watched. Commercial access, not military. We beach there, full crew. No splitting up yet."

Kael nodded, processing. "And the river?"

Grant's grin faded into something colder. "We'll need to hit the river later — but only after we're secure. Once we make landfall, I'll arrange some... help. Quiet, heavy, fast. We'll go upstream when it's time."

Valeria traced the estuary contours on the tablet. "Still tight as hell. Pánuco's got customs checkpoints, drone towers, snipers. It won't be quiet for long."

"We don't need long," Comstock said. "Just enough to open a window."

Sosa stepped in from the shadows, shoulder still bandaged but voice steady. "You've got ground units waiting?"

Comstock shook his head. "Not like you're thinking. No cavalry. No battalions."

Sosa frowned. "So what then?"

"I brought my Hellpack," Comstock said, jerking a thumb over his shoulder toward the three operatives still checking gear. "That's the team. Surgical, brutal, fast."

"There might be some local mercs keeping eyes out near the edge of the city," Comstock added, more as an afterthought. "But don't count on them. This fight's on us."

Sosa exhaled, jaw tight. "Then we go in loud, fast, and unforgiving."

Comstock gave a cold smile. "There's no other way."

Kael stood straight. "Then we land hard. Fast. No separation. Once we touch dock, you get us the rest."

Comstock nodded. "I'll make the call when we're ten klicks out. Until then—"

"Silent run," Kael finished.

They looked at each other—soldiers, rebels, killers, lovers—all about to gamble everything on a dock, a city, and a missing girl.

220

Infiltration Setup Recap

The map flickered under dim LED lights, casting ghostly contours across the table. Kael leaned in, jaw tight. Natalia stood beside him, arms folded. Comstock paced slowly near the far wall, flanked by Padre Luis, who watched silently, rosary wrapped once around his wrist like a tourniquet of faith.

Valeria pointed to the digital projection.

Landing Points:

• Marina El Dorado – current staging hub for Cartel Nueve Vidas. Still active, but surveillance is inconsistent.

• East dock access – partially abandoned. Minimal patrols. Likely booby-trapped, but offers a cleaner insertion if cleared.

"Too many eyes here," Kael muttered, tapping the Marina with a knuckle. "We can't storm it. We slip through it."

Comstock nodded. "That's why we use confusion. Divide the pressure. Split the boats."

Sea Assets:

• The Commodore – captained by Kael, with Comstock, Padre Luis, Natalia, and Valeria aboard.

• Support Vessel 1: A shrimp trawler — looks like a rust bucket, but it's got thirty Cárdenas shooters and a hidden 7.62mm deck gun beneath a canvas tarp.

• Support Vessel 2: A tourist ferry modified with about fifty Cárdenas fighters and carries most of the weapons for the sea assault.

• Support Vessel 3: A Cuban Coast Guard cutter outfitted with jamming gear, portable mortars, and Comstock's Hellpack — still running drills with the 30 soldiers they'll lead.

"Timing's the key," Comstock said. "Each boat moves as it was originally intended to be. Once we're close to the city limits, I'll coordinate river support. We'll get you up the Pánuco fast."

Kael nodded once. "Just get us to the edge. We'll do the rest."

Tactical Assignments:

• Sea Team One: Kael, Comstock, Padre Luis and the Hellpack will approach the hospital district by water, slip into the sewer line beneath the main highway, and use storm tunnels for breach. Padre Luis will stay mobile as spiritual and medical support, but he's carrying heat.

• Sea Team Two: Leonardo leads the assault team on the port's customs checkpoint. Grant's snipers will suppress rooftop threats from the ferry nest.

• Land Convoy: Will be led by Natalia, Valeria and Sosa. Still mobilizing from Mérida. Loud and deliberate. Old pickups, repainted Humvees, scattered desert patrol vehicles. Purpose: draw fire to the highway and away from the water-based breach teams.

Padre Luis made the sign of the cross and murmured, "May the saints walk with us."

Comstock cracked his neck. "Let's hope the saints don't mind a little blood in the water."

Doubts and Logistics

Kael studied the map like it was the face of a dying friend.

"We don't have enough trucks," he muttered. "We don't have enough trained fighters. Hell, some of our men still forget to flick the safety off."

Valeria crossed her arms. "We've got fire in their bellies. But not enough rounds in their belts."

Leonardo added, "And I don't know how many will actually pull the trigger when it matters."

Comstock had already stepped away, dialing a number on a satellite phone. He returned one minute later.

Private Call – Comstock's Ace

"I made the call," he said. "Our resupply hits Mérida International in 72 hours. Three C-17s inbound with over 40 pallets of gear."

Natalia lifted her head. "What kind of gear?"

Grant smirked.

"You'll have everything you need to break a city and burn a port."

Kael nodded. "Then let's start building the army."

Comstock cracked his neck. "We've got three days. Let's make them count."

They had seventy-two hours. Not to win — but to become something that might. The war room turned into a barracks, a dojo, a proving ground. Every table was cleared, every square of open floor used for drills. The Cárdenas loyalists—farm boys, ex-cops, former sicarios—were broken down and rebuilt in cycles of exhaustion and purpose. Comstock and the Hellpack led the sessions with ruthless precision. Call signs replaced first names. Tactics replaced fear. One moment, they drilled room clearing in mock hallways built from stacked chairs and flipped tables; the next, they were blindfolded and taught to identify enemy silhouettes by sound alone. Padre Luis walked among them, not as a priest but as a quiet sentinel— offering prayers, advice, and the occasional correction with a wooden cane that struck like a metronome.

Each night, the mission came into tighter focus. The convoy would roll out of Mérida just before dawn on Day Four, engines muffled and lights killed. Two main trucks were reinforced with steel plating. Others were disguised as livestock carriers and public transport. Natalia oversaw route planning with Sosa, marking risk zones and refueling points. Meanwhile, Valeria handpicked the infiltration gear and coordinated signal flares—color-coded, non-verbal, and burned into every man's memory like sacred rites.

No radios. No panic. Only movement, memory, and muscle.

At the shoreline, Kael and Comstock reviewed the sea launch. The Commodore was stripped and retrofitted—solar panels, hidden compartments, reinforced hull. Three support vessels waited nearby: a shrimp trawler gutted and packed with arms, a ferry boat modified to house two sniper nests behind tinted passenger windows, and a Cuban Coast Guard cutter fitted with jamming tech and guided by the Hellpack. The cutter, Comstock claimed, could shut down a one hundred square miles of enemy comms before they even reached the docks. All four boats would deploy at dusk, hugging the sea's edge like phantoms. Their arrival at Marina El Dorado would be silent, fast, and absolute.

But everyone knew the heart of the mission bled underground. Beneath the chaos, under the city, where storm tunnels led to the hospital's foundations — there, the real test awaited. The hospital breach team would slip through the belly of the beast in total silence. No comms. No second chances. Marisol's life, and possibly the fate of Veloxyn, hinged on a perfectly timed extraction. For now, they rehearsed it repeatedly in the war room — crawling through taped outlines of the tunnels, syncing watches, learning each other's breath. When the time came, it wouldn't feel like improvisation. It would feel like prophecy.

Mérida Airport – Three Days Later

The sun broke over the flat horizon like a blade being drawn. The air shimmered with morning heat. On the cracked tarmac of the old Mérida runway, dust whipped in slow spirals as Kael, Comstock, Valeria, Leonardo, Padre Luis and Lieutenant Mateo Sosa stood in a loose line, squinting upward.

A low rumble began in the east — not thunder, but something more mechanical, more deliberate.

Then they saw them.

Three hulking gray silhouettes, riding low and fast — C-17 Globemaster's, U.S. Air Force markings blacked out with black tape, no transponders, no comm signatures.

The sound hit like a promise.

Comstock grinned. "Right on time."

The planes came in heavy — one after another — sweeping over the treeline with a thunderous growl. Kael felt the vibrations in his ribs.

"Jesus," Sosa muttered. "That's beautiful."

From each cargo bay, the back ramp hissed open mid-flight. Giant steel pallets shot from the fuselage like rounds from a cannon.

Ten... twenty... thirty.

Parachutes bloomed above the jungle tarmac like gray flowers.

The supplies fell in perfect rows — a mechanical ballet against the blue sky. Some pallets spun, others dropped clean and vertical, chutes guiding them like the hands of angels or devils.

Kael shielded his eyes with a flat palm.

"They brought it all," he said quietly.

The pallets slammed into the red dirt fields outside the airport — some bouncing once, others folding in place like surrendered beasts.

Cárdenas fighters — a hundred of them — swarmed the LZ, slicing tarp, unbuckling cargo netting, pulling back metal sheeting.

What they found took their breath.

Eight Humvees, spray-painted matte brown, mud-caked but solid

Twelve Desert Patrol Vehicles — armed to the teeth. Each carried a mounted .50 cal on top and an M249 light machine gun rigged to a swivel mount just outside the passenger door. Extra belts of ammo were looped along the roll bars, and spare jerry cans, med kits, and smoke grenades were strapped to the side frames like battlefield jewelry.

Javelin launchers and spare fire-control systems

Mortars in foam racks

Thousands of rounds of ammunition — 5.56, 7.62, .50 cal

Field kits — medpacks, recon drones, comms arrays

Night vision goggles — real, Gen 4 thermal sets

Ballistic plates, Kevlar, gloves, radio headsets

C4 bricks, det cord, blasting caps

A cache of 200 American rifles and suppressed handguns

Leonardo let out a low whistle. "This isn't a drop," he said. "It's a damn resurrection."

Valeria opened one of the crates and held up a thermite charge the size of a soda can. "We could burn a small city with this."

Comstock cracked his neck. "Let's start with a port."

Phoenix — a symbol of rebirth and defiance — in quick, bold strokes, the red paint hissing as it dried over sunbaked metal.

Kael strode between the vehicles like a general in mid-campaign, barking orders as his boots kicked up gravel. "Bravo and Delta teams — you're with me on northern breach. If your rifle jams, switch to sidearm and keep moving. No one gets left behind." He stopped beside a young man struggling to load a belt into an M240. "Where you from?"

"Progreso," the kid answered.

Kael nodded. "Then you know what they did to your people. Don't forget it."

Nearby, Lieutenant Mateo Sosa — his bandages fresh but his voice sharp — coordinated the rest of the platoon, separating fighters by region, language, and known loyalties. "Yucatán boys with the SAWs. Veracruz crew on rear guard. Anyone who speaks

Mandarin or Cantonese, step forward — we'll need ears on the radios."

On top of a supply crate, Comstock raised his voice above the grind of drills and rumble of engines. His face was grim, his tone unforgiving. "Mortar teams — listen the fuck up. If you hit a hospital, a church, or anything with civilians inside, I will personally throw your dumb ass in the river. We are not blunt force. We are surgical. Say it with me— scalpel, not sledgehammer."

"Scalpel, not sledgehammer!" came the reply, ragged but strong.

Across the lot, a Cárdenas scout no older than ten sprinted into the yard, a bundle of battered field radios in his arms. Dust clung to his cheeks, and his Cárdenas patch was too big for his shirt. "These are the good ones!" he called out.

Valeria met him halfway, crouching low to take the radios with a soft smile. "Gracias, pequeño." She clipped two to her vest and passed the rest to Natalia. Her eyes scanned the vehicles — hardened machines for a war they hadn't asked for but would finish on their terms.

They were almost ready.

And the sky was beginning to burn.

The salty air at the Port of Progreso crackled with tension. Down by the docks, crews moved with quiet urgency, working by headlamp and moonlight. The Commodore—Kael's familiar 38-foot catamaran—rocked gently against the pier, her hull still streaked from the last escape. Two men in sweat-soaked shirts wrestled new fuel drums into place while another jury-rigged a cooling system to the starboard engine using salvaged tubing and duct tape. Valeria supervised the work with hawk-like precision, her voice clipped and fast. "If it dies mid-run, we all do. Make it count."

Nearby, three support vessels took shape from the shadows. The rust-bitten shrimp trawler creaked under the weight of its hidden cargo, while Cárdenas loyalists tossed tarps over crates and slid netting over deck hatches. The ferry—stripped of passenger benches and refitted with steel braces—now held rows of ammunition tins beneath fake luggage racks. A pair of engineers on the Cuban cutter fine-tuned its jamming array, the glow of their soldering torch painting orange streaks across the bulkhead.

Kael stepped aboard The Commodore, boots thudding against the deck. "How's the mount?" he called out. One of the scouts tightened the last bolt on the sniper platform — corrugated steel welded to the solar brace. "She'll hold," the man said, slapping the panel with a grin. "Just don't take a 50-cal to the face." Kael didn't smile. He just checked the angle, adjusted the sight line, and nodded once.

Divers surfaced off the stern, black suits gleaming under dock lights. "Clear," one reported, tossing a suction clamp onto the dock. "No trackers. Jammers are set." Meanwhile, Valeria crouched by the ferry's rear engine bay, shaking a spray can of orange paint. The stencil hissed out in sharp strokes — a phoenix rising through smoke. "Let 'em see who's coming," she muttered. She stood, wiped her fingers on her pants, and looked out toward the open sea. "We don't come back unless we finish it."

Back in the old command center, the core team gathered for the final call.

Kael stood at the head of the table, arms folded. Natalia and Leonardo flanked him. Valeria leaned on the back of a chair, chewing on a piece of sugarcane. Grant stood at the projector, fingers hovering over the screen.

The satellite phone rang once.

Kael answered.

Salvador's voice filled the room. "Is it time?"
Kael looked around at the team.
Then at the map of Tampico.
He spoke slowly.
"The convoy rolls at dawn. The boats sail after nightfall. Guerrillas in the hills descend when they see the smoke."
"And your bait?" Salvador asked.
Kael's voice was cold steel. "Already sharpening the hook."
A long pause.
Then the cartel patriarch said, "Hold nothing back."
"I wasn't planning to."
Salvador's voice turned to a whisper — a prayer and a war cry combined.
"Then bring the storm, mi hijo. Let them drown in the fire."

Predawn – Mérida's Edge
The city was silent before the storm.
A ghostly mist hung low over the cracked highways and overgrown fields outside Mérida, where the Cárdenas convoy idled like a beast coiled to strike. More than 80 vehicles lined the abandoned service road: Humvees, trucks, DPV's, armored pickups, motorcycles, and battered sedans painted in Cárdenas cartel colors — jungle brown, ash gray, and storm black.
A dozen flatbeds carried mortars under tarps. Mounted .50 cals gleamed beneath mosquito netting. The lead Humvee bore a phoenix decal burned into the hood with a blowtorch — the tip of the wing curling into the shape of a machete.
Inside each vehicle: a new generation of fighters. Some had trained with Kael. Others were gangsters reformed by purpose. A few were ex-

military with old grudges. All were armed, armored, and steady-eyed.

Kael walked the line in silence.

He passed squad after squad, checking gear, nodding to captains, adjusting optics. Every soldier looked at him like they were waiting for a word that hadn't been spoken yet — something sacred.

Natalia and Valeria stood nearby, watching. Leonardo smoked quietly by the front jeep.

Then Kael stepped onto the hood of the Humvee.

He didn't shout.

He didn't wave.

He just spoke — low and clear — into the dawn.

"They tried to bury us.

They poisoned our water.

Took our ports.

Stole our people.

But they forgot we come from blood.

From jungle.

From fire."

He paused, letting the silence rise.

"This isn't just about taking a city.

This is about who we are when no one thinks we'll survive.

We take Tampico.

We take our families back.

And we don't stop until the world remembers our name."

He raised a fist.

"¡Por los Cárdenas!"

And the road roared.

"¡POR LOS CÁRDENAS!"

Engines fired. Radios buzzed. Doors slammed.

And then — the convoy moved.

Simultaneously – Port Staging

Down at the coast, The Commodore rocked in place as crates were loaded by flashlight. Kael's smuggling flotilla was ready:
- The Commodore (lead)
- La Víbora (a shrimp boat with hidden grenade racks)
- El Norteño (ferry-turned-APC)
- Loba Azul (Cuban Coast Guard Cutter painted as a fishing vessel)

They moved like shadows across the decks.

Thirty to sixty men per boat, ten on the Commodore — too many for comfort, not enough for certainty. Some wore cracked t-shirts beneath their flak vests, remnants of past operations that still stank faintly of salt and gunpowder. Others wrapped their wrists in cloth and painted their faces in smears of ash and axle grease, transforming into jungle ghosts reborn for open water.

The waves rolled quiet and steady, black under a moonless sky. No music. No chatter. Just the low hum of engines and the occasional creak of wood under shifting weight.

On the Commodore, Kael stood at the helm, one hand on the wheel, the other gripping the rail. He didn't speak much. No one did. Beside him, Padre Luis watched the horizon like it might speak first — his face unreadable, fingers restless near his rifle strap. Comstock sat cross-legged on the roof, sharpening a blade with slow, hypnotic rhythm, each scrape a countdown. Padre Luis began moving between the galley and deck, offering quiet blessings and hand-squeezes, whispering prayers only the wind could carry.

Somewhere ahead, past the dark sea and the waiting tide, was Tampico. A city full of enemies. A daughter, mother, and SEXICO to save. A war to ignite.

But for now — just water, breath, silence.

A calm held so tight, it might shatter at the first gunshot

Grant Comstock paced the deck with a headset, coordinating satellite link-ups and field drone signals. He passed Kael a map marked with marine entry routes, sonar dead zones, and shallow choke points where fast turns could buy seconds.

"Comms blackout starts in twenty minutes," Comstock said. "From that point on, it's only signal beacons and gut instinct."

Kael nodded. "That's how I've always fought."

Comstock smirked. "Then may your instincts be angry bastards."

Overhead – Chinese Drone Watch Over Tampico

Miles away, above a nondescript jungle ridge, a Chinese BZK-005 drone buzzed lazily in a surveillance orbit. On its monitor feed: nothing unusual. Just highway heat signatures and normal port activity.

But what it didn't see were the Cárdenas guerrilla teams crawling through ravines beneath the radar.

Or the underground tunnel charges being wired under the Port of Tampico.

Or the dozen hidden rifle nests now lining the surrounding sugarcane fields.

Final Call – The Family Thread

Back at Torre Cristal, just before Kael boarded The Commodore, a final call came through. Salvador Cárdenas appeared on screen — his eyes shadowed by candlelight in the war chapel.

Behind him stood Santiago Cárdenas, his arm still in a sling, and Doña Teresa, Marisol's mother, praying silently with a rosary clutched in both hands.

Salvador didn't deliver a speech. He just looked at Kael.

"Bring her home, Kael.

Bring our blood back to us.

And if you fall…"

"…make the gods cry before you do."

Kael gave a single nod.

"Understood."

CHAPTER 20

Ghosts at the Gate

The docks were shrouded in salt mist and moonlight. Kael stood on the slick deck of The Commodore, tightening the final cargo straps across a waterproof crate marked "VT-4 | CLASSIFIED." Inside: thermite, NVGs, suppressors, and enough ammo to light up a coastline. Grant Comstock was already on board — crouched low by the comms panel, calibrating a frequency jammer and adjusting his thermal scope. "We'll be black to satellites once we leave the inlet," he said, without looking up. Kael nodded, eyes scanning the waterline. One boat down. Three more to go.

Down the Pier – Other Vessels

The next few hours unfolded like a war ballet — tense, efficient, and precise.

Cárdenas fighters moved aboard the ferry boat, a rust-worn civilian vessel now retrofitted for war. Beneath the faded paint and cracked benches, crates of ammunition, explosives, and Veloxyn-filled medkits were hidden with surgical care. Leonardo paced the deck, barking orders with the cadence of a man who'd bled for every inch of ground they were about to take.

"No one lights a cigarette. No one takes a shit without telling the guy next to him. This boat moves like it's hauling grandmothers and coconuts — not enough firepower to level half the city."

He slapped the hull twice. "You thirty, you're my hammer. The others are the smoke. We hit when the city's already choking."

Down the pier, the shrimp trawler creaked as it took on water and warriors. Fifty-plus men, many with jungle war paint streaked over their faces, loaded RPGs into false-bottom fish bins, and secured suppressed MP7s in coolers marked SQUID. From a distance, it was just another rust bucket crawling in for the morning catch — until the tide turned red.

At the far end of the dock, the Cuban Coast Guard cutter loomed — heavier, darker, bristling with jerry-rigged antennae and a thick backbone of hardened steel. Thirty Cárdenas loyalists boarded under the watchful eyes of the Hellpack.

Sergeant Reva "Sawtooth" Guerra moved through the formation like a shark circling blood. "I see a safety off before we're on the water, I throw you overboard. I see someone flinch at a grenade pin, I shoot you. We are not here to learn. We are here to kill smart."

Corporal Elias "Ghoul" Navarro adjusted the sling on his M249, then dragged a chalk line across the deck. "If you don't cross this line with accuracy and silence in your soul, you're a liability."

Ángel "Boomer" Valdés laughed from behind his bandolier, loading his M79 Thumper like he was rolling cigars. "Don't worry, boys. You'll be trained before we dock — or buried at sea."

Meanwhile, on The Commodore, Kael, Comstock, and Padre Luis stood under a lantern-lit canopy. The catamaran's twin hulls rocked gently, barely betraying the arsenal stowed beneath.

Kael glanced toward the shoreline. "They're almost ready."

Comstock checked his suppressed SR-25. "They better be. When the convoy draws first blood, we slip in silent and hit harder."

Padre Luis muttered a blessing over the waves. "May the saints hold the ocean still… and our hands steadier."

Kael gave a short, sharp whistle. Three tones. Across the boats, captains answered — head nods, clenched fists, blades tapped against metal.

The convoy would roar. The sea would whisper. And death would come between tides.

Southern Mérida – The Convoy

Across the city, at an abandoned cement yard turned rally point, engines began to hum. Natalia Ortega Henacho walked the line with her arms crossed, face locked in grim concentration. Beside her, Valeria checked tire pressure and barrel locks on the Humvees. Mateo Sosa, chewing a toothpick, directed two young fighters into the back of an old Ford Ranger retrofitted with sandbags and a turret. Vehicles ranged from pristine desert patrol rigs to ragtag farm trucks armored with scrap metal and Cárdenas cartel insignia painted in blood-red handprints. "It looks like a scrapyard mated with a militia," Valeria muttered. Natalia grinned. "Perfect."

They moved like a strange family — some veterans, others barely old enough to shave, all drawn into the storm for reasons ranging from vengeance to loyalty to sheer survival. Each face was a story waiting to end in glory or gunfire.

Sosa glanced at Natalia, his expression shaded with quiet respect. "Never seen this many different crews working' this clean," he said. She didn't smile. "They're not crews. They're believers. That's more dangerous."

Safehouse – 3 Miles Outside Mérida

That night, Natalia and Valeria rested in a half-collapsed hacienda on the edge of town. They shared a mattress on the floor in the middle of a living room next to a fireplace, breeze filtering through cracked blinds from a nearby window. Valeria was the first to break the silence.

"If we survive this…"

Natalia turned toward her, eyes soft in the dark. "We will."

"But if we do. Let's go somewhere. Cuba. Spain. That quiet village you always talk about."

Natalia brushed her fingers down Valeria's cheek. "I'd go anywhere with you, mami. Even to hell."

"We've already been," Valeria whispered. "Now we just need to make it back."

They kissed — slow and unhurried — a promise etched in flesh before dawn made it war again.

In the quiet after, Natalia whispered, "Promise me something."

"Anything."

"If we're separated again — you fight like hell. Don't wait for me. Don't look back."

Valeria brushed tangled hair away from Natalia's forehead and pressed their lips together once more.

"I'll never stop looking for you. But I'll burn everything between us and peace if that's what it takes to get there."

Unknown Location – Marisol Cárdenas

Far from them, locked behind steel and shadows, Marisol Cárdenas sat on the edge of a cot. A single flickering bulb buzzed above her. A tray of food had been slipped under the door — soup, flatbread, a bottle of water...

...and folded beneath the bread, a napkin. Her hands trembled as she unfolded it.

"You have friends here. Stay strong."

Her throat caught. Her eyes filled. She pressed the napkin to her chest, as if it were a lifeline made of cloth and hope.

"My SEXICO is coming," she whispered to the dark.

But even as she said it, she felt the cold truth tighten around her ribs. Her wrists still bore the raw lines of rope.

Her back flinched at the memory of electric currents. They'd tortured her. But they hadn't broken her. Not yet.

She closed her eyes and remembered the sea — remembered Kael's arms, the salt-wind, the hush between heartbeats. She held onto it like a matchstick in a storm.

Blood Roads and Broken Mirrors
Federal Highway 180 – Dawn

They rolled out at first light across the Gulf Coast Highway — Federal 180 — into a corridor soaked in blood, whispers, and old betrayals. This stretch of Mexico, 620 miles of salt, heat, and jungle rot, normally took 18–20 hours to cross. But this wasn't a normal day. And this wasn't a normal convoy.

They weren't just a band of rebels anymore. They were the spark of something bigger. Word was spreading in whispers across states and cities — something new was moving, something righteous, something Cárdenas.

It wasn't like they sent a note ahead. They didn't call Los Huesos Rojos, El Filo de Dios, or Cartel Nueve Vida to let them know they were coming. But spies would speak. Remnants would whisper. And sooner or later, someone would know.

All along the 180 Highway, cartel eyes watched from hills and rooftops. Radios clicked. Intel moved fast in this part of the country. Some welcomed what was coming. Some planned to resist. But all of them braced for fire.

Mission Parameters

They had to make it to Poza Rica — at minimum — before the heavy fighting began. That was the unofficial line. After that, it was fire and

238

blood. They weren't stopping to resupply. They were only stopping to fight.

Each commander carried sealed orders. Natalia's said: "Push to Tampico. Protect Marisol at all costs. Secure the airport." Valeria's said: "Guard the flank. Reunite if separated. Ignite the second wave." They both knew what it meant. Sacrifices would come.

The Convoy Composition
- 8 Humvees
- 12 Desert Patrol Vehicles
- 50 auxiliary vehicles: old taxis, refitted farm trucks, boxy delivery vans reinforced with welded steel
- Soldiers, ex-cops, smuggler loyalists, and farmers turned freedom fighters

The vehicles were staggered and spaced — a living chain across the road. Tactical gaps between each cluster to avoid pileups if ambushed. No one left behind. No one overloaded.

Each cluster had a call sign. Each squad had a rally chant. Each unit knew: if the Cárdenas flag dropped, you picked it up. Even if it meant dying to do it.

Natalia rode in a repurposed communications Humvee near the front. Forty vehicles back, Valeria watched the road from a patched-up Ford F-350 with a mounted gun and a cracked windshield. They were miles apart. But bound by something stronger than radio frequencies — a silent tether of love, blood, and the promise of peace.

At one rest stop, Valeria scribbled a quick note on the inside flap of her glove: "Mi amor — I feel you beside me. Every breath. Every second." She pressed her hand to her chest and then gripped the wheel. The wheels kept turning.

Back at Progreso – The Marina Shift

As the sun rose higher, boats began to slip silently out of the marina.

One by one.

A few miles apart.

Like knives leaving a drawer in slow motion.

The Commodore took point.

Other disguised vessels peeled off toward rendezvous coves and coastal holding positions, ensuring they weren't seen together.

They could've gotten there hours earlier than the convoy.

But that wasn't the plan.

They needed to arrive with the chaos, not ahead of it.

Kael stood beside the helm, wind teasing his hair, the scent of oil and ocean thick in the air.

Comstock leaned against the rail, chewing sunflower seeds and staring at the sky.

"Convoy's late," he muttered.

"They'll come," Kael said.

"Or they won't," Comstock replied, spitting a shell into the sea. "But we'll be where we're meant to be."

Dusk – Gulf Waters Afloat

As the last light of day dipped beneath the waves, Kael and Comstock sat on a cargo net strung between the twin hulls, their boots hanging just above the moon-glittered water.

The engines purred in low gear.

The breeze was thick with salt and destiny.

Kael stared into the horizon.

"What am I?" he asked quietly.

Comstock raised an eyebrow. "A man," he said, dry as sand.

Kael shook his head.

"No. What have I become? What am I doing? After everything in my past…"

There was silence for a moment.

Only the sound of the water.

Then Comstock turned toward him — eyes calm but heavy.

"My boy, I've been on this earth fifteen years longer than you. And let me tell you—no one really knows the answers to those questions."

He took a slow breath, voice low.

"But one thing I've come to realize? We don't live our lives for ourselves. We live for the people who survive us. The things we've done… they're our greatest teachers. So the ones we care about don't have to carry the same chains."

"You surrender to that idea, and you stop needing peace from the past. You make peace with why you're still breathing."

He looked out to sea.

"I see that connection between you and Marisol. That space in between yesterday and tomorrow — that pure presence."

"That's who you're living for, Kael. That's why you'll make it back."

Kael said nothing but nodded slowly.

He knew.

He pulled out a folded photo from his pocket — a shot of Marisol laughing, wind in her hair, taken back at El Conquistador.

He stared at it until his vision blurred with tears he didn't let fall.

"I'll bring her home," he said. "Or I won't come back at all."

Federal Highway 180 – 14 Hours In

It had been fourteen hours since the convoy had left the outskirts of Mérida.

Dust coated everything — the windshields, the boots, the faces of men who hadn't slept.

241

They'd lost a few trucks along the way: one to a broken axle, another to a blown radiator.

Two more had shredded tires and had to be rebalanced roadside with old spares and prayers.

They were expected delays. But frustrating, nonetheless.

No one complained.

Not out loud.

There was a weight in the air — a tension so tight it felt like the whole world was holding its breath.

Approaching the Papaloapan River

Now, they had reached it — the Papaloapan River, wide and brown, the air thick with humidity and tension.

The convoy slowed.

Each vehicle crept across the bridge one by one — Humvees first, followed by the six Desert Patrol Vehicles, then the patchwork line of taxis and farm trucks.

All weapons were loaded. Safety off.

Every gunner scanned the rooftops and tree lines like phantoms might emerge to strike.

Natalia's voice came low over the comms.

"Eyes open. Breath shallow. No second chances."

Moving towards Las Escollenas and Alvarado.

They passed through the quiet fishing town of Las Escollenas, windows shuttered, dogs barking in the distance, no civilians in sight.

It felt cursed.

Like a town that knew war was coming and chose silence over survival.

Then onto Alvarado — a town that once thrived on shrimp boats and sugar. Now it was something else.

Half abandoned. Half waiting to explode.

Walls were sprayed with anti-cartel graffiti.

Shattered glass crunched under wheels.

Natalia sat stiffly in the front Humvee, hand gripping the radio mic.

Valeria, forty trucks back, rolled down her window and let the wind slap her face.

They were close.

Too close.

And everyone could feel it.

Crossing the Papaloapan – The Trap Springs

The lead vehicles had just begun crossing when it hit.

Gunfire — from both the front and the rear.

The road behind them exploded into sparks as cartel and Chinese shooters opened up with AKs and belt-fed LMGs from tree cover and abandoned shacks.

From ahead, two burning vehicles blocked the far side of the bridge.

"CONTACT!" Valeria shouted, slamming the brakes on her F-350 just before the bridge's incline.

She threw open the door, landed in a crouch, and returned fire with her rifle.

A Cárdenas loyalist climbed into the truck bed and began hammering out bursts with a mounted .50 cal.

"CROSS! CROSS NOW!" she shouted into her comms.

Bullets pinged off the hood.

Tires shrieked.

An RPG whistled past, striking the guardrail with a blast that knocked a convoy truck off its wheels.

Push Through the Fire

The convoy began to surge.

Engines roared. Tires screamed.

Vehicles lurched forward, barreling over the bridge into a wall of gunfire and flame.

On the other side — two Cárdenas trucks were already engulfed.

One man down. Then another.

A third screaming as he crawled from the wreckage, dragging his leg and still firing.

Those who could still move scrambled — grabbing rifles, helping wounded, loading into surviving vehicles.

More than half the convoy made it across.

The rest were stuck in the kill zone.

Airstrike from the sky.

Then came the sound.

Whoosh… Whoosh… WHOOOSH.

From treetop level, two Chinese Changhe Z-10 attack helicopters emerged — dark, silent beasts bristling with ordnance.

They fired.

Rockets streaked down the length of the bridge.

Two vehicles — both loaded with ammo — exploded into a double fireball.

The shockwave ripped through steel and bone.

The center of the bridge collapsed.

A roaring metallic scream, a snapping of concrete and rebar, a chunk of roadway fell into the river below.

Separated by Fire

Natalia's Humvee skidded to a halt on the near side.

Valeria stood on the far end, the smoking wreckage between them, her face ash-streaked and blood-splattered.

Frantic voices filled the radio channel.

"VALERIA!" Natalia screamed. "VALERIA, DO YOU COPY?!"

"We're cut off!" Mateo's voice cracked. "She's still alive! I can see her!"

Inside the Humvee, Natalia pounded her fist into the door.

Tears rolled down her cheeks. Her voice was breaking.

"Mi amor—"

"Keep going," Valeria said softly, her voice steady. "Keep pushing through the ambush."

There was a pause. Her voice returned, this time with purpose.

"We'll take Highway 175… to 1480… to 1500. We'll rejoin 180 outside Veracruz."

"We'll pass through some old control zones. I'll try to rally help."

"Don't stop, Natalia. Not for me."

A click. Then silence.

Natalia slumped in the passenger seat, trembling.

"She's not gone," Sosa said beside her. "She's just fighting her own war."

Natalia nodded, eyes burning.

And then gave the order.

"Full throttle. All remaining units — we push north."

Aboard The Commodore – Gulf Inlet

Comstock's encrypted satellite phone buzzed once — then clicked into a secure line.

"Looks like there was trouble," the voice said. "The bridge just past Tlacotalpan—blew. Enemy knew you were coming. Hit hard."

"Convoy split. They're rerouting through Tlacotalpan. Might be a 20-to-30-hour delay depending on what they hit along 175 and 1500."

"Will call with updates."

Click.

The line went dead.

Comstock tucked the phone away and looked over at Kael and Padre Luis.

"The bridge is down," he said flatly. "They got split. Delayed. Won't reach Tampico for another one to two days minimum."

Kael stood up and started pacing.

His hands clenched unconsciously, jaw locked. He said nothing, but the muscle near his temple pulsed.

"She's not dead," he said finally. "She can't be."

Padre Luis didn't say a word. He only stared at the horizon, jaw grinding like a slow machine.

Comstock moved closer, voice like iron under velvet.

"She's out there. And she's not alone. You trained her for this. Hell, you helped train all of them."

Kael's eyes flicked to him.

"Then why does it feel like I'm already too late?"

"Because you love her. And love makes time bleed."

Meanwhile – Backroads

Valeria's lead truck bumped along the cracked backroad highway, her arm resting on the door, eyes locked forward — but her mind drifted.

Every word Natalia had whispered to her — beneath moonlight, in jungle hideouts, during stolen hours of peace — looped through her memory.

Soft skin. Gentle smiles.

A voice saying: "Promise me we'll live, mami. Not just survive. Live."

Valeria pressed her foot harder on the gas.

They stopped at two rural outposts — half-forgotten waystations in the Yucatán scrublands, places where the dirt tasted like ash and silence lingered too long. But the moment the convoy rolled in — dust trailing like a war banner — men emerged from the shadows. Some wore old Cárdenas sigils half-faded on their jackets. Others bore nothing but grit and the long memory of loyalty. They didn't salute. They didn't cheer. They just nodded, picked up rifles, and climbed aboard.

At the first outpost, three exiled Cárdenas lieutenants stepped from a rusted barn, pistols on their hips and machetes slung across their backs. One of them, a thick-necked man named Duran, walked straight to Natalia, and clapped her shoulder.

"We heard the phoenix was still burning," he said.

"Figured you'd come calling."

Behind him, a dozen more emerged — old fighters, disillusioned cops, and farmhands with weathered faces and fire in their veins. Some had been waiting years for this moment. Others decided on the spot. All of them swore the same thing: they'd rather die standing with Cárdenas than live kneeling to Wu or the Nine Lives cartel.

At the second stop, they found more than men. They found trucks — fleets of them. Stolen, salvaged, or donated in secret. Flatbeds, pickups, even a pair of armored cash transit vehicles stripped of logos and wired with improvised gun mounts. A Cardenas solider walked among them, hand on his sidearm, counting silently.

"We just doubled our reach," he muttered to Valeria. A young mechanic slid out from under one engine block, grease on his face and a rifle slung across his back.

"She'll make it to Tampico," he said, wiping his hands.

"Just don't ask her to stop fast."

The convoy grew by the hour, not just in numbers, but in purpose — a force of renegades, survivors, outlaws and true believers, rolling toward a reckoning.

They didn't arrive as saviors. They arrived as proof that someone was still fighting back.

And that was enough.

By the time Valeria hit the crossroads near Vega de Alatorre, her group had grown by 200 strong.

What had been an ambush — intended to break the Cárdenas cartel — had accidentally fused it back together.

A girl with a dirt-smeared face passed her a bottle of mezcal and whispered,

"My brother died in Mérida. We thought you were all gone."

Valeria took the bottle, raised it, and said,

"Then let them hear us coming."

Natalia's Regroup Point

Natalia and Sosa had made it to the intersection of Highway 180 and 1500, their battered column resting in the overgrown shoulder of the road.

They'd taken a second ambush outside Paso del Toro — lighter than the bridge attack.

One truck destroyed.

Three good men dead.

The team was exhausted.

Low on ammo.

Emotionally frayed.

They refueled from hidden drums. Cleaned wounds. Rechecked gear.

But the thing eating at them wasn't fatigue.

It was silence.

No word from Valeria.

No signal.

No hope.

"I'd rather hear bad news than none," Natalia whispered.

Sosa didn't answer. He just lit a cigarette and watched the sun dip behind a line of sugarcane.

Then — from over the hill — came the sound.

Engines. Lots of them.

Every fighter grabbed their weapon.

Sosa climbed on top of the Humvee.

Then they saw it.

Valeria's convoy.

Bigger. Stronger.

Rolling with unity and fire.

The road filled with flashing lights, Cárdenas flags, local militia, and police decals scribbled over with "Libre."

Natalia ran.

Valeria jumped down.

They crashed into each other's arms like magnets — kissing, touching, holding.

Foreheads pressed together like prayer.

Neither said a word for a long time.

They didn't have to.

Behind them, the merged convoy chanted something low and rhythmic, rising like smoke into the twilight:

"Cárdenas vive. Cárdenas lucha. Cárdenas vuelve."

(Cárdenas lives. Cárdenas fights. Cárdenas returns.)

Sosa stepped forward, nodding at Valeria.

"Told you she was just fighting her own war."

Valeria grinned.

"Now let's win it."

The road to Tampico was soaked in blood and bodies.

But now, it burned with something new—

Hope on fire.

Chapter 21

The Last Daughter

Marisol sat alone in the cold, stone-walled room. The silence pressed in like a second skin — thick, suffocating. Only the soft hum of electricity and the whisper of wind against the metal vent broke the stillness. But something had changed. She felt it — a shift in the air. A current of dread. The kind of stillness that comes before a storm, when every bird vanishes and the trees hold their breath.

She closed her eyes.

Through the concrete and steel, she could hear distant murmurs — the crackle of radios, boots grinding against gravel, foreign dialects barked in urgency. Something was happening. Something beyond the normal routine of confinement.

The balance was tipping.

She knew it in her bones — the Cárdenas were on the move again. They were re-arming. She could feel it through every tremor of the floor and every pause between voices outside her cell.

And they knew it.

The door swung open with a metallic groan that echoed like thunder in the confined space.

Two men stepped inside — ghosts stitched from betrayal and authoritarian power.

Lieutenant Javier Montalvo, a man whose uniform once bore the Cárdenas crest like a badge of pride. Now, stripped of loyalty, he walked with a calm malice. Once a protector of the bloodline. Now its betrayer.

And beside him — rigid, precise, and cold as marble — Colonel Sheng Wu, the Chinese military attaché who orchestrated foreign operations with the emotionless efficiency of a computer algorithm.

Javier's eyes didn't carry rage. Just strategy. He looked at Marisol like she was a crate of uranium — dangerous, but ultimately useful. Not a daughter. Not a woman. Just leverage.

Colonel Wu said nothing at first. He scanned the room like a surgeon prepping for a dissection — calculating every variable.

"You always were defiant," Javier said, circling her like a buzzard. "Now you'll be valuable."

He gave a short nod.

A sicario from Cartel Nueve Vidas, face half-covered with a blue skull bandana, stepped forward and backhanded Marisol across the spine.

The slap cracked through the room like a pistol shot. Her body twisted, the iron chain overhead groaning under her weight, but she didn't scream. Her jaw clenched. Her teeth bit back the pain like she had practiced in silence for days.

The soldier wheeled in a military-issue car battery, already scorched from previous use.

Wires trailed like venomous snakes. Terminals glinted in the overhead light.

They clamped one lead to her ankle. Another to her ribcage — just below a fading bruise.

Javier crouched beside her, calmly testing the charge. The faint click of the meter confirmed it was live.

In the corner of the room, a red light blinked to life on a mounted camera.

Colonel Wu stepped forward, his voice sharp and deliberate.

"Message for Salvador Cárdenas," he said in crisp Spanish. "Back off your convoys. Stop all troop movement and border supply lines immediately. Deliver the formula for Veloxyn, your cocaine and heroin routes, and all logistics. You have seventy-two hours."

Javier added, flatly, "Or your daughter dies slowly."

He flipped the switch.

The room exploded in sound.

Marisol's scream was not the kind taught to victims in films — it was deeper. A sound pulled from the marrow. Raw. Cracked. Primal.

Her back arched. Sparks danced along her side. Her hands curled into claws against the restraints.

Still — she refused to beg.

She bit through the scream halfway. Her throat convulsed. Her vision blurred to white. But in the storm of agony, one name pulsed through the electricity like a prayer tattooed to her soul:

Kael… find me.

Wu gave a slight nod to the camera operator. "Send it."

The light on the camera turned green.

Transmission initiated.

And Marisol collapsed into the chains — trembling, burned, but unbroken.

The command room was silent — the kind of silence that didn't breathe, didn't blink. It just sat there, heavy and suffocating.

On screen, the final frame lingered like a wound.

Marisol's face.

Bloodied. Swollen.

One eye purple and nearly shut, the other locked straight into the camera.

Terrified.

Defiant.

Unbroken.

No one spoke.

A Cárdenas lieutenant slowly lowered his tablet. Another leaned on the wall, visibly trembling. Even the air conditioning seemed to pause.

Salvador Cárdenas didn't move.

He stood at the center of the room, arms folded behind his back, his jaw clenched so tightly his teeth creaked. A vein throbbed in his temple. His breathing was shallow but controlled — the kind of breath forged by decades of war and the burden of empire.

One hand hovered over the console as if trying to will the image away. But the other... the other curled into a fist. A tremor ran down his arm, subtle but constant.

In the far corner, Santiago Cárdenas — ever the strategist — turned away from the screen. Not out of weakness, but out of respect. His fists were balled, too. But he knew the difference between rage and recklessness.

Mateo, by contrast, exploded.

He slammed his hand into a steel table, sending a laptop crashing to the floor.

"Give me a name and a plane, Papá. I'll take care of this now!"

The outburst startled two guards near the door. Salvador didn't flinch.

"They're baiting us," said Goya, arms crossed so tightly her knuckles turned white. "This isn't just about Marisol. They want more than just her. They want the whole damn house."

"Veloxyn. Cocaine. Heroin," said Colonel Duarte, Cárdenas cartel military chief, his voice gravel-coated and steady. "Every artery we own."

Goya turned his dark eyes to Salvador. "They'll kill her anyway. Even if we give them what they want."

Salvador finally moved. He stepped toward the screen and stared at Marisol's image. Something broke in his gaze — not his will, but a curtain behind it.

"They don't just want leverage..."

He turned from the screen. The light flickered across his face like an omen.

"They want the bloodline."

Gasps rippled through the room.

Santiago looked sharply at his father.

"You mean—"

Salvador cut him off with a slow nod.

"We've always known this day would come. The day they stop attacking the business and come for the name."

Mateo stood still now, breathing hard.

"What do we do?"

Salvador turned toward the war table, spreading out a satellite map of Veracruz and the Gulf corridor.

"We do what Cárdenas have always done."

He picked up a marker and drew a thick red arrow cutting across the jungle.

"We take her back."

His voice was different now. Not just the voice of a father.

But a warlord.

A king who had just been challenged for the throne.

"And when we do," he added, "the world will remember why they never should've touched a Cárdenas."

Route 180 – Veracruz Jungle Road

Rain fell in sheets. The kind of rain that didn't trickle — it hammered. Each drop like a nail from the sky. The windshield wipers of the beat-up Humvee struggled to keep pace.

Natalia Ortega Henacho gripped the wheel with one hand, burner phone clenched in the other. The truck hydroplaned slightly as it cut through the winding jungle road that carved toward Veracruz.

On the other end of the line, Salvador's voice was frayed. Heavy.

"She's alive… but they're torturing her."

He paused. The silence that followed was louder than the rain.

"They want Veloxyn. Cocaine routes. Everything. I had to tell you."

Natalia's hand tightened. "What?" she whispered.

Beside her, Valeria went still — posture rigid, lips parted slightly in silent dread.

"There's more," Salvador continued, voice almost inaudible. "Valeria… she's not just your second."

Natalia blinked. "What are you talking about?"

"She's Marisol's half-sister. My daughter."

A breath. Then:

"From an affair while on a business trip to Isla de la Juventud. 1995. Her mother was… someone I couldn't protect in Cuba. Her father worked for me. I kept it buried for Valeria's safety."

The rain fell harder. Thunder cracked across the treetops.

Natalia slowed the car to a crawl.

Valeria didn't speak. She simply stared out the window — face blank, heart spinning.

Natalia turned, slowly, eyes searching Valeria's. "You knew?"

Valeria shook her head. "I had pieces. Nothing like this."

A thousand things rushed through Natalia's mind.

Memories of shared nights. Whispered dreams. The way Valeria moved like a woman always looking for her reflection in others.

"I need both of you," Salvador said, softer now. "Now more than ever."

Natalia put the phone down.

Valeria kept her eyes forward, but the mask cracked. Her voice came, low and vulnerable.

"I always wondered why I felt tethered to her. Marisol. Like we shared something beyond the cause."

Natalia reached across the console and took her hand. The rain made their skin slick, but they locked fingers.

"You share blood," Natalia said. "But she's not the only one who needs you."

Valeria's throat moved. Her grip tightened.

"I'm done wondering who I am," she whispered. "I know now."

Natalia leaned forward and pressed her forehead to Valeria's temple, just for a second.

Then she pulled back and gunned the engine.

The truck tore down the road, jungle whipping by, headlights slicing open the storm.

Two sisters of war.

One bound by love.

The other by blood.

Now both bound by vengeance.

———————————

The Commodore – Off the Coast of Tampico

The sea had turned to glass. Black, endless, reflective. Only the occasional slap of a swell against the hull broke the illusion that the world had simply stopped turning.

Four vessels drifted in a loose formation, silhouetted beneath a cloud-blanketed sky. The moon barely pierced the overcast veil, leaving the flotilla suspended in a silence that felt holy. Or fatal.

The Commodore, Cárdenas flagship catamaran was leading the way. Its sails were furled, its lights extinguished, its crew trained in silence.

Kael Torres stood barefoot at the bow, shirtless, his breath fogging faintly in the salt air. His eyes locked on the distant coast, where the faintest silhouette of Tampico waited — dark and unaware.

Somewhere inland, Sosa's team was under fire.

Natalia and Valeria were threading the bypass.

256

And Kael… Kael was waiting.

He hated waiting.

Behind him, Grant Comstock adjusted the angle of a jury-rigged signal reflector, wired into a deep-spectrum sat-phone and concealed inside a weatherproof satchel.

"Secondary road movement confirmed," Comstock muttered without looking up. "Drone pattern unchanged. They're watching the coast, not the sea. Smart."

Kael exhaled, long and sharp. His knuckles whitened around the railing.

"They're late."

"We're staying dark," Comstock said, flatly. "One blip and the whole coast goes red."

Then — it began.

A low, bone-deep growl.

At first, Kael thought it might be thunder. But it rose too quickly, built too sharply.

From the southern horizon, two shadows tore across the water like predators. Sleek, fast, ghost-black.

"What the hell is that?" a Cárdenas gunner asked from the stern.

The growl became a roar, the kind that vibrated in your ribs and made your fingers twitch.

"Boats inbound!" another man barked. "Two marks, fast approach!"

The Cárdenas fighters snapped into position.

Weapons came up.

Tensions flared.

A boat crew swiveled a PKM to port.

Kael tensed — every nerve awake.

The Commodore's deck became a loaded chamber.

Comstock didn't move. He calmly clicked on the comms and spoke without emotion.

"Everyone calm the fuck down."

The silhouettes slowed.

Two SURCs — Small Unit Riverine Craft — coasted in, ghostlike, each armored and bristling with modern firepower.

Foam-wrapped buoys splashed into the water. One SURC latched on. A boarding line whipped up.

A helmeted commander climbed over the rail.

"Major," the man said, saluting with perfect posture.

Comstock didn't return it. He glared.

"Put your hand down. You want to get me killed?"

The commander dropped his hand instantly.

"We're under strict orders. Get you upriver. Raise hell. Extract clean. You don't leave the boats."

Kael stepped closer, eyeing the black SURC hulls —

Each one a floating fortress.

• GAU-19 .50 cal Gatling guns
• Mk 19 grenade launchers
• M240s
• Aft-mounted 75mm recoilless rifles
• Thermal scopes, radar baffling, and a strange, humming generator Kael didn't recognize

"Where the hell did you get these?" Kael asked.

Comstock stepped beside one of the boats, trailing his hand along the cold metal bow like it was sacred.

"These aren't friends," he said, softly.

He looked at Kael with a strange grin.

"But tonight…"

Lightning flashed behind the clouds, illuminating the water in quicksilver. The wind carried distant thunder from inland.

"…she's my mistress."

And for the first time in days, Kael smiled.

Not because he wanted to.

But because he finally saw how they might win.

Rain had finally stopped, but the roads still hissed under every tire. A convoy of Cárdenas vehicles — over thirty deep — idled beneath a flickering gas station canopy at the edge of town.

Natalia Ortega stood near the pumps, her boots caked in mud, staring at a roadmap spread across the hood of a Humvee. Beside her, Valeria lit a cigarette with shaking fingers, the flame struggling in the wind.

"Poza Rica is up ahead," said Lt. Mateo Sosa, arriving from the opposite flank. "Cartel activity is heavy near the toll booths. They've mined the center lanes."

Natalia traced a finger across an alternate route.

"If we cut through here—Highway 1800—we can split the convoy. One group goes loud, the other maneuver's around."

"We'll lose comms if we split," Valeria warned.

"We'll gain unpredictability," Natalia shot back.

Sosa cracked his neck. "You want to gamble lives?"

"I want to save my sister," Valeria snapped.

The words dropped like thunder.

Everyone went still.

Even Natalia blinked.

Valeria hadn't said it aloud until now.

Her voice had changed.

Not just pain.

Purpose.

Sosa raised his hands. "Then we better draw fire away from her captors before they know we're coming."

Natalia folded the map.

"Then let's burn a path straight through their heart."

Poza Rica – Just After Midnight

The city was a latticework of ruins and ambush zones. Rooftop snipers. Drone nests. Wrecked intersections set like traps.

Sosa's decoy convoy — half the desert patrol vehicles, two Humvees, a few beat up taxis and six retrofitted pickups — barreled straight into the mouth of hell.

They were met with a welcome party.

• DJI drones dropping mortar shells
• Rooftop cartel shooters
• Hidden RPG positions

A mortar struck the lead Humvee, sending it skidding into a roadside shrine. Smoke billowed. Screams followed.

Sosa pulled one of his men from the wreckage and screamed,

"Lay suppressing fire!"

They returned volleys with tracer rounds, cutting drones from the sky like insects. A rooftop shooter was obliterated by a lucky grenade.

But the price was high.

A DPV was engulfed in flame.

A medic bled out behind a taco stand.

And still… they pushed forward.

As they neared the edge of town, a police barricade waved them through — unusual.

Sosa hesitated.

Then the barricade was hit by a fresh drone strike. The officers fought back, shooting into rooftops.

They weren't enemies.

They were allies.

A resistance unit, hidden in plain sight.

As the Cárdenas convoy punched through, the police joined them — battered, desperate, but armed.

Sosa stared at the ragtag group in disbelief.

One of them, a weathered sergeant missing half his ear, grinned through bloodied teeth.

"You thought we all sold out?" he said. "Some of us still believe."

Sosa offered him a rifle.

"Then let's remind them what belief looks like."

At the barricade's edge, Captain Isidro Beltrán emerged from behind a scorched armored cruiser, his uniform torn and smeared with ash. He held a pistol in one hand, radio in the other, barking coordinates to his rooftop units as bullets cracked overhead. When he spotted Sosa, something passed between them — not recognition, but purpose.

Sosa jumped down from the lead Humvee, jogged across the rubble-strewn street, and handed the captain a bundle wrapped in canvas. Inside: two RPG launchers, a dozen fragmentation grenades, and spare radios. "They'll send more drones," Sosa warned. "Use these when they do."

Captain Beltrán nodded, handing the bundle to the nearest officer without breaking stride. Then he turned to a blood-splattered sergeant crouched behind a cruiser. "Round up six units — I want four patrol cars, two unmarked. Strip the lights. We move with them now."

The sergeant saluted without words and disappeared into the smoke. Within minutes, a half-dozen police vehicles screeched into position, their remaining officers climbing in with rifles, duct-taped shotguns, and vengeance in their eyes. Beltrán turned to Sosa. "Tampico falls, the region wakes up. Let's make sure they hear it."

Offshore – 10 Miles from the Tampico River

Onboard the SURCs, Comstock stood at the front of the lead boat, scanning the darkness with binoculars.

"Convoy made it through Poza Rica," he said into the comms. "Engagement confirmed. Friendly police joined the push."

Kael nodded.

"Valeria?"

"Unconfirmed."

Kael turned away, heart thudding.

The Commodore was now shadowing the coastline. They were close. Hours away at most.

Lightning danced again across the water.

The ocean whispered of reckoning.

Comstock pulled out a black notebook — dog-eared, stained, nearly torn. He flipped to a page that showed a crude sketch of the enemy compound.

"Colonel Wu thinks he's hidden."

Kael cracked his neck.

"Then let's make him visible."

The river would be the stage.

But blood would be the ink.

– A Hidden Compound

Inside the reinforced concrete facility where Marisol was kept, Lieutenant Javier Montalvo and Rafa reviewed the footage frame-by-frame.

He paused on Marisol's face.

Zoomed in.

Still defiant. Still refusing to break.

Wu entered, his expression unreadable.

"They're coming," he said.

Javier glanced at him. "Then let them. They'll drown in their own fire."

Wu stared into the dark.

"No," he said.

"They'll burn the sky to get her back."

Some wars are fought for land. Others for power.

But this one…

…was for blood.

Chapter 22

The River and the Fire

The convoy sat idle on Highway 180, engines low, heat bleeding off the hoods like sweat. Just ten miles from the Pánuco River bridge, the last stretch into Tampico lay ahead — a gauntlet they all knew was waiting.

It was just past 2:00 a.m. The sky was starless. The air was thick and quiet. A silence that vibrated with tension, like a wire pulled to its snapping point.

Natalia Ortega, Valeria, and Lieutenant Mateo Sosa stood in a tight circle around the hood of a Humvee. Their headlamps were dimmed to a dull glow, barely piercing the mist that hugged the jungle road. A battle-scarred map was pinned beneath a boot, fluttering gently in the breeze.

Around them, almost one hundred vehicles idled — desert patrol vehicles, Humvees with battered armor plating, rusted pickups bearing improvised steel plating, a few armored SUVs, old taxis and four weathered state police cruisers that had defected to the cause during the Poza Rica breakout.

Over seven hundred fighters waited in the dark — Cárdenas loyalists, exiled sicarios, former military, and farmers-turned-soldiers who had nothing left to lose and nothing left to fear.

The air smelled like diesel and adrenaline. Sweat ran like rivers under body armor. Somewhere in the distance, a dog barked once, then went silent.

They'd lost two Humvees and a DPV to drone strikes earlier in the night. It still stung — the kind of pain that hadn't had time to settle into grief. But they had enough. Enough to make it count. Enough to take it back.

Tampico knew they were coming.

Natalia leaned over the map, her voice barely a whisper. "We send in the state police units first, one at a time. They're not expecting the cops to be with us."

"They'll assume it's routine patrol," Valeria added, her voice steady despite the cut above her brow. She brushed matted hair from her eyes. "Each cruiser takes four men — two in the back, two in the trunk. Full suppression kits. Quiet comms."

"They cross the bridge and scatter into the grid," Sosa said, tracing three streets with a cracked fingertip. "Calle Herradura, Calle Obregón, Calle Reforma. Hit three angles and give us cover fire when we punch through."

He looked up. "We only get one chance at this."

Then came the call. The one that would shatter radio silence.

Natalia keyed the comm. Her voice was low, calm, final.

"Cárdenas. Kael. We're in position. Ready to move."

Hacienda del Jaguar — Cárdenas Farmland, Altamira

On the outskirts of Altamira, the Cárdenas estate — once a quiet farm operation under assumed names — had transformed into a fully operational forward base.

The avocado trees were gone. In their place: armored SUVs lined the irrigation trenches, mounted .50 cal trucks sat beneath fruit sheds, and the northern access road had been mined with command-detonated explosives.

Salvador Cárdenas stood beneath the rusting water tower, one boot braced on the concrete rim, a Cuban cigar pinched between his fingers.

He heard the crackle in his ear.

"Natalia?"

"We're staged. Dark. Clean. We begin in thirty."

Salvador didn't hesitate.

"Copy. We roll in ten. See you at the Expo grounds."

He turned to his drivers, raising a single finger. "Roll them."

The engines came alive like hounds shaking off chains.

Across the fields, lights flicked on. Men scrambled onto tailgates. Radio calls laced the air. A hundred voices wove into one message:

"It's time."

Offshore — The Commodore Flotilla

Three miles off the coast, The Commodore cut gently through the chop, sails furled, engines dead. The four-boat flotilla floated in silence — cloaked in darkness and ready to strike.

Above, the clouds obscured the stars. Below, the sea held its breath.

Kael Torres stood on the upper deck of the lead catamaran, bare forearms braced against the railing, watching the coast of Tampico flicker with distant pulses of orange. The flashes came in clusters, like someone lighting matches inside a storm.

Onboard the ferry, Leonardo Barragán had gathered seventy Cárdenas fighters across the boats. Most were quiet. Focused. Some prayed. Others sharpened blades or checked sights for the hundredth time.

Below deck on the Commodore, Grant Comstock barked final checks on the two SURC riverine assault boats moored beside The Commodore. He moved like a man half-mechanized — efficient, unreadable, locked in.

Kael descended the stairs into the operations bay.

"Time?"

Comstock didn't look up. "Twenty-six minutes."

Kael nodded, then stepped to the secured comms console. He pulled on the headset, voice low.

"Cárdenas. Natalia. We are moving in thirty."

There was a beat of silence. Then her voice came through — calm as thunderclouds.

"Copy."

Kael placed the handset back in its cradle.

"We take this town back," he said. "We get Marisol."

Pánuco River — Bridge Crossing

Twenty-six minutes later, the first of four state police cruisers rolled silently across the Pánuco River bridge.

The night was still. No spotlights. No resistance. No sound but the rolling rubber of worn tires and the slow creak of ancient steel.

Each vehicle carried four Cárdenas fighters — two patrol officers in the front, two Cárdenas fighters in the back seat and two hidden in the trunk, rifles clutched tight against their chests.

They drifted into the city grid one by one:
• Calle Herradura
• Calle Obregón
• Calle Reforma
• And a shadowed service lane choked in ivy and broken fences

Within twenty minutes, they were positioned across Tampico's eastern flank, ready to strike from within.

The Cárdenas infiltration had entered the lungs of the city.

Ten minutes later, the first wave of Humvees, armored farm trucks, taxis and DPVs began crossing the bridge.

And that was when the sky fell.

Eastern Gate — City Limits of Tampico

The night cracked open.

A distant whine gave way to a banshee scream — and then the first mortar dropped.

A Chinese Type 87 82mm round screamed down from the clouds and exploded fifty meters ahead of the convoy, vaporizing an empty checkpoint station and sending shrapnel into the city.

The second round hit harder — it struck a farm truck filled with ten Cárdenas loyalists.

The explosion tore the vehicle in half, its back wheels flipping skyward. Bodies launched into the road like ragdolls. Screams erupted — cut short, raw, human.

A third mortar detonated beside the lead Humvee carrying Natalia and Valeria.

The blast flipped the vehicle onto its side. Doors sheared off. The windshield spiderwebbed in an instant. Shrapnel tore through tires and side panels, sending nearby DPVs swerving to avoid collision. A few men rushed over and pushed the Humvee upright.

Glass rained down like ash.

"They've zeroed the road!" someone screamed over the comms. "The whole corridor is locked in!"

The bridge lit up like a runway to hell.

For 1,000 meters, the road became a kill zone — mortar after mortar, placed with cruel precision.

It wasn't chaos. It was coordination.

Deliberate. Surgical. Timed.

The enemy had planned for this.

And still…

The Cárdenas convoy pushed forward.

Not because they believed they would survive.

But because there was no other way.

Two Miles Past the Bridge

The mortars faded.

For one fleeting breath, the world was only smoke and silence. No gunfire. No orders. No screams. Just the low groan of burning metal and the thrum of engines trying to hold the line.

Then came the bullets.

Gunfire erupted from the industrial district — buildings, rooftops, scaffoldings.

Tracer rounds lit the air red and green, streaking across the night like dragonflies made of fire. Every building became a hive, every alley a mouth spitting death.

An RPG screamed from a parking garage and slammed into a desert patrol vehicle at full speed. The blast flipped it end-over-end. When it landed, it didn't stop burning.

Natalia's Humvee, already scarred from the earlier blast, lost its rear axle to a mine. The whole rig buckled and skidded sideways into a drainage ditch.

Valeria was already halfway out the window, rifle in hand, laying down suppressive fire with cold precision.

The convoy surged into the city like a wounded animal, thrashing, howling, bleeding — but still moving.

They returned fire from every angle.

Men in the truck beds opened fire with M249 SAWs, the deafening rattle of the belt-fed guns filling the street as brass clattered like hailstones against the metal floor. Every burst sent muzzle flashes strobing against the buildings — illuminating faces contorted with focus and fear. Nearby, two fighters dragged a bleeding comrade from the open bed of a pickup, shouting over the roar of gunfire as they ducked behind an overturned produce cart. One man pressed a bloodied hand to the wound, yelling,

"Stay with me! You're not dying in a fruit stand, hermano!"

An RPG screamed from the second floor of a crumbling cantina, the trail of smoke curling into the humid air. A split-second later, another launched from the Cárdenas side — both warheads crossing in midair like infernal arrows before disappearing into separate impacts. One struck a rooftop water tank, sending a geyser of black water and steel into the air. The other obliterated a corner balcony where an enemy lookout had just raised binoculars.

A sniper's shot rang out — a sharp, surgical crack. The round pinged off the side mirror of Sosa's truck, missing his skull by inches. He dropped instinctively, glass shattering against his face.

"Sniper! West wall, third floor!" he barked, rolling off the cab and drawing his sidearm. Valeria's voice crackled over the radio:

"I see him — watch for the reflection. He's repositioning!"

Then came the fire. A diesel tank on the hood of a farm truck took a round and went up in a whoosh of heat and light. The flames painted the alley in deep amber and flickering shadows, casting monstrous silhouettes as the fighters scrambled through smoke and soot. For a heartbeat, it looked like the whole block was burning — and still, they kept fighting.

They weren't pushing through.

They were breaking in.

A city under siege by its own ghosts.

Pánuco River — 500 Meters from Bridge 180

The two SURC boats raced upriver, wakes slicing through the water like knives.

Kael Torres crouched at the bow of the lead boat, eyes sharp, face unreadable. He tracked the skyline for movement, counting flashes of gunfire by their pattern.

Comstock stood at the GAU-19, body poised like a coiled spring. His eyes flicked between a thermal scope and the riverbank.

Behind them, two Navy operatives checked belts of ammo and lined up frag launchers.

"Five-story structure," Kael said, nodding upriver. "Two o'clock. Adjacent to the river. That's their platform."

He didn't finish the sentence before the first mortar trail lifted from the rooftop.

"Mortar team confirmed," Comstock said, already swinging the GAU-19. "Clearing it."

The riverine boat slowed just enough to steady aim —

Then Comstock opened fire.

The Gatling gun erupted — a thunderclap in the dark.

.50 caliber rounds cut through the rooftop, shredding sandbags, tiles, and silhouettes. The entire platform stuttered under the weight of it.

Kael locked into the Mk 19 and let loose — four 40mm grenades sailed upward like glowing embers.

When they landed, the entire upper floor went concave.

From the stern, a navy operative fired the 75mm recoilless rifle — the shell hit the building like a divine hammer.

Concrete erupted. One side of the rooftop caved in completely.

Down the shoreline, Cárdenas convoy fighters saw it.

And for the first time that night, they screamed in joy.

Pánuco Bridge — The Beast Awakens

The mortar barrage had gone quiet. The rooftop gun nest was a smoldering hole in the skyline.

From the south side of the bridge, Cárdenas fighters watched in awe as the two SURCs roared up the river — weapons flashing, turrets swiveling, men screaming war into the night.

"¡Vamos, cabrones!" a young soldier cried, slamming a fresh mag into his rifle.

The convoy surged forward again — no longer crawling. Now it charged.

It wasn't just a push. It was a counter-invasion.

Back on the River

Kael scanned the rooftops when he saw it , a low-flying shadow, cutting through the black like a shark.

"Helicopter!" he shouted.

A Chinese Z-10 attack chopper surged from behind a warehouse, rotors thumping low and fast.

Rockets fired.

Two streaks toward the second SURC.

Comstock spun the GAU-19 and roared into it, spraying the sky with red-hot tracers.

Kael lined up the Mk 19 again and fired three rounds in quick succession. One missed. One hit the chopper's stabilizer.

The third struck its side chassis.

The bird exploded in midair — flames bursting from its core. It spun, caught a support beam on a riverside billboard, and crumpled into the water with a final scream of metal.

A geyser of flame and smoke launched thirty feet in the air.

Someone cheered on the second boat.

Comstock didn't. He just grinned.

"That's air denial."

Kael shouldered his rifle.

"Next stop — hell's front gate."

North End — Industrial Corridor, Tampico

Smoke hung over the road like a low ceiling. Ash clung to the air. The smell of diesel, blood, and gunpowder was thick enough to chew.

Natalia and Valeria crouched behind the twisted carcass of a disabled Humvee, steam hissing from its shattered hood.

They were covered in soot, grime, and blood — not all of it their own. The mortar barrage had eased, but the city hadn't stopped screaming.

Gunfire echoed from all directions. RPGs flashed across alleyways. Somewhere to the south, a convoy vehicle burned — the heat visible in the rippling night air.

Three Cárdenas fighters huddled behind them, wide-eyed and shaking. One clutched a cracked radio, the other dragged a duffel bag stuffed with RPGs and bandoliers.

Natalia exhaled slowly. Her voice was low, clipped.

"We're already in the city."

Valeria grinned through the blood on her lip. "Why the hell not?"

Natalia keyed her mic.

"Convoy, this is Natalia. If you're close, unload. Hit everything that shoots. Everyone moves. Now."

She dropped the mic. Looked at Valeria.

"Let's go."

City Rooftop Assault – Five-Story Killhouse

The building ahead loomed like a monolith — five stories of crumbling concrete, its face scarred with old graffiti and fresh bullet holes.

Two stairwells. No lights.

They kicked open the rear of the Humvee and pulled gear:

• Two RPG launchers
• Six rifles
• Frag grenades

• Spare magazines

• A medical wrap Valeria didn't bother to use

Natalia split the fighters into two flanking groups.

She and Valeria took the west stairwell.

It smelled like bleach and rot — someone had tried to clean something terrible here and failed.

By the third floor, a shotgun blast tore through the drywall inches above Valeria's head.

"Down!" Natalia shouted.

Valeria hit the floor and returned fire in a smooth roll — three tight bursts. The shooter staggered, dropped his weapon, and fell backward down the stairs.

They didn't stop.

They reached the fifth floor. The door was unmarked.

Gunfire echoed from the other side. A language — a rhythm. Natalia raised three fingers. Valeria nodded.

They moved.

The door burst inward.

The top floor was hell.

A dozen men inside — half wearing Cartel Nueve Vidas skull masks, the other half in Chinese PLA uniforms. Mortar and RPG rocket crates stacked along the wall. A tactical table lit with drone feeds.

Chaos.

Natalia shot the nearest soldier through the neck. Valeria dropped to one knee and hosed the left flank with automatic fire.

A cartel soldier screamed, "¡Mujeres arriba!"

Bullets tore into the walls. One grazed Valeria's thigh — spun sideways into a stack of crates.

Natalia ducked, flanked right, and put two rounds into a PLA comms officer before launching a frag into the far corner.

The room erupted in smoke, screams, and the high whine of a feedback loop.

When it cleared, thirteen bodies lay still.

Valeria stood, limping, rifle smoking.

Natalia kicked the rooftop door open. "Let's finish it."

Rooftop — Sicarias Ascend

From the fifth-story perch, the city unfolded like a battlefield map lit by fire.

Convoy vehicles pushed down Calle Lerdo de Tejada. Shooters advanced behind scorched buses and shattered storefronts. Enemies held rooftops three blocks ahead, pinning Cárdenas fighters with suppressing fire.

Natalia dropped to one knee, RPG launcher resting against her shoulder.

"My turn."

The rocket hissed — then roared. It struck the top floor of a warehouse. The blast ripped a hole through its corner, sending a rooftop sniper sailing into the street below.

Valeria, still bleeding, steadied her rifle on a pipe vent and sent five clean shots into another rooftop. One figure dropped. Then a second.

A third shooter got off a burst — slamming two rounds into the rooftop wall inches from Valeria's face.

She ducked.

Grinned.

Then stood back up.

"Missed."

Interior – Black Site Holding Room, Tampico

A flickering light bulb buzzed overhead, casting shadows that jumped like ghosts on the walls.

Marisol Cárdenas sat chained to a steel chair bolted to the floor. Her lip was split. One eye swollen nearly shut. Blood dried along her temple.

But she was upright. Breathing. Conscious.

And she was listening.

Gunfire. Closer now. Echoes of grenades. A shout. A scream. Then silence. Then more gunfire.

The storm was coming.

The door creaked open.

Two men entered — one in Nine Lives cartel fatigues, the other in a Chinese PLA field jacket. Both wore expressions that had seen too much and understood too little.

The PLA man knelt beside her. Voice flat. Accent hard.

"They won't get here in time."

Marisol's eyes met his. One was nearly closed. The other, burning.

"I hope you're right," she whispered.

He stood.

A tray clinked. A syringe was prepared. The cartel man snapped on gloves.

Marisol didn't look at them.

She looked at the wall. Toward the sound of her city rising.

A scream. An explosion. Another RPG.

The sound of fire. Of resistance. Of hope.

The PLA officer leaned in. "What did you say?"

She smiled — blood cracking in the corner of her mouth.

"I said…"

"You should run."

The Black Site — Storm Drain Ingress

The two SURC boats had drifted into shadow beneath the Marina Club de Tampico, hidden in the water's black reflection.

From the lead boat, Kael and Comstock stepped off first, boots landing in the ankle-deep shallows with practiced ease. The surf hissed against the hull, whispering secrets in the dark.

Behind them, a dozen Cárdenas loyalists jumped into the water, rifles slung tight, moving like men who had nothing left to lose. Padre Luis brought up the rear, rosary beads wrapped around his wrist like a battle talisman, a short-barreled rifle cradled in his arms.

A voice barked from the deck of the SURC — sharp, furious.

"Comstock! You're not authorized to disembark!"

It was the Navy commander — helmeted, leaning over the railing with an M4 in one hand and a headset jammed against his ear.

Comstock didn't even look back.

"Authorizations in the results," he muttered. "Cover the waterline."

The commander swore but didn't follow. The SURC's GAU-19 turret swiveled toward the treeline as the boat reversed into a holding pattern, engines barely audible.

Kael signaled with two fingers. The strike team fanned out, moving like shadows across the darkened beach, every step drawing them deeper into the belly of the operation. Padre Luis whispered a prayer in Spanish as they crossed the sand, the moonlight catching the edge of his rifle barrel.

This wasn't just an infiltration. This was an omen.

They moved silently through back alleys and overgrown lots. The city moaned around them — alive with fire and vengeance.

"Two blocks more," Comstock whispered. "Intel says storm drain, west wall. Reinforced entry."

Kael nodded. They crossed a drainage bridge, turned into a shadowed alley, and stopped.

Before them: a concrete wall topped with razor wire. A low grate gaped at the base — rusted but intact.

"This is it."

Kael tapped his earpiece. "Comms dark after breach."

He adjusted his rifle. Checked his sidearm.

This wasn't a mission anymore. It was retrieval.

He looked at the crumbling structure. Saw the scorch marks. The burned signage.

She was in there.

He stepped forward, voice low.

"We go in quiet."

Tampico Expo Grounds – Command Staging Center

The once-glamorous Tampico Expo Center now looked like a wounded giant — cracked glass, fire-scorched beams, and walls pockmarked by stray bullets.

What had once hosted black-tie galas, municipal fairs, and corporate trade shows had been stripped to its bones and reassembled into a field command post.

Cárdenas convoy vehicles poured into the crumbling lot from three directions — Humvees trailing smoke, pickups with bullet holes punched through their hoods, armored SUVs dragging shards of streetlamp cables and torn-up sidewalk.

Men leapt off the back of trucks, rifles slung across their shoulders, sweat glistening beneath body armor caked in soot. Others stumbled, wounded, supported by medics or fellow fighters.

Inside the once-glass grand hall, the chandeliers were gone.

In their place:

• Hanging lanterns and rigged LEDs

• Folding tables stacked with maps, gear, and blood-soaked field reports

• A giant laminated city grid laid across the center floor, now marked with red pushpins, black tape, and dozens of blood stains

Mateo Sosa shoved through the chaos, dropped his gear on a folding chair, and went straight to the main comms table. Sweat poured from his brow, his uniform stained with dust, smoke, and someone else's blood. He didn't hesitate, just leaned in, breath ragged, and muttered,

"We're in. West gate was held. Convoy split worked."

The room didn't freeze, but it pulsed—like the breath before a final exhale. Salvador Cárdenas looked up from the map table, his sharp eyes meeting Sosa's with the kind of gratitude that didn't need words.

"You made it," Salvador said, voice gravel thick.

"I thought they clipped your wings back in Poza Rica."

Sosa grinned, eyes flicking toward a distant corner where blood was being scrubbed from a helmet.

"They tried. Sent drones, RPGs, rooftop assassins, and mortars. But we punched through."

"Plans changed. So did the road." Sosa smirked, wounded fighters by the wall. "Feels like the world's coming back together, piece by piece."

Salvador stepped forward and placed a hand on Sosa's shoulder. "We wouldn't be standing here without you. Not today." Then he looked toward the window, where smoke still rose in the distance. "Let's finish what we started."

"Valeria and Natalia have rooftop coverage at Plaza Hidalgo," he reported. "They're feeding grid targeting. Eastern flank suppressors are cut off, but they're holding."

Salvador Cárdenas didn't lift his eyes from the map. He stood like a mountain — still, grim, composed. One hand rested on a pistol. The other hovered over a cluster of red-circled buildings five blocks from the river.

"The black site's here," he said. "Kael and Comstock are en route."

Sosa frowned. "We've got no contact since insertion."

"Keep it that way," said Goya, emerging from behind a sandbagged terminal. "If they're close, any ping gives them away."

Moments later, Santiago Cárdenas entered dragging a handcuffed sicario by the collar — blood dripping from his temple, mouth gagged with a strip of Cárdenas-blue cloth.

"Caught him running east. Said Cartel Nueve Vidas is falling back toward the refinery."

"They're not retreating," Salvador said without pause. "They're consolidating."

The room buzzed with overlapping voices — field updates, weapon counts, incoming wounded, signal disruptions, and sniper locations being plotted by hand.

A Cárdenas scout yelled from the rooftop:

"Two more transports inbound! Looks like the rest of Sosa's column made it through!"

Goya's eyes narrowed. "Who's still outside?"

"Natalia. Valeria. Still up. Still killing."

Salvador checked his watch. 3:42 a.m.

The city wasn't just burning.

It was breathing Cárdenas air again.

———————————

Flashback — Aboard the Commodore (Days Before Ambergris)

The cabin was bathed in warm amber light — part moon, part oil lamp. Curtains fluttered at the open window, the wind carrying salt and jasmine across the sheets.

Kael Torres lay shirtless, one arm folded under his head, eyes closed but alert.

Marisol Cárdenas curled beside him, tracing slow, lazy circles across his chest with her fingers — not for comfort, not for seduction, just to feel he was real.

Minutes passed in silence.

"I used to think I had time," she said, her voice half a whisper. "Time to fix things. Time to run. Time to not be… this."

Kael opened one eye. "What stopped you?"

"You," she said simply. "And this."

She reached down and slid his hand gently across her stomach.

He felt it — the faintest tension under her skin.

"I'm late," she said. "And I don't care."

Kael's breath caught.

"Are you sure?"

"No," she admitted, a small smile tugging at her lips. "But I want to be."

He turned toward her, brushing hair from her face with a tenderness born of war and scarcity.

"I'll protect you," he whispered. "Both of you. Always."

She closed her eyes. "I know."

Outside, the ocean whispered lullabies to the hull.

Inside, for one brief night, the future felt like it was possible.

Rooftop — Southeast Corner of Plaza Hidalgo

Smoke drifted across the rooftop in slow, snaking ribbons. The sounds of war had dulled to a low chorus — the percussion of distant RPGs, the staccato whisper of suppressed rifles, the ragged roar of engines cutting tight corners through narrow streets.

Natalia sat with her back against a busted air conditioning unit, her rifle laid across her lap like a sleeping animal. Blood had dried on her knuckles. Her cheeks were streaked with ash.

Beside her, Valeria lay prone, scanning the skyline through the cracked scope of a borrowed rifle. Her thigh was wrapped in a strip of bandage — stained dark, tied rough. She hadn't said a word about it.

Below them, Cárdenas forces moved like wolves through the city grid — peeling around barricades, leaping fences, claiming intersections in brutal, efficient bursts.

But the resistance wasn't gone. Not yet.

Natalia reached into her vest, pulled out a cigarette, and held it up. Valeria glanced sideways.

"Didn't know you smoked."

"I don't." Natalia flicked the unlit cigarette away. "Just wanted to see if I still could."

Valeria exhaled through her nose — a laugh more breath than sound.

"Bad sign when this feels like the calm part."

Natalia turned to look at her. "How bad's the leg?"

Valeria flexed it once, winced. "Through and through. Didn't hit bone."

Natalia nodded. "Good. I'm not carrying your ass."

Valeria smirked. "I always figured you liked me for my body." They both chuckled. Not because it was funny. But because it was real.

Silence fell again — that strange silence you only find in the middle of war. Not peace, exactly. But the eye of the storm. The kind of quiet where your soul checks its reflection.

Then Valeria spoke.

"You ever think about after?"

Natalia didn't answer right away.

She stared at the city. At what used to be streets, markets, weddings, and lives. Now just rubble and movement and flags made from torn shirts.

"I didn't think there would be an after," she said. "Not for people like us."

Valeria turned her head. "But now?"

Natalia looked down. Then at her. Her jaw shifted. Her voice came soft.

"Now I think… maybe."

Valeria reached out. Her fingers found Natalia's, pressing together in the dust between them.

"We finish this," Valeria whispered. "Then we see what after looks like."

Natalia didn't say anything.

She stood. Loaded a fresh mag.

And stepped into the smoke.

Chapter 23

The Blood Vault

Interior – Black Site, Lower Level
The first shot was muffled.
The second was not.
It cracked through the corridor like a hammer splitting bone.
Marisol Cárdenas jerked upright, muscles seizing, eyes wide. The rusted chain from her wrist restraint dragged across the concrete floor with a metallic hiss, echoing like a serpent warning of death.
Her gaze locked on the steel door.
Heavy boots pounded against the hallway outside.
Someone shouted — Mandarin. Sharp. Urgent.
Then came more gunfire. Not frantic volleys — no. These were clean, short bursts. Controlled. Executions.
Then a scream — guttural, real. A man dying slow.
Then silence.
She held her breath.
Her pulse thundered in her ears.
Kael, she thought. Please.
The silence stretched — until the door clicked. Not opened. Just… unlocked.
The bolt released with a soft metallic thunk.
Her eyes locked onto the seam.
But no one entered.
She stared at it. Waited. Counted to ten. Then twenty. Her breathing stayed shallow, her spine straight. Every nerve stretched taut, every instinct screaming for her to move — but she didn't. Not yet.
Then another scream outside. Closer.
Then gunfire.
Multiple weapons. Different calibers.

A fight.

She recognized one voice amid the chaos — unmistakable, arrogant, sharp: Colonel Sheng Wu.

The same man who had electrocuted her. Who'd stared into her eyes with surgical coldness while ordering pain as if flipping a switch.

But now… he wasn't yelling at her.

He was screaming at his own soldiers.

He's fracturing, she realized. Breaking away. Going rogue.

Then came a sudden burst — a grenade or flashbang — then a rush of movement. Heavy boots thudding away from the cellblock. The floor trembled beneath her.

Then… silence again.

A deeper silence. The kind that fills after gods leave and devils retreat.

Marisol didn't wait.

She slid across the floor to the sidewall.

Gunfire cracked through the concrete like distant thunder — sharp, rhythmic, relentless. Somewhere above, boots pounded against steel grating. Shouts in Mandarin. A scream. Then silence.

Marisol held her breath.

She was chained to the wall — wrists cuffed in front her, cold steel biting into the brick. They'd given her just enough slack to sit or kneel, nothing more. Her legs were stiff, back sore from hours — maybe days — of this position. The only light came from a swinging bulb overhead, casting warped shadows along the floor.

Then the door groaned open.

A Chinese soldier stepped in.

But something was wrong.

He didn't storm the room or bark orders. He just… staggered forward, like a drunk in a dream. One hand gripped his rifle, the other dangled useless at his side. His face was blank — not angry, not focused. Just vacant.

Marisol froze. Her breathing shallow. Her pulse sharp and erratic.

The soldier took two more steps.

And then he stopped. Wavered.

Dark red began to spread across his chest. First a dot. Then three.

Blood gushed through the front of his uniform in silent bursts. He dropped his rifle. Stared down like he didn't understand. Then — slowly, like gravity had forgotten him for a moment — he fell forward.

Flat. Face-first.

The thud shook the room.

He landed just a foot away.

Marisol stared at the corpse.

Three bullet holes were punched through his back. Whoever had taken him out was close — maybe watching. Maybe not. It didn't matter. Her eyes were on the sidearm holstered at his hip.

It had landed just barely within reach.

She twisted her shoulder, stretched her leg, teeth clenched from pain and effort — and managed to nudge the weapon closer with her foot. Again. Once more. Finally, it slid far enough.

With trembling fingers, she snatched it.

The weight felt like fire and freedom.

She turned and aimed awkwardly at the chain bolt behind her. One shot. Then two.

Metal screamed and shattered.

She spun, dragging herself toward the utility cart in the corner. Finding the keys. Yanked them free. Her hands were shaking as she unlocked the last cuff and let it clatter to the ground.

Marisol slumped forward, free for the first time in what felt like forever.

The gun still in her hand.

And blood drying on the floor

Her hands trembled — but not with fear.

Not anymore.

She crouched beside the wall, back pressed into shadow. The sidearm was cold in her grip, but her finger knew where to rest.

She remembered.

She pointed it toward the door.

And waited.

Long enough for the adrenaline to plateau. Long enough for the quiet to start whispering questions.

But she didn't let them in.

The silence pressed like a weight.

Then… nothing.

No footsteps. No orders.

No one coming to save her.

So, she saved herself.

She crept toward the steel door — easing forward, breath thin, body tight.

It was slightly ajar now, a two-inch invitation.

Through it, a trail of blood.

Dark streaks. Dragged boot prints across the tile.

The stench of cordite lingered, fused with smoke and copper and something more primal.

She slipped through.

The corridor opened like a wound.

She took two steps. Stopped. Pressed her back against a column.

Then it hit her — not panic. Not hope.

Memory.

Flashback – The Commodore, Night Waters

The night was soft — tropical wind brushing the catamaran like a lover's breath.

Kael Torres had handed her the pistol as if it were sacred. Not a tool of death, but a key to autonomy.

"You don't squeeze," he'd said, voice low. "You press. Like a heartbeat. Controlled."

She remembered how it felt in her hand — heavy but promising.

He'd gestured toward a floating melon bobbing off the stern.

"Focus on your wrist. All the strength's there."

First shot — too low.

Second — off-center.

Third — clean.

Hitting the crate several times.

Kael laughed, proud and surprised.

"You're a natural."

She had smiled. Watching the pieces drift away in the silverlight.

That night, she felt more than capable.

She felt dangerous.

Back to Present – Black Site, Stairwell 2A

She ducked under a stairwell, curled in the wedge between concrete and steel.

For a moment, she let herself shake.

Then it passed.

She pulled her knees in tighter. Kept the sidearm pointed low.

Finger along the frame. Trigger untouched. Just like he taught her.

All Marisol could hear now was distant outside gunfire.

She wasn't a prisoner anymore.

But she wasn't free yet.

She looked up the stairs. Then down the hallway.

She saw the blood. The open silence. The smoking vents.

And she knew —

She would never go back in that chair.

Not ever again

Approach – Streets Near the Black Site

The storm had passed, but the city still looked like it was drowning.

Rain slicked the pavement in a mirrored sheen, reflecting the orange glow of scattered fires. The moon was gone, swallowed by smoke.

Kael Torres and Grant Comstock moved like wolves — low, fast, deliberate — down opposite sides of a smoke-stained boulevard.

Two blocks ahead loomed the objective:

The black site.

It wasn't marked on any satellite maps. Not even Cárdenas intel had precise layouts. But through enough whispers, captures, and Comstock's quiet sorcery, they'd learned what mattered.

It was a repurposed medical facility, twisted into a fortified nightmare. Chain-link fences wrapped it like barbed cloth. Concrete towers topped with thermal cameras rose from the corners.

And inside… Marisol.

Kael spotted a Chinese soldier near the outer gate — slack posture, head bobbing slightly. The man looked half-awake, shell-shocked.

Kael didn't hesitate.

He crossed the distance in five quiet steps. Drew his K-bar in one clean, silent motion.

The blade sliced across the soldier's throat with surgical grace.

Warm breath escaped in a gurgle. No sound. No alarm.

The man collapsed, one hand grasping the air — already gone.

Across the street, Comstock gave a short nod and flicked two fingers forward.

They moved.

Outer Perimeter Breach

Comstock reached the corner fence first. A single cut from his carbon saw popped the chain-link gate from its latch.

Kael followed, stepping over a puddle of blood still glistening from the soldier's fall.

Inside the yard, the light was lower. The darkness deeper.

The black site was quieter than expected.

Too quiet.

They passed rows of rotting equipment, half-sunken in the muddy terrain. Two abandoned data vans sat side by side, their antennas snapped and hatches left open to the elements. A pair of scorched Dongfeng Mengshi armored vehicles came next, one still trailing a faint curl of smoke from beneath its hood. The tires had blown out, and the windshield was shattered inward. Farther down, a mobile medical unit stood with its doors ajar, the interior stripped bare. No movement. No personnel. Just the stale echo of something that had been evacuated in a hurry — or not at all.

Diesel fumes mingled with the stench of cordite and burning plastic. The metal tasted different here. Bitter.

Kael raised his fist.

Stop.

At the far end of the yard, a figure stepped from shadow — tall, lean, dressed in a stripped-down Chinese field uniform. No medals. No rank.

But unmistakable.

Colonel Sheng Wu.

Two guards flanked him. Neither moved.

Kael lifted his rifle — and froze.

This wasn't a long shot.

This was personal.

He slung the rifle across his back.

Dropped his shoulder pack.

Cracked his neck.

Wu smirked.

"Merida," he growled. "You cost me that city."

Kael didn't speak.

He just stepped forward, boots silent in the blood-wet dirt.

Wu unbuttoned his coat and let it fall.

Tension rippled through the air like static.

Then they ran at each other.

The clash was bone and fury.

Kael ducked a wild haymaker and drove his elbow into Wu's side. The Colonel responded with a snap kick to Kael's inner thigh that buckled his knee.

They twisted into the mud, fists landing like mallets.

Wu's strikes were clinical — military-grade, born of thousands of drills and reinforced with discipline.

Kael's were wild — feral, forged in Fallujah and Mosul, hardened in jails, alleys, and the back rooms of betrayal.

Blood spattered the yard.

Wu landed a clean hook across Kael's temple — it split the skin and sent Kael stumbling.

Kael surged forward and cracked his forehead into Wu's mouth.

Both men staggered.

But neither fell.

Elsewhere in the yard, the two guards raised rifles —

Too slow.

Grant Comstock opened fire.

Two bursts.

Two men dropped.

The third turned to run — Comstock clipped his leg and let him crawl.

He holstered his sidearm and leaned on the hood of a scorched truck, watching the brawl.

"You made it farther than I expected," Wu said in English, voice cold as stone. "But not far enough."

Kael didn't answer. He dropped his rifle, drew his fighting knife with one hand, and cracked his neck with the other. Wu smiled — slow, deliberate — then pulled off his jacket, revealing a sleeveless combat rig beneath. The scars on his forearms told their own stories.

They collided like war gods.

Kael struck first — a tight elbow-hook combination meant to break the jaw. Wu slipped the blow and countered with a spinning heel kick that smashed into Kael's ribs. The impact sent him staggering, but Kael recovered, surged forward, and tackled Wu into a portable air defense console. Wires snapped. Glass shattered. Sparks flew.

They grappled — elbows, knees, bone-on-bone — a brutal exchange with no finesse left, just pain and will.

Wu grabbed a loose cable and whipped it across Kael's back. Kael growled, headbutted Wu, then drove him backward toward a server rack. But Wu reversed, hooked Kael's leg, and slammed him to the ground with a judo throw.

Kael rolled, knife flashing, slicing Wu's thigh open — deep.

Wu hissed but didn't falter. He landed a punch to Kael's throat, followed by a brutal stomp to his chest. Kael wheezed, staggered to one knee — but it wasn't enough.

Wu grabbed him by the collar, lifted him halfway off the ground, and smashed him down on a metal grate. Kaels body echoed with steel and breathless pain.

Kael tried to rise.

Wu kicked the knife away and dropped to one knee, pinning Kael's arm beneath his knee and driving an elbow into his face — again. And again. Blood sprayed across the floor.

Breathing heavy, face flecked with crimson, Wu finally stood over him — towering, dominant.

"You're brave," he said in Mandarin. "But bravery is only useful… if you win."

Kael ducked Wu's next strike, spun, and slammed the Colonel into the side of an armored vehicle.

"I'm not here to kill you," Kael hissed, nose inches from Wu's bleeding face. "I'm here to break you."

Wu coughed blood and smiled. "Then you're already too late."

Kael struck again — a brutal elbow to the jaw, then a knee to Wu's ribs. Wu staggered, but countered like a serpent, snapping Kael's wrist and slamming him into a crate. The fight devolved into grapples and throat shots, each blow trading years of pain and memory.

"You don't get to walk away," Kael hissed, jamming his thumb into Wu's eye socket.

Wu roared — not in pain, but in rage. He snapped Kael's head back with a savage palm strike, then lifted him by the throat and slammed him against the wall so hard the concrete cracked.

Kael fell — knees first, then face-first. He tried to push himself up, but his body wouldn't answer.

Wu stepped over him slowly, breathing hard now, one hand dripping blood.

"You are not the storm," Wu said, his voice like thunder from a distant mountain. "You are the last gust of a dying age.

Wu stood over Kael's broken form, hands bloodied but steady, eyes burning like coals in the flickering ruin of the command center. Outside, distant explosions shook the night sky, but here — in the heart of the black site — time had stilled.

"You don't understand what's coming," Wu said, his voice low, reverent. "You think this is still about borders. About cartels. About flags. But that world is gone."

He stepped forward, placing one boot on Kael's chest, pressing just enough to draw a groan from deep inside him.

"I am the new covenant," Wu continued. "Not a tyrant… but a shepherd. This chaos — this blood and fire — it's birth, not death. We are delivering the world from its sickness."

He crouched, close enough that Kael could see the constellation of scars across Wu's jawline.

"Empires fall, soldier. You of all people should know that. America, China, Europe, Japan, Australia was a story. I'm what comes after."

Wu stood again, spine straight as a blade, looking not just at Kael, but through him — as if already seeing the next battlefield.

"You'll die with your myths," he whispered. "And I will rise with the future."

_____

Interior – Black Site, Corridor 3C

The violence outside felt miles away.

Inside the dim corridor, Marisol Cárdenas crouched behind a corner, listening to chaos.

Boots. Bursts. Shouts.

But underneath it all, something else:

A voice.

Not out loud. Not in the world.

Inside her.

His voice.

"Move."

She blinked. Looked down.

Still alone.

But she didn't hesitate.

She moved.

Hallways of the Dying Lab

Marisol Cárdenas moved like a shadow—lean, fast, silent. Her bare feet touched cracked tile like she belonged to the building.

The air inside the black site was different now. Not just smoke and blood and fire—though all those things lived here. Something else had arrived. Something electric.

Hope.

She kept the pistol low, sweeping corners like Kael had shown her. The hallway flickered under failing fluorescents, some blinking in agony, others dead altogether.

Trash fires burned from tipped-over file cabinets. Crumpled papers scattered like leaves in windless air. Wires sparked from the ceiling, some coiled like snakes above her head.

The building was gasping.

Dying.

She stepped over three bodies.

Marisol moved through the corridor like a phantom of war. Her bare feet made no sound against the cracked tile, and her pistol swept each corner with a practiced calm that only survival could teach.

The air was thick — not just with cordite and rot — but with something more: the scent of collapse.

This place was dying.

She moved through it all — steady, unflinching.

Three bodies blocked her path:

• One Chinese soldier, eyes wide, face frozen in fear

• One cartel shooter, mask split in half by shrapnel

• And one still alive, slumped against the wall

He groaned in Mandarin, clutching his abdomen. Blood bubbled through his shirt, his lips, his fingers. His eyes met hers.

There was no plea. Just acknowledgment.

She stepped over him.

Not out of cruelty.

Out of resolve.

This was no longer about vengeance.

It was about forward motion.

She turned the final corner.

And then — light.

A rush of damp air hit her like a memory.

She was in the loading bay.

Half the roof had collapsed. Smoke vented through the breach. The outside world waited just beyond a crumpled steel gate.

She saw movement — a scuffle. A blur.

Kael Torres, bloodied and battered, was on the ground.

Colonel Sheng Wu loomed over him, a combat blade in his hand, eyes lit with hatred.

Wu pinned Kael with a boot to the chest.

Kael fought to rise — muscles straining — but he was losing.

Wu raised the knife.

Marisol didn't hesitate.

She stepped into the opening, pistol already raised.

Her voice cracked the sky.

"LEAVE MY SEXICO ALONE!"

She fired.

The first three rounds shattered the silence, kicking up sparks and concrete near Kael's sprawled body. He flinched instinctively as rounds slammed into the ground beside him, dust erupting around his face.

The fourth and fifth tore past Colonel Wu's head — one grazing the edge of his jaw, the other whistling past his ear like a sonic dagger.

Wu turned sharply, eyes narrowing, just as the sixth through eleventh rounds tore through the air, each one fired in panic, not precision. But she was closing the distance — walking forward as if the act of firing could drown her fear.

The twelfth round hit the truck and shattered the windshield. The thirteenth hit the ground near Wu's boot.

The fourteenth cracked into a steel beam behind him.

The fifteenth — the final round — buried itself into his shoulder.

Wu staggered back with a grunt, gripping the wound. Blood seeped through his tactical uniform, dark and immediate. He locked eyes with Marisol, half in disbelief, half in fury.

stood there, empty pistol still aimed at his chest rising and falling like she might never breathe again.

Wu dropped his knife, spinning away from Kael. Wu hit the ground, rolled, then scrambled into the shadows beyond the bay.

Gone.

For now.

Marisol ran to Kael, dropped to her knees beside him.

He was breathing — barely — blood trickling down from his temple.

He looked up, eyes glassy, and smiled. "I'm okay," he muttered.

She cupped his face. Her palms were shaking, but her voice wasn't. "You better be. Because I am done watching this world tear itself apart."

Kael coughed and tried to sit up. "And you still shoot like a pirate."

She laughed through the tears. "Damn right."

She pressed her forehead to his.

"I thought I lost you."

"You didn't," he whispered. "You found me."

Dawn – Tampico in Ash and Silence

By morning, Tampico barely looked alive.

296

Smoke floated over rooftops like exhausted ghosts. Flames still licked the edges of old refineries and half-fallen church spires. The streets were slick with water, oil, and blood.

Bodies lay scattered in parking lots and intersections. Cárdenas, Cartel Nueve Vidas, Chinese soldiers. The city looked like it had tried to exhale and choked on the cost.

Gunfire still popped in the distance. But it was rare now. Controlled. Pockets of resistance folding in on themselves.

Men slumped against walls, sleeping with rifles in their arms like children clutching teddy bears.

A strange calm settled. Not peace.

Survival.

The Cárdenas flag flew again.

Men were returning.

Some in trucks. Some on foot.

Old sicarios, men thought dead, appeared from safehouses and tunnels. Locals waved them through. In a few corners, people wept when they saw the banner raised again.

The Tampico Expo Center became more than a command post.

It became a symbol.

A warning.

The cartel wasn't gone.

It had been reborn.

Across the scattered frequencies — rooftop radios, squad comms, old transistor bands — came a burst of static.

Then a voice.

Clear. Familiar. Strong.

Marisol Cárdenas.

"This is Marisol Cárdenas.

I'm alive."

That was all.

But it was enough.

Cárdenas fighters stood taller.

Others wept — or whispered her name like a benediction.

In one church, someone rang a bell.

The war wasn't over.

But something deeper had shifted.

The future had a voice now.

Rooftop – Plaza Hidalgo

High above, Natalia Ortega knelt beside a half-crushed HVAC vent, binoculars pressed to her face.

Beside her, Valeria lay flat on her stomach, her rifle resting across a broken pipe. Her thigh was wrapped tight with two layers of gauze and a makeshift tourniquet.

Around them lay a dozen enemy dead. Stripped of gear. Used for supplies.

"See anything?" Valeria asked.

"Smoke," Natalia muttered. "Not ours."

Valeria closed her eyes. "We held."

Natalia didn't respond for a long beat.

Then: "We did."

They had taken this rooftop twelve hours earlier. They had held it through the night. Through waves of enemy fire. Through snipers. Through mortars. Through silence.

Natalia looked toward the horizon, where the sun was trying to rise through smoke.

Valeria opened one eye. "They stopped firing."

Natalia sipped water. "That's a bad sign."

Valeria smirked. "Or it means we won."

"We'll know soon enough."

Now, they listened to the city's heart — and it still beat.

Tampico Expo – Rally Point

The Expo building stood tall again.

Scarred. But upright.

Cárdenas flags flew from the balconies. Crates of ammo were stacked against stairwells. Medics treated the wounded in repurposed conference rooms.

And something was changing.

Men were returning.

From safehouses. From caves. From memory.

Old sicarios emerged with grizzled beards and quiet stares. Former lieutenants who had disappeared months ago walked

in without a word. They didn't salute. They didn't ask questions.

They came home.

Comstock – Unknown

No one knew where Grant Comstock had gone.

Not Kael. Not Natalia. Not even the Cárdenas radio crews.

Some said he disappeared under a sewer grate. Others claimed they watched him walking across a rooftop in silhouette just before sunrise.

No one saw him leave.

But they all knew:

Wherever war was breaking — Comstock would be nearby.

Waiting.

Watching.

Whispering to the darkness.

_____

Safehouse – Fourth-Floor Office, East Sector

Kael and Marisol holed up in a former courier depot, now half-collapsed and soaked in the scent of ash and rust.

The fourth floor had once been an office. Now it was a fortress — windows shattered, the stairwell booby-trapped with a tripwire, a mattress dragged against the door.

There was an old breakroom fridge. Inside: a stale loaf of bread, three bottles of water, a jar of garlic olives and a package of questionable deli meat.

They took what they could.

Kael moved through the rest of the dimly lit office, HK416 tight in his grip, boots crunching over broken glass and discarded shell casings. The air smelled like dust, sweat, and stale electricity. A broken ceiling fan spun lazily above, clicking like a metronome for madness.

He crouched behind a desk marked with peeling labels in Spanish, opened the top drawer—nothing but old receipts. The second drawer stuck halfway, splintered from an earlier scuffle, but he forced it open with a grunt.

Inside: a half-drunk pint of Parrot Coconut Rum, beads of condensation still clinging to the bottle like it had been cracked open yesterday. Kael cocked his head. He grabbed it.

"The fuck?" he muttered, amused.

He checked the bottom drawer—seven mini bottles of Fireball Cinnamon Whisky rolled toward him like guilty little soldiers reporting for duty. He picked them all up, then glanced over at the blood-smeared whiteboard on the far wall, still listing shift rotations and satellite download codes.

"What kind of office was this?" Kael said aloud, chuckling to himself. "Cartel IT support with a drinking problem?"

Kael went back into the office Marisol was in, sat on the floor, back against the wall, gauze wrapped around his ribs. Blood still crusted his hairline. Marisol sat cross-legged beside him, a blanket over her shoulders, the pistol still tucked in her waistband like a declaration.

They didn't speak for a while.

Eventually, she looked up.

"You didn't come for me," she said.

Kael blinked, weary. "No?"

She shook her head.

"You came for us."

He smiled — slow, broken, but true.

He didn't need to reply.

The sun dipped low.

Tampico exhaled.

Fires still burned in gutters. Glass still cracked underfoot. But something had shifted in the city's rhythm. The chaos was no longer wild.

It was coiling.

Consolidating.

Enemy patrols still roamed. Chinese soldiers moved in pairs now — not squads. Some abandoned checkpoints altogether. Others went silent, as if they were unsure who was giving orders anymore.

Kael watched from the cracked window of the fourth-floor office. Marisol sat behind him, patching her arm with an old medkit.

He saw it in the movements — the hesitation.

"Wu's gone freelance," Kael muttered. "He's not reporting to command anymore."

Marisol didn't look up. "He's going cartel."

"Yeah." Kael's jaw tightened. "He's building something worse."

A new cartel.

With foreign funding.

With international muscle.

The flicker of a trashcan fire gave the room a dull gold glow.

They sat together on the floor, backs against a bullet-pocked filing cabinet, passing the bread, deli meat and garlic olives between them like a peace offering from a forgotten world. Kael pulled the pint of Parrot Coconut Rum from his vest and cracked the cap. Marisol toasted with one of the Fireball shots, tapping it lightly against the bottle.

"To surviving," she said.

"To you and the little one," Kael replied, nodding toward her stomach. His voice softened.

"You think the little one will have your fire or my bad habits?"

Marisol's smile deepened — warm, mischievous, and just a little bit nervous. She looked down, then back up at him.

"Little ones," she corrected softly.

Kael froze, bottle halfway to his lips. "Wait— what?"

She nodded, eyes glistening. "Twins. Found out right before I was taken from San Felipe. I didn't know how to tell you… not like this."

A wave passed over him — equal parts awe, fear, and something ancient and protective.

He set the bottle down slowly. "We're having twins."

She leaned in and rested her forehead against his. "Yeah, Kael. We're having twins."

Marisol rested her head against his shoulder, warm breath brushing his neck. "Hopefully neither. But if they get your eyes… they'll be dangerous."

Kael kissed the top of her head. "If we make it out of this, we're naming them something absurd. Like Rumball. Boy or girl."

She laughed. "Deal. But only if we don't die eating this questionable deli meat and olives."

They clinked bottle and of whiskey again, and in that moment—just for a heartbeat—the war faded outside the window. Inside, they were just two people trying to hold onto something real, something human.

Kael sat back on the couch, boots off, shirt undone, breath shallow.

Marisol sat beside him — legs tucked under her, arms crossed against the cold.

For the first time in days, there was no war between them.

No distance.

No secrets.

Just silence.

Kael reached for her hand. She gave it.

They didn't speak. They didn't need to.

He leaned in.

So did she.

The kiss was soft. Deep.

Earned.

They moved like they had once on a boat in St. Maarten — slow, reverent, lost in each other.

Clothes fell away. Wounds forgotten. Breath mingled with breath.

They moved together like ocean and storm — equal, chaotic, beautiful.

There was no war in that moment.

Just heat.

And gravity.

And a need that had never really left them.

It wasn't just sex — it was survival wrapped in sweat and skin. In the ruins of an office building, with tracer rounds flickering in the distance like dying stars, Kael and Marisol moved together like it was the last night they'd ever be alive. Her hands shook with adrenaline, his breath came in broken gasps — not from fear, but from needing her more than the next heartbeat. Explosions rumbled outside, but inside, their bodies clashed in a rhythm so primal it felt like war made them gods for a moment.

Making love in a war zone wasn't about tenderness. It was desperation and defiance — moaning against cracked concrete walls, trembling beneath the sound of chopper blades, biting lips not to cry out too loud. It was erotic in a way nothing else could be — viral, electric, dangerous. Two orgasmic souls intertwined like the world was ending, because maybe it was. And if it did, at least they would've gone out inside each other.

Kael felt her body beneath his like gravity had a name — Marisol. The heat of her skin made him forget the blood on his hands, the bone-deep exhaustion, the men he'd killed just hours ago. Every time her hips met his, it was like pulling himself out of a grave. He gripped her like she was the last real thing left in a collapsing world. If I die tomorrow, he thought, at least I died inside heaven.

Marisol's thoughts were less rational — more feral. The crack of gunfire in the distance, the scent of oil and sweat, the tension in Kael's jaw when he looked down at her — all of it fed something she didn't know she'd buried. This is what it means to be alive, she realized, nails digging into his back. To be wanted even when the world is burning. She bit his shoulder, not gently, and felt him groan low in his throat. It wasn't about dominance. It was about being chosen, even here, even now.

Outside, the war screamed. Inside, they moved like no one was watching — like the walls themselves were afraid to interrupt. Every thrust, every breath, every muffled cry was a rebellion against death. They didn't just come together to feel good.

They collided and made love to remember they were alive.

Gunfire crackled in the distance.

A mortar landed somewhere west, its thunder swallowed by buildings.

Kael didn't flinch.

Neither did Marisol.

She lay against him, skin warm, head on his chest. His arm around her shoulders.

The fire popped once.

Then again.

They didn't move.

They were still alive.

They were still together.

For now — that was enough.

She whispered:

"We can only be one now… or none."

Kael kissed the crown of her head.

"My SEXICO."

They stayed like that.

And when Kael finally spoke again, it was with a softness rarely heard from men like him:

"Get some sleep, love. We need to move soon."

Outside, the city waited.

Inside, they breathed.

And in the silence between those breaths, something deeper than war began to stir.

Something like a future

Chapter 24

Blood and Asphalt

Just past midnight, after a few restless hours of sleep on a couch beside a dying trash can fire, Kael and Marisol decided to move.

They were on the fourth floor of an abandoned office building, the kind that might've once housed insurance brokers, a courier depot or tech startups, now gutted and ghosted by war. Earlier that night, they had curled up on a lopsided leather couch, drinking whatever they could find—half a pint of Parrot Bay coconut rum and seven mini bottles of Fireball cinnamon whiskey pulled from an office drawer Kael had laughed at like it was a joke only the apocalypse could deliver.

The buzz had faded into a slow ache behind their eyes, but the warmth it gave—and the memory of tangled limbs and whispered laughter in the dark— lingered. The couch reeked of mildew. The windows were barricaded with file cabinets and shredded blinds. But for a few hours, it had felt like a kind of refuge.

Kael stretched his back and looked toward the stairwell. The air was thick with dust and diesel. Somewhere in the distance, something exploded—too far to matter yet, but close enough to quicken the pulse.

He glanced at Marisol. "Ready?"

She tightened her ponytail and nodded. "Let's go before the city remembers we're still alive."

The streets outside were alive with shadows and death. Tracer fire painted red and green streaks across the sky, like a twisted fireworks display for a country tearing itself apart. Sirens cried in the distance, followed by muffled booms that trembled in the soles of their feet.

They moved slowly. Controlled. Breathing shallow, sweat pouring down their faces in the thick heat of the Mexican summer. Kael's shirt clung to him like a wetsuit. Marisol's hair was damp, matted to her face, but her eyes were locked forward—focused, determined.

As they stepped out into the shattered street, the silence was heavy, broken only by the distant crackle of gunfire and the buzz of flies. They moved quickly, boots crunching over broken glass and shell casings, eyes scanning for movement. One by one, they began stripping weapons and tactical gear off the fallen—friend and foe alike. Bloodied vests, loaded mags, sidearms still warm. In war, morality came second to survival.

A block away, gunfire intensified. They rounded a corner—and froze.

The intersection ahead was a war zone. Chinese defectors and cartel sicarios were locked in an all-out firefight, using burning vehicles and fallen debris as cover. Smoke coiled upward in ghostly streams. In the middle of the chaos stood Colonel Sheng Wu, shouting commands like a general from a lost empire.

Wu's unit—no longer loyal to Beijing—now bore hybrid patches: a crimson serpent coiled around a golden cross and Chinese star. His alliance with the Cartel Nueve Vidas was official.

But facing him—Major Lee Ho, lean and unflinching, rallied the loyalist forces trying to reestablish order.

A civil war within a foreign army, playing out on Mexican soil.

Kael cursed under his breath.

Wu's eyes swept the dark—and locked on Kael and Marisol.

"There!" he roared. "Alive! I want the girl intact!"

Twenty men broke off. Tactical gear, laser sights. Running straight at them.

Kael grabbed Marisol's hand. "Run."

They bolted.

Bullets sliced past. Brick dust filled the air. A fruit stand exploded behind them, oranges bouncing into the street like shrapnel. Kael pulled her into a half-collapsed Pemex gas station, ducking under twisted metal and shattered glass.

Inside, everything reeked of oil, blood, and rot. An overhead bulb flickered like a dying heartbeat. Metal shelves lay overturned; bags of chips and candy scattered across the floor like forgotten offerings.

Kael checked his mag. Fifteen rounds. Marisol crouched behind the rusted coffee machine, Glock ready.

Boots. Outside.

Dozens.

No exit. No backup.

Kael moved beside her, close enough to feel her breath on his neck. He touched her shoulder. She turned.

"We stand. Back-to-back," he said.

She nodded.

"I love you," she whispered. "In case we don't walk out."

Kael's jaw clenched. "Then let's make damn sure we do."

The first wave poured in.

Screams. Muzzle flashes. Chaos.

Kael dropped the first two. Marisol took a shot to the chest plate but didn't flinch—she kept firing, pivoting with him.

Back-to-back.

Bullets danced around them. Glass shattered. A grenade clinked to the floor—Kael spotted it, kicked it under a checkout counter.

Boom.

The blast blew half the wall open. Smoke poured in.

A cartel soldier rushed through the haze—Kael put a round through his eye. Marisol dove left, rolled, and came up shooting. Another man fell.

Kael took a shot to the ribs. The vest stopped it—but it knocked him sideways. He stumbled, caught himself, and rose again, blood on his lip.

"Kael!" Marisol shouted, fear in her voice.

"I'm good," he grunted. "Keep firing!"

Kael yanked spare magazines from the pouches on his vest, the Velcro tearing loud in the night. He slammed one into his rifle, checked the chamber, then passed two to Marisol without hesitation.

She reloaded with smooth precision, her hands steady, eyes scanning the shadows. Beside the bodies, they worked in rhythm—loading, locking, breathing—readying themselves for whatever came next.

More enemies spilled in. One screamed a prayer as he charged. Marisol dropped him with a double-tap.

They kept spinning. Firing. Fighting.

Until it was quiet.

Only the hiss of a leaking gas line. The drip-drip-drip of blood onto tile. The static crackle of a radio no one would answer.

Kael leaned against a support beam, chest heaving. Marisol stood barefoot now—her sandals lost in the chaos—blood splattered on her thigh, face streaked with sweat and ash.

She limped toward him. Her eyes scanned his vest. A dent over his ribs—charred, but not pierced.

"You okay?" she asked.

He nodded slowly. "Armor held." " Go grab those boots off that dead solider."

" In a minute Marisol replied."

She pressed her forehead to his chest, letting her breath slow.

Then her eyes caught something scrawled across the far wall, barely visible under soot and bullet holes:

"EL JUICIO VIENE." Judgment is coming.

She pointed. "What does that mean?"

Kael looked at the bodies, the blood, the shattered fragments of the world around them.

He said, "It means we keep moving."

They exited through the back that had been blown open during the firefight, down a ruined alley and toward the canal. Up ahead, the glow of muzzle flashes flickered like fireflies—Major Lee Ho's loyalists pushing back against Wu's traitor regiment.

Kael spotted a break in the fence. A concrete drainage ditch led toward the old sewer tunnels.

"We take the tunnels," Kael said. "Bridge is too exposed."

Marisol nodded, already moving.

They dropped in, boots splashing through warm, fetid water. Rats scattered ahead of them. The air was thick with rot and mold, every breath a challenge. Somewhere deeper inside, water echoed in rhythmic drops, like the ticking of some underground clock. Kael swept the tunnel ahead with his tac light, the beam slicing through shadow, catching glimpses of graffiti, bone-white roots, and spent shell casings.

Behind them, Marisol adjusted her rifle and kept pace, the fatigue buried beneath adrenaline. Neither spoke—they didn't have to. The mission had shifted from extraction to survival.

They emerged near the far end of the canal, just beyond a sloping concrete spillway half-choked with debris and ash. The night above had not calmed— tracer fire cut across the sky like red comets, and the distant pop of mortars thudded in their chests. They kept low, weaving through the charred skeletons of buildings and overturned cars, trying to stay in the seams of darkness.

A squad of enemy fighters sprinted across an adjacent lot. Kael motioned Marisol down, waited until the danger passed, then moved again. Gunfire cracked behind them. They didn't stop.

They were 2 miles from the Expo when headlights burst over the ridge—too fast, too low. Kael raised his rifle, but the truck swerved and braked hard in front of them.

"¡Torres!" someone shouted.

Lieutenant Sosa leaned out the window of a dust-covered pickup, eyes wide with disbelief. "Get in!"

Without hesitation, Kael and Marisol vaulted into the bed of the truck. The engine roared and tires kicked gravel as the truck peeled off toward the Expo. Marisol held the side rail with one hand, her other still gripping her rifle. Kael crouched beside her, keeping watch as buildings-streaked past in a blur of flame and chaos.

The truck roared down a narrow avenue lined with the skeletal remains of office buildings. Every few blocks, flames danced in shattered windows, casting flickering shadows across walls riddled with bullet holes. Civilian cars, long abandoned, had been turned into makeshift barricades.

Kael sat in the bed of the truck, one arm around Marisol, the other gripping his HK. His ribs ached beneath the plate that had saved his life. Sweat stung the cut above his brow.

Sosa drove like the devil was on their tail.

"We're riding through El Cobre sector," he yelled over the engine. "Wu's defectors pulled back last night, but Nueve Vidas still has snipers and drones in the area."

As if on cue, a crack! echoed from a rooftop. A bullet pinged off the side mirror.

"Shit!" Sosa shouted, jerking the wheel.

Kael stood, braced against the roll bar. "Second story, green building, east corner. Move!"

He lifted the rifle. One clean shot. The sniper fell back through a broken window.

The truck jolted forward. Another shot rang out—this time from the front. Marisol ducked instinctively.

"Roadblock ahead!" Sosa barked.

A cartel technical—flatbed pickup with a mounted machine gun—sat crooked across the avenue. Two men jumped out and opened fire. The windshield spiderwebbed instantly.

Kael didn't hesitate.

He climbed to the roof of the cab, bracing as the truck skidded sideways. He fired three controlled bursts—two rounds tore into one gunman's chest, the third clipped the other's leg. Marisol, crouched beside Sosa, fired through the shattered windshield to finish him.

They blew past the wreck, tires screeching.

Behind them, a rocket slammed into a wall, throwing up a plume of dust and flame. The concussion rocked the truck. Kael held on, teeth gritted.

"We've got five more blocks to the Expo Center," Sosa shouted.

Kael dropped back into the bed and locked eyes with Marisol.

"You good?"

She nodded, eyes hard. "I'm with you."

Six blocks away, atop a five-story office complex riddled with shrapnel scars, Natalia and Valeria lay prone behind a concrete parapet.

Natalia scanned the chaos through a thermal scope. "That's them," she muttered. "Sosa's truck just cleared El Cobre."

Valeria shouldered a scoped Galil. "Visual?"

"Eastbound, heading for the safehouse."

Below them, cartel scouts moved in the alleys like wolves. A trio of silhouettes moved toward the intersection—one carrying a shoulder-fired rocket.

Natalia locked on with her suppressed rifle. "Not tonight."

She exhaled.

Thud. Thud. Thud.

Three bodies dropped in perfect sequence.

Valeria didn't speak. She was watching Kael's truck now—eyes tracking every twitch, every potential ambush point.

Natalia stole a glance at her.

"You okay?"

Valeria smirked faintly. "You ask me that after every firefight."

"I'm not asking about the fight."

Valeria lowered her rifle. For a brief second, her fingers brushed Natalia's gloved hand.

"After this," Valeria whispered, "if we make it out—promise me we go back to the farm. Just for one day."

Natalia didn't answer.

She just kissed her—quick, fierce, and wordless—then picked up her rifle again.

"They're clear. Let's move."

Two miles blurred into two minutes. As they approached the main gate of the Expo Center, floodlights flared on. The Cárdenas banner flapped against a scaffold overhead, and the battered gate was held by armed fighters—loyalists, alive and holding. The pickup screeched to a halt inside the barricade.

Before the truck even stopped, Salvador Cárdenas was already running toward them—Goya on his heels.

"¡Marisol!" he shouted.

She jumped down before the wheels fully stopped, and her father caught her in a crushing embrace. For a second, the war vanished. There was only the sound of a father's breath hitching, the fierce grip of a man who thought he had lost everything.

Kael dropped from the bed and nodded to Goya, who pulled him into a quick hug, then grinned. "Took you long enough."

Word spread fast. Fighters emerged from tents and rooftop posts, pouring toward the truck like survivors greeting legends. There were tears, claps on the back, the chaotic sound of laughter rising against a backdrop of burning sky.

Marisol stood in the center of it all, dust-streaked, blood on her collar, hair wild—alive.

Kael just watched her from a few steps back, the rifle still slung, heart still pacing like it hadn't caught up to the moment.

She turned, met his eyes, and walked over. Slowly. Purposefully.

Then she kissed him—hard, full of fire, full of everything they'd survived.

The war wasn't over.

But they were home.

The rooftop had gone still. Natalia exhaled slowly, her rifle across her knees, eyes scanning the streets below. Smoke curled into the night like black silk, rising from broken buildings and burning cars. Her hair was damp with sweat and grime, matted to her forehead. Valeria sat beside her, her thigh pressed lightly against Natalia's. The rooftop had been theirs for hours—their perch of survival, their last vantage point over the battlefield.

But now… it was time to move.

"Two mags left," Natalia muttered, checking her vest.

"One and a half," Valeria replied, holding up a cracked clip, then snapping it into her weapon with a practiced click. "We won't make it far like this."

"We don't have to," Natalia said, rising to a crouch. "Just far enough."

They exchanged a look. That rare, quiet kind—more than sisters-in-arms, more than lovers in a war zone. A bond forged in blood, fire, and the silent promises made between kills.

As they stepped out of the office, the stairwell reeked of dust, cordite, and mildew. Descending in silence, they passed bodies scattered across the lower levels—some Cárdenas, some rival cartel, some barely recognizable. Before hitting the street, they paused to search the dead.

Natalia knelt beside a collapsed soldier slumped against the wall, peeling back a flak vest crusted with blood. She found two loaded pistol mags and four rifle magazines. Valeria checked another—nothing but a shattered radio and an empty holster.

"Scraps," Natalia muttered.

"Still counts," Valeria said, sliding a mag into her thigh rig.

They exchanged a glance, weapons checked nerves taut. Then they stepped into the night—and into hell.

Climbing down a shattered stairwell, they hit the street and headed west, toward the distant Expo Center. No time for stealth. The firefight had shifted northeast, but random bursts of gunfire still crackled in every direction. They jogged low past hollowed storefronts and burned-out sedans, ducking behind dumpsters and walls when necessary.

Halfway down Calle 23, a group of rival cartel soldiers emerged from an alley—five men in mismatched body armor, weapons raised.

"¡Mierda!" Valeria hissed.

Natalia opened fire first, her rounds thudding into two of them before they hit the ground. Valeria followed up with a grenade she'd found earlier—it skipped once on the asphalt, then detonated, sending shrapnel and fire into the rest.

They ran, hearts pounding. Footsteps behind them. Shouting.

Rounds zipped past their heads, slamming into walls and light poles. Natalia turned on instinct, dumped her last full mag into the shadows, then ducked into a narrow gap between two buildings. Valeria followed, panting.

"We're almost dry!" Valeria yelled.

"I know."

They reached a burned-out van and dropped behind it. Natalia checked her pockets. One mag. Six pistol rounds. Two knives.

Valeria looked over at her, eyes wide, lips parted as if she wanted to say something... but didn't.

"Don't do that," Natalia whispered. "Not here."

"We may not get another chance."

"You always say that."

"Because it's always true."

Natalia looked away, then back again, her voice softer now. "We'll make it. We always do."

Valeria leaned in, pressed her forehead to Natalia's. "But if we don't... I want you to know something."

Natalia's breath caught.

"I love you," Valeria said. "Not just in the way we survive together. Not just in the mission. You are... the only peace I've ever known."

Tears welled in Natalia's eyes before she could stop them. She smiled—broken, bloody, real. "Then you better live, cariño. So, I can hear that again somewhere with clean sheets and no mortars."

They kissed. Fierce and desperate and full of everything they couldn't say.

Then footsteps thundered from behind.

"¡FUEGO!"

The street lit up as a hail of bullets cut through the pursuing enemy.

Padre Luis came into view, rifle in hand, cassock flapping behind a tactical vest. Four trucks skidded to a halt behind him, Cárdenas fighters jumping out, weapons blazing.

"¡VAMOS!" he shouted. "Get them out of here!"

Natalia and Valeria were already moving. Two fighters lifted them by their arms and shoved them into the bed of a truck. Padre Luis jumped in beside them, laying suppressive fire with a rifle, using it like he was giving a sermon as the convoy peeled away.

Behind them, the street dissolved into fire and fury. Screams echoed, enemies scattered, and the Cárdenas loyalists surged forward like a tide reclaiming the broken city.

The Expo Center loomed ahead like a fortress—battered but holding, lit by floodlights and fires. As the convoy rolled in through the front gate, fighters ran alongside, cheering.

Kael was already there. So was Marisol. Goya. Leandro. Sosa. Dozens of familiar faces.

The truck stopped and Natalia jumped down, barely landing before she was surrounded. Valeria stumbled after her, limping from a graze she hadn't mentioned.

Kael hugged them both. Goya clapped them on the back. Marisol stepped in, tears in her eyes, and hugged Valeria like a sister.

"You made it," she whispered.

Natalia just nodded, too tired to speak.

The chaos blurred. Arms guided them toward water, medical kits, a cot near the rear of the building.

The Expo Center pulsed with a strange combination of grief and victory.

Valeria sat beside Natalia and leaned her head on her shoulder.

"We made it," she murmured.

Natalia touched her face. "We always do."

Outside, the night raged on.

But for now—just for now—they were safe as well.

CHAPTER 25

The Serpent's Nest

The marina lay still beneath a sky veiled in war smoke and salt. The moon had long since disappeared behind a gauze of clouds, and only the dim glint of navigation lights flickered like static over black water.

A warm wind pressed off the Gulf, rustling mooring lines and tugging at the Cárdenas flags flanking the docked vessels. Even the water held its breath.

On the edge of the longest pier — where Cárdenas cartel boats sat in loose formation — Grant Comstock stood aboard one of the SURCs: a Small Unit Riverine Craft that had days ago shredded Chinese mortar nests with .50 caliber and grenade fire.

Now it sat silent — a sleeping monster.

Comstock leaned against the turret mount, helmet tucked under one arm, satellite phone pressed to his ear. His voice was low, clipped, and focused.

"I'm telling you, it's bigger than we thought," he said.

"Wu's not just a rogue colonel anymore. He's building something."

Wind tugged at his collar, the lines on his face sharp in the dim blue light.

"He's got Cartel Nueve Vidas behind him. El Filo de Dios too, at least in part. But they're not cartels anymore. They're zealots with a global supply chain. He's fusing warlord ideology with drug logistics — and he's got the money to do it."

He paused, listening as static cracked across the encrypted channel. A gull screamed overhead and vanished into the fog.

"It's worse than a cartel," he continued.

"It's a hybrid. A sovereign paramilitary state — Chinese logistics, Mexican corruption, and black-market capital. And I don't think Beijing is unified anymore. Some of these PLA units are breaking off. Freelancing. Selling themselves to the highest bidder. Wu is just the first."

His jaw clenched as he spoke. He wasn't speculating. He was warning.

Out in the dark, a shadow shifted across the water — large, low, deliberate.

Comstock's eyes tracked it without blinking.

"In the last forty-eight hours I've counted three Y-20 heavies and four Y-9 tactical birds landing at the Tampico Airport. They're not stopping. Troops. Comms vans. Drone command modules. Satellite dishes big enough to cook a cow. I even spotted two containerized power units running silent ops on borrowed gridlines. It's growing."

A beat of silence. Then a reply — muffled, clipped, urgent.

Comstock's expression didn't change. But his tone did.

Colder.

"Copy. Understood. Returning to platform."

He clicked off the phone, slid it into a waterproof pouch, and sealed the Velcro flap.

A US Naval officer stepped into view from the deck ladder below.

"Sir?"

Comstock turned, eyes scanning the bay.

"Prep my gear," he ordered. "I've been called back to the USS Portland — LPD 27. She's loitering forty miles out. We will rearm, resupply, and pick up the rest of the hardware."

The officer hesitated. "What hardware?"

Comstock's mouth curled just slightly at the corner.

"Enough to break the spine of a false empire."

He stepped down from the turret deck, boots thudding against steel, and moved toward a waiting command jeep parked near the fuel station.

Behind him, the SURC's mounted weapons gleamed under the flicker of moonlight:

• GAU-19 .50 cal Gatling — heat-scored from the last mission

• Mk 19 grenade launcher — oiled and reloaded

• 75mm recoilless rifle — its blast plate tightened with new bolts

It wasn't just a boat.

It was a promise.

───────────────

Back at the Expo Grounds, a quiet fell over the group—not heavy, but reverent. The kind that settles over warriors when something deeper than victory is spoken aloud.

Goya stepped forward, raising his glass high. A salute to the man who brought her back. To Kael Torres. The man who walked through fire and didn't blink. You saved the boss's daughter, hermano." A chorus of nods followed—glasses lifted, a few claps on the back, even from Sosa, who rarely showed emotion.

But Marisol raised her hand, steady and unshaking. "No," she said. "That's not what happened."

The group quieted.

"I saved myself," she continued. "Back at the hospital when they came for me—Wu's men—I didn't scream or run. She paused; eyes fixed on the fire. "Then a guard came in. I thought he was going to kill me. But before he could even speak, he dropped— three shots in the back. Someone had taken him out."

The group leaned in, silent.

"I crawled to his body, grabbed his sidearm, and shot the chain off my wrist. I snuck out through

321

the side hall, found a fire escape, and made it to the street."

She looked around the circle, gaze unflinching.

She paused, eyes scanning the firelight around them. "And when I made it outside, Kael was down. Wu was standing over him, gun in hand. I didn't hesitate. I emptied the clip. I didn't stop shooting until he stumbled and ran off."

Natalia stepped forward. "You... killed?"

Marisol nodded once.

"Yes when I was at the hospital when they took me."

"It cost me something," she said. "But it gave me something else."

Her voice didn't tremble. She didn't ask for their approval.

They looked at her not with judgment—but with quiet recognition. That was the price. And she had paid for it.

Goya's mouth opened but no words came.

Valeria blinked slowly.

Sosa looked away.

Even Salvador tensed.

Silence rippled through the group— deeper than respect. Awe.

Valeria gave a low whistle. Natalia just nodded, as if she'd known it all along.

Valeria stepped forward, her arms crossed.

"You held your ground."

Marisol nodded.

"I didn't want to. I was shaking so badly I could barely breathe. But I heard his voice. I remembered his hands on mine, showing me how to line up a shot. And I thought—if I don't fight for myself, who will?"

Kael looked at her, jaw tense, then down at the fire. The flicker lit up the bruises on his cheek, the dried blood on his collar. He didn't say a word.

Salvador's expression shifted—half pride, half something deeper. A father seeing a different daughter than the one who left. One who had crossed some line that could never be uncrossed.

"She's Cárdenas now,"

Goya said under his breath.

"All the way through."

Natalia raised her glass again.

"To those who fought for her—and to the woman who fought her way back."

They drank again.

A slow wind passed through the compound, stirring ash and heat, tugging at tarps and ammo belts. In the distance, dogs barked, and the low rumble of distant explosions reminded everyone that this was only one night in a long war. But it was their night.

Cárdenas broke the silence once again.

"Tomorrow, we fortify. We'll need new routes, intel, water lines—" He stopped mid-sentence, then turned back to Marisol.

"But tonight… you rest. You've earned it."

Marisol glanced at Kael again.

"All of us have."

Kael didn't speak. He just reached out and took her hand.

Natalia and Valeria exchanged a look—one of recognition, not just of love, but of shared damage. Of survival.

Goya blew out a long sigh, then smiled and slapped Sosa on the back.

"We live another day."

Padre Luis wandered up from the side lot, a rifle slung across his chest and a cigarette burning low between his fingers.

"Someone say 'amen' to that."

A few chuckles rolled through the group, light, grateful. For a moment, they weren't just sicarios or soldiers or ghosts of a broken war—they were people again.

Cárdenas broke the silence.

"We've taken most of the city. But the airport is still under foreign control," he said.

"Chinese rogue units are landing every night— Wu's last supply lines."

Natalia's eyes narrowed.

"Then we hit it next."

Kael stood.

"We'll need recon. Fast, quiet."

"I'm coming,"

Marisol said immediately.

Cárdenas turned sharply.

"You're not leaving my sight again."

His voice wasn't angry—it was broken. He had nearly lost her once. He wouldn't risk it again.

Marisol didn't argue.

Kael, Natalia, and Valeria exchanged looks.

"We'll go," Kael said.

"We're used to darkness," Valeria added.

Natalia gave a small smirk.

"We're war dogs, remember?"

Kael chuckled. "It's time to stop being dogs. You should take the Commodore. Sail out. Find something else."

Natalia and Valeria exchanged a long glance. A smile passed between them—intimate, private.

"Maybe someday," Natalia said.

"But not until we finish what we started," Valeria added.

───────────────

Hours later, the three of them moved like phantoms through the ruins on the edge of General Francisco Javier Mina Airport.

The city gave way to cracked tarmac and hangars lit in red from emergency backup power. Chinese patrols moved with robotic precision, rifles at the ready. An air traffic tower flickered in the dark like a broken tooth.

Kael crouched behind a downed bus, watching the rotation pattern of a PLA security units.

Natalia unslung her suppressed rifle.

Valeria adjusted her earpiece.

Kael whispered,

"We go quiet. In and out. No mess unless it finds us first."

Then they disappeared into the night.

The wind hissed low across the broken tarmac as Kael, Natalia, and Valeria crept along the eastern fence line, slipping through a gap cut into the razor wire hours earlier by Cárdenas scouts. Motionless. Silent. Shadows in the shadow of war.

They moved in a triangle formation—Kael forward, Natalia flanking left, Valeria rear right—keeping tight to the exterior wall of a crumbling hangar. A spotlight swept overhead. They dropped flat, hearts thudding, breath slow.

A pair of Chinese guards, barely out of their twenties, stepped around the corner—laughing in low Mandarin.

Kael signaled. Three fingers. Then two. Then one. He rose.

The blade slipped between the first man's ribs before the guard even had time to gasp. Natalia swept in behind him, covering the second man's mouth as Valeria slit his throat clean. Both bodies dropped silently.

No gunfire. No alarms.

They slipped into the first warehouse. The interior was vast—high ceilings, stacked pallets, the chemical stink of narcotics strong enough to burn the eyes. Rows upon rows of vacuum-sealed cocaine bricks, fentanyl capsules, and Veloxyn crates rose to the roof.

Natalia scanned with infrared.

"This isn't just product," she whispered.

"This is inventory for a new empire."

In the far corner, a group of PLA troops in partial body armor loaded supplies into a heavy transport truck. Then a familiar voice echoed through the warehouse.

"Double the loadouts. Priority on Zone Delta. Wu's men are overrunning the north perimeter."

They ducked behind a forklift and peered through a cracked plexiglass panel. Major Lee Ho stood near the rear exit, flanked by two aides and six armed soldiers. He was younger than Kael had expected—maybe early 40s—but his posture was pure command. Cold. Precise. Focused. He barked in Mandarin, gesturing toward the runway. Off in the distance, the pop-pop-pop of distant gunfire rolled through the night.

Wu's men were fighting Lee Ho's forces.

"They're eating each other alive,"
Valeria whispered.

"And the winner gets Tampico,"
Kael muttered.

Then they saw it. Beyond the storage crates, another group of troops unloaded something from a black cargo container. Metal clanked. Hydraulic gears hissed. Exoskeleton rigs. Kael's eyes narrowed. Each frame was built to support a human body—amplifying strength, speed, and endurance. Soldiers in the suits were lifting crates three times their weight and testing mounted weapon arms.

Even worse—robotic quadrupeds stood in rows along the wall. Like dogs—but wrong. Their limbs were made for speed. Their backs bore mounted machine guns and multi-spectral cameras.

Valeria whispered,

"They're not just arming soldiers. They're building supers."

Kael clenched his jaw.

"They're prepping for something big."

Natalia turned.

"We need to go."

They slipped out a side loading bay, careful not to trip motion sensors. Back through the fence. Back through the rubble. By the time the sun began to rise, they were back at Cárdenas HQ—filthy, adrenaline-drenched, and burning with urgency. Kael grabbed the encrypted field radio.

"Get me Comstock. Now."

Kael stormed through the outer corridor of the expo compound, boots echoing off concrete. His face was drawn, jaw locked, eyes scanning the sky above as if waiting for it to catch fire. He raised the encrypted field radio and keyed in Comstock's signal.

"Hellpack One, this is Cárdenas Command. Do you copy?"

Before the static could break, Salvador Cárdenas approached from the shadows near a broken column, drink in hand.

"Wait," he said. His voice wasn't calm—it was coiled.

Kael lowered the radio slightly. Cárdenas took one last swig and hurled the glass against the ground. It shattered, mezcal soaking the dirt.

"They've got my city's airport," he growled. "They're flying out my product. Fentanyl. Veloxyn. Cocaine. Billions of dollars worth of empire built over decades… slipping away on every landing gear."

He turned toward the others. His eyes were fire.

"It would take us years to rebuild what's in those warehouses. Years of risk. Years of blood."

He pointed toward the north.

"We take the airport. Tonight. We end this."

Kael met his eyes.

"Then let me finish the call."

He brought the radio to his mouth again.

"Hellpack One, we have visuals. The airport is hot—exosuits, robot dogs, heavy narcotics, and weapons inventory. Major Lee Ho is on-site. Wu's forces are fighting him north of the tarmac."

A pause.

Then Comstock's voice crackled through, calm and ice-cold.

"Don't you worry, Kael. I'm on my way. Riverine boats are loaded. And I brought some… extras."

Kael almost smiled—but didn't.

As he lowered the radio, he felt Marisol's arms wrap gently around him from behind, her chest pressed to his back.

"Don't go," she whispered. Her voice was soft. Breaking.

"You don't have to be the one."

Kael reached up and touched her forearm. Just once.

"I already am."

From behind them, Salvador Cárdenas stepped forward.

"You've done enough," he said. "I'm ordering you to stand down."

Kael turned, calm but unyielding.

"I can't. If Comstock's coming in, I'm the only one who can get him in—and out."

Silence fell over the courtyard again. Then Cárdenas looked at his daughter. He saw it in her eyes: the grief, the pride, the love. He gave a single nod.

"Then don't fail."

Kael's voice was steady.

"I won't."

Later that morning, the compound stirred with a different energy—less celebratory, more alert. The scent of coffee mingled with burnt concrete. Outside,

Cárdenas fighters reorganized sandbags and patched bullet holes. But inside the central briefing room of the Expo Center, Salvador Cárdenas had already assembled a tighter circle.

Kael, Marisol, Natalia, Valeria, and Padre Luis gathered at his call. The door was shut behind them. Goya stood watch outside, arms folded.

Salvador lit a cigarette, then stamped it out almost immediately.

"There's something we need to retrieve," he said. "Before someone else does."

He opened a steel case on the table—inside, a partial schematic of the San Felipe de los Monte's hospital. He pointed to a wing not marked on the standard blueprints.

"West wing. Sublevel three. Not open to patients. Not even the regular staff. It was sealed under emergency protocols after the Chinese raid."

"What's down there?" Kael asked, eyes narrowing.

"Data," Salvador replied.

"Research protocols, chemical samples, encrypted drives tied to Veloxyn's secondary synthesis pathway."

Marisol blinked.

"I didn't even know there was a sublevel three."

"You weren't supposed to," Salvador said.

"Only two scientists and my late consigliere knew about it. The rest was compartmentalized."

Natalia folded her arms.

"And you think the Chinese haven't found it yet?"

"I don't know," he said, grim.

"But I doubt they know what they're looking for. The lab door is triple-sealed. You'll need this."

He slid a biometric key, shaped like a thumb drive, across the table.

Padre Luis picked it up and turned it over.

"Are going in quiet or loud?"

"Quiet. If they haven't found it, you don't want to lead them there."

Valeria spoke up.

"And if they have?"

Kael answered before Salvador could.

"Then we go loud."

Salvador nodded.

"Get what you can. Files. Drives. Chemicals. If the Chinese or Nueve Vidas get that synthesis data… Veloxyn won't just be a cartel asset anymore. It'll be theirs. And that can't happen."

Marisol looked toward the hospital's direction—still scarred on the horizon.

"Then we go now," she said.

And no one disagreed.

They left within the hour.

Kael drove a battered armored SUV while Natalia rode shotgun, scanning the broken streets with her rifle across her lap. Marisol, Valeria, and Padre Luis sat in the back, gear loaded, tension thick. The city was quieter than usual, but not still—distant gunfire echoed sporadically, and the occasional plume of smoke reminded them they weren't alone in the ruins.

The hospital loomed ahead like a haunted skeleton. Its northern facade had collapsed, exposing rebar and cracked tile. The main lobby was empty— ransacked and scorched. Kael parked behind the emergency wing, near an access hatch half-covered in rubble.

"Back entrance," Padre Luis said, pointing.

"Leads to service corridors."

They moved in fast, flashlights flickering as they passed overturned gurneys and scorched stretchers. Blood stains still marked the floors. Marisol's pulse quickened as they passed the maternity

330

ward—memories flashing like gunshots—but she pushed them aside.

Sublevel access was tucked behind a supply room. Kael moved a collapsed metal shelf, revealing a steel-reinforced door with no visible handle.

"This is it," Marisol said quietly.

Padre Luis inserted the biometric key. A soft click. Then another. The door hissed open—air pressure equalizing—and the smell of antiseptic and chemical solvents spilled out.

They descended a tight stairwell to Sublevel Three, with weapons raised. The hallways below were pristine but dark, illuminated only by backup LEDs pulsing low along the walls.

"Jesus," Valeria whispered. "This place looks untouched."

"Which means we're not the first ones here," Natalia said.

As if on cue, a faint noise echoed from down the hall—metal clinking against tile.

Kael signaled them to split—he and Marisol veered left, while the others flanked right.

The lab door appeared ahead: triple-sealed, as Cárdenas had said. Next to it, a slumped body in a Cárdenas jacket—one of the missing scientists. A clean bullet hole through the forehead.

"They found it," Kael muttered.

Padre Luis rushed to the body. "Still warm."

Valeria moved to the door and keyed in the biometric trigger. The door resisted… then clicked open.

Inside: a small, high-tech lab. Shelves of vials. Racks of drives. One small terminal still glowing with low power.

Natalia and Marisol moved fast, pulling chemical samples into a sealed case. Marisol accessed the terminal.

"Encrypted. I can pull the drives, but we'll need Salvador's key to decrypt."

"Do it," Kael said. "Fast."

Footsteps echoed behind them.

"Company," Padre Luis said, raising his rifle.

The footsteps were not coordinated. Not military.

Padre Luis peeked through a narrow wall slit and frowned. "Cartel foot soldiers. Not Chinese. And not ours."

Kael signaled for silence.

Outside the lab, the shuffle of boots and casual laughter echoed. A group of four young rival cartel members, barely more than teenagers, wandered in through a blown emergency stairwell. One had a machete on his hip. Another held a small revolver, loose in his grip like a toy. They were looters, not tacticians—drawn by rumors, not strategy.

"Check this out," one said in Spanish. "Some science shit."

"Think there's drugs in here?" another whispered.

They were half-laughing, stepping carefully, looking more confused than dangerous—like kids stumbling into a lion's den without realizing it. The kind of mistake you don't make twice.

Kael didn't move. Neither did the others.

Natalia's hand hovered near her trigger. Padre Luis shook his head slowly. No noise. No kills. If these idiots went missing, it would raise questions. Let them wander out.

The looters passed through the far exit, talking about hitting a pharmacy next.

Kael finally exhaled.

"Let's go," he said. "Now."

They loaded the last of the canisters and hard drives into an insulated carry crate. Valeria and Padre Luis took point while the others fell into formation.

The sublevel exit opened out into the old ambulance loading bay—overgrown, exposed, and quiet.

Too quiet.

As the group emerged, a low electronic whine buzzed through the air. Marisol froze.

Kael's gut dropped. "Exos."

From across the lot, Colonel Wu stepped into view—flanked by two operatives in matte-black exoskeleton suits, reinforced with hydraulic joints and shoulder-mounted optics. Behind them came another squad of Chinese soldiers, moving fast and precise.

"DOWN!" Kael yelled.

The firefight erupted in a thundercrack.

Rounds hammered the concrete. Sparks burst from the Humvee's armor plating. Natalia dove behind a planter wall but cried out—hit clean through the side.

"Val!" Marisol screamed.

Padre Luis tried to pull her back but caught a round in the leg, dropping hard beside her. Blood sprayed. He gritted his teeth and kept firing with one hand.

Kael laid down suppressive fire with his HK416, picking off two of the Chinese flanking soldiers. Valeria fired her last mag and dragged Natalia toward cover. Marisol was already hauling open the rear hatch.

"Get them in!" she yelled.

Kael hit the ignition. The Humvee roared to life. Marisol jumped into the driver's seat. Padre Luis and Natalia were hauled into the back by Valeria and Kael. Crates slammed in next to them. Bullets whistled around them.

They peeled out of the loading dock, tires screaming, rounds hammering the steel armor.

Behind them, Colonel Wu didn't run.

He charged.

His exosuit hissed with hydraulic force, each step thunderous as he sprinted after them. A grenade exploded behind him, but he emerged through the smoke untouched.

Kael popped the roof hatch, swung the .50 caliber turret around, and braced.

"Drive, Isa!"

Marisol floored it, dodging debris and weaving through ruined streets. Wu was still gaining—his suit pounding like a freight train, supported by drone scouts tracking their escape.

Kael lined up the shot.

The .50 cal opened with a deafening roar, shells flying from the chamber in a stream of fire and smoke. Concrete shattered around Wu. He ducked, raised a metal-clad arm as rounds sparked off his shoulder.

Still he came.

Kael adjusted, then hit center mass. The second burst slammed into Wu's chest plate, knocking him back ten feet. The exosuit staggered, then collapsed to one knee, trailing smoke.

Kael didn't wait. He fired again. This time the .50 cal punched through the right leg of the suit, shredding servos, and hydraulics.

Wu collapsed.

Kael kept his finger on the trigger until the weapon clicked empty.

Silence.

Then Marisol screamed. "We're not clear yet!"

A drone swooped low. Valeria leaned out the rear window and blew it apart with a lucky rifle shot.

Kael dropped into the seat next to Marisol, blood on his neck and hands.

"You good?" she asked, breathless.

He looked at her—wild-eyed, alive.

"Better now."

They didn't speak for a while. Just the hum of the engine, the wheeze of Padre Luis in the backseat applying pressure to his leg, and Natalia barely conscious but alive.

The crates sat between them like precious relics—samples and secrets that could tip the war.

Behind them, Wu's exoskeleton smoldered. The city trembled.

And the war for Veloxyn was only beginning.

The Humvee tore into the compound like a wounded animal, tires screeching, smoke trailing behind it. Fighters scrambled to open the gates as the vehicle slid to a halt near the medical tents.

The doors flew open.

Kael and Valeria leapt out first, yanking open the rear doors. Natalia lay across the back seat, her skin pale, her side soaked in blood. Padre Luis groaned, gripping his leg, soaked in red to the boot.

"MEDICS!" Kael roared.

A team rushed forward. Stretchers were dragged from nearby. Salvador, Goya, Leandro, and Sosa appeared at a sprint from the central building.

Valeria didn't wait—she pulled Natalia into her arms, ignoring the blood, her cheek pressed against hers. "Stay with me. You're not done, do you hear me?"

Natalia blinked once, her lips trembling. "Not… done…" she whispered.

They carried her toward the largest triage tent, canvas flapping from the downwash of a circling drone.

Inside, medics barked commands. Valeria refused to let go until they physically pulled her away.

They laid Natalia on the operating table. Scissors sliced through her blood-soaked top, exposing the wound—shrapnel embedded deep near her ribs. As they worked, she coughed violently.

A spray of blood hit the side curtain.

"Lung's hit!" a medic shouted.

Valeria's hands flew to her mouth, and she staggered back a step. Tears streaked her cheeks. She reached out but stopped, trembling. Padre Luis was rushed in behind her, still conscious, biting down on a strip of gauze while they tourniqueted his thigh.

Salvador put a hand on Valeria's shoulder. "She's strong. Let them work."

Valeria nodded—but didn't move.

Outside the tent, Salvador turned to Kael and Marisol, voice firm but low.

"Bring the crates. Now. You, Goya, Leandro, Sosa—get everything from the Humvee and follow me."

Kael threw open the back hatch. Inside were three reinforced cases—two full of vials, one heavy with drives and encrypted documents. Goya took the heaviest. Leandro and Sosa grabbed the others.

They moved quickly across the cracked courtyard, past rows of resting fighters and repair crews, toward the large conference room inside the Expo Center's central building.

The room was once used for pharmaceutical trade shows—now transformed into a war council chamber. Maps covered one wall. A projection screen glowed with satellite intel. Cárdenas cartel lieutenants hovered around the perimeter.

Salvador pushed open the doors. "Clear the table."

Kael and the others set the cases down.

"Let's see what we bought in blood," Salvador said.

Behind them, Valeria remained at the tent entrance, eyes locked on the thin white curtain where medics fought to keep the woman she loved alive.

Salvador Cárdenas shut the heavy conference room doors himself. The echo of the latch locking echoed like a final seal.

Only Kael, Marisol, Sosa, Goya, Leandro, Padre Luis, the Hellpack and Valeria remained.

No aides. No guards.

Salvador turned to face them, his expression iron. "What I'm about to tell you," he said, "doesn't leave this room. Not ever."

They nodded—one by one. Kael leaned forward. Marisol folded her arms. Goya and Sosa straightened. Valeria wiped the blood from her cheek but said nothing.

Salvador stepped to the head of the long table, hands planted firmly on its surface.

"Veloxyn," he began, "is not just a cartel drug. It's never been just that. What I'm about to tell you— very few alive know."

He paused, then continued, his voice lower, heavier.

"Decades ago, I was approached by operatives linked to DARPA and to the CIA. They told me a story about a compound—a synthetic stimulant developed in Nazi Germany during World War II. A variant of methamphetamine. Hitler gave it to his soldiers to keep them alert, fearless, aggressive."

He looked up, locking eyes with Kael.

"After the war, the Americans captured one of the Nazi scientists. He had perfected a stabilized version of the compound—one that enhanced endurance, focus, and pain tolerance beyond anything we'd seen. But it was addictive. Damaging. Too wild to control."

"So the U.S. tried to refine it," Salvador continued. "They wanted a version that was stable, non-addictive. A performance enhancer that could be administered without long-term side effects. They called the project Veloxyn."

"MKUltra," Kael whispered.

Salvador nodded. "That was the name. MKUltra was the umbrella program. Veloxyn was one

337

of its hidden trials. During the late '60s and early '70s, the CIA tested it on subjects across the country. Mental hospitals. Military volunteers. Even patients with terminal illnesses. And what they found…"

He exhaled, leaning back.

"Was that Veloxyn didn't just enhance strength or focus. It started reversing symptoms. Alzheimer's. Parkinson's. Cancer. Even severe diabetes. The drug's stimulant properties triggered immune and neurological regeneration at a cellular level. What began as a drug for war… became a potential cure for the world."

The room was dead quiet.

"But," Salvador said, raising a finger, "they couldn't separate the euphoria. The feeling of invincibility. That rush—like methamphetamine. It made people addicted and reckless. Violent. They were close to solving it… but then MKUltra got shut down. The research was buried. The scientists scattered."

"And that's when they came to you," Sosa muttered.

"In the '90s, yes," Salvador said. "Some of those scientists resurfaced—many disillusioned. They approached me in private, through proxies. They offered to refine my drug production processes— cocaine, marijuana, synthetic amphetamines—but their real goal was Veloxyn. They called it by a different name then, but I recognized the pattern. I saw the opportunity."

"They helped us begin trials—quietly. Using trusted doctors across Mexico, South America, and some European countries with Cárdenas ties. Patients with terminal or degenerative illnesses. We watched. We refined. We adapted."

He looked at Marisol.

"You, hija, were working on the newest strain. You just didn't know what it really was."

She stared, wide-eyed. "You told me it was to manage adrenaline. Combat fatigue."

"Partly. But the goal was to remove the addictive profile. Make Veloxyn a pharmaceutical-grade miracle. Something the FDA and its cousins around the world could approve. Something that would change medicine forever."

Kael's brow furrowed. "And then what?"

Salvador stepped back. "Then the Cárdenas family would step away from the drug war. The cartels. The shadows. We would go public. Partner with companies like Bristol-Myers Squibb, Eli Lilly, Procter & Gamble. We would become legitimate. Trillions. Legacy. Redemption."

He looked at all of them now. "That is why Veloxyn matters. That is why the Chinese want it. Why the Nueve Vidas want it. It's not just a weapon. It's a cure. And we are the only ones who have ever come close to perfecting it."

Silence.

Then Kael stood slowly. "Then we protect it. And we finish what you started."

Chapter 26

Operation Chimera

The war had paused—but it hadn't ended.
Outside the crumbling walls of the Tampico
Expo compound, the city shivered with uneasy quiet.
Distant mortar smoke still lingered in the sky like
bruises on God's canvas. The ground was damp with
the residue of blood and rain.
But behind the rusted maintenance shed—just
west of the primary fuel depot—time collapsed.
Kael and Marisol found each other in the hush
between breaths.
Here, the world did not spin.
Here, the sirens did not wail.
Here, nothing existed but them.
Kael pulled her close. Marisol came willingly,
pressing her face into his chest like it was the last safe
place left in the hemisphere. Their bodies found each
other the way gravity finds mass, naturally, inevitably.
They kissed, slow and breathless, their mouths
speaking a language older than the war, older than the
blood in their veins.
"I keep thinking," Marisol whispered between
kisses, "that this moment… might be the last time I
feel peace."
"Then let's make it count," Kael murmured.
Her hands slid beneath his jacket, fingers
clawing at the tension buried in his back muscles. His
arms wrapped around her with the quiet ferocity of
someone who had already lost too much.
Their foreheads met.
Their breathing synced.
"I used to dream of escape," Marisol said, voice
cracking with softness. "Of drifting away from all
this… on a boat… just us. No bullets. No names. No
fear."

Kael's thumb brushed her cheek.

"Then dream it again. After this, we find the sea."

"You promise?"

"If we survive tonight—I'll build us a sailboat with my bare damn hands."

She laughed, but it caught in her throat. Her body pressed tighter into his, her eyes glinting with something fragile.

Something permanent.

"Kael…" she whispered.

"I know," he said. "Me too."

Her hands dropped to her belly—subconsciously, instinctively. Kael followed the motion with his gaze.

She didn't need to say it.

He already knew.

Not just a future.

A bloodline.

A war within a war.

The silence broke with bootsteps—measured, deliberate. Gravel shifted. Fabric brushed fabric.

"Kael. Marisol."

Goya.

Her voice cut through the moment like a machete through sugarcane. Not cruel—but decisive.

They pulled apart like teenagers caught under the bleachers. Marisol wiped her eyes. Kael cracked his knuckles and rolled his neck like he could stretch the moment back into place.

Goya stood there smirking, arms crossed.

"Comstock's on the line. Says he needs you now."

Kael nodded, already shifting gears.

The soldier reloaded behind his eyes.

He turned to Marisol one last time.

"I'm coming back," he said, voice low.

"You'd better," she whispered, brushing the collar of his shirt flat. "I'll be here."

Then she pulled him into one last kiss—hard and fast.

A goodbye.

A promise.

He turned without another word and walked toward the command tent.

Marisol didn't watch him leave.

She watched the wind.

Tampico Expo – Outer Corridor – 03:38 Hours

The concrete groaned under Kael's boots. Every step felt heavier now—not with doubt, but with purpose. The walls of the compound—once hollow echoes of a lost expo center—had become the bones of resistance. Radios crackled. Runners moved like nervous veins beneath floodlights.

Kael passed a Cárdenas technician handing out grenades like flyers at a revolution.

He didn't stop.

Didn't blink.

He entered the outer corridor where the comm tent waited—but someone stood in the shadows, just before the flap.

Salvador Cárdenas.

A half-empty drink in one hand. A storm in the other.

"Wait," the old lion said.

Kael paused. Tension hummed between them like an unstruck chord.

Cárdenas took a final swig and hurled the glass against the concrete. It shattered, mezcal bleeding into the dirt.

"They've got my city's airport," Cárdenas growled. "They're flying out my product—fentanyl,

Veloxyn, cocaine. My empire, bleeding into the sky with every takeoff."

He turned fire in his eyes.

"It took me thirty years to build that infrastructure. Thirty. Do you know what it takes to bribe, bury, and bully your way through every port, every inspector, every banker from Jalisco to Beijing?"

Kael said nothing. He didn't need to.

"And now… it's slipping away on every landing gear." Cárdenas spat. "While we watch."

He pointed north, toward the airport's ghost lights blinking in the far dark.

"We take it back tonight. No more waiting. No more planning. We end it."

Kael held his gaze.

"Then let me make the call."

He raised the encrypted field radio and keyed in the signal.

"Hellpack One. This is Cárdenas Command. Do you copy?"

Static. Then a crackle. Then—

"Don't you worry, Kael," came Comstock's voice, cool and clear like a winter river. "I'm on my way. Riverine boats are loaded. And I brought some… extras."

Kael nearly smiled—but his eyes didn't.

As he lowered the radio, Marisol stepped out from behind the columns and wrapped her arms around his waist, pulling herself flush against his back.

"Don't go," she whispered. "You don't have to be the one."

Kael reached up and touched her forearm.

Just once.

"I already am."

Salvador stepped forward again. Voice lower now. Less fire. More weight.

"You've done enough, Kael. You've given us this moment. I'm ordering you to stand down."

Kael turned to face him, calm but immovable.

"I can't. If Comstock's coming in, I'm the only one who can get him in—and out."

Silence.

Then Cárdenas turned to his daughter.

He saw it in her eyes—the grief, the pride, the legacy.

He gave a single nod.

"Then don't fail."

Kael nodded back, jaw tight.

"I won't."

And with that, he stepped through the curtain of command lights and out into the war again.

Later that evening the interior of the comms tent felt like a war bunker crossbred with a spaceship. Blue light flickered from portable monitors and encrypted tablets, casting surreal glows across crates of radio gear, maps, and empty coffee tins. The hum of static filled the space like a held breath. Somewhere outside, a generator sputtered under strain.

Kael entered with the weight of purpose in his stride. His silhouette cast a long shadow on the canvas wall, drawing eyes and muting conversations.

A Cárdenas tech—a lanky man in a blood-smeared poncho—handed him a headset. "Line secure. He's waiting."

Kael nodded once. Slipped the headset on. "Comstock."

The response came like flint against steel. Low, steady, lethal.

"Meet me at Bridge 180. Pánuco River crossing. One hour."

Kael's brow furrowed. "You said we had until dawn."

"Plans changed. Comstock continued, his tone shifting slightly. "Wu's already started loading Cárdenas product onto transport planes. Looks like they're trying to lift it out before we bring the hammer down."

Kael's brow furrowed. "So we hit the planes?"

"No," Comstock replied. "We don't want to blow them up directly. That product's worth billions and I don't want to tip the apple cart with Cárdenas. I know he needs and wants the product secure." Plus, we don't have the gear to crater an entire airport with reinforced runways."

Kael glanced toward the makeshift war map inside the expo center. "So what's the play?"

"We got intel—five Chinese military transports are inbound. Type Y-20s. Cargo birds. Big. Heavy. Vulnerable on descent."

He paused.

"We're gonna let them land."

Kael's eyes narrowed. "Say again?"

Comstock came through clear. "Those planes will be our bombs. We hit them as they approach over the river. We will be directly under their glide slope. They will be only about eight hundred feet in the air. They will be like glide bombs and turn the tarmac into a firestorm. That'll send the message and trap Wu's operation mid-exit."

Kael nodded slowly. "Turning their reinforcements into their funeral pyre. Understood."

"We'll be watching the skies," Comstock added. "Time it right, and we'll light up the whole damn runway."

Kael paced slowly in the tent; eyes fixed on a digital map.

"So, we hit it before the hive finishes moving?"

"Exactly," Comstock said. "Burn the nest while it's still fat with product."

Kael tapped a rhythm on the edge of a crate with his finger—fast, measured, like syncing his pulse with the mission.

"Who's the crew?"

"You. Natalia. Valeria, Sosa, and Padre Luis" Comstock replied. "No other lieutenants. No other Cárdenas brass. No one who thinks in empires. Just the ones who know how to cut throats in the dark." In addition, bring about 8 vehicles fully armed and packed with men for an attack on the airport.

Kael's voice crackled through the comms. "Comstock, Natalia's out. Took two hits—she's in the med tent. She's not coming on this op."

Kael keyed his mic. "You running solo on this, or you got back up?"

Comstock's voice came through, cool and steady. "Negative. Picking up the Hellpack now. We'll be in position by the time you roll."

"Bring a rifle. And your resolve."

Kael didn't smile.

"I've got both."

The line clicked dead.

Kael removed the headset slowly, as if grounding himself. Then he turned, stepped into the pale edge of morning filtering through the flap.

The sky was bleeding toward dawn, washed in smoke and sulfuric light. The glow didn't feel like sunrise. It felt like ignition.

Expo Courtyard – Tactical Staging

Valeria stood beside a loaded Humvee, rolling her shoulders as she clipped a new mag into her CZ BREN. A bandage on her forearm still bled through the gauze.

Padre Luis sat on a flipped ammo crate, wrapping her ribs with a roll of combat tape, teeth clenched.

Neither asked questions when Kael approached.

They'd already packed.

"Bridge 180," Kael said. "Comstock wants a special team. No politics. Just pain."

Valeria gave a curt nod.

She tightened the knot in her wrap and stood with a wince. "Let's go carve our initials into history."

Kael looked toward the northeast—the city still cloaked in haze, the river glittering in the distance like a wound that refused to close.

He tossed his bag into the Humvee.

"Then let's go meet the devil."

Five minutes later the sun was just beginning to rise, casting a molten glow across the compound. Dust swirled in the morning light as engines growled to life. Eight vehicles stood lined up and ready—armored pickups, SUVs, and technicals, each fully loaded with Cárdenas fighters and weapons.

Kael walked the line, doing a final visual inspection. Heavy machine guns—M240s and .50 caliber Browning mounts—were bolted to reinforced roll bars. Each vehicle had men strapped in, packs loaded, ammo crates stuffed under seats. One truck, squatting low under the weight, was laden with two 82mm mortars and over 300 rounds. The suspension groaned, the rear axle nearly buckling.

"Tell me that thing's going to survive the trip," Sosa muttered.

"Barely," said Valeria, checking the straps herself. "But if it does, it'll be worth its weight in hell."

All of the eight vehicles had special designations:

One carried the core team—Kael, Valeria, Sosa, and Padre Luis.

Six served as main attack force, filled with the Cárdenas squad's best shooters and the mortar teams.

One was left empty, engine running, staged as a decoy. If spotted from the air or intercepted, it would draw fire—maybe even trigger an ambush of the ambushers. It would take off a minute before the rest of the convoy.

Kael climbed into the lead vehicle, gripping the dash as the door slammed shut.

Marisol was there too—at his side but not behind him. Her hand was on her abdomen. A silent promise to herself.

As Kael mounted into the passenger seat, she called out.

"You come back to me, Torres."

Kael looked up and held her gaze.

"That's the only reason I'm going."

Valeria revved the engine.

She then chambered a round.

Kael shut the door.

"Let's move," he said.

Engines revved. Radios clicked.

And the convoy rolled out, dust spiraling behind them like a ghost no wind could scatter.

The decoy sped off out of the compound. The seven-vehicle convoy rolled out of the Expo Center gates in a staggered column, tires chewing up the battered road as they headed northeast—toward the airfield.

Toward Comstock.

Toward war.

Salvador Cárdenas stood on the balcony above the launch strip, arms crossed, silent.

Pánuco River Crossing — Bridge 180

04:49 Hours

Fog rolled over the river like a living thing—thick, slow, merciless. The kind of fog that soaked through your uniform and whispered to your nerves. The bridge itself was a skeleton of war—concrete scarred by mortar blasts, its guardrails pocked with bullet holes. Charred husks of vehicles lined the sides, some flipped, others rusting in place like forgotten tombstones.

Kael stood at the southern edge, bootheels just shy of where the asphalt turned to decay.

He scanned the distance.

Beyond the smoke, the river shimmered in pale gray under a bruised sky. The world felt like it had forgotten how to breathe.

Mist clung to the steel underbelly of Bridge 180, where the river whispered beneath, sluggish, and dark. Kael, Valeria, Sosa, and Padre Luis stood at the base of the crossing, surrounded by concrete pillars scarred from older battles.

A faint rumble echoed upriver—then headlights cut through the fog.

Then—there they were.

Two SURCs.

Comstock's boats.

Comstock stood at the bow of the lead craft, one hand gripping the side rail, the other holding a tablet. On the other SURC stood his handpicked squad—the Hellpack. Three figures, armored and masked, emanating the silent precision of apex predators.

The boats slid to a gentle idle near the shoreline. Comstock leapt off first, boots landing in a splash of mud and river foam.

Kael met him with a quick nod. "Right on time."

Comstock grinned. "Aren't I always?"

The rest of the Hellpack readied the other SURC. Reva "Sawtooth" Guerra—close-quarters killer, tomahawks strapped to her back. Elias "Ghoul" Navarro—the heavy gunner, carrying an M249 like it was a sidearm. And Ángel "Boomer" Valdés—the demolitions expert, his vest packed with enough high-ex to level a building.

Comstock turned to the Cárdenas men. "Alright, listen up. You're heading to the far end of the airport. That's where they're loading the product onto the Chinese transports. Do not engage until the SURCs open fire. You wait for our signal—got it?"

The Cárdenas sergeant nodded. "Understood."

Comstock pointed inland toward the airport perimeter. "You stay on the west flank. We'll keep the north. The 75s on these boats are going to shell the runway and the cargo bays. You do not want to be anywhere near our arc of fire."

He shifted his gaze to the mortar team. "You'll set up near the jungle edge—grid echo-bravo-seven. Once we start, you rain hell on the eastern quadrant. That's where the bulk of their infantry is dug in— Chinese and cartel both."

Sosa stepped forward. "And us?"

Comstock gestured toward the boats. "You're with us. Kael, Sosa, Valeria, Padre Luis—you're riding in the first SURC with me. The Hellpack will take the second. We hit from the riverbank and push up once the transports are down."

Kael exchanged a look with Valeria. She gave a single nod.

The Cárdenas squad drove off quickly, vanishing into city to flank the airfield. The mortar team moved with purpose, crates of 82mm shells clutched in shaking hands.

Kael slung his rifle and jumped into the lead SURC, taking position beside the recoilless gun. Padre Luis followed, his cassock flapping as he climbed in. Valeria took the rear port gunner's post. Sosa climbed up to man the M240.

Comstock vaulted in last, spinning the ignition. "Let's wake the sky."

Behind them, the Hellpack checked the belts and ammo on the second boat. Ghoul cocked his M249. Sawtooth checked her rifle. Boomer gave a low whistle and strapped in beside a crate of shaped charges.

The SURCs pulled away from shore, their wakes splitting the Pánuco River wide.

War was minutes away.

"Planes are coming in," he said without preamble. "Chinese, cartel-aligned. Heavy cargo. Troop rotation. You know the type."

Kael didn't speak. He just nodded once.

"We're going to shut them down," Comstock continued. "Not delay them. Not intercept. Drop them."

He pulled out a folded map and spread it over the hood of the vehicle.

"In exactly fifteen minutes aircraft will begin final approach into Tampico. Altitude? Eight hundred to a thousand feet on the glide slope. We'll be in the river—floating just beneath that descent path." It's foggy outside. The planes following will not see what happened to the lead plane until it is too late. We try and take down two to three planes.

Valeria's eyes narrowed. "You're going to fire from the river?"

Comstock gave a small smile.

"GAU-19. Mk 19. Surface-to-air uplinked targeting. We'll let them know we're here."

Valeria gave a quiet whistle. "Hell's coming upstream."

The wind picked up slightly. It carried the smell of fuel. Of rain. Of war.

For a few minutes, the river was quiet—but the air was pulsing with the weight of what was coming.

Two SURC boats drifted just below the tree line, low in the Pánuco River's current, like predators waiting to strike. Onboard: Kael, Valeria, Padre Luis, Sosa and Comstock—each armored, armed, and locked in.

Comstock stood near the GAU-19 Gatling gun, eyes locked on the darkened skies. The other SURC mirrored theirs about 50 meters to the east—The Hellpack's post, quiet but ready.

"Remember," Comstock barked to the Cárdenas troops over the comms, voice low but sharp.

"Don't step foot on that airfield. You fire from the streets, from the trees. Stay on the edges. The tarmac's going to be hell."

Then—the hum.

Faint at first. Then louder. Engines. Lights. Approach.

Comstock leaned into his headset. "Here we go. Get your eyes up."

The glow of a descending aircraft shimmered through the clouds—a massive Chinese military transport, wide-bodied and heavy. Its landing gear extended. Too smooth. Too routine.

Kael's voice crackled.

"Target locked."

Comstock grinned without warmth. "Just as it passes us—light it the hell up."

The roar exploded all at once.

Kael's SURC opened fire first—Comstock at the helm of the GAU-19, his fingers tight on the butterfly trigger. The six-barrel Gatling cannon spun up with a mechanical shriek, then roared like thunder. .50-cal rounds tore across the sky, lighting up the belly of the incoming transport plane with ribbons of glowing death.

The rounds struck home—shredding aluminum, severing hydraulics, and punching straight through the fuselage. Inside the plane, Chinese soldiers—still seated and strapped in—jerked violently as the rounds hit. Some were torn in half where they sat. Others convulsed, bodies twitching and recoiling like they'd been electrocuted. A fine pink mist sprayed across the interior walls, streaking the inside of the transport with gore.

Kael swung into position behind the Mk 19 grenade launcher. He locked eyes on the midsection of the aircraft and fired.

The first 40mm shell hit just behind the cockpit. A bright orange explosion bloomed outward like a shockwave wrapped in fire. The second and third rounds struck near the wing root—blasting open panels and igniting internal fuel lines.

The sky lit up in staccato bursts, each shell painting the transport in fire and ruin.

Valeria leaned over the rail beside Kael, unleashing bursts from her suppressed CZ Bren, picking off scattered troops near the rivers edge and nearby buildings scrambling for cover.

Sosa fired short, disciplined bursts from his SCAR-H, every round a surgical cut through chaos.

Padre Luis, kneeling at the starboard corner of the boat, muttered a prayer as he laid down cover fire with his M4, each round fired with conviction.

The aircraft wobbled in the air, half its belly gutted open. A fireball pulsed out from within, briefly illuminating the silhouettes of dead men still strapped to their harnesses, bouncing like broken marionettes in the cabin's collapsing frame.

"Direct hit!" Comstock bellowed. "She's going down hard!"

Behind them, the Hellpack's SURC echoed with fire—Ghoul's M249 screaming, Boomer preparing the shaped charges, Sawtooth crouched with her tomahawks drawn, waiting for boarding range.

The sky wasn't just lit with fire.

It was fire.

The transport shuddered, twisted violently—and tried to pull left.

Too late.

The plane clipped the edge of the tarmac, overcorrected, spun 180 degrees, and slammed into the runway, dragging across concrete like a dying beast. A split-second later—

BOOM.

The fuel ignited in a roar that shook the streets of Tampico. Flames rose high, black smoke curling like a funeral banner across the sky.

Kael looked across the water, eyes narrow. "Message delivered."

From the SURCs, the 75mm recoilless rifles launched in sequence—artillery rounds hammering the tarmac with thunder. Concrete split. Hangars crumbled.

Then Comstock saw the other plane coming in. Smoke still rose from the wreckage of the first transport when a second

Y-20 screamed low over the trees, its landing lights cutting through the smoke like spears.

Inside the SURC, Comstock yanked the feed tray on the GAU-19 open, smoke curling from the overheated barrel cluster. He grabbed a fresh belt of .50-cal rounds and hissed through his teeth.

"Reloading!" he barked. "Kael—get on the recoilless!"

Kael was already moving, vaulting over crates as he dropped behind the 75mm recoilless rifle mounted toward the bow. The barrel still smoked from its earlier use, but it was clean and ready. He adjusted the scope, tracking the descending plane.

The Navy gunner on the SURC hesitated, glancing at the painted markings on the approaching aircraft.

"Sir, that's a Chinese military bird. If I fire—"

"It'll be a declaration of war," Comstock growled, already on the comms. "Copy. That's why you don't shoot."

He switched channels.

"Hellpack Two, this is Hellpack One. New target. Light up that transport.

"Copy that, Hellpack One," came Ghoul's voice over the comms, calm as death.

From the second SURC, the response was immediate. The Hellpack's GAU opened in a steady roar. Bright tracers arced upward, stitching across the night sky.

Kael steadied the recoilless rifle aimed it about five meters above the cockpit and pulled the trigger.

The 75mm shell tore through the sky like a comet, striking the cockpit of the aircraft with a bone-cracking explosion. Fire and metal erupted along the belly of the plane. The rear engines flared, then stuttered, then detonated midair.

The transport lurched, pitched sideways, and began a slow, spiraling descent—flames trailing behind it like a falling star. Shards of metal and fire rained down on the SURC's. Everyone trying to find cover as the plane passed overhead.

Inside, silhouettes moved—figures scrambling, then flailing as gravity took over. The plane clipped a radio tower on the edge of the runway and exploded on impact, a rolling wall of flame lighting up the jungle edge.

Comstock slammed the GAU feed shut and chambered the new belt.

"That's two," he muttered. "Let's make it five."

The sky above the runway was chaos and cinders. Flames still licked at the wreckage of the second aircraft as black smoke spiraled upward into the breaking dawn like a nuclear mushroom cloud. The mist that had cloaked the jungle minutes earlier was beginning to burn away, revealing the full scale of the devastation.

Then—another shape.

The third Y-20 appeared low on the horizon, just a mile out, moving slow. But it wasn't descending. It was veering off—tilting away from the runway, arcing wide over the coastline.

Kael squinted into the rising light. "They saw the fire. Or caught the last transmission before impact."

"Doesn't matter," Comstock said, already moving. He dropped to a weapons crate at the rear of the SURC and flipped it open, pulling free a FIM-92 Stinger missile launcher.

He turned to Kael. "Kid, you've got about sixty seconds to get this thing in the air and shoot that bastard down."

Kael met his eyes. "You think I forgot?"

Comstock smirked. "Was kind of hoping you didn't."

Kael dropped to one knee and powered the Stinger on. The infrared seeker spun up, tone sharp in his headset. The aircraft—now angling hard toward the sea—was well out over the coast, but still in range.

Kael tracked the target. Locked.

He squeezed the trigger.

The missile tore from the tube with a shriek, trailing a column of smoke. It curved upward, homing in with lethal precision.

Seconds later, it struck the aircraft's left wing.

The explosion lit up the morning sky, a burst of flame and sheared metal. The engine flared, then blew apart. The entire wing folded, broke, and peeled away from the fuselage.

The transport spiraled, a giant flaming arrow crashing toward the sea. It slammed into the Gulf in a plume of foam, oil, and fire—sending a shockwave across the water.

Padre Luis lowered his rifle and crossed himself. "May their souls rise as quickly as their orders fell."

Kael lowered the empty launcher, eyes still on the smoking impact.

"That's three," he muttered.

Comstock nodded. "Then let's get to four."

Inside the airport, chaos erupted.

Wu's loyalists and Lee Ho's splintered forces began scrambling, shouting in two languages, taking up defensive positions along terminals and blast walls. Some ran for remaining aircraft, desperate to escape but the runways strewn with the wreckage of their comrades and twisted burning metal.

Panic bloomed across the airfield.

Some men fired at shadows. Others boarded planes still grounded, hoping to flee before the next shell hit. But most knew—

They were trapped.

They were outflanked.

And the Cárdenas cartel was coming.

The city was now a war zone.

And this… was just the first strike.

Far across the city, back at the Cárdenas compound near the Expo Center, Marisol stood on the rooftop, barefoot, wrapped in a blanket as the first light of morning cracked the horizon.

Then she heard it.

Gunfire.

Then a roar so loud it shook the windowpanes. A distant flash lit the sky like lightning—but this was no storm.

Her breath caught in her chest.

She clutched the edge of the railing; eyes locked toward the north.

"Kael…" she whispered, her voice cracking with fear—and awe.

"Don't die before you see the world you're helping build."

Chapter 27

The Battle for Tampico

Kael, Valeria, Comstock, Sosa, Padre Luis, and the Hellpack disembarked from the SURCs in a staggered wedge, boots crunching against shattered glass and broken asphalt. The river behind them churned with smoke and heat, the fading echo of battle rolling through the air like distant thunder.

Their gear was slick with river mist and sweat. Valeria adjusted her sling, scanning the rooftops. Her face was tight, focused. Kael checked the mag on his rifle and motioned them forward. Comstock brought up the rear, eyes sharp behind smudged sunglasses, a sidearm at his hip and a steel-case satphone clipped to his plate carrier.

The Hellpack moved like a shadow unit—silent, surgical. Sawtooth flanked left, tomahawks swaying on her back. Ghoul moved center, the M249 slung low, finger brushing the trigger guard. Boomer brought up the far right, eyes constantly scanning, demo charges strapped across his chest like a vest of sleeping dragons and rifle in hand.

They moved through the war-torn veins of the city—rubble-lined streets filled with shell casings, spent mortar fins, and the burned-out husks of technicals. The early light bled across crumbling facades, casting long shadows, and exposing the raw wounds of the fight for Tampico.

In the distance, the control tower of the airport loomed like a scarred sentinel. Plumes of smoke still curled from the tarmac. Somewhere beyond those runways, Wu's remaining forces were regrouping.

Kael slowed at a corner, held up a fist, then crouched near a collapsed billboard. "Two clicks out," he said. "We cut through the service road, hit the fence line behind the north cargo terminal."

Comstock nodded. "Air defenses are down, but they'll still have spotters. Keep it low. Keep it fast."

Valeria raised her rifle and exhaled. "Let's finish this."

And without another word, they moved—threading the ruins of a city on the brink.

The sun was up now, bleeding through smoke-streaked skies. Gunfire cracked in the distance—measured bursts from AKs and suppressed rifles, the steady percussion of a 75mm recoilless rifle echoing from somewhere just west of the terminal.

The city felt like a chessboard already half-burned.

As they advanced, the smell of spent brass and diesel hung thick. They passed a row of dead Cárdenas fighters—some still clutching their rifles, others slumped over crates. One had been cut in half by shrapnel.

Kael paused, scanned the rooftops, then waved them forward.

Then they saw it.

Movement—low to the ground. Controlled. Fluid.

Not human.

"Eyes up," Valeria hissed. "We've got metal."

Down the street, robotic quadrupeds crawled from the alleyways like mechanical wolves.

Model: QX-7 Specters—four-legged hunter-killers, low-slung, matte-black, each with a belt-fed 5.8mm mounted on their backs and thermal target acquisition systems glowing faintly red.

Then they charged.

Three dozen Specters. Full sprint. Straight at them.

"MOVE!" Kael shouted.

The street became fire and fury.

Comstock opened up with a suppressed .308, dropping two dogs before they leapt. Valeria hit the flank with grenades. She moved like smoke, head shotting one, then two, then ducking as rounds chewed up the brick wall behind her.

But they kept coming.

Across the street, Sosa and Padre Luis took cover behind an overturned technical, pinned down by another wave of Specters that had flanked through a blown-out parking garage. Their movements were sharper, faster—adapting.

"Seven more—two o'clock!" Sosa called, leaning out just long enough to drop one with a burst of fire.

Padre Luis chambered a fresh mag into his rifle, muttering to himself. Then louder—his voice growing into a roar.

"O, LORD OF WAR AND MERCY, GRANT ME THE FIRE OF GIDEON, THE WRATH OF ELIJAH—AND A CLEAN SHOT THROUGH THESE DEMON MACHINES!"

The Specters paused. Their optics flared red. One turned its head and—impossibly—mimicked the Padre's prayer in a garbled metallic stutter:

"...fire of Gideon... wrath... Elijah..."

Padre Luis blinked. "Madre de Dios."

Then he opened fire.

Rounds shredded through two of the machines. Sosa flanked the last three, laying suppressive fire while Padre Luis charged, holy fury in his voice.

One Specter lunged—but Padre Luis drove his rifle butt into its jaw, spun, and dumped ten rounds into its processor core.

Hydraulic fluid sprayed across his chest like blood.

Sosa stepped over the wreckage, panting. "You okay, Padre?"

Luis looked at the smoldering wreck, raised his hand in blessing, and said, "Even the Devil builds his dogs... but today, they kneel."

On the far flank, the Hellpack moved like a storm. Twelve Specters burst from a blown-out bus terminal, charging across the open lot in a coordinated kill pattern—sensor eyes pulsing red, guns spinning up. Ghoul stepped forward without hesitation, bracing his M249 against a concrete divider and unloading a sweeping arc of fire. The belt-fed beast roared, sending a torrent of rounds into the lead wave, splitting metal and bone-like alloy in a storm of sparks and smoke.

Sawtooth didn't flinch as two bots peeled off and lunged toward her position. She dropped low, let the first leap, then pivoted into its side, driving both tomahawks down into the machine's spine. The blades dug in, hissed with heat. The Specter thrashed—then she wrenched the axes free and beheaded it in one fluid spin. The second charged, jaws snapping. She ducked, drove an elbow into its core, then kicked it into Boomer's blast radius.

Boomer was already waiting. "Bad dog," he muttered, and triggered a charge he'd planted on a support beam seconds earlier. The explosion ripped through the lot, sending a trio of Specters skyward in molten pieces. The last two bots scrambled, confused. Ghoul picked them off with controlled bursts, sending one toppling in a shower of brass, while the other spun out—legs shattered, systems fried. The Hellpack stood breathing hard, surrounded by smoking wreckage, not a scratch among them.

One Specter launched from a balcony— slamming Kael to the pavement.

He rolled, hands bloody, rifle kicked away. The dog pinned him, its jaw unit snapping, fangs of reinforced titanium gnashing toward his throat.

Kael screamed, reached for his thigh rig.

Pulled the knife.

Stabbed hard.

Right into the sensor cluster.

A spurt of hydraulic fluid burst across his chest as the dog spasmed—twitching, whirring, then going still.

Kael kicked it off and stood, gasping, drenched in coolant.

"Clear!" he shouted.

"No you're not!" Comstock yelled back.

Valeria had been forced into a blind corner behind a collapsed storefront. Five Specters had them pinned—one taking rounds but still charging. Another launched into the air, teeth open.

Valeria, slamming the bot into a wall. She screamed in pain as metal claws tore into her shoulder.

Valeria dropped her last mag and fired from point-blank—headshots into the dog's sensor plate. Sparks flew. Its body convulsed. Dead.

Another Specter rounded the corner.

Then—fire from behind.

Kael and Comstock came in blazing, rifles singing.

Thermite grenades arced through the air—boom, boom—white-hot flame engulfing two more Specters, melting them from the inside.

The rest scattered, retreating, legs broken or trailing sparks.

Silence returned, broken only by the hiss of burning metal.

Kael exhaled slowly and dropped to one knee beside the robotic dog that had nearly ripped his throat out. He reached down and gripped a jagged fang of titanium lodged in the creature's ruined jaw. It came loose with a metallic click.

He stared at it—still warm, streaked with coolant and his own blood.

Without a word, he slipped it into his vest pocket.

Kael stood. Comstock approached, reloading.

"We're a half-click from the south tower," he said. "And they know we're coming now."

Kael looked down the street—scorched, steaming, littered with robotic carcasses and fractured humanity.

He nodded once.

"Then let's finish this."

South Hangar, Tampico Airport

The smoke from the tarmac had begun to clear, and what remained of the Chinese and cartel defenders had scattered into alleys, safehouses, and burning wreckage. What was left of the resistance was a skeleton force—injured, disoriented, retreating.

But Kael didn't trust silence.

They regrouped at the south edge of the airport—Kael, Comstock, Valeria, Sosa, Padre Luis, the Hellpack and a group of Cárdenas fighters moving low through shattered hangar rows and air traffic corridors.

Then Comstock froze and lifted his hand.

"Movement," he said.

Across the cracked taxiway, inside a partially collapsed hangar, shapes moved—dark, disciplined, and too fast.

"Those aren't stragglers," Valeria said.

They inched forward—then saw it.

Nine Chinese helicopters, still operational, were spinning up quietly in the shadow of the hangar complex. Troops were boarding fast, loading crates, weapons, and tech cases with choreographed precision.

But what made Kael pause… was how they moved.

Exosuits.

Not the crude cargo-assist rigs they'd seen earlier—these were tactical frames: integrated armor, spinal compression boosts, servo-assisted limbs, and HUDs lighting up in violet overlays.

The soldiers weren't just moving.

They were gliding. Hunting.

"Shit," Comstock muttered. "They're not retreating. They're extracting."

Kael checked his mag. "Let's make it costly."

They moved in.

The firefight hit like a thunderclap.

Cárdenas men had opened from the flanks, cutting down two unarmored soldiers instantly. But the exo-suited troops turned fast—returning fire with inhuman precision, shrugging off small arms like raindrops. One Cárdenas man took a full burst to the chest—his body lifted and spun, landing hard and lifeless.

Kael ducked under a fuel cart, firing a three-round burst that struck one of the suits' shoulder ports. Sparks flew, but the soldier barely staggered.

"Comstock!" Kael shouted over the comms. "We need a hole in that armor!"

Comstock sprinted past, dropped behind a tire stack, and yelled, "You want an edge? Suit up."

He pointed to a discarded exoskeleton—a damaged unit near the hangar door, half-loaded and missing its primary HUD.

Kael didn't hesitate.

Comstock helped him slide in—locking the spinal brace and triggering the hydraulics. It groaned, sparked... then powered up.

Kael stood—his vision augmented, strength doubled, weight no longer an issue.

Then—Wu emerged.

Wearing a full military-grade exosuit with reinforced plating, red insignia on the shoulder, and a gauntlet-mounted flechette launcher. His helmet retracted just long enough to show his face—calm, detached, surgical.

Kael stepped into the open, locking eyes.

Wu didn't speak.

He just charged.

Their suits collided with bone-rattling force—metal grinding, pistons hissing. Wu struck first, slamming Kael into a wall of crates. Kael's HUD blinked with warning. He countered with a rising elbow, followed by a short jab to Wu's rib plate.

Wu didn't flinch. He spun and kicked, sending Kael sprawling to the ground, suit groaning under the impact.

Overhead, the helicopters roared—all nine beginning their liftoff in waves, blades carving through the smoke.

Wu turned his back to Kael—leapt thirty feet into the air, clearing the hangar like a predator born for flight.

He grabbed the landing gear of the lead helicopter mid-ascent, one arm still dripping with oil and blood.

Kael pulled himself to his feet, raised his rifle—but the choppers were already rising fast, fanning out into formation as they vanished into the sky.

Wu looked down at him as the bird carried him away.

He was gone.

Again.

The sky was silent now.

The nine helicopters had vanished into the morning haze, leaving behind the smoldering wreckage of a city reclaimed—but not yet won.

Kael stood at the edge of the runway, exosuit sparking at the shoulder, smoke curling off the joints. His rifle hung low, forgotten in one hand.

He stared up into the space where Wu had disappeared, eyes fixed on the fading contrails.

"He's not running," Kael said quietly.

"He's positioning."

Comstock stepped up beside him, breathing hard, scanning the ruins of the hangars.

"That wasn't an escape," he said.

"That was a maneuver."

Behind them, Padre Luis helped Valeria sit against a supply crate. Her arm was still bleeding, but her eyes were sharp.

Valeria looked at Kael, then toward the eastern skyline, where another column of smoke rose in the distance—black against gold.

She exhaled slowly.

"He's not done," she said.

"Neither are we."

Chapter 28

Ghost Empire

Tampico Airport — Just After Sunrise
The smoke was thinning.

But not gone.

It hung over the tarmac like a veil between worlds—what was, and what had been shattered just hours before. Acrid and metallic, the scent clung to skin, hair, and memory. The morning sun tried to break through, sending fractured beams across the shell-pocked concrete, but even light seemed reluctant to bear witness.

Kael Torres walked slowly at the head of the group—his boots crunching over shattered lenses, spent casings, and the carbon-scored fragments of machines that had once hunted them. Beside him moved Grant Comstock, silent and sharp-eyed, always scanning. Valeria, Sosa, Padre Luis, and the Hellpack followed close, speaking little, their eyes heavy with sleepless hours and fresh scars. None of them limped, but all of them bore wounds.

The wreckage of the battle lay everywhere—craters, shredded bodies, crushed drones still twitching in death spasms, and exosuit limbs fused to asphalt by napalm or grenade fire. A robotic dog blinked its last flicker of light against a broken tarmac lamp. Its targeting lens stuttered, flickered, and then went dark.

The heat rising off the tarmac shimmered like a mirage, warping the twisted skeletons of the downed transport planes. One lay split open at the fuselage, its cargo doors blown clean off, blackened containers of weapons and ammunition melted into chemical puddles around charred crates and snapped harnesses. The stink of scorched rubber, jet fuel, and something acrid—something medical—hung thick in the air. Smoke from the wreckage still spiraled lazily into the sky, catching the morning sun in hues of copper and blood.

Kael walked slowly past the ruin of the first aircraft, boots crunching over spent shell casings and fragments of human bone. He stepped carefully around the engine nacelle, blown open like a cracked ribcage. Inside, the remains of Chinese soldiers sat frozen in twisted postures—limbs fused to buckled metal, helmets melted into their skulls. A pair of them looked like they had tried to unbuckle in the final seconds, caught mid-motion by the blast.

Valeria stood ahead, rifle low, gazing at the second downed aircraft that had plowed through the outer fence and come to rest against a line of shipping containers. "All that firepower, all that training," she murmured. "Didn't matter. We turned them into tombs before they ever touched the ground." She didn't say it with pride—just observation. Sosa crossed himself quietly beside her, while Comstock scanned the smoke-blurred runway through his scope. "Let this be a warning," he muttered. "Anyone else thinking of landing in my sky better reconsider."

Padre Luis moved slowly through the wreckage, his boots stepping delicately over scorched metal and the remnants of shattered lives. In one hand, he held his rosary; in the other, a small flask of holy water which he sprinkled over the twisted bodies and scorched insignias. "Eternal rest grant unto them, O Lord," he murmured, eyes heavy with grief. "And let perpetual light shine upon them." His voice barely carried over the crackle of smoldering debris, but each word landed like a blessing on cursed ground. He paused beside a burned flight helmet, made the sign of the cross, and whispered, "May your souls be freed from the chains of men's war."

Cárdenas cartel flags were being raised over every outpost in sight—torn banners re-sewn, hoisted over radar towers, taped to antenna masts, nailed to the walls of ruined hangars. It wasn't organized. It wasn't ceremonial. It was instinctual. Reclamation by symbolism.

Atop the air traffic control spire, a Cárdenas tech team was wiring a hijacked Chinese comm relay to the booster array, tapping into what remained of the eastern corridor's digital backbone. The signal flickered once—then caught. Data lines bled back to life. The secure net hummed.

The city was theirs again.

At least for now.

Kael paused at the edge of a collapsed hangar. Dust and ash gusted faintly as he crouched beside a half-melted exosuit—its left side charred, its right side twisted into unrecognizable shapes. A shattered optic unit blinked once and then died. One arm was missing. The helmet lay cracked open like a dropped skull, blood and coolant pooled around what was left of the operator's head.

In the ruins, glinting silver and char-black, lay a dog tag—half-melted into the chest plate. Kael knelt, brushing ash aside, and read the remnants of the inscription.

A name. Chinese characters. Then: "Unit 514 — Experimental Field Division."

His jaw clenched. He remembered that number.

"Jesus," he muttered.

Footsteps behind him.

Comstock approached, rifle slung, face unreadable. He looked down at the ruin beside Kael and exhaled slowly through his nose.

"They didn't expect to see what they saw," he said quietly.

Kael didn't answer. He stared at the dog tag for another breath, then slipped it into a pouch on his vest—not as a trophy. As a warning.

The sound of approaching engines rumbled in the background—Cárdenas vehicles, armored pickups, and repurposed troop carriers cresting the edge of the airfield.

The second wave was arriving.

Kael stood and turned toward the smoke-washed skyline. Somewhere up there—beyond the clouds, beyond the drone of retreating aircraft—Wu was still out there.

Still watching.

Still waiting.

Minutes Later

The second convoy arrived like a bruised heartbeat—steady, defiant, and marked with loss.

Armored SUVs, Humvees pockmarked with fresh bullet scars, and trucks that had clearly been salvaged from the earlier siege all rolled onto the cracked tarmac. Their wheels crunched over spent shells and shattered steel. Steam hissed from radiators. The scent of diesel mixed with blood and sweat.

Salvador Cárdenas stepped out first.

The head of the cartel wore black boots, a dark collared shirt now streaked with ash, and a heavy silver ring once worn by his own father—a symbol of legacy, power, and the cost of both. He didn't speak as he descended from the SUV. He didn't need to.

His eyes scanned the airfield. The blackened edges of blown-out hangars. The silhouettes of Cárdenas fighters standing guard along the perimeter. The faint glint of a fallen exosuit caught the morning sun.

He took a long breath. Then another.

Leonardo Barragán climbed out next, trailing a scent of gunpowder and cigar smoke. His hand instinctively rested on the grip of his sidearm. Goya followed, adjusting a cracked shoulder plate, his boots still flecked with dried blood. Lieutenant Sosa brought up the rear, silent, scarred, and squinting toward the control tower.

They walked side by side, unhurried, across the runway as the wind kicked up ash around their feet.

Cárdenas spoke first—his voice gravel and thunder.

"We've waited years for this."

He didn't raise his tone. Didn't need to. The moment spoke for him.

Kael stepped forward, flanked by Valeria, Sosa, Padre Luis, and the Hellpack. He gave a curt nod. "The airport is secure. PLA remnants fled north. Wu got out, but he left most of his supply behind."

Cárdenas glanced to the hangars.

His men were already peeling back the blast doors, rifles up, nerves taut. Inside, rows upon rows of crates stood untouched—stacked high, labeled in Chinese and cartel code, sealed with polymer wrap and reinforced aluminum corners.

Leonardo whistled low. "That's a goddamn city of contraband."

Goya blinked. "Cocaine, Veloxyn, fentanyl, AR mod-kits, thermobaric charges, maybe even new prototype units."

The Hellpack ran a hand along one of the crate labels. "They were building a fortress here. A forward base for something bigger."

Valeria added, "There's armor. Exosuits. Spare servo limbs. Regenerative gel packs. They weren't just distributing—they were evolving."

Kael opened a smaller container—rows of tactical comms helmets and encrypted biometric scanners inside. "Wu took what he needed," he said. "But most of it's here. Enough to rebuild or rearm five divisions."

Cárdenas stared at the haul for several seconds, then smiled.

Not wide.

Not cruel.

Just… satisfied.

371

"This is the foundation of something new," he said, stepping into the hangar's center. "Mexico doesn't get a second chance very often."

He turned to face them.

"But this is one."

Then he raised his arms to the soldiers now gathering in a rough circle.

"Light the fires. We'll honor the dead tonight. And after that…"

His eyes locked with Kael's.

"We build new empires."

The Cárdenas men roared—not wild, not drunken—but like soldiers. Their voices echoed through the half-ruined airport with eerie finality.

And beneath the thunder of their celebration, Kael could still hear the whisper of engines overhead—Wu disappearing into the horizon.

He wondered how many more would come.

———————————

Later That Night — The Pyre Ceremony (South Tarmac, Near the Old Fuel Depot)

The sky over Tampico had turned a deep, ember-stained violet.

Smoke from the wreckage still curled upward in lazy spirals, but on the southern edge of the airfield—near the remnants of the fuel depot—they made space for the dead.

It was sacred ground now.

The Cárdenas cartel laid out seventy-three bodies, wrapped not in silence but in the symbols of war. Some were draped in the crimson-stitched Cárdenas insignia. Others bore the faded olive fatigues of guerrilla fighters who had answered the call weeks earlier. Each body was positioned with care. Each weapon—slung, placed, or held—told a story.

There were no trumpets. No hymns.

Only fire.

Kael stood at the front, arms crossed over his chest, face unreadable. Marisol stood beside him, wrapped in a dark shawl that fluttered in the wind like a wing waiting to break free. Her expression was solemn, her hand occasionally brushing against Kael's, tethering them to each other as the night pulled taut around them.

Natalia and Valeria stood together in the second row, both wearing bandages beneath their clothes, both holding torches. Natalia now barley able to walk.

Valeria's shoulder throbbed, but she refused to show it.

She had dressed her own wound again—tight, clinical, with only a half-smirk when Natalia offered to help.

Now, in the firelight, her posture was stiff with pride and pain.

Salvador Cárdenas arrived last. No security. No escort. He walked slowly between the rows of fallen, pausing at each face, each silent name. He nodded once for each.

When he reached the final body, he bent down and whispered something.

No one heard the words.

But the wind seemed to be still for a moment.

Valeria stepped forward and raised her torch. She said nothing at first, just stood there, silhouetted in flame, her gaze sweeping across the mourners.

Then she spoke.

Her voice wasn't loud.

It didn't need to be.

"They didn't fall for a flag," she said. "They fell for the people behind it."

The wind carried her words like ash.

"No one asked them to be heroes. No one promised they'd survive. But they stood. They fought.

And they kept standing even when they knew they wouldn't make it."

She turned to face the flames.

"They didn't die for a cartel. They died for each other."

Kael moved then. He lit the first pyre.

The torch hissed as it touched soaked kindling. Flames crawled upward, crackling through wood, cloth, and memory. Others followed—Goya, Sosa, Natalia. Within minutes, five pyres roared like orange beasts into the night sky.

Smoke rolled like waves, hiding the stars.

Then Kael froze.

One of the bodies—wrapped in a Cárdenas flag stitched with initials—had something dangling from its neck.

A necklace.

Not military. Not cartel. Not tactical.

It was silver. Faded. The chain broken and clumsily repaired.

It was her necklace.

Marisol's.

The one she had worn during their first dance in Puerto Rico. The one she had given to a young courier—the teenager who had volunteered to carry coded documents back east weeks ago.

No one had seen him fall.

Until now.

Kael's breath caught in his throat.

He didn't cry.

But something inside him dimmed, folded, changed.

He didn't say a word.

He just watched as the necklace glinted once— then vanished in flame.

Behind him, Comstock turned away from the fire and slipped into the shadows. No announcement. No farewell.

He was simply gone again.

A ripple of awareness moved through the group, but no one said a word.

It was just what Comstock did.

He came. He burned bright. He vanished.

Just like the ghosts they all were becoming.

Tampico — Just After Midnight.

Airport Control Compound, East Grid.

The fires from the pyre still licked at the night sky when the lights began to die.

First it was the perimeter floodlights—each one flickering once, then cutting out in sequence like dying stars. Then the control tower screens blinked. The signal repeater on the ATC spire sparked twice—then went black. A Cárdenas tech ran to the console, hands flying across the keys.

"I've lost the uplink," he said. "We're blind on civilian and military frequencies."

"What about internal?" Goya barked.

The tech shook his head. "Gone."

All at once, every device within the Cárdenas war compound lit up.

Screens.

Comms units.

Helmet HUDs.

Even the old projector in the war room, still patched into a makeshift command relay.

The screens all went white.

Then a face appeared—blurry, synthetic, digitally scrubbed. Almost human, but not quite. The voice that came with it was calm, filtered through a distortion layer that made it sound like it was speaking from the other side of a grave.

"You think this is over."

Kael, Marisol, and Salvador Cárdenas had just returned to the hangar-turned-operations-center when the image hit.

The voice continued.

"You've taken land. You've flown a flag. But you haven't silenced me."

The camera panned back.

And then came the horror.

A Cárdenas lieutenant—young, barely twenty—was bound to a steel chair. He was shirtless, his tattoos marked him clearly as a Veracruz loyalist. But his body trembled violently. His arms were limp, eyes red and wide, veins already darkened like rivers filled with oil.

The screen zoomed in as Wu stepped into frame.

No exosuit. No tactical gear. Just a plain black shirt. Hair slicked. Calm eyes.

In his hand: a syringe.

Kael's jaw tightened. "This isn't a broadcast."

"This is a fucking ritual," Salvador muttered.

Wu didn't address the camera directly. He didn't monologue. He didn't sneer.

He simply spoke with clinical precision.

"You're fighting with fire and rifles. But I'm building a future that can't bleed."

He knelt beside the boy in the chair. The camera zoomed in as the needle pierced his neck.

The boy screamed—but it came out silent. Foam bubbled at the corners of his mouth. His body shook with violent spasms, muscles contracting in unnatural patterns. His veins turned jet black, pulsing up his neck and down into his chest.

Kael took a step forward—as if he could stop what was already recorded.

Valeria turned away.

Natalia didn't.

The boy convulsed—twice more—then slumped forward.

His heart stopped onscreen.

Then, slowly, Wu looked into the camera.

"This is Veloxyn X," he said. "You've seen its shadow. Now you'll meet its rage."

The screen cut to static.

Then black.

Not a sound remained.

No one moved.

Only the flicker of backup generator lights buzzed in the distance.

Marisol's voice was the first to break the silence.

Soft. Controlled. Terrifying.

"We end it. We end him."

Chapter 29

When the Sky Turned Black

For a few stolen days, war forgot them.

The Hotel Arenas del Mar had once been a boutique luxury resort—a cliffside refuge carved into the edge of the Gulf with sprawling decks, split-level infinity pools, and cabana lounges sculpted from white stone. Now it was the most secure command outpost in the Yucatán.

Satellite dishes had replaced rooftop gardens. Combat drones hovered where champagne used to flow. Snipers nested beneath umbrellas.

But it was quiet. For now.

The sun kissed the coast like it didn't remember the fires. Kael and Marisol walked the beach in bare feet, fingers laced, trying to rebuild something they'd lost back in Puerto Rico and St. Marteen. The rhythm of the waves, the laughter from a distant hammock, the taste of rum and salt—it all pulled them back to that week where everything felt possible.

Kael and Marisol wandered into the surf, letting the water lap at their knees. She reached down, scooped a handful of wet sand, and let it drip between her fingers.

"I used to think I'd die before I ever saw the world look like this again," she said.

Kael looked at her.

"What does it look like?"

She smiled faintly.

"Like it might be worth saving."

He stepped behind her, arms wrapping around her belly. She leaned back into him. He rested his chin on her shoulder.

"I felt them move again," she whispered.

Kael closed his eyes. For a moment, the tide, the heat, her skin—it was all he knew.

"Twins," he said, still stunned.

She nodded. "Two hearts. One war."

But the sea couldn't wash away the war.

Not for long.

Natalia walked barefoot into the suite's stone bathroom, hair wet from the saltwater pool, and a towel slung low around her hips. Valeria sat on the window ledge, in nothing but a Cárdenas tank top, legs curled beneath her, cleaning a sidearm.

"You think we'll ever be civilians again?" Natalia asked.

Valeria did not answer immediately. She slid the mag into place, set the pistol down, and looked out at the waves.

"Civilians die with their eyes closed," she said. "We don't get that luxury."

Natalia smiled.

"But we could sail," she added. "Disappear."

Valeria turned, and smirked. "Is that a proposal?"

Natalia stepped closer.

"No," she whispered. "That's a threat."

They laughed—low, tired, real.

And then Natalia kissed her.

Slow. Long. Like they might never come up for air.

Later by the poolside cabana under the late afternoon sun, the poolside bar at Hotel Arnas shimmered like an oasis pulled from a forgotten dream. The war—just hours behind them—felt a continent away.

The Cárdenas inner circle had begun to gather.

Goya arrived with tactical maps rolled under his arm, already planning the next blockade. Leonardo brought a crate of Cuban cigars and fresh intel from the western corridor. Two Cárdenas lieutenants— former sicarios now acting as coastal administrators—

discussed supply chains over grilled snapper and beers.

The Hellpack lounged near the edge of the water, shirts off, drinks sweating in their hands, weapons propped lazily against a nearby table like they were just tools from another job.

Sawtooth reclined in a chair with her boots up, sipping a mezcal margarita through a steel straw. "I don't trust any bar that doesn't have bullet holes," she muttered with a grin, eyeing the luxury around them.

Boomer had claimed the grill and was flipping some stolen steaks like a man born to barbecue. "I could get used to cartel hospitality," he said, tossing a piece of sizzling meat into his mouth without flinching.

Ghoul stood waist-deep in the pool, a beer in one hand and an M249 in the other, barrel still slick with jungle moisture. He stared out toward the sea, unreadable. "War's never far," he muttered. "But today… it can wait."

Nearby, under the shade of a palapa, Padre Luis sat cross-legged on a lounge chair surrounded by four Cárdenas soldiers. He wasn't drinking—just swirling a glass of coconut water, rosary beads draped around his fingers like a second skin. "When the blood dries," he said gently, "we must remember why we bled. And more importantly—what we do with the breath we still carry."

The soldiers listened, quiet and sunburnt, heads bowed. The padre continued, voice soft but firm, "God sees the hearts of killers. He sees yours. The question is—can you?"

In the background, laughter from the Hellpack rose like smoke into the gold-streaked sky. For now, peace held.

Kael and Marisol arrived late.

She wore a white sundress. He wore nothing tactical.

Comstock toasted the air with a mezcal bottle. "Our rebels look like gods now."

Cárdenas grinned. "We are still monsters. Just washed."

They sat. Ate. Smoked. Laughed.

For a brief hour, it felt like something new.

Something almost human.

Upstairs, on the balcony of their shared suite, Natalia and Valeria sat in lounge chairs, wine glasses in hand, legs tangled as they watched the tide roll in.

"I dream about Barcelona sometimes," Valeria said. "But we both know where we'll be in two weeks."

Natalia nodded. "Covered in blood."

Valeria smiled. "And still reaching for each other."

Then she set her wine glass down and looked out at the horizon, sun painting the waves in gold and gray.

"Even paradise feels like a lie," she whispered,

"When you've memorized the weight of a rifle."

Natalia did not speak.

She just reached for her hand—and held on.

The next morning Cárdenas, Leonardo, and Goya had converted a tactical tent beside the control tower into a war room. A large digital map of eastern Mexico flickered behind them.

Cárdenas workers moved briskly across the airfield—dragging away bodies, torching the remains of enemy vehicles, and stacking Veloxyn crates with cartel tags freshly printed in red and gold.

The airport was functional again.

So was production.

Salvador Cárdenas leaned over the table, tapping coordinates.

"Once Veracruz falls, I am backing Sosa as governor of the corridor. Mérida to the Gulf. Full legitimacy. He has earned it."

Sosa, standing nearby, simply nodded. "I'll make them fear peace more than war."

Cárdenas did not answer right away.

He placed a hand briefly on Sosa's shoulder—strong, but not showy. His eyes stayed fixed on the tactical map, even as Goya leaned closer and murmured:

"Let's hope he holds the line."

Cárdenas did not smile.

He just said, "He'd bet."

But one shadow still lingered.

Mateo 'El Venado' Cárdenas—Marisol's younger brother—had gone dark.

Last seen near Poza Rica, he hadn't responded to encrypted pings, cartel runners, or even his mother's voice on direct comm.

Cárdenas stared out toward the mountains, eyes narrowed.

"Something's wrong," he said. "He doesn't hide. He hunts."

————————————

Comstock's Quarters — 08:14 Hours

Comstock lit a cigar, flipped open his encrypted sat phone, and stared at the blinking alert.

Incoming transmission: USS Portland, LPD-27.

He answered.

The naval commander's voice was clipped, direct.

"Comstock, we have eyes on two PLA container ships—Type 071 LPD-class. Heading for Veracruz. No official manifest. No insignia."

Comstock went still.

"Reinforcement fleet?"

"Looks that way."

He ended the call, stood slowly, and pulled on his tactical vest.

Then he hailed Kael.

"We need a sit-down. Full table. Cárdenas, Marisol, Sosa, Natalia, Goya—everyone."

Kael answered immediately. "Wu?"

Comstock's voice dropped to a whisper.

"He is building an empire in Veracruz. And he just called in his army."

Two Days Later — War Council, Arenas del Mar

The morning light filtered through the salt-streaked windows of the repurposed hotel banquet hall. Maps, satellite photos, and encrypted comms covered the long mahogany table where the Cárdenas inner circle sat.

Salvador Cárdenas took his usual place at the head. Around him: Leonardo, Goya, Sosa, Kael, Marisol, Natalia, Valeria, Comstock, and the Hellpack who stood beside the main monitor, flipping through tactical imagery pulled just hours earlier.

Comstock tapped the screen.

"Let's start with this."

A high-res satellite image flickered to life.

Two massive PLA container ships—Type 071 LPD-class—sat one hundred miles off the Veracruz coast, loitering in blue water, not transmitting identification. No docking activity. No flight paths. Just… waiting.

"Rogue fleet," Comstock said. "No public manifests. No radio chatter. If they move, they will do it under cover of darkness and cloud cover."

Kael leaned forward. "So, what are they waiting for?"

Comstock clicked again.

"This."

A new image appeared—a rail station near the industrial port in Veracruz, less a hundred yards from the port. Half-covered by tarps and scaffolding were heavy transport trains, lined in a series of loading bays.

"They're preparing to move whatever comes off those ships by rail. No trucks. No risk of air interception. Fast. Hidden. Efficient."

Cárdenas lit a cigar. "So… distribution is ready. He just needs the product."

"That's not all," Comstock added. Another image flashed a grainy zoom captured from a surveillance drone.

A convoy.

Thirty-eight vehicles, moving south along Highway 180, cutting toward Veracruz from the north. Armored pickups. Fuel tankers. Utility rigs. All unmarked.

"Here's the riddle," Comstock said. "We do not know who they are. They are encrypted. No comms. No cartel identifiers."

Goya frowned. "You think it's Lee Ho?"

Sosa shook his head. "Lee Ho does not move quietly. He broadcasts his firepower."

Natalia tapped the edge of the table. "Then it's either reinforcements Wu called in…"

"…or Mateo," Marisol finished.

Silence.

Cárdenas stared at the image. His jaw tightened. "Still no word?"

Leonardo shook his head. "He is alive. We have had sightings. But no contact. No replies. Nothing."

Comstock looked around the room. "Whether it's Lee Ho, rogue PLA, or Mateo building a third front—we need eyes on that convoy."

Kael nodded slowly. "I'll lead the recon team."

Cárdenas raised an eyebrow. "You sure?"

Kael's voice was calm. "If it's Mateo, he won't fire on me."

The sun was sliding low over Tampico, bleeding orange across the cracked windows of the hotel conference room. Maps were spread across a long table, some tattered and coffee-stained, others printed just days ago from military satellite feeds. The mood was electric and tight, like the storm before the hurricane.

Salvador Cárdenas stood at the head of the table, fingers pressed into the map of Veracruz. His eyes scanned every ridge and river like a general plotting his final campaign. Around him, the war family had gathered.

Kael leaned against the wall, arms crossed. Comstock sat with his boots on the table, casually drinking espresso from a chipped cup. Marisol, flawless even in combat wear, had her hair pulled back in a tight braid, eyes locked on the coastline. Sosa flipped through pages of tactical reports. Goya leaned forward on his elbows, silent but burning with intent. Padre Luis clutched his rosary but said nothing yet. The Hellpack stood scattered—Boomer cleaning his grenade bandolier, Sawtooth carving a small cross into the table with a combat knife, and Ghoul flipping through a stolen Chinese field manual.

"Veracruz is a nest of snakes," Cárdenas said flatly. "Wu's remnants, Nueve Vidas stragglers, and now rumors of Russian-supplied mercs near the old naval yards. We can't just walk in."

"We don't walk," Kael said. "We hit hard, hit fast, and stay liquid."

"From where?" Sosa interjected. "The main highways are watched. Drone activity's heavy between here and Poza Rica."

Goya pointed at the map. "There's still movement along Route 1800, but they're setting up sandbag positions here and here. We'd be ambushed before we made it halfway."

"What about the air?" Marisol asked. "We still have that Black Hawks in storage."

Comstock shook his head. "Too risky. Chinese radar has picked up everything lately. That's a shoot-on-sight risk."

Boomer grunted. "Then how the hell do we get there? Dig a tunnel?"

That's when Kael and Comstock locked eyes.

Kael pushed off the wall. "We don't go around. We go through. The ocean up the river."

Comstock smiled. "You thinking what I'm thinking, cowboy?"

"SURCs," Kael confirmed. "Load up, ride quietly, hit the Gulf, and slip up the Rio Grande."

Padre Luis straightened slowly. "I know that river like the lines on my palms. I grew up on the outskirts of Veracruz—my family fished it, baptized their dead in it. You take me on that water; I'll get you home."

Cárdenas looked at him with surprise. "You're from Veracruz?"

Luis nodded. "Before I was a priest, I was a fighter in those hills. After that a mercenary for Executive Outcomes in Africa. Then a sinner by the sea. God never forgets his rivers."

Sawtooth smirked. "Alright preacher, let's baptize some bullets."

Ghoul laughed under his breath. "And maybe some war criminals."

Cárdenas stepped back from the map. "Alright. We take the SURCs. Load heavy, keep it fast. We move tonight."

Comstock raised his glass. "Then let's go give Veracruz a sermon they won't forget."

Kael looked around the room. Every face, every scar, every story—etched into the war they now carried. He grabbed his rifle from the table.

"Let's ride the river."

And just like that, the storm began to move.

Arenas del Mar — Marisol's Balcony (Later That Night)

The war room had emptied, but Marisol stayed behind, standing barefoot on the balcony above the sea, her hands resting over her belly.

The air was warm. The ocean was steady.

But her mind was a storm.

Mateo.

El Venado.

Her brother. Her wild shadow. The one who danced with knives as a boy and never once feared the dark. She had seen him bleed for the family. Kill for it. Laugh through it. And vanish into it.

Now… silence.

Not even her mother's voice had drawn him home.

She looked down at the soft swell of her stomach. The twins kicked once—light, subtle.

She closed her eyes.

"Don't make your uncle someone I have to kill."

A tear slid down her cheek before she could stop it.

Behind her, the wind lifted the hem of the Cárdenas cartel flag that had been draped over the railing.

And still, the ocean rolled.

Río Grande — 1 Mile from Insertion Point (04:37 Hours)

The jungle was still, moonlight bleeding through the canopy like smoke.

Then—gunfire.

From the tree line, less than thirty yards away, a wall of muzzle flashes erupted, lighting the riverbank in staccato bursts.

Exosuited fighters.

Nine Lives cartel gunners.

Wu's perimeter patrol.

They weren't falling for the old river infiltration tactic—not again.

"AMBUSH!" Comstock roared.

The jungle exploded with chaos.

.50 caliber fire from the boat's mounted guns ripped through the trees, shredding palm trunks and bark into splinters. Shell casings clattered like hail against the hull.

Kael pivoted behind the Mk 19 grenade launcher.

Thump. Thump. Thump.

40mm grenades launched in succession, exploding in airbursts that rocked the shoreline.

But the enemy was close. Too close.

The rear SURC caught a direct hit to the fuel cell—a thunderous crack followed by a fireball that lit up the night. Men were hurled into the dark water, flames licking up behind them.

Kael felt the blast in his chest. His heart pounded as instinct took over.

"TURN US AROUND!" he shouted.

Comstock yanked the wheel, veering into the chaos. The forward boat looped back, weaving through debris and floating bodies.

Natalia pulled two drenched Cárdenas men aboard while Goya returned fire with short bursts, blood spattered across his arms.

Shell casings rained down into Natalia's vest— one dropped between the plates and burned into her chest.

She cried out, jumped up, slapping at her gear.

Valeria, crouched beside her, went pale. "Are you hit?"

Natalia ripped open the vest—just burned skin. Nothing worse. She gritted her teeth and gave Valeria a nod.

"No bleeding. Let's go."

Ahead, a recoilless 75mm round screamed through the air—direct hit to one of the enemy exosuits.

Boom.

Steel, hydraulics, and shredded meat exploded across the treeline.

The boat surged forward, now overloaded— Kael, Comstock, Natalia, Valeria, Goya, Padre Luis, and the Hellback and half the original rear crew crammed into one vessel.

Men fired from both sides, rifles barking as the last rounds sent the jungle into retreat.

The jungle snapped with rifle fire and the roar of engines as Wu's exoskeleton-clad soldiers emerged from the mangroves like armored beasts. Hydraulic joints hissed. Servo motors growled. Bullets pinged off the heavy plating that wrapped their torsos like mechanical muscle. From the lead SURC, Ángel "Boomer" Valdés let out a low whistle.

"Well shit," he muttered, taking a 40mm grenade and slapping it into his M79. "Looks like Christmas came early."

"Left bank!" Reva "Sawtooth" Guerra shouted, raising her AA-12. The fully automatic shotgun thundered in her grip, unleashing a wall of slugs that slammed into one of the exo-soldiers mid-charge. The impact staggered it—just long enough for Elias "Ghoul" Navarro to hose it down with his M249 SAW, rounds punching into weak joints until the suit collapsed under its own weight.

"They're using IR to track us!" Ghoul barked. "Pop the flares!"

Sawtooth was already moving. She slapped a flare launcher onto the rail and fired into the tree line.

A bright burst of magnesium lit up the riverbank, temporarily blinding the enemy's optics. Boomer used the moment to lob two grenades behind the nearest boulder—both detonating with a thump that sent one of Wu's men flying backward into the river, armor cracked open like a crab shell.

"Do not let 'em cross!" Comstock shouted from the front of the boat.

"Working on it!" Boomer yelled. "Goddamn cockroaches in robot suits!"

"More like tin cans with anger issues," Ghoul added, switching mags with muscle memory and lighting up a second wave.

As tracer fire lit the river like a concert from hell, the Hellpack held their line—synchronized, savage, and surgical. Every movement spoke of experience. Every kill was executed with brutal precision.

Then—silence.

The boat rounded the next bend, finally out of the kill zone.

Kael stood, smoking barrel in hand, watching the tree line vanish behind them.

So much for secrecy.

Comstock spat into the river. "Well… they know we're here now."

Kael checked his sidearm. "Good. Saves us the trouble of knocking."

Three miles Away — Wu's Forward Command Post, Veracruz

The jungle was quiet, except for the low, constant hum of surveillance drones circling overhead.

From his mobile command deck—half-buried in the hillside of an abandoned concrete facility— Colonel Wu watched the river curve in the distance.

Then—a flash.

Bright. Wide. Red orange against the blackness of pre-dawn.

One of the boats had gone up. The explosion painted the trees in silhouette for half a second.

Wu's face didn't change. But his breath did.

He stepped closer to the open hatch and listened.

A burst of enemy chatter cut through the encrypted PLA channel—scrambled, but not enough.

"...Kael... Comstock... on foot... advancing west shore... jungle..."

Wu's eyes twitched.

He did not flinch. He just clenched one armored fist—and brought it down on the metal table in front of him.

CRACK.

The table snapped in two, steel warping beneath the exosuit's amplified strength. Sparks shot out from a spilled data pack. A lantern clattered to the floor.

Still breathing hard, Wu turned to one of his lieutenants.

"Let them come," he said in Mandarin. "Let them walk."

Western Shoreline — Minutes After Insertion

The survivors of the ambush had reached land.

Kael, Comstock, Natalia, Valeria, and Goya. Padre Luis and the Hellpack moved quietly up the bank, rifles ready. Water dripped from their bodies, dark rivulets running off tactical gear and soaking into the jungle floor.

They crouched beneath a thick canopy of ferns, listening.

Voices echoed faintly in the distance—Spanish. PLA accents. Cartel slang. Patrols close by, but not close enough to reveal their exact location.

Kael signaled: silence. hold. move slow.

The adrenaline that had kept them wired moments ago was now draining, replaced by sharp breath, wet fabric, and the raw awareness that they were inside enemy territory with no exit plan.

Natalia leaned in toward Kael and whispered, "Feels like Mosul."

He gave her one look.

"No," he said. "Mosul had better cover."

They began to move.

Shadows among shadows.

Footsteps kissing wet leaves. Rifles angled. Eyes up. Every second carried weight.

The jungle welcomed them like a sleeping serpent.

―――――――――――――――

Dawn — Hillside Lookout, West of Veracruz

By sunrise, they had climbed 300 feet up a narrow ravine and found a crumbling stone house overlooking the valley.

It looked like it had once belonged to a farmer—or maybe a smuggler—half-swallowed by vines and weather, but the roof held, and the windows framed a perfect vantage point of the city below.

From this elevation, they could see everything:

Veracruz Marina.

The industrial rail junction.

The refinery smokestacks.

And in the distance, faint but clear—the airport control tower, still flying no flag.

They would move at night.

Until then, this was shelter.

Inside the house, the team stripped off soaked gear and found dry corners to rest and regroup. Natalia, Valeria, Sosa Goya, and Padre Luis sat near the broken fireplace, patching a ripped pack and quietly watching Comstock, who stood near the window, sipping from a tin mug. The Hellpack laid a few claymores mines and trip flares around the perimeter.

Valeria finally asked the question lingering in all their minds.

"Why are you even helping us?"

Comstock did not look at her. He just stared through the cracked window at the city below.

"Because Cárdenas, for all his sins... always respected the game."

Natalia tilted her head. "What game?"

Comstock turned to face them.

"The unspoken one. Cárdenas paid taxes. Did not shoot at cops. Did not overthrow states or destabilize cities. He built—not burned. He moved product, yes, but he employed people. Paid salaries. Ran ports. Bought hospitals."

He sipped again, eyes cold now.

"The others? Los Huesos Rojos. Nine Lives. Wu? They torture teachers. Shoot mayors. They peddle fear and traffic human lives like cattle. You back that kind of chaos, you don't get to rebuild. You just... rot."

Goya nodded quietly.

Valeria asked, "So we're friends?"

Comstock smirked. "Today." He turned back to the window. "Tomorrow? That is a different story."

The air shifted slightly.

Natalia looked toward Kael, who was checking his gear by the door. "And what about you?" she asked. "You gonna be our friend tomorrow?"

Kael did not answer right away.

Then, with his eyes still down:

"I did not come looking for this. Any of it. I would rather be on the Commodore. With Marisol. And the twins."

Silence.

All three turned to him.

"Twins?" Valeria grinned.

Natalia's eyes went wide. "Wait... you're serious?"

393

Kael gave a rare, honest smile. "Yeah. Two of them."

Goya slapped his shoulder. "¡Coño! You are a cartel commander and a daddy now?"

Even Comstock raised an eyebrow, pausing mid-sip.

He let them celebrate for a beat, then turned toward the back of the house and said flatly:

"I need air."

He stepped outside, lifting his encrypted satellite phone and slipping into the shadows near a moss-covered wall. His face turned hard as steel as the call connected.

"Yeah. It's me. The Cárdenas crew is all here. Kael too."

A pause.

"They have got no idea Cárdenas once trafficked bodies out of Honduras with Nine Lives. I do not care if it was years ago. It is going to matter soon."

He ended the call.

Chapter 30

The Wolves Are Watching

The sun had long since dipped behind the haze of smoke and steel, casting a dull crimson glow across the hills. After hours of rest in the abandoned hillside house, Kael stirred to the distant crackle of gunfire. The sounds came in pulses—bursts of automatic fire, then silence, then the low boom of something heavier. Artillery or mortars, maybe both.

He moved to the edge of the hill and raised a pair of battered binoculars. Through the smoky air, he could make out a convoy—about forty-five vehicles, mostly technicals and armored pickups—engaging with a splintered formation of Chinese rogue forces and cartel fighters along Highway 1800. Muzzle flashes lit up the edge of the city like fireflies on a warpath.

"They're pushing into Veracruz," Kael said, handing the binoculars to Goya. "That's our window."

Under the cover of darkness and the chaos erupting on the far side of the city, the team began moving. Natalia and Valeria moved like cats, slipping between ruined buildings, their pistols tucked tight under their worn jackets. Comstock stayed back, covering the rear with his suppressed rifle slung across his chest, eyes scanning every rooftop.

As they rolled through the broken streets of Veracruz, the Hellpack moved like shadows beside Kael, Natalia, Valeria, Padre Luis, and Sosa. Reva "Sawtooth" Guerra scanned every alley with her shotgun raised, while Boomer muttered about possible ambush points, fingering the grenades on his chest rig. Ghoul took rear security, his SAW M249 sweeping windows above as the group passed crumbling buildings tagged with rival cartel symbols and scorched by war. Padre Luis whispered quiet prayers for the city's lost souls, while Valeria kept her hand near her sidearm, eyes sharp. Kael led from the front, Comstock a few feet behind—silent, focusing each step bringing them closer to the stronghold.

In a trash-strewn alley, they found a few old taxi cabs—sun-faded yellow with cracked windows and a crooked front bumper. Nearby, a clothesline flapped in the wind, hung with weathered jeans, sun-bleached button-downs, and a few floral-print blouses stiff with dust.

"We need to blend in," Natalia said. She grabbed a long dress shirt and tied it over her tactical gear.

Kael changed into a loose short-sleeve and pulled a straw hat low over his brow. "I look like I sell coconuts to tourists."

Valeria smirked. "No. You look like a tourist who gets robbed buying coconuts."

Comstock slid on a pair of aviators missing one lens. "We are a fashion disaster and a half. Let's roll."

Sosa was already pulling down a weathered flannel shirt and a straw hat, chuckling. "Think I'll go farmer chic."

Ghoul grabbed a black hoodie and a pair of loose cargos. "This one smells like old tacos," he muttered, pulling it on anyway. Boomer found a jacket stitched with a faded Veracruz soccer logo and gave a mock salute. "Local hero now."

Sawtooth tossed her tactical vest under a tarp and buttoned up a blue blouse. "How do I look?" she asked flatly.

"Like someone who could still kill me with a butter knife," Sosa said.

Padre Luis swapped his bloodied clerical shirt for a light guayabera, then slung his rosary back around his neck. "A priest must always dress for the people," he said solemnly, though a hint of a grin tugged at the corners of his mouth.

By the time they emerged from the alley, Kael, Natalia, Valeria, and Comstock were already waiting — similarly disguised, weapons hidden beneath layers of thrift-store anonymity. They all looked like tired locals, travelers maybe, except for the hardness in their eyes.

"Let's move," Kael said. "We've got work to finish."

With the team disguised, they loaded into the cabs. Goya took the wheel of one, his face smeared with grease to dull the shine of sweat. The engine sputtered to life, coughing smoke as they rolled downhill toward the marina.

About a mile out, the lights of the checkpoint came into view.

Kael held up a hand. "Kill the lights. Coast the rest of the way."

They drifted forward, the engine silent now. Five men manned the checkpoint—three outside smoking near a stack of fuel drums, two inside the small hut watching the distant firefight to the west.

Kael turned to the team. "Three outside—hand and knife. Comstock takes the hut."

"Copy that," Comstock said, already unslinging his rifle.

Valeria rolled her neck. "I haven't knifed anyone in two days. I'm getting rusty."

Natalia nudged her. "You always say that right before you show off."

Kael slid from the passenger seat, blade in hand. Goya mirrored him on the far side. Natalia and Valeria melted into the shadows, flanking wide. They moved in sync—no words, no signals. Just years of training and blood-borne instinct.

Kael reached the first guard and drove the blade under his ribs, catching the man's body as it folded. Goya spun and cut the second. Valeria swept in behind the third, her knife glinting once before it vanished into the dark.

A sharp hiss—then two soft thumps.

Comstock's rifle barked once, twice. The men inside the hut slumped forward, still staring at the monitor as their blood bloomed across the screens.

"Checkpoint's clear," Comstock radioed.

Kael wiped the blade on his shirt and looked toward the marina. Floodlights framed the dockyard in harsh white, and beyond that—the masts. The boats. The sea.

"Move in," he said. "Quiet and fast. We get what we came for… or we die trying."

As they neared the sprawling container yard that bordered the marina, the group slowed to a crawl. The lights were blinding—brutal flood beams mounted to the dock cranes, cutting across rows of stacked shipping containers. The noise was industrial, almost indifferent to the chaos unfolding just miles away. Hydraulic hisses, the whine of diesel engines, and the groan of heavy steel being moved filled the night air.

Kael held up a fist.

Without a word, the team grabbed a few weather-worn burlap sacks and a shredded gray tarp from the corner of a rusted storage pallet. They climbed up three containers high, careful to stay in the shadows between cargo stacks. There, huddled beneath the tarp and sacks, they concealed their silhouettes—just shapes in the clutter. Eyes in the dark.

Above them, small recon drones buzzed past, their IR sensors scanning the container rows with mechanical indifference. No one dared breathe loud enough to be heard.

Then they saw it.

"Jesus…" Goya whispered.

What they had expected to be two Chinese cargo ships turned out to be four—massive, black-hulled transports sitting low in the water. Kael squinted. "They must have sailed in formation. Close enough to mask radar returns."

On the docks below, chaos was organized.

Chinese marines barked orders in Mandarin as crates of exoskeleton suits—sleek, armored, terrifying—were offloaded from the first two ships and placed onto reinforced rail cars. Nearby, Type 99 main battle tanks rolled forward under their own power, treads grinding over steel plates. Norinco Tiger armored vehicles were staged like a spear tip, their cannon barrels wrapped in tarp but unmistakable.

"It's not a shipment," Valeria said. "It's a fucking invasion."

Dozens of rail cars were already loaded, Kael counted one hundred eight one cars before they curved out of view. The train's twin locomotives at the head of the line were roaring, the engines hot and ready to pull.

Comstock tapped his comms and broke protocol.

"This is Comstock, code Sierra-Ghost-Alpha, broadcasting on black channel. Immediate contact. I repeat—requesting real-time relay to the USS Portland."

Static. Then a voice crackled back. "Portland copies. Hold position. What's your SITREP?"

"Four Chinese transports. Repeat—four. Rail line nearly full. Armor, exosuits, infantry weapons. Entire mechanized division."

"Stand by."

They waited in silence.

Natalia whispered, "What the hell are they planning?"

Kael answered, voice low and calm. "They are leaving. Veracruz is lost, and they know it. They are not staying to fight in a city where every building is a sniper's nest. This—" he gestured toward the train "—this is a strategic withdrawal. They're heading inland. Regroup. Regenerate. My guess? They'll ride those rails straight into cartel territory… probably Nueve Vidas. Secure new partners. New fronts."

Goya muttered, "Then we're gonna have a bigger war than anyone's ready for."

Thirty minutes passed. The first rail convoy jolted, then rumbled forward—headlights sweeping through the dockyard like a ghost train on fire.

Then he appeared.

Colonel Sheng Wu, crisp in his officer's coat, emerged from a command vehicle and strode to the dock's edge. He barked new orders. The first two ships began to pull away from the berth, while the remaining two advanced to dock.

More men. More weapons. More fire.

Comstock's voice cracked with urgency as he reopened comms. "This is Comstock again. We've got second-phase unloading in progress. Need immediate action. I can get coordinates."

"Copy. Send GPS lock now."

He pulled a compact rangefinder from his chest rig and marked both vessels. The data fed into his comm pad—distances, GPS coordinates, and thermal signatures relayed up the chain.

A pause. Then the Portland's comms officer returned, voice clipped and grave.

"USS Michael Monsoor (DDG-1001) is four hundred miles out—exiting Pascagoula yesterday morning. Target lock authorized. Eight Tomahawk cruise missiles inbound. Two per ship."

Kael looked up.

Even under the tarp, the air felt electric. The beginning of something seismic.

He looked to the others.

"Let's watch the sky."

Distant gunfire still echoed from the west—sporadic now, like the final gasps of a dying firefight.

But a different sound crept in behind them. Heavier. Closer.

The low rumble of boots. Not just a squad. Dozens.

Kael tensed, eyes narrowing. From their perch atop the shipping containers, he peered down toward the service road threading through the stacks.

Shapes emerged. Four—no, five dozen armed men in ragged gear, moving tactically but fast. Flashlights off. Weapons drawn. Some carried RPGs over their shoulders, others marched with M4s, AKs, and suppressed SMGs.

Goya's brow furrowed. "Wait… that can't be—"

He dropped from the ledge and moved cautiously toward the figures, one hand raised.

A dozen weapons snapped toward him. Then one man stepped forward.

Young. Muscular. A bulletproof vest over a white tank top soaked in sweat. His hair was matted from heat, but the swagger was unmistakable.

Mateo Cárdenas.

"El Venado," Goya muttered.

Mateo blinked in surprise. "Goya?"

"You're a hard man to find, Teo."

Mateo's eyes narrowed. "You're supposed to be in Cuba. Or dead. What the hell are you doing here? You working for Nueve Vidas now?"

"No," Goya said. "Kael's here. Natalia, Valeria, Sosa Padre Luis, and the Hellpack too. We have been hiding on top of the stacks, watching the docks. Planning."

Mateo's jaw clenched. "Of course you are. Always sneaking in at the last second, stealing my thunder." He motioned angrily toward the ships. "You know how long I've been tracking this shipment?

401

Trying to prove to my father that I can run the organization one day. This was supposed to be my op."

Goya raised both hands in a calming gesture. "You will get the credit, Teo. We are just here to stop a goddamn invasion. We have already got naval strike inbound. eight Tomahawks. Two per ship."

Mateo blinked. "Tomahawks?"

"They are coming. But those bastards are unloading faster than expected. We need to stall them."

Moments later, Mateo and his men climbed up the containers and joined the team.

Natalia's eyes lit up when she saw him. "Nice of you to join the party."

"Next time, leave me a damn invitation," Mateo snapped, though the edge in his voice softened when Valeria offered him a half-smile.

Kael knelt beside them, scanning the dockyard through a monocular. "They are prepping the second train. Wu is directing with pinpoint speed."

"We're outnumbered," Natalia said, "but if we stall them long enough, the strike will land while the cargos still stacked."

Mateo looked at the racks of RPGs his men carried. "We don't have long. We hit them from the shadows. Fragment them. Kill the rhythm."

"Hit and vanish," Kael confirmed. "Small groups. Fire, relocate, fire again."

Goya chambered a round. "Stir chaos. Make them think we are more than we are."

Mateo smirked. "Time to make a little thunder."

Kael gave the nod.

They slipped into position—wolves in the shadows of steel.

And then… the first RPG streaked through the night, roaring like a devil let loose.

The gunfire erupted in jagged bursts, echoing off the steel walls of the shipping yard like thunder trapped in a cage.

Colonel Sheng Wu did not flinch. He knew.

Knew exactly who had triggered the ambush. Knew the style. The rhythm. That signature western arrogance layered over jungle-born precision.

"They never quit," he muttered in Mandarin, his voice a venomous whisper. "Like mosquitoes. Fire ants. Always biting."

He ducked behind a forklift as bullets sparked off its side. Around him, hundreds of Chinese marines began to mobilize, sweeping the yard in disciplined waves. Orders rang out. Weapons lifted. Flamethrowers hissed to life. The ground trembled with motion.

Wu's hand went to his sidearm. Then he froze—eyes narrowing.

A shadow leapt from the top of the containers. Not dropped. Leapt.

Kael.

Landing hard, his boots cracking against the steel with force that sent up a puff of dust. His side burned. His lungs begged for air. But none of it mattered.

He was done running.

From behind, Natalia gasped. "Kael!"

Padre Luis watched in disbelief as Kael launched himself off the shipping container, boots hitting the ground hard as he sprinted toward Wu without hesitation.

The old priest clutched his rosary tight. "Santa María, madre de Dios… he's got the soul of a lion and the brains of a papaya." He crossed himself quickly. "Señor, if you must take him today, at least let him take Wu with him." Then under his breath: "And please… do not let him get shot in the face again. He just healed."

Valeria reached for him, but Comstock stopped her, his voice tight. "No. He knows what he's doing."

Comstock dropped to one knee and began firing—tight, controlled bursts—covering Kael's advance. Each shot lanced through smoke and chaos, buying precious seconds.

Wu stood tall, watching Kael come for him.

The Colonel cracked his neck to the side and charged.

Two bulls in a China shop. Two sovereign warriors bred in opposite hemispheres of war, violence, and consequence.

They slammed into each other with a force that knocked a metal cargo drum off its base. Blades flashed. Fists blurred.

They rolled—one on top of the other—a brutal, desperate ballet with no rhythm except violence. Kael drove a knee into Wu's ribs. Wu elbowed Kael's throat. Blood flecked the sand. A grunt. A roar. A cracked tooth.

Wu twisted, pinning Kael, and drove a Chinese combat knife into Kael's thigh.

Kael screamed, shoved him off, staggered back—only for a ricocheted bullet to catch him in the side of the vest, knocking the wind from his lungs.

He dropped to one knee.

Comstock sighted through the scope—no shot. Too many bodies. Too much movement.

Kael's vision blurred. Wu stalked forward, eyes gleaming.

And then—

The sky cracked.

A sonic boom. The sound of steel splitting the heavens.

Eight Tomahawk cruise missiles shrieked overhead, silent at first, then screaming with the fury of retribution.

In the half-second of silence before the impact, Kael looked up.

Wu did too.

One missile hit the lead ship—mid-deck—detonating with a blossom of fire that turned night into day. The second punched through the engine room of the sister ship, sending shrapnel and men sailing into the air like rag dolls. The third smashed into the staging zone on the dock, obliterating a line of armored vehicles mid-transfer, scattering scorched debris across the pier.

The fourth tomahawk slammed into the bridge of the third vessel, instantly vaporizing its command center. The fifth struck a fuel reservoir along the quay—igniting a fireball so massive it sucked the air from the lungs of men two blocks away. The sixth and seventh missiles found their marks on the other two Type 071 LPD transport ships leaving the dock with clinical precision, carving through hull and steel, leaving nothing but molten wreckage and screams echoing over the harbor.

The eighth missile veered right—its guidance system compromised. It streaked over the bay in a smoking arc, dipped low, meant for the docked vessel near Wu—overshot, veering just yards off target and exploded on the dock.

Padre Luis watched from the rooftop, clutching his rosary. "Seven seals broken. One spared by grace. Even God has a sense of mystery."

The yard erupted in a rolling fireball. Tanks flipped. Cranes buckled. Shockwaves roared through the cargo stacks.

Wu was hurled backward—smoke-trailing, spinning, the shockwave lifted Wu off his feet and hurled him like a ragdoll into a collapsed forklift and vanished behind a wall of flame.

Kael collapsed beside a container wall, ears ringing, skin seared by proximity. Blood from his thigh soaked into the dirt.

Kael barely had time to cover his head. Screaming Chinese marines were thrown across the yard. Flames belched into the sky, shrapnel rained like hail.

The sky still trembled from the last echoes of the missile strike. Smoke curled into the heavens, dark and oily, as fires gnawed at the edges of the dockyard.

Wu stood again.

Staggering. Bleeding. Alive.

Around him, what remained of his marine battalion rallied. He barked a rapid series of commands in Mandarin, face twisted with fury and shame.

They began to load what they could—damaged vehicles, crates, weapons—onto the second train already warming on the tracks.

Wu climbed aboard the last flatbed.

As the rail cars began to roll out, Wu turned and stared back at the fire-wreathed yard.

Behind them, what remained of Wu's army scattered—burning, screaming, retreating into the shadows of a broken dock.

Above them, fire rained like judgment.

The third—meant for the docked vessel near Wu—overshot, veering just yards off target.

It hit the dock.

The team moved through the wreckage, bloodied and limping. Every breath they took was soaked in ash and adrenaline.

Kael lay motionless near a burned-out container wall, his leg wrapped in a blood-soaked tourniquet. His body convulsed with shallow breaths. His eyes fluttered, but he wasn't looking at anyone—he couldn't. His mind drifted somewhere between now and the void. He felt Comstock's arms wrap around him, dragging him to cover. Valeria and Natalia appeared moments later, weapons ready, eyes wild.

"Is he—?" Valeria began.

"He's alive," Comstock growled. "But we need to move. Now."

"Jesus," Valeria whispered, dropping to her knees beside him. "He's ice cold."

Comstock pressed two fingers against Kael's neck. "Pulse is weak. Fading."

Natalia tore open a trauma pack and knelt beside them, hands moving fast—pressing gauze, checking pupils, muttering under her breath like a prayer she didn't believe in.

Around them lay the remains of an abandoned invasion: Thirty Tiger armored vehicles, a dozen Chinese tanks, and crates of weapons, ammunition, and sleek black exosuits—stacked in perfect rows, untouched by the chaos.

"This is a fucking arsenal," Goya muttered.

Comstock stood, scanning the wreckage with grim focus. "We do not have time. Everyone grab a Tiger. We are getting him to Tampico. Now."

Valeria moved, almost running, boots echoing off scorched pavement. "I'll find one with a working med bay in the rear."

Mateo Cárdenas stepped forward, dusted in ash, his rifle slung and forgotten.

"I'm staying," he said.

Comstock looked over. "This isn't the time for ego, Mateo."

"This isn't ego," Mateo replied. "It's purpose. We've got survivors scattered, Cárdenas loyalists hiding, civilians trapped. This place is a mess. I can rebuild it. I have to."

He looked down at Kael—barely breathing, eyes half-lidded, face pale—then turned away. "Get him out of here. Save him. I'll handle Veracruz."

Padre Luis dropped beside him, rosary beads clutched tight in one hand, the other pressing down on the wound.

"Oh Lord," he muttered, "I know this one's sinned with women, guns, and rum—but if you're taking requests today, maybe hold off just a little longer."

Sawtooth knelt nearby, pulling Kael's plate carrier loose with sharp hands. "He's got a pulse, but it's slipping."

Boomer ripped a pressure bandage from his kit. "Not today, hermano. You aren't dying on us in the middle of my kill count."

Ghoul scanned the perimeter, rifle up. "Clear the flank. We're not losing him while I'm on overwatch."

Padre Luis, still praying over Kael's chest, added, "If Saint Jude has an inbox, consider this a priority submission."

And Kael—barely conscious—cracked the faintest grin.

Comstock and Goya lifted Kael between them—dead weight, limbs dragging. He didn't groan. Didn't flinch. Blood smeared across the floor beneath him.

Valeria backed up the Tiger armored vehicle to the edge of the wreckage. "Let's go! He does not have long!"

The team loaded Kael in, packed the med kit, and sealed the rear door. The engine roared to life.

Comstock climbed into the front seat, adjusted the mirrors, and gave Mateo one last nod through the smoke. No words.

The armored convoy turned north—toward Tampico—grinding over twisted steel and scorched earth.

Behind them, Mateo stood alone among the firelit skeletons of tanks and war machines, the rising sun casting a hard glow over what was left of Veracruz.

And Kael… was slipping into darkness.

Chapter 31

The Ashes and the Tide

A week had passed since the decisive battle of Veracruz.

The whole of the Cárdenas territory had been reclaimed.

What began as a war of survival had shifted—into a revolution of consolidation.

Thousands lost. Cartels shattered. Governments buckled.

Wu was missing. Nueve Vidas wounded. El Filo de Dios burned.

The Cárdenas name, once whispered with fear and reverence, now carried something more dangerous: momentum.

But for now, the trouble lingered up north—along the fractured border.

And to the west, where soldiers, guerillas and cartel sicarios waited in fractured strongholds.

Here, in the calm space between chaos and rebuilding, something rare bloomed.

Peace.

The sea breeze moved in steady rhythms, brushing through the palm trees like the earth exhaled relief.

A soft bolero hummed from a speaker tucked beneath a thatched cabana.

Seagulls wheeled overhead.

Waves lapped at the shoreline, washing over broken shells and footprints slowly fading into memory.

Kael stirred in a hammock strung between two salt-bleached posts.

His body felt like stone. Heavy. Etched with fire. He was sore and bruised.

Every cut still burned at the touch.

His head was heavy. His chest ached like a cave had collapsed inside it.

But he was breathing.

He blinked against the warm light. The scent of citrus and smoke hung in the air, familiar and faintly narcotic.

Pain lived in his bones like a guest who had overstayed its welcome. But he was breathing.

He'd been unconscious for seven days.

They had told him it was a miracle.

Kael groaned, voice dry and cracked. "That… was a hell of a nap."

The air around him stirred as someone stood.

He looked slowly toward the sound.

Across the sand, under the shade of the old roof, sat the last people he trusted in the world:

Natalia. Valeria. Goya. Marisol, Sosa, Padre Luis, The Hellpack, Salvador Cárdenas, and Comstock, shirt half-unbuttoned, sunglasses crooked, a half-finished Old-Fashioned sweating in his hand.

They were playing cards and drinking in the lazy glow of post-war calm.

Cigars. Mezcal. Bare feet in the sand. Tactical scars hidden beneath linen and laughter.

Comstock had his classic Old Fashioned in one hand, two aces in the other. A fresh line of sweat trickled down his temple.

Padre Luis leaned back in a creaky wooden chair, one boot kicked up on a cooler of Tecate. He raised a half-empty bottle of mezcal in the direction of the card table and muttered, "Even the Apostles drank wine at the Last Supper. Who am I to break tradition?" He took a deep pull, wiped his mouth with the sleeve of his black linen shirt, and crossed himself—half out of habit, half in jest.

"You quoting scripture again, Padre, or just makin' it up as you go?" Reva "Sawtooth" Guerra smirked from behind her sunglasses, shuffling the

411

deck with one hand while flicking ash off her cigar with the other.

"A little of both," Padre Luis said. "Saint Paul wrote many letters. Mine just happen to be distilled."

Laughter rippled through the table.

Boomer chuckled, dragging chips toward his pile. "I swear the priest's got the best poker face of any of us."

"You try giving last rites to sicarios for twenty years and see how well you bluff," Padre Luis replied, eyes twinkling.

Ghoul tapped a finger to his temple. "Still think he's counting cards. Or getting divine intervention."

"God deals me what I need," Padre Luis said, sliding two cards toward the center. "And tonight, He's dealing flushes."

Valeria threw down her hand and groaned. "How is he winning again?"

"Because he's not afraid to bet it all," Natalia said with a grin, lighting another cigar. "Same way he walks into battle."

Sosa leaned back, hands behind his head. "That, or God really likes whiskey."

Cárdenas said nothing—just watched them, his old eyes filled with the quiet ache of things lost and the fragile joy of what remained.

Kael tried to sit up and groaned again.

Kael whispered, barely audible. His throat was dry as bone.

"…Marisol…"

Across the deck, Marisol froze mid-laugh.

Her glass slipped slightly in her hand. Then her whole body turned.

"Mi amor?" she said. Then louder, urgent. "Kael?"

She ran barefoot across the sand, nearly slipping as she reached the hammock.

Kael opened one eye fully. A crooked grin slid onto his cracked lips.

"…Mi SEXICO," he rasped.

She collapsed beside him, wrapping her arms around his chest so gently it broke him.

"You bastard," she whispered, sobbing. "They said you might not wake up. That it might be weeks. Or… longer."

His arms came up slowly—trembling, aching. But they held her.

"Woke up… for you."

"You always say the right thing when your half-dead."

Laughter followed the tears.

Behind them, Comstock lifted his glass lazily. "Welcome back, warlord."

Goya raised a bottle. "I had twenty bucks on you waking up by Thursday. Pay up, Cárdenas."

Valeria shook her head with a soft smile. "He's still got it."

Natalia wiped something from her cheek and said nothing.

Kael took a deep breath and let it go.

The hammock creaked. The sea murmured.

For the first time in what felt like forever… he was home.

And Marisol held him like she'd never let go.

Marisol helped Kael sit upright, one arm slung carefully over her shoulder, her other hand pressed to his ribs like she could hold him together just by touching him.

He winced as the hammock rocked. "I feel like I got thrown off a building. Then hit by the building."

"You kind of were," Valeria said, strolling over barefoot from the poker table, mezcal glass in hand. Her swimsuit top peeked out from beneath an oversized men's shirt tied loose at her waist. "We all saw it. Overly dramatic."

413

Kael squinted at her. "Did I at least look cool?"

Natalia snorted, leaning against the nearest palm with a quiet smile. "You looked like you were trying to headbutt a shipping container."

"You almost won," Goya added, sipping his beer. "Then you passed out like an old goat."

Padre Luis leaned over the poker table, squinting at his cards, a half-empty bottle of tequila nestled against his vestments. He glanced up as Kael groaned in the hammock nearby.

"You looked like a saint falling from the sky, mijo," the priest called out, raising his glass with mock solemnity. "A bloody, broken saint... who forgot how to land."

The table chuckled.

Sawtooth smirked and tossed two chips into the pot. "Nah, he looked like a busted scarecrow doing parkour. Respect for the commitment, though."

Ghoul didn't look up from stacking his chips. "I had five hundred pesos on him not getting up. Should've known better."

Boomer threw down a terrible hand and groaned. "Bro, you flew through the air like a damn piñata — and hit the ground like it owed you money."

Kael winced as the hammock swayed. "Did I at least look cool?"

Valeria leaned back in her chair, raising a mezcal glass. "You did. For a second. Then it got sad."

Comstock, holding a losing hand and a winning drink, grinned. "Next time, try not to make the Earth flinch when you land."

Padre Luis clinked his bottle against the rosary draped around his wrist. "Salud to the flying fool of Veracruz."

Laughter echoed under the shade of the worn awning, cards flipping, drinks clinking, the war for a moment just a memory.

Kael groaned and rolled his neck. "Should've let me die."

Marisol kissed his temple. "Shut up. You're the father of my children. You don't get to die anymore."

Everyone paused—briefly—and looked at her.

She smiled softly, placing a hand on her belly.

The message didn't need repeating.

Kael nodded slowly, something flickering behind his tired eyes.

Even pain couldn't bury the awe.

Comstock lifted his glass again, half toasting and half shielding emotion. "To stubborn bastards and beautiful consequences."

The sun dipped lower, casting long shadows across the sand.

Salvador Cárdenas stood slowly from the poker table.

He stubbed out his cigar with ceremonial care, turned toward the group, and rested both hands on the back of his chair.

His voice came steady, but low.

"I have known war most of my life. I have seen men build empires and destroy them in the same breath. But what we did here…" He looked at Kael. Then Marisol. Then at each face around him. "It changed something."

He paced slowly toward the fire pit in the center of the courtyard, his sandals whispering against the stone.

"We lost good people. Friends. Sons. Brothers. Lovers."

Natalia looked down. Valeria's fingers twitched beside hers.

"But we also saw what happens when courage meets loyalty," Cárdenas continued. "When hearts lead hands. When family fights for each other instead of against the world."

He raised his glass one last time.

415

"To the ones who never came back. And to the ones who did."

They all lifted theirs.

"To scars," Goya said.

"To survival," Valeria added.

"To what's next," said Marisol.

Kael lifted his drink slowly. "To the ones we love. And the ones we will make damn sure never get taken from us again."

Their glasses clinked in soft chorus.

Behind them, the flames from the firepit crackled higher as logs settled deeper into embers.

And with the heat dancing on their faces, a sense of quiet gratitude passed through them—not loud or ceremonial.

Just real.

Just family.

Cárdenas took a deep breath, gazing out toward the ocean.

"Tonight," he said, "we dance. We drink. We remember."

He looked back toward Kael, then down at Marisol's hand on his chest.

"Because tomorrow…" he said quietly, "we begin again."

The sun had slipped behind the palms, its afterglow setting the horizon on fire. Lanterns were strung between bamboo poles and branches, flickering like fireflies caught in a dance. The music came next—low and pulsing, pulled from Marisol's old playlist: a sultry blend of trance, Latin percussion, and slow-burning beats.

Someone lit a circle of torches near the shoreline.

Another uncorked a bottle of rum with a pop that echoed like a celebration bell.

Expensive champagne flowed like Niagara Falls—uncorked without ceremony, foaming over the rims of crystal flutes and repurposed tumblers alike. The good stuff. Victory vintage.

Padre Luis poured some into his tequila, crossed himself, and muttered, "Jesus turned water into wine. I am just multitasking."

The Hellpack howled with laughter as Ghoul raised his glass in mock reverence. "To holy mixers and unholy hands."

Kael leaned on a walking stick Goya had whittled from a palm frond branch. Each step was deliberate. His thigh still pulsed with fire, and his ribs felt like they had been tightened with steel wire—but he made it to the edge of the dance circle.

Marisol stayed by his side. Always.

Her sundress fluttered in the sea breeze, hips swaying gently as she rocked to the rhythm of the music. Her eyes, dark and shining in the torchlight, never left him. He could hardly believe she was real.

Across the fire, Comstock was already moving with his signature swagger—dancing badly but with confidence. He held a drink in each hand, hips shifting to the beat like a drunk cowboy trying to stay on a wild horse.

Two women from the Cárdenas compound took turns laughing at him, spinning circles just out of his reach.

Valeria emerged barefoot, hair loose around her shoulders, dressed in an open linen vest and white bikini bottoms. She extended her hand toward Natalia with theatrical elegance.

From the matte black Arena Match AMU208-120 compact high-performance loudspeaker, connected to Marisol's Bluetooth, a familiar pulse began to rise.

The slow synth climbs and drifting vocals filled the salt air like magic conjured from memory.

It was Valeria's favorite club trance track.

"Drifting Away" by Akille & Juna Rose.

Valeria's head snapped toward the speaker, eyes lighting up like a fire had sparked behind them.

Her lips parted. "Oh, hell yes."

Natalia looked over, instantly suspicious. "Valeria…"

Valeria did not answer. She just grabbed Natalia by the hand, pulling her up with a mischievous grin and absolutely no patience.

They began to dance.

There was no announcement. No crowd. No performance. Just movement—intimate, slow, magnetic.

Their bodies brushed gently in rhythm, melting together with each beat.

Hands slid along hips. Lips found skin. The space between them disappeared as they drifted deeper into each other, drifting away, just like the song.

They kissed softly—then again, more deeply.

It was not lust. It was liberation.

Wanting to drift away from here. From war. From scars. From blood and orders and old pain.

Valeria pressed her forehead to Natalia's.

"I needed this."

Natalia's fingers moved gently through her hair. "So did I."

The music pulsed around them, building to its high point.

"Maybe we just… go," Valeria said. "Disappear for a while."

"Where?"

Valeria smiled, brushing her thumb across Natalia's cheek.

"Does it matter?"

Natalia closed her eyes, breathing her in. "No."

They swayed like a secret shared under moonlight.

Valeria rested her head on Natalia's shoulder, her voice barely above the waves and synths.

"Let's leave. Just ninety days. No guns. No cartel. No war. Just... us."

Natalia pulled her closer and nodded.

"We'll figure out the specifics tomorrow."

They kissed again—longer, deeper—then simply held each other there, surrounded by music, firelight, and the kind of peace they did not know they'd been waiting for.

They embraced in happiness.

That they could drift away—together.

From the table nearby, Marisol smiled and leaned her head on Kael's shoulder.

Goya lifted his beer in a silent salute to the two women swaying in the sand. "About damn time," he said.

No one else interrupted. No one made a joke.

They all just let the moment exist—real and beautiful—as the music carried them into twilight.

They were free.

Kael smiled.

He had not seen that look on Natalia's face in weeks—maybe ever.

Marisol watched them too, then leaned closely and whispered in Kael's ear. "Do you think if we danced like that, the universe would finally leave us alone?"

Kael turned his head, smiling through the pain. "No. But at least we'd look good getting chased."

Marisol laughed, full-bodied and joyful.

She turned, faced him squarely, and said, "Then dance with me."

"I can barely stand."

"Then sway."

So, he did.

They moved together just off the firelight, slow and imperfect. Kael leaned on her a little too much, and she leaned back without hesitation. Their bodies were not doing choreography—they were telling stories. Every scar had a verse. Every kiss a bridge. Every breath a chorus.

Her hand slid around his waist, and he winced.

She smiled. "You are supposed to say 'ow' in rhythm."

Kael chuckled, gritting his teeth. "Working on it."

They danced through the pain—limping, laughing, glowing.

A few songs later, across the way, Natalia dipped Valeria low into the sand, both laughing like they were seventeen again. When Valeria stood, she pressed a kiss to Natalia's collarbone, then her jaw, then her lips—slow and reverent, in front of everyone.

Nobody said a word.

No one needed to.

The circle simply opened a little wider for them.

Back at the drink table, Goya raised a beer in their direction.

"To women who could kill you… and still make you smile about it."

Just beyond the glow of the firelight, the poker table broke into soft applause and hollers at Goya's toast.

"Damn right," Sosa muttered, raising his glass. "I'll drink to that—hell, I'll drink to anything that isn't another mortar round."

Padre Luis lifted his glass of smoky mezcal, now half gone, and made a swirling cross in the air. "To holy assassins, divine temptresses, and the blessed chaos they bring. And to the tequila they force us to drink in penance."

Boomer snorted. "You call that penance?"

Padre Luis did not miss a beat. "Son, I was a mercenary in Angola. This is spa day with Jesus."

The Hellpack burst out laughing.

Sawtooth leaned back in her chair, boots kicked up on a crate. "I've been shot at, stabbed, electrocuted—and none of it was as dangerous as that look Valeria just gave Natalia."

Ghoul nodded solemnly, eyes hidden behind dark glasses. "She was aiming center mass with her heart."

"Felt it from here," Boomer added, popping the cap off another beer with his bandolier buckle. "If I die tonight, let it be from secondhand passion."

The group erupted again.

Padre Luis held up his rosary dramatically. "If you all heathens keep going, I'm going to need another bottle. Or a miracle. Whichever arrives first."

Comstock, walking past with a cigar, clapped the Padre on the shoulder. "Let's split the odds and order both."

They all laughed again, then turned to watch Kael and Marisol sway in the shadows—imperfect, aching, alive.

For one night, no one had to wear armor.

Even Cárdenas cracked a grin from his distant table, sipping tequila and watching his empire move with joy under torchlight.

He did not interrupt.

Not yet.

Not tonight.

Tonight was for the living.

A few minutes later, Kael and Marisol quietly slipped away from the celebration, hand in hand.

No one stopped them.

Everyone knew where they were going.

Goya gave a mock salute. Natalia winked. Valeria just smiled.

Comstock raised his glass and muttered, "Finally. I thought we'd have to draw a map and light the path with tracer rounds."

Sosa snorted. "Ten bucks says they don't even make it to the room before it's go time."

Boomer leaned back in his chair, arms behind his head. "I give 'em thirty seconds before furniture gets broken."

Ghoul kept his eyes on his cards, deadpan. "I timed them last time. Forty-two seconds to clothes-off, five more to regret nothing."

Sawtooth slapped the table, laughing. "Romance is alive, boys."

Padre Luis took a long sip from his tequila bottle, lifted his rosary, and declared, "May the Lord bless their union… and multiply it. Many, many times. Mexico needs more beautiful chaos."

They disappeared into one of the guest rooms off the resort's main villa—one Kael had not seen before, decorated in pale blue and sun-bleached driftwood, with white linen curtains drifting gently in the sea breeze.

"This one's got the best view," Marisol whispered as she closed the door behind them.

Kael dropped slowly onto the bed, wincing as the mattress accepted his weight. His bandages were frayed. His shirt clung to dried blood and sweat.

"You gonna patch me up?" he said, teasing but tired.

Marisol raised a brow. "You bet your ass I am. I just graduated nursing school."

Kael smiled, then winced again. "Just don't puncture a lung, alright?"

Marisol leaned in slow face just inches from his, her breath synchronizing with his like they'd rehearsed it in a past life.

She did not kiss him right away.

She just… breathed.

Inhaled his exhale.

Took it deep into her lungs.

Then gave it back.

As if life itself were a rhythm they could pass between them.

As if she needed to breathe him in to remember who she was.

"I can barely move," Kael whispered.

"Good," Marisol murmured. "You just lay there. I'll do all the work."

They both giggled—honest, awkward, beautiful—like high school kids sneaking off at a party.

Marisol pulled back just enough to slip his shirt over his shoulders, moving slowly, careful not to reopen any wounds. Her fingers traced the bruises across his ribs, the cuts along his hip, the stitches at his thigh.

Each touch was a kiss in disguise.

When she slid her dress off, it fell to the floor like a wave pulling back from the shore. No drama. No flash. Just gravity and need.

Two naked bodies.

One broken, the other healing him.

Falling into each other like stars folding back into space.

Marisol lay beside him, skin pressed to skin and gently ran her fingertips along his chest—down his sides, across the muscle of his arm, back to his face. She kissed his eyelids. His jaw. The edge of his collarbone.

She whispered in Spanish—soft prayers and dirty poetry both.

Kael's breath caught as her hands explored him. Not frantic. Not aggressive.

Worshipful.

She kissed his scars. Let her lips linger over every patch of skin that had survived something violent.

Her hands slid down and up again, igniting him without pressure—just presence. As if her body was saying, You made it. You're still here. Let me remind you what it feels like to be loved, not just needed.

Kael reached up with one good arm, threading his hand into her hair.

She looked down at him, eyes full of wildfire and rain.

They moved together—not with urgency, but with reverence.

Slow. Deep. Real.

Two people stitching themselves back together with touch.

And when she finally sank into him, he whispered her name like a spell.

"Marisol…"

She kissed his throat.

"Mi SEXICO," she breathed. "Mine. Always."

Outside, the music played on.

Inside, the only sound was breath.

And the sound of two souls coming home.

It was just after 7 p.m.

The sun was dropping low over the water, melting into the horizon in hues of gold, crimson, and violet. The light did not seem real—too perfect, like something out of a dream or a movie. Even Kael, hardened by fire and trauma, could not look away from it.

The way the waves glowed beneath it.

The way Marisol's face shimmered in that light.

She walked beside him slowly, barefoot in the sand, a loose sundress flowing around her legs. There was something deeper in her now—a quiet radiance. A presence that whispered motherhood without a word being spoken.

Kael glanced over at her and smiled through the dull ache in his ribs.

She looked like peace.

424

Her hand held a tall glass of a cucumber cooler, non-alcoholic. She sipped it slowly, savoring the moment.

Kael's grip was firmer, cradling a double Blue Hawaiian, half ice, half therapy. The painkillers hadn't touched the nerve pain in his leg. But this helped. Somewhat.

Ahead of them, the beach flickered with golden light and the hum of a growing celebration.

Over two hundred guests filled the sand and the torchlit pavilion—Cárdenas loyalists, fighters, friends, and family. Just as many armed personnel circled the perimeter, dressed in casual beachwear but eyes sharp, weapons tucked beneath loose linen.

The scent of woodsmoke and sweet marinade filled the air.

A massive wild pig rotated over a pit fire, skin crisping to perfection under the slow turn of steel rods. Smoke drifted upward in lazy spirals.

Off to the right, on a raised platform built from polished driftwood and adorned with old cartel banners, Comstock sat like a retired war god.

One arm cradled a double Old Fashioned, the other a dirty martini.

Tucked under each bicep were two stunning Mexican women, laughing at everything he said whether it was funny or not.

Kael grinned. "Of course."

Marisol rolled her eyes with a soft laugh. "He's completely incorrigible."

Near the east bonfire, Natalia and Valeria leaned against an open weapons crate, surrounded by a circle of fellow sicarios and sicarias.

They were deep in storytelling—battle scars on display, comparing entry wounds, bruises, and near-death moments from the past two months of hell.

Each tried to outdo the next:

425

• A bullet graze that came within millimeters of the jugular

    • A roadside bomb deflected by a car door

    • A knife fight in a cult chapel gone sideways

Padre Luis stepped into the circle, half-drunk and fully blessed, rosary in one hand, mezcal bottle in the other.

"Grenades? Bullets? Blasphemy!" he boomed. "One time, in Veracruz, I dodged a narco's machete with nothing but the power of Christ and a full bladder. Wet my pants, yes—but the Lord gave me wings."

Laughter rippled through the group.

Reva "Sawtooth" Guerra raised her tomahawk and pointed at the scar running from her bicep to her wrist. "Padre, next time, use one of these. Works better than holy water."

Valeria lifted her shirt to show the puckered scar near her ribs. Natalia shook her head. "Still not as bad as the church grenade. That shit nearly took my jaw off."

Ángel "Boomer" Valdés exhaled a puff of smoke from a crooked cigar. "I once accidentally blew up a bridge with my own pack still on it. Had to dive into a river, swim with broken ribs, and pop my own shoulder back into place."

"Did the job get done?" Sosa asked, amused.

Boomer shrugged. "Bridge is gone. I'm still here."

Elias "Ghoul" Navarro, calm as always, simply pulled his shirt aside to reveal a twisted patch of scar tissue over his ribs. "Close-range burst from a .50 cal. Still got shrapnel in my lung. Whistles when I breathe too hard."

Padre Luis made the sign of the cross, eyes wide. "And you people think I'm the crazy one."

Then he raised his bottle and added with a wink, "But if we all live through tonight, someone

426

better make some damn babies. This cartel needs a new generation of psychopaths baptized and ready to sin."

The whole circle howled with laughter, even Valeria.

Natalia grinned. "You first, Padre."

He winked. "I'll stick to being godfather."

They all laughed—loud and real.

Not because it was not painful.

Because they'd lived to tell it.

At a long-carved cedar table near the dance floor, Salvador Cárdenas sat in quiet confidence, dressed in a deep navy guayabera, gold watch catching the last rays of sunlight.

At his side was Leonardo, freshly shaven, bruises still faint on his cheek.

Goya leaned back in his seat, laughing deep and low. Beside him, their wives clinked glasses, radiant and unburdened for once.

It was as close to heaven as any of them had seen in months.

But none of them knew the devil had already stepped onto the sand.

Later that night, the celebration began to slow—just slightly. Music faded into softer rhythms, and most of the guests made their way to the fire pits or drifted toward their rooms, pairs disappearing into the shadows of palapas and hammocks. The sky above stretched clear and endless, punctuated by stars burning clean through the coastal haze.

Kael moved with a slow, steady limp. Marisol held his arm, her hand resting just above his heart. He had not stopped smiling since the light touched her face—that glow, the unmistakable aura of a woman carrying life.

They joined the others: Comstock was already there, dancing with Marisol first like a gentleman from another era. Kael grinned as he swapped in to dance with Valeria. Natalia grabbed the two beautiful women Comstock had draped over him earlier and spun with them in playful circles, laughing loud and free. By the bonfire's crackle, Padre Luis swayed in half-time, a cigar clamped between his teeth and a flask in one hand. He lifted it heavenward and declared with a grin, "First the war ends, now babies? Dios mío, you better start building more cribs and fewer coffins!"

The Hellpack wasn't far—Reva "Sawtooth" Guerra stood up from the poker table, wolf-whistled, and pointed her beer toward Kael. "Daddy Kael in the house!"

Ángel "Boomer" Valdés raised both hands like a preacher. "We'll baptize the baby in tequila and chaos."

Elias "Ghoul" Navarro just nodded from the edge of the firelight, chewing on a matchstick. "If it is a girl, she is gonna be deadlier than both parents combined. If it is a boy—he will probably inherit that limp."

Everyone laughed. Padre Luis crossed himself theatrically. "Holy Mary, Mother of God, pray for us sinners—and for Marisol's hips to survive her pregnancy."

Even Comstock cracked a smile, twirling back into the circle. "That's it—we need a bigger compound."

The moment held—wild, raw, joyful. War-beaten hearts glowing in firelight, bound by something deeper than blood.

They moved as a unit—rotating partners, touching hands, trading laughter, each letting go a little more with every song.

Warriors. Survivors. Friends.

When the track ended, they drifted to the open-air bar.

Comstock gave both his ladies a gentle pat on the backside. "Give me a few minutes, darlings. Old man needs a second to remember who the hell he is."

They laughed and peeled off as Comstock rejoined the circle.

At the bar, they ordered drinks—Kael and Marisol with their arms still around each other. Comstock sipped both a bourbon and a martini without hesitation, his sunglasses still on despite the dim tiki lights.

They talked about the last two months—the betrayals, the gunfights, the miracles. They traded stories like medals.

Natalia leaned over the bar, knocking twice on the counter. "Tequila. The good kind. And bring a glass for my woman." She grinned at Valeria, who was already holding up two fingers for mezcal.

Valeria smirked. "I fought off a robot dog with my shoulder. I deserve top shelf."

Sosa showed up with a mild limp and a bandaged forearm. He tossed a pack of cigarettes on the bar. "I'm not even a smoker," he said, "but if there's ever a night for bad decisions…"

Padre Luis appeared from nowhere, robes tied off, rosary swinging slightly. He grabbed a bottle of rum from behind the bar without asking. "For healing the body," he declared, raising it like a sacrament, "and for making more little warriors in the image of our chaos."

The Hellpack spread out like a myth walking into a cantina.

Sawtooth Guerra banged her tomahawk against the bar for attention. "Whiskey. Neat. And do not you dare water it down."

Boomer grinned and pulled a grenade from his belt like it was a bottle opener. "I will take a beer. And a reason not to start throwing fireworks."

Ghoul sat in silence, then finally spoke—his voice low, almost reverent. "I want the strongest thing you've got… and a quiet minute to forget."

Marisol rested her head on Kael's shoulder. He rubbed her back absently, still processing the weight of everything—but lighter now, surrounded by the only family he had left.

Comstock raised his bourbon. "To the ones who made it."

"And the ones we'll never forget," Padre Luis added, pouring rum into his glass, then crossing himself.

They all drank.

And for a moment, the war felt far away.

Then Comstock leaned back against the bar.

"I'm leaving tomorrow," he said.

Natalia and Valeria both turned toward him. "What?"

"Yeah. Last SURC boat's supposed to pick me up around 1200 hours sharp. Portland's pulling back out into deeper waters. I have got more chaos to chase."

Padre Luis let out a long sigh, sipping his rum like it was communion wine. "Then we send you off proper. With fire. With ocean. With heart." He raised his glass solemnly. "And at least one sacrilegious blessing."

Kael nodded. "Let us all meet at the docks tomorrow. Say goodbye the right way."

Valeria clinked her glass against his. "I am in. Wouldn't miss it."

Natalia rested her head on Valeria's shoulder. "I want to see the legend off with a kiss and a curse."

Sosa checked his watch and stood, the smile fading from his face. "I wish I could. But Cárdenas just made me Governor of the South. I fly out tonight."

Kael reached across the bar and shook his hand. "Then be the kind of governor they write songs about."

Sosa smirked. "Only if they're banned in three countries."

The Hellpack raised their glasses in silent agreement—Reva "Sawtooth" Guerra gave Comstock a nod, Ghoul just muttered "Respect," and Boomer grinned. "We will be there. Even ghosts need a farewell."

Comstock saluted them all with his glass, his eyes scanning each face—etched with blood, loyalty, and something like peace.

"Tomorrow, then," he said. "At the edge of the world."

Chapter 32

The Gift and Departure

The next morning was eerily quiet, almost holy in its stillness.

No alarms. No radios. No foot patrols. Just ocean breeze and scattered coffee cups.

Most of the Cárdenas command staff had already left—Cárdenas, Leonardo, Goya—back to their own territories and operations. Only a dozen or so bodyguards remained. The storm had passed.

Kael, Marisol, Natalia, and Valeria climbed into one of the Tiger armored vehicles and rolled down the coastal road to the marina. A few bodyguards followed in an armored SUV behind them.

Behind Kael's Tiger, the second vehicle started up—a desert-camo Humvee with the Hellpack climbing in like it was just another mission. Reva "Sawtooth" Guerra rode shotgun, a lime from the bar still clutched between her teeth as she tightened the strap on her tomahawk harness. Ángel "Boomer" Valdés tossed his bag of grenades in the backseat like it was beach gear, while Elias "Ghoul" Navarro settled into the turret mount, sunglasses on, scanning the coast like he could see into tomorrow.

Padre Luis climbed into the front passenger seat, robes fluttering, a bottle of mezcal tucked under one arm and a half-lit cigar between his fingers. He raised the bottle, blessed it in the air, and took a swig.

"If God didn't want us drinking at farewells, he wouldn't have turned water into wine," he declared to no one in particular, then crossed himself backward.

The convoy headed toward the marina, rolling slowly along the coast. No radio. No chatter. Just the hum of engines and the taste of salt in the air as the sea came back into view.

They were sending off a legend—and they knew it.

The last SURC riverine boat waited at dockside—camouflage gray with the U.S. flag faded on the hull. The crew saluted as Comstock approached in his signature black shirt, glasses on, pack slung.

Comstock stood near the dock with the sun baking down, sweat glistening on his neck beneath his half-buttoned shirt. He looked over at Kael with that ever-present glint in his eye.

"You still got a couple million stashed on The Commodore?" he asked casually, like he was asking for a beer.

Kael nodded. "Yeah. Still locked under the deck plates. Marisol and Padre Luis can go grab the bags."

Marisol kissed Kael on the cheek and started toward the marina ramp with Padre Luis trailing, cigar in one hand, rosary in the other. A few minutes later, they returned hauling two heavy duffels—unmistakably stuffed.

Comstock unzipped the bags, pulled out neat bricks of cash—$50,000 each in crisp $100 bills—and began stacking them like building blocks of destiny.

He turned to the Hellpack first. "Reva, Ghoul, Boomer—five bricks each. That's $250K apiece. You earned every fucking cent."

Boomer whistled low. "Guess I'm finally getting that tequila distillery in Culiacán."

Reva winked. "Or I'm buying a shark."

Ghoul just nodded, accepting his bricks in silence with a smile that did not quite reach his eyes.

Then Comstock held out five more bricks. "Padre."

Padre Luis accepted the bricks of cash like it was holy scripture. "For what purpose, mi hijo?"

"Build a church," Comstock said. "Right here in Tampico."

Padre Luis raised the a brick high in both hands. "In the name of the Father, the Son, and the Holy Dollar—may it be glorious and non-sequential." He kissed the money like a relic and muttered a prayer in Latin that ended with: "Bless this currency and the empire that minted it."

Kael looked into the bags. "What about the rest?"

Comstock zipped it up and shoved it into Kael's chest. "It's yours, kid. You have got a war to rebuild. And maybe a future."

Kael stared at him a second, then nodded. "Natalia. Valeria. Lock it back in the Commodore."

The girls moved quickly, hauling the bag down the dock as the others gathered around.

Everyone shook hands. Marisol hugged him long. Valeria whispered something in his ear that made him laugh. Natalia slapped a tracker on his shoulder and said, "Just in case you need backup, from a legend."

Then it was time.

Comstock climbed aboard the SURC. The engine roared to life. He gave one last wave—two fingers to the temple, then out to the horizon.

By the time the clock struck noon, the SURC was gone vanishing into the shimmer of the Gulf like a myth retold.

The Hellpack loaded into their vehicle, cash in hand, still stunned and grinning. Padre Luis followed in a rusty Jeep with a pistol strapped to the side and his holy duffel in the back seat. They waved once— then rolled out, heading back into the sun-drenched chaos of Mexico.

And just like that, the team was gone… but the revolution rolled on.

Back at the dock, Marisol, Natalia, and Valeria cleaned and prepped the Commodore—her white hull still gleaming, sails folded, decks washed.

Kael moved slower than usual, but his hands were steady as he walked Natalia and Valeria through every part of the boat again.

"Engine controls are simple. GPS routes are loaded. Frequency's pre-set for emergencies. Sails are tight."

"We know," Valeria said softly. "You showed us before—when we sailed to Isla de la Juventud."

They smiled at the memory.

Later that day, they dropped anchor just offshore in shallow water.

Kael dove in with the speargun and brought back a red snapper, a snook, and three speckled trout.

On deck, Marisol, Natalia, and Valeria sat in bikinis, feet swinging over the cargo net, toes skimming the sea.

They talked about the water. The stillness. What it felt like to float.

Kael returned soaked and laughing, fish in hand. They grilled them on the small deck unit, opened cold drinks, and watched the sun burn the horizon into orange flames.

Marisol took a sip of red wine—just a few drops.

"It helps with digestion," she said with a smirk.

They all laughed.

———————————

Back at the dock, Marisol and Kael stepped off the Commodore.

Kael paused, turned, and stood in front of the boarding ladder.

Valeria frowned. "What are you doing?"

Kael looked at them both, then down at the boat.

"She's yours now."

Natalia blinked. "What?"

Valeria shook her head. "Kael—we don't have anything."

Kael looked at Marisol. Then back.

"You have each other," he said. "And you've got over a million in cash, a small armory, and burner phones stored in the hull. That is more than enough to get lost for a while."

Valeria's lips trembled. "Are you serious?"

Kael nodded. "You keep talking about disappearing. This is your chance."

Marisol stepped forward. "I will tell my father I ordered you on an extended vacation. We will cover your tracks. Be in touch in a couple of months. No one will question it."

Natalia turned to Valeria, eyes wide.

Valeria grinned through the tears.

"Come on, mi amor," she said. "We keep saying it. Let us do it. Three to six months. Just us."

They hugged Kael and Marisol hard—weeping, laughing, kissing their cheeks.

"We love you guys," Natalia said. "You are family. Always."

Kael untied the mooring line and gave the bow a shove.

The Commodore drifted slowly away from the dock.

They stood at the edge, waving as Natalia and Valeria disappeared toward the open sea—two warriors finally drifting into peace.

On the way back from the marina, Kael and Marisol stopped in town—just the two of them, hands interlocked, strolling under soft afternoon light.

Two Cárdenas bodyguards trailed a few steps behind, dressed casually, eyes alert but relaxed.

They wandered in and out of small shops, admiring beach dresses, sunglasses, artisan jewelry.

Marisol clung to Kael's arm like the world could not touch her—and maybe, for a moment, it couldn't.

She stopped outside a maternity store, drawn to the pale fabrics and soft displays in the window. Tiny shoes. Blankets embroidered with clouds and stars.

Her face lit up.

"I can't wait," she whispered.

Kael smiled and pressed a kiss to her temple. "Me neither."

The day after Natalia and Valeria set sail, the coastline felt quieter. Lighter, somehow. Kael and Marisol lingered at the edge of the marina, watching the surf roll in, their hands intertwined, fingers still warm from the night before.

Neither of them spoke for a while.

They did not need to.

Eventually, Marisol leaned into his shoulder and whispered, "Let us disappear too. Just for a few hours."

Kael smirked, his body still aching from wounds and restlessness. "Only if there's good food at the end of it."

Marisol led him up the narrow coastal road into town. Their pace was slow—his limp still pronounced, but more human now, less wounded predator and more man still learning how to stand after falling so far.

They wandered the sunlit mercado, ducking into boutique shops with driftwood wind chimes and handmade sandals, palm-frond hats and woven blankets dyed in ocean hues. Tourists had not yet returned in full force, but a few wandered through like zombies in bright shirts, unaware of how close this place had come to crumbling.

Marisol paused outside another small maternity shop.

In the window: a white cotton onesie with embroidered waves, a matching set of baby shoes no bigger than her palm.

She placed her hand on the glass.

Kael watched her from behind, memorizing the curve of her body in the sunlight, the way the light laced her hair in gold.

She turned and smiled. "Do you think we'll be okay?"

He stepped beside her, eyes on the reflection of them both.

"Not right away," Kael said honestly. "But we'll get there."

They went inside. She bought the onesie.

They returned to the Arnas just before sunset.

The sky burned orange, the sea calm.

Soft music played from the bar's outdoor speakers—a slow Caribbean rhythm, half love song, half lullaby. They did not need to speak. They just held each other and danced, barefoot in the sand outside the resort entrance.

Kael sat on the deck with a blanket draped across his lap, Marisol beside him. She poured them each a drink—his laced with painkillers, hers a cucumber-and-lime spritz. They clinked glasses.

"To survival," she said.

Kael shook his head. "To escape."

They sipped.

In the background, soft Caribbean jazz filtered through the open doors of the lounge. Somewhere, someone was frying plantains. The smell drifted through the air like an offering.

Marisol took Kael's glass, set it aside, and curled up in his lap carefully.

Her ear found his heartbeat.

"I don't need to save the world," she whispered. "I just want to raise our kids somewhere no one knows our names."

Kael ran his hand slowly through her hair. "Then we will build that place. Brick by brick."

She looked up at him, her eyes soft, a little sad. "Promise?"

Kael kissed her forehead.

"I promise."

Later that night, with the tide lapping the edges of the beach, they danced alone under the stars. No music this time—just their breathing, the sound of water, and the occasional chirping of crickets.

Kael held her with the gentlest strength.

She rested her head against his chest.

Their future was a mystery.

But right now?

They were still here.

Still holding on.

And as the wind picked up, Marisol whispered something he would not forget.

"We didn't survive this war to become ghosts."

Kael smiled against her hair. "No. We survived it to become legends."

They kept swaying until the moon rose fully over the water.

And the sea, once again, pulled everything quiet.

The bonfires crackled softly now, casting golden rings of light around fading footprints and half-buried beer bottles. The musicians had gone quiet, their instruments resting in the sand like sleeping animals. Only the hush of the waves and occasional laughter from the patio kept the night alive.

Kael and Marisol sat side by side in a cabana strung with soft lights, tucked away from the main path. Her head rested on his shoulder, her legs draped across his lap, a warm linen blanket covering them both. His arm curled protectively around her back, fingers tracing absent patterns into the thin cotton of her sundress.

Neither of them had spoken for several minutes.

They just… existed.

Wrapped in warmth, salt, and survival.

Kael finally broke the silence, voice rough but calm. "When the war ends, what do you want to do?"

Marisol stirred. "Plant something. Maybe orange trees."

Kael smiled. "Oranges, huh?"

"I always wanted a grove. Something that blooms. Something that stays."

She turned and looked at him fully.

"And you?"

Kael's eyes narrowed at the question—not in confusion, but in restraint. He had never allowed himself to think that far ahead.

But he answered.

"I want to write."

Marisol blinked. "Write?"

"Yeah. Not a novel. Nothing grand. Just… the truth. What happened. For us. For them." He nodded toward the future she carried. "So, they know how it started."

She leaned in and kissed him, slowly and gratefully.

"I'd read it," she said softly.

He chuckled. "I hope so. You will be in every chapter."

Kael ordered a double ginger pom, something sharp and warm to numb the deep ache still living in his ribs.

He drank it slow while they danced.

His forehead rested against hers.

Their eyes locked soul to soul, deeper than language could reach.

Before going upstairs, he ordered another double to be sent to their suite.

They returned to the suite just before midnight.

The windows were open, letting in the breeze. The sky beyond the terrace was a velvety dome of stars. The smell of salt and smoke lingered in their clothes, their hair, their skin.

Kael stood shirtless at the mirror, replacing the bandage on his side. Marisol moved behind him in the reflection, arms wrapping slowly around his waist, her cheek resting between his shoulder blades.

She whispered something in Spanish. He did not catch it all—but he felt it.

She was praying again.

This time, not for survival. For the future.

They got into bed. She laid her head on his chest. His fingers moved through her hair. Their breathing matched.

And as her eyes fluttered closed, she whispered one last thought:

"You're still mine."

Kael kissed the top of her head and answered without hesitation.

"Always."

Outside, the sea hummed in agreement.

And the last candle flickered out.

The world ended in a whisper.

Later, they lay in bed, a breeze lifting the curtains.

The TV played quietly in the background—headlines about war and chaos:

- Tariffs crushing trade routes
- The Ukrainian frontlines shifting again. The U.S Bombing Iran.
- Middle Eastern oil diplomacy unraveling
- Mexico still destabilized, its government fractured and Ice Agents in America raiding every taco and fruit stand. People protesting in the streets.

Kael muted the sound.

Marisol turned toward him, took his hand, and placed it gently on her stomach.

"Rub my belly three times," she whispered, grinning, "and you can make a wish."

He chuckled and did as he was told.

They kissed softly. She laid her head on his chest.

And together... they fell asleep.

At 2:41 a.m., the night was still. Waves lapped against the seawall. A pelican skimmed the black water. In the quiet suite at the edge of Arnas del Sol, Marisol Cárdenas stirred in her sleep, her hand finding Kael's chest like a compass rediscovering north.

Then—

CRASH.

The door exploded inward.

Splinters. Gunfire. Shadows.

Kael was on his feet before his eyes were fully open, instincts overriding pain. He grabbed the HK45 from the nightstand, aimed, fired.

Pop. Pop. Pop.

Three masked men dropped instantly—headshots, clean and brutal.

But more kept coming.

A flash grenade detonated just outside the balcony. The light washed the room in white heat.

Kael roared, covering Marisol's body as another burst of automatic fire shattered the windows. Blood sprayed across the linen curtains. The bed splintered behind them. Marisol was screaming—not from fear, but fury.

She rolled out from under Kael, reached the drawer, pulled the Glock she had hidden days ago. Fired.

Bang. Bang.

One attacker stumbled back, bullet through the collarbone.

442

But another man, armored and silent, stormed in from the side and slammed the butt of his rifle into Kael's temple.

CRACK.

Kael collapsed, dazed, vision shattering into static.

Two men grabbed Marisol.

"No!" he groaned, crawling toward her.

She kicked. Bit. Tore at the mask of one man until he screamed in pain.

Another rifle struck her in the ribs hard. She dropped with a cry.

Kael reached for her.

Their hands touched—barely.

Then they pulled her away.

Through the shattered balcony doors.

Down the stairs.

Into the surf.

Ribbed military boats waited—three of them.

Kael tried to rise, but his legs would not work. His head pulsed with every heartbeat like it was trying to explode. Blood filled his mouth.

He saw Marisol one last time—her body limp, her arm swinging.

And then she was gone.

Swallowed by the tide.

The shadows retreated.

Silence fell again.

Kael collapsed on the bloodied tile floor, facing the sky, the memory of her still on his hands.

Then—blackness.

Two weeks passed before Kael Torres opened his eyes.

He awoke in a dim, cool room, his body heavy, bandaged, broken.

His ribs were taped, one orbital bone fractured, the side of his skull stitched and swollen from the ambush. Every breath felt like dragging sand through his chest.

A nurse stood beside him. Others followed. Quiet voices. Sterile movements.

They dressed him slowly. Slipped a light button-down shirt over his bruises. Gave him a tray of warm food he barely tasted.

Then one of them spoke softly in Spanish: "Señor Cárdenas wants to see you."

They walked through long, quiet corridors—stone hallways lined with iron sconces, flickering with low flames despite the daylight outside. Kael's boots echoed with every step. The deeper they went, the more it felt like descending into something sacred… or sinister.

The Cárdenas estate—Hacienda Santa Gracia—was carved into legend.

Warfare had been planned here. Cartels had risen and crumbled at this table.

And Kael was walking back into it—half-alive, half-haunted, wholly changed.

The air smelled of oak. Blood. History.

Kael knew this place.

Hacienda Santa Gracia.

Not just a mansion.

A myth.

A war room.

A crucible.

They reached the great hall, its arched ceilings soaring like a cathedral. There, at the head of a twenty-foot table carved from a single slab of mahogany, sat Salvador Cárdenas. He did not rise when Kael entered.

Instead, he calmly lit a cigar, the tip glowing red as he exhaled a slow plume of smoke.

As Kael approached, Cárdenas lit a cigar with slow, ceremonial ease.

Then, silence.

A long one.

444

Finally, Cárdenas spoke.

In a massive sunlit room with arched windows and dark wooden beams, Salvador Cárdenas sat alone at the head of a long mahogany table.

"Where are Natalia and Valeria?" he asked without looking up.

"And Comstock?"

Kael, still dizzy, answered slowly explaining the Commodore, the cover story, the escape. Cárdenas said nothing in reply. Just nodded slightly, as if it had all been expected.

Then he placed the cigar between his lips and stared at Kael.

"Do you know why I sit at the head of this table?"

Kael said nothing.

"Do you know why I'm the emperor of this empire?"

Still nothing. Kael just looked at him—eyes sunken, face expressionless.

He was not sure if he was awake… or still somewhere in the bleeding dark.

Cárdenas tapped his fingers on the tabletop with slow precision.

"It is not because I am the most ruthless.

And it is not because I am the smartest."

He leaned forward, voice tightening.

"It's because I come from a place of proper perception."

He let the words hang.

"You think you are free in America.

You think the Emancipation Proclamation freed you.

But in 1913, the Federal Reserve was created— and your enslavement began again.

The entire nation became a debt farm."

His eyes locked on Kael, sharper now.

"Consumers… you call them. But what are they really?

Slaves to a number.

A credit score created by corporations you never gave permission to.

TransUnion. Equifax. Experian.

Who told them they could decide what a man can and can't own?"

Cárdenas stood now, pacing slowly behind the chair.

"Your country parades like it's benevolent… then tells the world what it can and cannot grow.

What if I told Florida they could not sell oranges?

Or Idaho potatoes?

Or California almonds?"

He smiled faintly.

"Yet they tell us we can't sell our number one export."

He took another long drag from the cigar.

"More Americans die every year from alcohol-related deaths—car accidents, liver disease, chronic addiction.

But no one is shutting down Budweiser.

No one is outlawing Kentucky bourbon."

He paused.

"And what of weapons? Your country is the largest arms producer on Earth.

The top ten weapons manufacturers in America are all publicly traded.

Worth over a trillion dollars combined."

His voice deepened.

"Fifty thousand dead in Palestine since October 7, 2023.

What are they using and dropping on them?

U.S. F-15s. U.S. JDAM bombs.

All made in the States.

All paid for by your taxes.

And who are the top shareholders of those companies?"

He took a step toward Kael, eyes burning now.

"You created two lives with my daughter.

Two lives your country will try to exploit, label, enslave, or erase."

Cárdenas turned and waved Kael forward.

"Come."

Kael followed him through the archway into a vast, marble-floored parlor.

He knew this room. He had been here before—during war councils, mission briefings, cartel gatherings.

But this time was different.

The doors opened wide.

Inside, the room was full: dozens of sicarios, elite commanders, old-guard lieutenants, and new blood standing in silence. All eyes turned as Kael entered.

Marisol was gone.

His children were somewhere out there.

And the man who once wanted peace… had just inherited an empire.

Cárdenas placed a hand on Kael's shoulder.

He looked him dead in the eye.

"It's about time we talk about your future."

The doors closed behind them.

To Be Continued......
SEXICO: Rise of The Ouroboros
Coming Winter of 2025

Comstock's parting shot:
"Normally I don't drink. But when I do, it's because someone has to die…. or fall in love, I prefer the latter."

447

www.ingramcontent.com/pod-product-compliance
Lightning Source LLC
Chambersburg PA
CBHW050120030726

47505CB00007B/1969

* 9 7 9 8 9 9 9 8 8 6 8 3 0 6 *